TARNISHED JOURNEY

SOUL DANCE BOOK FOUR

ANN GIMPEL

Edited by
ANGELA KELLY
Edited by
DIANE EAGLE KATAOKA

CONTENTS

TARNISHED JOURNEY

SOUL DANCE, BOOK FOUR

Historical Paranormal Romance
By Ann Gimpel

COPYRIGHT PAGE

BOOK DESCRIPTION, TARNISHED JOURNEY

Long before Germany rounded up Romani and sent them to prison camps, the Netherlands declared them undesirables. Yara's caravan disbanded when she was fifteen to avoid being driven out of the country. Ten years have passed, and she's been alone for most of that time hiding in caves and abandoned buildings. It's been a lonely life, but at least she still has one.

Stewart conceals his true identity for the best of reasons. He's not actually Romani, even though he's been a caravan leader for many years. In a bold and desperate move, he joins a small band of shifters and Rom to fight the Reich's chokehold on Europe. When they're crossing the border into the Netherlands, vampires attack.

Yara senses Romani near her cave. The stench of vampire comes through loud and clear too, along with shifters. While not nearly as bad as vampires, her people have always steered clear of them. Another type of magic plucks at her. She can't identify it, but it draws her from her hiding place. That decision tilts her world on its axis when she comes face to face with Stewart's raw masculinity and savage presence. She could still turn tail and run. If she stays, it doesn't require magical ability to recognize her life will change forever.

CHAPTER 1

Stewart Macleod paced in a rough circle, skirting the collection of shifters and Romani gathered in small groups. He'd declared a rest break, but everyone was too keyed up to sleep. A few of the shifters were combing the forest for food for the rest of them. The shriek of a vulture on the hunt told him Meara wasn't far away. It had been drizzling all day, and now fog was moving in. He encouraged it with a bit of magic. Anything that would shield their presence might help.

They'd avoided Hannover and Osnabrück as they transited the northern portion of Germany, selecting backroads that had stressed their truck's ability. There'd been a few places where they'd all had to get out, but luck had been with them. They hadn't broken an axle or even had so much as a punctured tire.

The Netherlands border wasn't far. Crossing it would push one problem—Nazis—to a backseat. Vampires would still plague them, but he hadn't sensed any since they'd passed Hannover. Was it because the Reich was using every single one of the fell creatures they could get their hands on?

The more he thought about it, the likelier it seemed. Vampires reveled in blood and death. Sex ran a hot second. The Nazi prison camps provided lush opportunities for both feeding and fucking, a resource far too rich to be ignored. Vampires might disparage the Reich, but they weren't above using them to meet their needs.

A corner of Stewart's mouth twisted downward into a grimace. Hitler and his henchmen believed they had vampires under their thumbs, but they'd be in for a rude awakening someday.

Och aye, and we can only hope 'twill come sooner rather than later.

For once no one was bothering him. No questions. No "Hey, Stewart, come here for a moment," requests.

It gave him a much-needed opportunity to flesh out his plan for getting the group across the border and examine it for holes. Critical elements he might have missed. They'd be abandoning the large transport truck soon—not much choice, even though not having it created other problems. Every road had border crossing guards, and they prowled the terrain near their stations. The Nazis knew good and well that once someone moved into the Netherlands, they were home free.

The safest way across was on foot for the Rom and in shifted form for everyone else. He ticked off names of the principal players. Tairin, Elliott, Jamal, Ilona, Meara, and Gregor were shifters. All wolves except for Meara, whose other form was a vulture. Nivkh and two other bear shifters traveled with them as well. That left himself, Michael, Cadr, Vreis, and Aron, along with three other Rom from Michael's caravan.

He thought about his own caravan hidden behind a magical barrier a short distance outside Munich. It was hundreds of miles away, and he hoped to hell they'd be safe. He hadn't always been a caravan leader. In truth, he'd only adopted the Romani mantle a mere century before. Or perhaps it had been two. Regardless, he'd pulled off the deception swimmingly—until a few days ago. Jamal was sharp. He'd asked pointblank what Stewart was, having intuited his magic didn't match Romani energy patterns.

Fortunately, Jamal had the good sense not to keep nagging

once Stewart told him that topic was off-limits. He swallowed a snort. Romani magic had dwindled until only a very few had much left. But Jamal was a shifter, and an old, canny one at that. Leave it to a shifter to call him out on his long-running deception.

Before the Nazi problem heated up, he'd toyed with the idea of translocating his entire caravan to Scotland, but he'd waited too long. He hadn't understood how the Reich solidified its power-base so quickly—until he discovered their mass hypnotism was fueled by vampire coercion.

A squawk from Meara's vulture was followed by a flash of light as she shifted midair and somersaulted to his side, landing lightly. Silver-gray hair fell to the ground, providing both cover and warmth. Her shrewd amber eyes still held an avian cast, and she looked more raptor than human as she regarded him.

"Mind if I join you?" She quirked a brow.

He met her gaze, not fooled by her words. She was one of the first shifters and always had a motive. "Ye're not asking a question. Not really," he countered. "State what's on your mind."

The prickly jab of magic pierced him as she surrounded them with warding. Along with it came the odor of clay baked under a sun far hotter than it ever got in Germany—or the British Isles. Rosemary and fresh cut hay joined the clay scent, the combination the scent of many of her castings. Whatever she had to say, she apparently wasn't interested in being overheard.

"Everyone's too worried to pay us much heed," he said, keeping his tone neutral. The vulture shifter could be touchy and had a short fuse.

She shot a pointed look his way. "Do you want them to listen in when I inquire whether now is the time to reveal what you are?" Without waiting for him to respond, she went on, "Laying that aside for a moment, we must firm up the details of how we shall tackle the border. The shifters will take their animal forms. Crossing the border unnoticed should go smoothly for them—"

"Unless a vampire notices," he cut in.

"Unless a vampire notices and chooses to act on the knowledge," she corrected him. "Shifters are immune to vampire mind control. They've pretty much left us alone because of that, preferring to focus on more tractable prey."

Stewart waited. Meara clearly had a plan of her own for spiriting them across the border into the Netherlands. One she was about to share. Perhaps it was less risky than his.

"You're quiet," she observed.

"Ye're far from done. If I interrupt every few seconds, ye'll never finish."

The corners of her mouth twitched, but didn't quite form a smile. "True enough. All right then. By my count, eight of us are stuck in human bodies. Seven if we take you out of the equation, but bear with me."

He made come along motions with one hand, ignoring her gambit about taking himself out of the equation. She sensed he was different, much as Jamal had, but he'd been evasive in the face of her earlier probing. Was she hunting for information?

"What is your true name?"

Stewart started, not expecting the question. He shook his head. "'Tisn't important. I havena used it for centuries, and no one remembers who I was."

Meara frowned, drawing her gray eyebrows into a single line. "Surely your gods would. Shifters don't have such things, but the Celts had them in droves."

"Aye, true enough. If any recall who I was, none have chosen to speak with me for a verra long time."

He cut the flow of his words. Part of his plan hinged on those same gods, who'd discounted him for hundreds of years, still being tethered to Earth and capable of responding to a summons for aid. It was one of the biggest unknowns in his strategy, and one he hadn't spent much time worrying about. They had to get to Scotland first—a place that would strengthen his magic sufficiently the gods might take notice of him once again.

The way things were going, Scotland was far from a given.

Even if the Celtic gods had left for other worlds, the British Isles would still concentrate his power, and everyone else's as well. But without the Celts, no amount of magic would be enough to subvert the Nazis and their war machine.

Meara narrowed her eyes. The gesture made her look even more like a vulture. "Skipping your name, you were a Druid high priest, correct?"

"Good guess. I was the highest-ranking Druid in Britain. 'Tis why I'm close to immortal."

She narrowed her eyes further. "What does *close to immortal* mean?"

He shrugged. "I'm not exactly certain. Danu, Gwydion, Arianrhod, and a few of the others got into an argument over events at one of the Druid temples. We had an overabundance of corrupt priests, and I had to sanction them. Not one of the proudest moments in our priesthood, but—"

"Sanction as in kill?"

"Aye." An image of bodies smoldering atop a pyre flashed through his mind. He pushed it aside.

"Interesting. I had no idea Druids were so bloodthirsty."

"We're not." Defensiveness raced through him like a hot tide. "Times might have been different then, but some transgressions deserve death no matter what the era."

"Now it's me who's doing the interrupting. You brought this up to answer my question about immortality. Go on. I'll bite my tongue."

Stewart had a hard time imagining her sitting on her opinions, but kept that thought to himself. "Not so much more to tell. Druid priests provided a buffer between the Celtic gods and everyone else. The gods dinna wish to deal with anyone but me after the problem I described earlier, so they told me I'd live a long time."

"That's it?" Meara's nostrils flared. "No rough estimates?"

Stewart shook his head. "After the first five hundred years or so, I stopped expecting to drop dead and just went with the flow. Modern times have made it harder to slip out of sight and reappear elsewhere. 'Twas one of the reasons I opted to masquerade as a Rom. They're wanderers and more likely to escape notice. I've had to change caravans a few times, but luck—or something—has been with me. I've run into freshly leaderless caravans at just the right time. A dollop of coercion mixed with a dash of compulsion were enough to put me in charge."

He stopped to consider his next words. "Other than bullying my way in, I've never taken advantage of the Rom in my caravans. I needed a position where people would accept my magic, and the Rom never questioned me. I couldna verra well be a shifter. Druidry has seen a bit of a resurgence, but naught where I could lose myself and be invisible. Not much in the way of other magic wielders left in the world."

"You forgot vampires." A feral expression etched into her ageless face.

"As if I could. Ye asked me all these things for a reason. What do ye have in mind?"

"I've been playing with a few options. It would be safer for the Rom to be invisible, but that level of expended magic fanned out over a large area is sure to attract vampires, if any are in the region."

"What does any of that have to do with exposing myself as a Druid?"

"I was hoping you'd have some special magical tricks at your disposal."

"Tricks that would reveal I couldna be Romani if I employed them, eh?" Stewart cleared his throat. "Nay. Sorry. I havena any magic bullet that will transport the eight of us who are not shifters across the border. We'll have to pray our good fortune holds. I dinna expect we'd get this far without notice, yet we have."

"You're planning to leave the truck on this side, right?"

"Aye. Too difficult to find a route past the border that won't entail searches and requests for papers. None of us have them except the driver, and those are stolen. The communications network turns slowly, but by now the name on his identification might be on a list that would alert a border guard."

"I've cut that deck a few ways. We'll need transport on the other side. It's either that or a very long walk to the docks in Amsterdam where we can find a ship. More than sixty miles through settled country, places where a pack of wolves and a few bears would stick out like mismatched shoes and stockings."

Stewart raked a hand through his hair, but his fingers snagged on his braids. "I thought about Amsterdam, but 'tis crawling with officials. Far better if we angle north and try for a ship around Harlingen."

"So my estimate of sixty miles was conservative. That's even more reason to hang onto the truck. Shifters can still take to their animal forms to cross the border, which would leave Rom in the truck. Not so big a challenge to make it appear no one is there when the border guard checks the back, and I can magic up the driver's papers to make certain they're not flagged as stolen."

"I doona like it. What if the guard is one of the SS who've parleyed with vampires and holds some of their magic? Worse, what if the guard *is* a vampire?"

Meara looked askance at him. "Have you seen even one vampire actually working for the Reich? Never mind in a menial, boring position where they'd be standing beside a little booth for hours checking an endless procession of vehicles?"

Stewart winced. "Nay. Mayhap I'm overreacting, but this border idea was mine, and I'm the one who'll have to live with it if we lose anyone during the crossing."

Her harsh expression softened. She stopped walking and laid a hand on his arm. "The odds of all of us making it across aren't good. You have to know that."

"I do, but I doona wish to add to the risks."

"How were you thinking we'd cross the Netherlands once we

put the border behind us?" Her question was soft, but her penetrating gaze never left him.

"Stealing a vehicle—or two." When he said it out loud, the words pinged sourly. Talk about danger. And an immediate one at that. Even if they removed the plates, most cars were easy enough to recognize.

"Stealing, eh?" She snorted. "You've traveled with the Rom so long, you think like one. We'd need at least two vehicles. Probably three to accommodate everyone, which means we'd have to split up. Nothing like three stolen cars caravanning across the country."

Breath whistled through his clenched teeth. "Ye made your point. We'll chance it with the truck. Ye just overflew the area. I bet ye have a suggestion about which border crossing station we should approach."

She rolled her eyes. "I like to think I'm not quite that transparent."

"Why go through a quarter hour of conversation? Why not just tell me what ye wished to do?"

"It's always better if we come to agreement. No one likes being force-fed another's ideas. Turns out we can remain on the road we left before this break. It's as good as any other, and I didn't sense vampires. Which isn't to say some couldn't show up between now and nightfall—"

She snapped her fingers, but before she could say anything, he spoke up. "No reason to wait for nightfall if we don't need darkness to shroud ourselves. Vampires are strongest at night, so we're better off rounding everyone up and going right now."

"You read my thoughts. I'm off to work on the driver's papers. See you on the other side." Light flashed around the vulture shifter just before she vanished.

Stewart hustled back to the group and rattled off names. "Change of plans. Into the truck with you."

Cadr jumped to his feet. Loose black trousers were tucked into a battered pair of leather boots, and a heavy navy-blue sweater was tossed over a lighter woolen top. Curly dark hair fell to his shoulders, and his blue eyes crinkled with concern at their corners. "Och aye, and I thought we were waiting for the dark to better hide ourselves."

"'Twas my original plan as well, but Meara talked me out of it. I was going to leave the truck and chance it on foot, but she helped me realize how badly we'll need transport big enough to hold all of us once we cross the border."

Cadr cocked his head to one side. "Are the shifters still crossing as animals?"

"Aye, 'twill be just us Rom in the truck. Ready your magic. We'll weave a ward to render ourselves invisible." Stewart loped toward the truck, still calling names. By the time he got there, the rest of the Rom were loaded into its cavernous bed, and he joined them.

Meara lifted the canvas and stuck her head inside. "Drape the blankets over yourselves. Rather than invisible, try a spell that makes the lot of you appear dead."

Michael shifted his swarthy, thickset body and nodded in her direction. "Brilliant. Most people are uncomfortable enough with death, they won't wish to examine corpses too closely."

She cracked a rare smile. "Not just corpses. Dutch citizens returning to their native soil for burial." She dropped the canvas panel, and the truck's beefy engine roared to life.

"Thank you." Stewart directed his telepathic comment to the driver.

"Why thank me? It's my truck. None of you could figure out how to drive it on short notice."

"Because if it weren't for us, ye could join the other shifters and cross in your bear form."

Laughter rolled through Stewart's head. When the shifter stopped chortling, he said, *"Yeah, like a bear in the middle of winter isn't something that would make folk sit up and take notice. We're supposed to be asleep."*

Stewart almost thanked him again for interrupting his hibernation cycle, but didn't. The less magic expended right now, the better.

"Will we be all right?" Aron asked, his gray eyes pinched with worry. At sixteen, he was the youngest of them. Ilona was his sister, but she'd very recently become a shifter because there were no other options to call her back from a borderworld inhabited by Romani spirits.

"Come here." Stewart beckoned. "Ye can join me beneath my blanket."

Aron scooted across the truck's rough bed. "Thank you. I'm scared."

"Rightfully, so, lad," Michael said. "It's not as if you haven't had a rough go of it between the Nazi prison camp and vampires feeding off you."

Aron straightened his thin shoulders and pushed long, dark hair out of his face. "Meara fixed the bad places in me. Vampires can't find me anymore."

Stewart heard a tremor in the lad's voice. "Ye said the words," he exhorted. "Now ye have to believe them."

"Yes, sir."

Stewart arranged a blanket, lay on it, and motioned for Aron to lie next to him before he draped another blanket over them. The truck pitched and rolled on the dirt road before getting back on asphalt. It wouldn't be long now.

"Open your minds to me," Stewart instructed and wove a spell with all their various magics. Death was easier than invisibility. He even added the stench of decaying flesh to make it more realistic.

The truck rumbled to a stop, and he heard a guard demanding papers. Aron edged closer, and Stewart's heart went out to the boy. In many ways, crossing on foot would have been easier. At least movement provided an outlet for the adrenaline that had to be pouring through everyone scattered across the truck's bed.

Heavy footsteps moved around the truck, and Stewart tightened the web he'd woven around them all. Next to him, Aron flinched and started to shake.

"They can't see me anymore, can they?" Even his telepathy was breathless.

"Ssht. Remain still."

Meara's intervention might have moved Aron beyond vampire gunsights, but the lad was still sensitive to their presence. That had to be what he meant by *they*. Stewart sent a thread of power outward. He'd been so focused on protecting everyone inside the truck, he hadn't bothered to check who was headed their way. After Aron's reaction, he wasn't surprised to find vampires.

Goddammit!

The bastards were close enough, he could smell their rotting blood stench. He followed up the English curse with a string of Gaelic ones, but kept them locked in his head.

Vampires would enjoy dead cargo, but maybe not long dead. Stewart upped the ante on the rotten carcass smell until he wanted to gag.

Someone pulled back a corner of the canvas and dropped it in a hurry. "Whew! That's terrible."

"Are you certain?" a second voice demanded. "I'm hungry."

"Not for those you aren't," the first voice responded.

The canvas was pulled back a second time, followed by the truck's springs complaining as someone jumped into the bed. "Pick me up on the other side of the border," the vampire who'd just entered their truck called cheerily to his companion. "Easier to find something back here than to grab any more humans. They're touchy as scalded cats. Superstitious too."

"Have it your way. I'm hungry, but not that desperate. Meet you in the Netherlands an hour or two past nightfall. Jump down when you're done. I'll find you," echoed from next to the truck. Its engine whined, and the gears ground as they engaged. Tires thumped as they rolled through the gateway and into a country free from Nazi domination.

One problem at a time, Stewart told himself. Getting the crossing behind them was huge.

He'd just begun to reshape their shared magic to snare the vampire when Aron bolted upright and launched himself at the creature. His lips were drawn back from his teeth, but no sound emerged. Even terrified, he understood the necessity of not drawing undue attention to their truck.

The vampire's eyes widened and it crooned, "Our Nosferatu goddess is smiling indeed. Look at that luscious morsel." Red hair cascaded down broad shoulders, and eyes the shade of raw emeralds glimmered with hypnotic charm.

"I'm no one's morsel," Aaron snapped and wrapped his limbs around the vampire, grappling with it.

"Love it, just love it when there's a bit of a challenge." The vampire's mouth opened to display its fangs.

Aron twisted away from the deadly incisors, but the vampire was fast.

Before it could sink its teeth into Aron, Stewart wrapped power around the vampire, coil after coil of shiny cord, but it didn't slow the creature down.

"I've got this," Cadr grunted and lurched past Stewart with a silver blade drawn and ready.

Sensing the deadly metal, the vampire twisted away from Aron, leering with extended fangs. "Now you're making me angry. You don't want to do that. I can make short work of the lot of you."

"Really?" Michael pulled a silver blade of his own and shot forward. "Try it, vampire."

Aron made another grab for the vampire, this time from behind. He clung to the creature, ripping its flesh with his nails while he grunted from the effort. He slowed the vampire down just enough for Cadr and Michael to attack from opposite sides.

Two silver blades. Two death blows.

Stewart's power crackled around them, rich with the scents of a restless ocean and the cool northlands. Finally, he had enough strength to immobilize the godless creature. What hadn't been sufficient before, worked now. The vampire's life force ebbed as black, stinking ichor spewed from it, staining the truck's floorboards. Vreis yanked blankets away before the thing's blood could stain them.

Stewart hissed out a breath. A dead vampire held its own set of problems, but it had sealed its fate when it jumped into their vehicle. What would happen when its companion couldn't find it, tracked it by smell, and discovered it was dead?

A shudder tracked down Stewart's spine. Not much rattled him, but he hated vampires. Living forever was one thing. Living forever as a blood-sucking abomination, something else entirely.

The other vampire could identify their vehicle, which stuck out like a sore thumb. Not so much in Germany where the war was in full bloom, but he doubted there were many transport trucks in the Netherlands.

Guess we're about to find out.

Cadr pulled out his blade. "Dead." He drew his lips back in a satisfied snarl.

Michael retrieved his blade as well. "None of those insidious beetles are crawling out of it, so this can't be one of the truly old ones. What do you want to do with him?" He looked at Stewart and directed a stream of magic to eradicate black blood pooling around the thing. It might not have been ancient, but its flesh withered quickly. Mottled bones emerged as the vampire revealed its true age in death.

Rather than answering, Stewart used telepathy to talk with the driver. *"Turn the truck so we're headed south. Lose it in the first forest road you can find."*

"Got it." The driver's voice was tense. *"That bastard is dead, right?"*

"Aye, quite dead," Stewart replied.

"Well?" Michael prodded and rocked back on his heels.

"We'll do our best to conceal what's left of his carcass in the forest and magic it up so it takes time for his buddy to find him."

"Maybe we should wait for the other one. Kill him too." Vreis raised a dark brow.

"If it were only the one, I might agree," Stewart said. "But these bastards travel in packs. Our priority is to get out of the Netherlands, not engage another nest in a full out war."

He added magic to Michael's to obliterate what he could of the stinking, oozing remains. They'd need something close to divine intervention to get all of them across this country without vampires tracking them, but returning to Germany wasn't an option.

CHAPTER 2

$\mathcal{Y}$ara de Vos slunk deeper into the cave where she worked her magic. Power had been bombarding her for the past hour. Some she recognized, but not all. It was the *not all* that made her nervous. Shifters were close. So were vampires and Romani, but powerful enchantments were afoot. Supernatural energy she'd never run across before.

Beyond picking up magic, she'd sensed emotion. That particular skill made her a decent fortuneteller, not because she had seer ability, but because she read people easily.

She inhaled, blew out the breath, and did it again to manage her growing anxiety. Worry wouldn't do her any good. Neither would giving in to helplessness—or anger at her situation.

She avoided doing anything that identified her as a gypsy. So far, her spells and tricks had kept her alive and out of prison. The Dutch government wasn't kindly disposed toward those like her. The *Woonwagenwet* or Caravan Act of 1918 had labeled caravan dwellers as antisocial parasites who refused to work. By the time 1930 rolled around, gypsies had been branded as undesirables. That was ten years ago. She'd been fifteen at the time, and her caravan had disbanded.

It was either that or be rounded up and subjected to brain-washing designed to "civilize" her and her kinfolk, whatever that meant. Her mother was long since dead, and her father a chronic drunk. She'd remained with one sister for a couple of years after her caravan broke up, but a sweet-talking Irishman had convinced Ilse to run off to Ireland. She'd sent letters, not often, but her sister stopped writing back six months ago. Yara was worried about her, but there wasn't much she could do from the wrong side of the North Sea.

She shook her head. She'd been on her own for a long time, stealing what she needed since no one would hire her. She closed her teeth over her lower lip. That last part wasn't entirely true. She could have found work in the brothels that peppered Amsterdam, but the specter of men pawing at her every night twisted her stomach into an ugly knot of tension.

She'd never been hungry enough or cold enough to regret her decision.

At least for now, she had her cave and an abandoned shepherd's hovel, no doubt deserted because one of the walls had fallen in. Between the two and an occasional foray into nearby towns, she managed. Summers were easier since she could filch produce from tilled fields, but she'd grown skilled at taking more than she needed and drying both fruit and vegetables to hold her through the cold months.

Somehow, she'd made a life for herself, and she'd done it by being cautious and shrouding herself in *don't look here* spells. They were easier than full-on invisibility and had much the same effect.

The magic she'd sensed earlier returned with a vengeance. Closing her eyes to hone her attention, she sensed a vampire on the hunt. What was it with their resurgence, anyway? She'd never met even one of the wicked creatures until a few months back, and now the German-Netherlands border was crawling with them.

Yara concentrated. Fear and anger met her probing mind.

Whoever the vampire had targeted was fighting back. She clenched one hand into a fist. *Good.* The bastards almost had her once, but that was before she understood their facility with mind-control.

She'd escaped by a fluke. Another vampire showed up, just as uncommonly beautiful as the first one. She'd been certain she was seconds away from being turned, but the duo pulled so much power it made her dizzy and vanished, leaving her with her mouth hanging open. Not for long, though. She'd snapped up what had to be a gift from whichever goddess watched over incompetents and fools and retreated to her shepherd's hut, winding strong wards around it and herself. After that, she'd been far more careful. The vampire's eerie beauty had drawn her. No more. Vipers were beautiful too—and just as deadly.

At least they kill cleanly. That vampire would have recreated me, and I'd have had centuries to kick myself for being stupid.

Eyes open again, she pushed her magic outward, but couldn't determine what was happening. Against her better judgment, she edged toward the cave's entrance. She wanted to know what was going on, and the grotto's earthen walls dampened everything. It was why it was such a good hiding place.

The unfamiliar magic surged. Her vision wavered, turning inward, and the spirit world flickered. It was almost as deadly a place as running into a vampire, but far easier to escape from. She shook her head hard and commanded the spirits of the dead to stay put. Stuck between worlds—dead, but not—they were a restless bunch.

Pulling her patched woolen cloak tighter around herself, she stepped into a fading day. Trees and shrubs grew thickly around the cave's entrance, and she sprinkled magic to hide its doorway from animals or people. Her stomach growled, protesting she hadn't eaten for hours, and she tugged a strip of dried apple from a pocket, stuffing it into her mouth.

The zing of expended power was much stronger here.

Curiosity sparred with reticence to get too close to the vampire's unmistakable emanations. Maybe she could help, but she sensed at least half a dozen Romani, one shifter, and the thing she couldn't identify.

Vampire energy throbbed, flaring hotly.

Damn it!

Was the creature killing the gypsies? Worse, were they gypsies she'd known before they'd gone their separate ways? She'd run into some of her old caravan mates, had even traveled with an aunt and uncle for a time after Ilse left—until they'd all become too nervous about being caught.

Easier to escape notice as a woman alone—or a couple. No one wore the flamboyant clothing or jewelry that had identified them as Romani, and their wagons were long gone. Traded for a variety of nondescript vehicles. Most of her kin had dark hair and dark skin, though, which was hard to hide in a country where most were blonde and blue-eyed. She was an anomaly with her flame-colored tresses and light eyes. It was why she could have found work as a prostitute.

Yara balled her hands into fists. She should at least try to help. Power pulsed and streamed from a spot that wasn't static. It moved away from her, following a western trajectory.

A car. They're in a car.

Her steps faltered. No way could she catch up with a moving vehicle. Grateful for an excuse to not face off against a vampire, she sent her magic outward. Maybe she could discern what was happening. If anyone was jettisoned from the car, then she'd risk revealing herself to help them. She latched onto the vampire's nasty, oozing energy. Out of all the magic crashing around her, that was the one that could be her undoing.

Yes. And the one I must keep track of.

Since her near-brush with disaster, she'd always put distance between herself and vampires fast. It was hard to force herself to remain still, watchful and waiting.

The vampire doesn't know I'm here.

It's busy.

It can't hurt me.

Mesmerizing waves of vampire sludge crashed over her. When she caught herself taking a step forward, she wrapped a hand around a nearby tree trunk. It was wet and slimy, but it anchored her in the real world. The one she aimed to remain in.

At least none of the other magical sources had flickered and died. And there was still only one vampire. Because she was focusing so intently on it, she noticed a difference in how its power felt. At first, she thought she'd imagined it, but the vampire's life force was definitely waning.

Which meant the bastards could be injured. Maybe even killed.

After her first run-in with them, she'd have sold her soul for access to the lore books that had been in her caravan for generations. She knew less than nothing about vampires, including this new information that they could be wounded, perhaps slain.

What had happened to the lore books? The caravan's leader said he planned to sequester them somewhere safe, but old parchment was sensitive to mold and mildew. Maybe he'd kept them in their trunk and—

It doesn't matter. Her mental voice was stern. Even if gypsy lore died out of the world, there wasn't a thing she could do to stop it.

Yara followed flickering vampire energy as it pulsed weakly, and then faded to nothing. She wanted to jump up and down, shrieking her joy at a major victory over something truly evil, but knew better than to give her location away.

The mix of magics was still on the move. Without overthinking things—so she couldn't talk herself out of it—she sprinted toward its location. If the vampire were truly dead, she'd spit on its corpse. The specter of seeing Romani—her people— heartened her. That odd magic still shimmered in the midst of them, but if it meant them harm, she'd have felt the red-tinged throb of fear.

One of the car's inhabitants was a shifter, but that didn't bother her. No love lost between shifters and Rom, but they left one another alone. What did it mean that a shifter had thrown in his lot with a bunch of gypsies?

Lots of mysteries lay ahead, and she ran faster, using magic to muffle branches that snapped beneath her pounding feet. Water squished through a hole in one of her boot soles. She needed new boots, had needed them since last winter, but they were hard to pilfer. They had to be the right size, or at least close enough, and the few pair she'd found that might have worked had been even more worn than the ones on her feet.

A major roadway, one that led to a crossing station, wasn't far. Had the car come from Germany? It made sense, given the direction it was traveling.

Oh-oh.

She skidded to a halt. The car left the main road and was headed right for her. She'd switched from the forest to an ancient, little used dirt track because it was easier than wending her way in and out of thickets. This near the border, most folk were in a hurry to put either Germany or the Netherlands behind them, and she'd never seen a vehicle on this road before.

She moved to the side of the road, uncertain whether to draw attention to herself. Something might be amiss with the car; the engine was noisy with a labored sound. Better if it stopped on its own and its inhabitants got out. That way, she could ascertain if the vampire were truly dead. She couldn't sense its energy anymore, but the things were sneaky.

Headlamps lit the dying day, and the vehicle—a huge truck, not a car as she'd thought—pulled into view. At least it explained the way the engine sounded.

Magic snared her, the magic she couldn't identify. She tried to pull away, but this brand of power was almost as insidious as vampire energy. It felt cleaner, though, and the ball of fear that had lodged in her throat when she realized she couldn't escape began to loosen.

The truck rumbled to a stop not ten paces from her, and the canvas sides covering the back parted. People poured out. The driver stepped down from the high cab. Tall, broad, and burly with shaggy, dark hair, it was the shifter she'd sensed. He ignored her and made his way to the back. Someone dropped a pile of bones that had to be the dead vampire into his outstretched arms.

"Ugh. God but he stinks," the shifter complained.

"How do you think it smells back here?" Someone she couldn't see countered. "Between Stewart's spell to make it look like we were dead and rotting and the vampire, it's enough to put a man off his feed for a week."

She faded into shadows, still uncertain, but a slightly built young man made a beeline right for her. Romani to his core, he had curly dark hair and arresting gray eyes.

"Who are you?" He locked gazes with her. "We sensed you while we fought the vampire. Or Stewart did, anyway. Are there gypsies here? Where's your caravan?"

Yara didn't bother denying her Romani roots. Other Rom had ways of knowing these things.

A tall, spare fellow clad in a tartan hurried toward them. Red hair hung in braids that reached past his waist, and he trained astute dark eyes on her.

Yara took a step back, and then another. This man was the source of the magic she couldn't identify. "What are you?" she blurted, and then clapped a hand over her mouth. She might have chosen to live alone, but it was no excuse for being rude.

"My name is Stewart, and I'm a Romani caravan leader." Compulsion flowed beneath his words.

She narrowed her eyes and considered calling him out on an obvious untruth. Before she could craft something that wasn't quite as insolent as her previous question, he saved her the trouble.

"All ye need know is I willna harm you," he said into her mind. Soothing magic accompanied the words. He switched to spoken speech. "Is your caravan close, lass?"

Yara rolled her eyes. "You don't know much about gypsies in the Netherlands, huh?"

"No. We thought we'd be safe here," the young man said. He stuck out a hand. "My name is Aron."

"If ye could hit the high points," Stewart prodded. "About Romani and this country."

"Sure." She extricated her hand from Aron's. "Rom have never been exactly welcome here, but things got a whole lot worse in 1930. We were branded undesirables. All the caravans disbanded, and we've been living as best we can."

"What happens if the authorities figure out what ye are?" Stewart asked.

"They imprison you under the guise of helping you learn proper ways to live." Yara didn't bother concealing the derision that lined her words.

"So the sooner we're out of here, the better," Aron muttered.

"Might not be as easy as all that, lad," Stewart replied.

"What's this?" Another man bustled up. This one was stocky and dark-haired with tanned, leathery skin. "I'm Michael." He extended a hand, and she shook it. "Where's the rest of your caravan, woman?"

Yara inhaled sharply. "No caravan. Just me. No caravans anywhere in Holland. Not anymore. Where have all of you been living, anyway?"

"Germany." Michael narrowed his dark eyes to slits. "We've kept to traditional ways. No radios. I did read the occasional newspaper, but never kept up on the news—until lately when our survival was threatened by the Reich."

"Where were you when your caravan disbanded?" Stewart asked.

"Not far from Amsterdam. I was with my sister then. She and I traveled to this location, and I've remained here."

"What happened to her?" Aron spoke up.

"Hush." Michael sent a pointed glance at the young man.

"It's all right," Yara said. "She left for Ireland, but that was a long time ago. Maybe eight years."

"Do ye know if she got there?" Stewart drew his brows into a thick, worried line.

"Yes. It's only been recently I stopped hearing from her. Either that or the post office in Enschede figured out I'm Romani and—"

"General delivery to a postal station?" Stewart cut in. At her nod, he went on. "Ye must have wanted to keep in touch with her verra badly to risk showing yourself in a public location."

Heat rose from her chest and swept over the top of her head. "I did. That's the only place I ever let anyone see me. If they'd asked me any questions, I'd never have returned, but the lines are long and the clerks overworked. No one looked twice at me, but I helped that along with spells."

Magic converged on them. Shifter magic. Yara stood straight and raised her hands to summon power. Why wasn't anyone else preparing to defend themselves? "Shifters approach." She kept her voice low.

Aron waved a dismissive hand. "They're our friends. One is my sister. Things have changed—a lot."

"Your sister?" Yara focused a beam of magic at Aron. Perhaps she'd misjudged when she pegged him as Romani.

He rolled his eyes, having sensed her examination. "You got it right the first time. Her boyfriend, Jamal, had to make her a shifter to save her life. It's a long story, but—"

"Indeed it is, and we shall save it for another time," Michael cut in sternly.

"Aye," Stewart concurred. "We must be gone from here soon. Afore the vampire's partner is done feeding and comes looking for his companion."

Yara snapped her head up, looking for the shifter who'd taken the vampire. "Is there some way to hide the dead one? It is dead, right?"

"Aye, lass. 'Tis dead," Stewart concurred. "No good way to hide it, though, and his associate saw our truck. We must pick a path quickly afore our options dwindle to nothing."

The shriek of a large bird drew her attention to the sky. An enormous black vulture with magic sheeting from it circled to land. Must be another shifter. In addition to knowing next to nothing about vampires, she also didn't know much about shifters. Including the various animals they could share a bond with.

Thick underbrush crackled, and a group of black and gray wolves moved toward them. Yara marshalled her instinctive fear, reminding herself they were all part of the group she'd stumbled onto. The wolves hastened toward the rear of the truck and jumped inside. More rustling, and a pair of shaggy, brown bears followed them.

Breath hissed through Yara's clenched teeth. At least they weren't milling around showing their fangs and snarling. She glanced upward, noting the vulture's position as it spread its wings, intent on landing. The wolves and bears might make her nervous, but the vulture was far more daunting than any of the other shifters, and had significantly more magic.

The air turned incandescent, taking on a shimmery aspect and pulsing with power. Scents rose around her. Yara understood that part. Every magic wielder's castings held a particular scent. Her own magic had always reminded her of pine trees after a downpour, sweet and tangy with undernotes of vanilla.

Bright light flashed, so intense she shut her eyes. Along with the light came the smell of clay baked under an intense sun, mingled with rosemary and new-mown hay. Yara pried her eyes open expecting to see the vulture rocking from foot to foot. Instead, a tall, angular woman stood before her. Long, silver-gray hair hung to the ground. She may have looked human, but her amber eyes were pure raptor. Intense, searching.

Power scoured Yara from the crown of her head to her toes. It prickled and burned, but she held herself still as the bird shifter took her measure. The woman was ancient and stronger than Stewart, the one who'd tried to pass himself off as Romani, but wasn't.

"Interesting," the woman muttered. "Where'd you come from, girl?"

Yara bristled. "I live here."

"'Tis just her, Meara." Stewart stepped forward, joining them. "No caravan. No other Rom. I checked with magic."

"What?" Yara rounded on him. "You didn't believe me?"

He shrugged. "Not much reason to believe anyone ye doona know, lass. Sheathe your claws. I dinna mean aught by it. Have ye a name? Or should I call ye lass and have done with things?"

Something about Stewart, his words or his soft brogue, caught her off-guard. No one had apologized to her for anything in a very long time. She held up both hands. "Sorry. I always did have a short fuse. I'm Yara de Vos."

"I am called Meara," the bird shifter said, "but that one already named me." She tilted her chin at Stewart, her nostrils flaring. "I smell dead vampire. I don't need to know what happened, but we must mask its presence from its kin. They'll be along—"

"Sooner rather than later," Michael muttered.

"I can't do much about concealing it forever, but I can buy us an hour or two." Still scenting the air, Meara moved away from them.

"I'll add my magic to the mix." Stewart trotted after her. "That might extend our window for an additional hour."

"Can you move it away from this location?" Yara called after them, but neither Stewart nor Meara turned around.

"Why?" Michael asked.

"Because I live here, and I'd just as soon not deal with those undead monsters."

"Why not come with us?" Aron asked.

Surprise slapped her, and her mouth gaped open. She shut it with a snap.

A slender woman with long, dark hair and Aron's gray eyes raced toward him. She must have been one of the shifters who'd disappeared into the wagon, no doubt to don clothing. Reaching them, she scooped Aron into a hug. "I'm so glad you're all right. When I smelled vampire, I feared we'd lost someone." A long, woolen skirt clung to her, topped by a gray tunic and a black cloak. Apparently, these Rom were downplaying traditional clothing as well. All to the good if they planned to traverse the Netherlands.

"Your brother was very brave." Michael beamed at the pair. "He would've taken the vampire on singlehandedly, silver or no."

The woman glanced up from hanging onto Aron. "I'm Ilona," she told Yara. "Until very recently, I was Romani, just like you."

"I'm Tairin, and this is Elliott." Two more people who felt far more Rom than shifter joined them. Tairin had beautiful, tawny curls that fell to her waist and liquid dark eyes with amber centers. Elliott's hair was dark, and his eyes a deep, reflective blue. Both wore thick, dark, woolen clothing similar to Ilona's.

Another man hurried their way. This one was pure shifter with hair the same color as Tairin's and eyes that matched hers as well. What was he? A parent or a sibling?

"I'm Jamal." He extended a hand. "Tairin's father and Ilona's mate."

Yara grasped it, enjoying his warm, firm handshake. When she let go, he moved to Ilona's side and wrapped his arms around her and her brother.

"I heard Aron suggest you join us." Michael focused his attention on her. "It was a decent idea. Nothing to hold you here, and a gypsy without a caravan is an affront to nature."

The corners of Yara's mouth twisted into a sad smile. She knew that expression so well, she repeated it in Dutch. "Can I have a few moments to think things through?"

"Not much longer than that," Michael cautioned. "We must be on our way as soon as Meara, Stewart, and our driver return."

She nodded. "I understand. If I'm not back, leave without me."

Resisting the temptation to remain with the group, she strode briskly into the forest, heading for her grotto. If she did leave this place, everything she wanted to bring with her was there. It was safer than the shepherd's hovel.

Am I really considering going with them?

Her thoughts raced feverishly. She knew what she had here, and it wasn't very goddamned much. Survival hung by a thread, and had for all the years since her caravan split up. When she tried to conjure even one argument to remain where she was, nothing came.

The lack of reasons to stay put surprised her. She'd been fine by herself. Well, maybe not fine, but not *unfine*, either. Now that she'd come to a decision, she moved faster. If things didn't go well, she could always return here. By then, any hoopla around the dead vampire should have played itself out.

She didn't have much to lose. If the group were intent on harming her, she'd have picked up on it. Besides, she wanted to know how Romani and shifters ended up allies. She raced into her cave and scooped up her few possessions.

The prospect of no longer being alone was heady.

Yara tried to rein in her enthusiasm, but it refused to retreat. She hadn't had anything to look forward to in years. To finally be part of a group of magic wielders again was too tempting an offer to refuse.

Remain vigilant, her inner voice cautioned.

Yara pushed it aside. Vigilance would keep her mired right where she was. Leaving was a gamble, but one she was willing to take.

CHAPTER 3

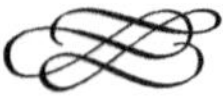

Stewart felt the gypsy woman, Yara, leave. She was medium height, but had an arresting presence that transcended her patched clothing and half-starved appearance. Hair the color of a ruddy sunset was drawn into a bun, but flame-colored strands mingled with gold hung around her face. Her eyes were incredible, a blue-violet that shaded lighter and darker with her moods.

She had strength of character too. Most Rom were lost without their caravans. Living in groups had become an ingrained way of life for them since their origins back in India. Her news about gypsies becoming *persona non-grata* in the Netherlands surprised him, but well over a century had passed since he'd left the British Isles. A lot could happen in that much time.

"Do you require my presence?" the bear shifter who'd carried the carcass asked Meara.

She shook her head. "Return to the group, but do what you can to remove all traces of vampire stench before you do so."

"I'd have done that anyway," the shifter groused and stalked out of the clearing muttering in German.

Stewart barely spared him a passing glance. He was still lost in thought about Yara.

"Your attention is wandering." Meara's voice cracked like a whip before she returned to chanting over the vampire's remains. Fire sizzled along what was left of it, cleansing and purifying its evil.

Stewart redirected the flow of his magic, weaving it in with Meara's. Between the fire and the fact that the vampire hadn't actually died in this particular spot, they might get lucky. For a while.

"Wonder how many other Roma are wandering around Holland," he muttered.

"A lot of them from the sound of things." Meara dropped her hands to her sides. "There. Not much more we can do here."

"At least the gypsies here have had a few years to develop skills to conceal themselves."

Meara glanced at him. "You sound bitter."

"I am. I've become fond of the Rom in the years I've traveled with their caravans. Their magic dates to the beginnings of the world."

She shrugged. "So does shifter power and the odd hybrid magic you possess. The woman determined you were different immediately. How the hell did you conceal yourself from—?"

He made a chopping motion with one hand. "She has power the likes of which I've never seen in a Romani. She's empathic, able to delve deep into what people are. And without much apparent effort from the looks of things."

"Pfft. That's always been part of Rom magic."

"Not to the extent Yara has it. Nowhere close."

"I'll have to take a closer look—if she decides to join us. Are we still headed for that northern port city?"

"Harlingen?"

"Yes, that's the one you identified before."

"I still think it's a good idea," he replied. "As we angle north, the settlements are smaller, and the odds of covering our tracks improve. Come on." He tossed one more layer of obfuscation over the vampire. It had stopped smoking at least, but an unmistakable burned smell permeated the area. "Can ye get rid of that stench?"

Meara shook her head. "No. It will die out soon enough. I've done everything I can, including obscuring our scents. It's one thing for the vampires to locate their fallen kin. That will happen eventually, but I'd just as soon they didn't latch onto anything overly obvious to track us. If I'd realized that nest outside Dachau had more members, I'd have taken more care with the fires and spells I fashioned there."

Vampires were exceptional trackers. Stewart thought it unlikely they wouldn't be able to glean enough information to come after them, but he kept his opinions to himself. If it happened, they'd deal with it. The truck was a much bigger problem. While probably not the only transport vehicle in the Netherlands, it was large, clunky, and recognizable.

They hastened back to the rest of the group. Michael stood next to the truck making hurry up motions with both hands. "Everyone's inside," he informed them. "We need to get moving."

"Did Yara join us?" Stewart's words surprised him. He'd been thinking about her but didn't realize he'd spoken out loud.

He clamped his jaws together to keep further speculation from escaping his control. He'd been intrigued by Rom in several of his caravans, but had never acted on any of the attractions. It wouldn't have been fair. Women needed to see him for himself before he bedded them, and that would never happen in a caravan where he masqueraded as Romani.

"Not yet." Michael shrugged. "It's quite a leap of faith for someone who's been living alone as long as she has. That's why I'm still out here. I wanted to offer reassurance in case she returned but harbored ambivalence."

"And here I thought you were still standing here to protect her from me." Power crackled around Meara, and she swung her body in a full circle. "She's coming. I feel her magic. It's distinctive, but I haven't the time to sort it out just now."

Michael snorted. "You can be a bit on the overwhelming side, but now I feel just plain stupid. I could have employed power and looked for myself, but didn't."

"Not stupid. Instinctive and wise," Meara retorted. "Enough expended power will draw vampires."

"But you just—"

Meara cut off his words with a withering glance. "I'm about to take to my bird form. If anyone tracks my energy, it won't lead them back to the rest of you." She focused her attention on Stewart. "That was why I inquired about our route. I'll overfly things and be in contact telepathically with what I find."

"Fair enough. We'll drive through the night," Stewart said. "I'd rather put as much distance between ourselves and the vampires as we can. Here's hoping there's not a curfew in this country like there is in Germany."

Bright light flashed, joining the sunbaked, rosemary scent of Meara's magic. When his vision cleared, the vulture was airborne, her wings pumping hard. "Good to have a forward scout," he muttered.

"Indeed. I've come to appreciate shifters in a way I never thought possible," Michael said.

"Comes of keeping an open mind." Stewart jerked his chin toward the sound of boots pelting toward them. "Get into the truck. Yara and I will be there soon."

Michael nodded and trudged toward the back of the truck. Worry flowed from him, but he had it well in hand before he lifted the heavy canvas cover and climbed into the back. Part of any caravan leader's job was to project confidence, so your people didn't lose hope. That had become progressively harder as Germany sank into a war touting Aryan supremacy as the sole standard for survival.

A war where everyone who wasn't blonde, blue-eyed, and part of the master race was at risk of imprisonment…

Magic had to survive. If it didn't, the world would devolve into chaos.

Yara came into view and cut off the troubling flow of his thoughts. Her arms overflowed with cloth bags. He hurried toward her, intent on helping.

"Guess ye're planning to stay," he joked and tugged a couple of sacks out of her hands.

Color stained her thin cheeks. "Silly of me, but I hated to leave anything behind. I may not have much, but—"

"'Tis all right. I ken well enough. I was teasing. None of us have aught by way of possessions. We planned to return to our caravans near Munich, but changed our minds after we attacked a German prison camp on the outskirts of Berlin."

"Were you successful?" A savage tone lay beneath her words, as if she were rooting for them to have slain as many Nazis as possible.

"We were." They reached the truck and he helped her inside, handing her belongings to her before jumping onto the high bed.

The engine was already running, and the truck began to roll. *"Angle northwest,"* he told the driver.

"Not toward Amsterdam?" The bear shifter sounded surprised.

"Meara and I decided on Harlingen on the northern coast. Sorry. Meant to say something, but the vampire got in the way."

"Glad I asked," the driver grumbled. *"Harlingen is probably safer. I used to drive a delivery truck. My route included the Netherlands, Belgium, and France. The easiest port used to be Havre, but France is crawling with Nazis."*

"The country will be occupied soon enough," Elliott spoke up. "Apologies for listening in, but you didn't bother to shield your telepathy, and I've seen France overrun in visions."

"No apologies needed," Stewart said.

"Are Nazis coming here too?" Yara trained her unusual eyes on Elliott.

"Yes. I can't tack the time down exactly, but it will be soon. A few months at most."

"Oh. Maybe a good thing I'm leaving then." Brave words, but they lacked conviction, and she sounded sad. "I might have listened in on your conversation with the driver too. Harlingen is a reasonable choice."

Stewart motioned to Yara, who sat surrounded by her things. Maybe talking would help her feel less isolated from the rest of them. "Tell us about yourself, lass."

A crooked grin made her look young and vulnerable. "Funny, but I was about to ask you the same thing. Who are all of you? And why are Rom and shifters working together? Doesn't it violate some long-ago edict?"

"Fair enough," Tairin said. "I can see why you'd be curious about us and wondering if you made the right decision."

"Not so much that. I know this country. If it turns out to be a bad call on my part, I can always retreat to my cave. Maybe. Travel will become even more dangerous if the Nazis show up."

Cadr eyed her speculatively. "If ye werena planning to stay, ye'd not have brought all those things."

"No point going into any venture unless you have hopes for its success," she countered. "As for my things, they're all I have, and I couldn't stand the thought of leaving any of it behind." She scrunched her face into a thoughtful expression. "I do want to know about you, though."

"I understand about abandoning things," Tairin said. "Long ago, my caravan discovered my mixed blood and kicked me out. I had a small sack with me. Not much, but it was all I could carry and still travel." She hesitated before continuing. "Someone stole it, and it made what came next much easier because I had nothing left to lose."

Stewart's heart went out to the shifter. She'd revealed what she was several weeks ago to up their odds of destroying a nest of vampires. Rom weren't strong enough to withstand vampire mind control tactics. Shifters were, so she'd hunted down her long-lost father, the man who'd abandoned her, to demand help.

Something about his last thought jolted him, and he held up a hand. "Aron. Come closer."

"Why?" The young man angled his head to one side.

"Ye attacked the vampire."

"Yeah. So what?"

"So he wasn't able to control you. You're Romani. You should've been an easy mark for him."

Understanding flared on faces ringed around the truck's bed. "Do you suppose that thing Meara did to him changed him somehow?" Ilona asked and focused a worried expression on her brother.

Magic shimmered as several of them reached to examine Aron.

"Sheathe your power. The vampires havena gone away." Stewart kept his voice low, but made certain the command was obeyed. "Aron, come close enough for me to touch you."

This time, Aron slithered across the expanse of truck bed separating them, and Stewart placed a hand over the back of his head. Directed magic, anchored by touch, wouldn't seep outside the truck. He took his time, probing carefully. Aron's primary ability was future-seeing. It was intact, but Stewart located places Meara had made alterations in the overall warp and weft of Aron's magic.

He removed his hand.

"Hey! Am I a shifter now?" Aron asked excitedly.

"Nay. Not even close," Stewart replied. "Meara transformed the areas where vampire magic made you even more susceptible to their hypnosis."

"The thing that happened after they fed on me, right?"

"Exactly," Stewart concurred. "Anyway, she not only got rid of their insidious incursion into your free will, she made certain they couldna mesmerize you at all."

"Good to know. Means I can fight them all I want."

"It does not," Ilona said sternly. "They can still sink their fangs into you and turn you."

"Aw, Sissy. I was just joshing." Aron crawled back to the blanket he'd been lying on.

"Some of you were Rom and now you're shifters." Yara spoke up. "Is that an easy transformation?"

"No," Michael answered. "Nor is it sanctioned by either of our people. Tairin began with mixed blood. Her mother was Rom, and you've met her father, Jamal. Elliott and Ilona became shifters because they were dying. Linkage with a bond animal was the only way to save their lives, and the sole condition where transformation is allowable."

"I see, but Aron wants to be a shifter."

"Who wouldn't? He grinned. "It'd be like having the ultimate imaginary sidekick."

Ilona ruffled his hair. "My wolf just pointed out that it's far from imaginary."

"Why'd you come to the Netherlands?" Yara asked. "There's lots more I want to know about all of you and how you ended up together, but—"

"This country will be occupied by the Reich in a few months," Ilona broke in. "So will France. At least according to Stewart, our magic will be stronger in the British Isles, and we'll have a better chance of sabotaging the Reich from there."

"At first, we'd planned to stage raids on prison camps—in between taking on vampire nests—but the logistics of traveling in Germany were harder than we anticipated," Tairin added.

Yara narrowed her eyes in thought. "Stewart told me you attacked a prison camp. I'm not seeing how moving across the North Sea will give you any advantage, no matter how strong your magic becomes. Not that I'm questioning a strategy you've decided on as a group." She lowered her gaze to her hands. "Sorry, I spoke out of turn."

"Ye dinna. All opinions are welcome." Stewart dragged his attention away from her, but it wasn't easy.

"Vampires joined forces with the Reich. Did you know that?" Elliott asked.

A muted gasp escaped Yara. "No. I couldn't figure out why there were so many of them all of a sudden, but that explains it."

"Hitler believes he can control them." Michael snorted. "He has no idea what he's up against."

Stewart nodded. "Aye, they're only playing along because 'tis advantageous. Gives them access to blood and death in the prison camps."

"Doona forget all the sex they can handle." Cadr jumped into the conversation.

A blush etched into Yara's fair skin, and Stewart sent a pointed glance Cadr's way. "Och. Sorry if I was a wee bit blunt," Cadr said.

"Blunt is fine," Yara retorted. "It's better than beating around the bush and having your words misinterpreted."

"I've likely spent more time in close quarters with vampires than any of the rest of you," Jamal said. "They were common as caravans in Egypt. They'll tire of Hitler and his rants. When that happens, we may gain an unlikely ally, so long as we don't make the mistake of trusting them."

"We'll never fight on the same side," Stewart cautioned. "Best we can hope for is they'll launch their own war against the Reich. Hopefully, they'll weaken them enough to amplify our efforts."

"There is that angle," Jamal agreed. "And it's a good one."

"I know who's shifter and who's Rom," Yara said looking at Cadr, "and I know some of your names, but—"

"Sorry. I should've given my name afore I spoke. I'm Cadr and this is my brother Vreis."

Voices rose and fell as everyone in the wagon introduced themselves. "Will ye remember who everyone is?" Stewart asked.

"Yes. I'm very good at that," Yara replied. "I could have peeked into your minds and culled names that way, but it seemed rude."

"Your magic is odd for a Romani," Aron piped up.

"Hush." Ilona trained gray eyes on her brother. "That wasn't polite."

"People have told me that my whole life." Yara turned her hands palms up. "It's the way of the world. Me being different made other Romani nervous, but I was good with the Tarot cards, and telling fortunes came easy since I read people so well. The gadjo didn't trust any of us, so they treated me like one more gypsy."

"And your leader welcomed the coin you brought in." Michael's deep voice rumbled.

"Of course, he did. I miss him. He was wise and fair."

"Were you born in the caravan?" Michael prodded.

She nodded. "Yes. My mother died when I was twelve giving birth to what would have been my little brother—if he'd survived—but he died right along with her. After that, it was my two sisters and me and Father, but he drank a lot. So much, he wasn't good for anything. The caravan leader gave up on him, but didn't kick him out because then my sisters and I would've been orphans—"

"—and another would have taken over your wagon and stock," Stewart finished her sentence.

"Yes." She blew out a tight breath. "Turns out that happened anyway. My oldest sister claimed sovereignty and took the wagon and team when the caravan was breaking up. It was all right. I didn't want them. I didn't want anything that might identify me as Romani, and wagons are a dead giveaway. I was fifteen at the time. My other sister was a year older. She and I stuck together until she met an Irish man. He was as poor as we were, but had a silver tongue, truly the soul of a poet. He talked her into running away with him to Galway, where he was from.

"She and I wrote. Not often, but a few times a year. I haven't received anything from her for eight months now, and I'm beginning to worry." She furrowed her brow. "Galway is probably a long way from where we're going, huh?"

"Aye, lass," Stewart replied. "That it is. I'd thought northern Scotland as good a goal as any other with its Highlands and islands. Did your sister have your same magic?"

An unreadable expression crossed Yara's face, but it was gone before he could interpret it. "No. Nor did my oldest sister. Ma's power was weak as dishwater. And Father was drunk so much of the time, it was impossible to tell what type of power he commanded. Rom magic is dying, withering. Once we were far stronger—"

"Aye, I'm well aware of all that. Do ye have an explanation for the source of your magic?" Stewart redirected her away from what was turning into a rambling philosophical commentary, but gently.

"Of course, I do, but it shames me." She tipped her chin at a defiant angle.

"Nay, lass, 'twould be your Mum who'd bear the shame for her choices. Did she never tell you who your Da was?"

Yara shook her head. "It wasn't as if I didn't ask. Not in that way because I was too young to know much about sex then, but I realized I was different and I peppered her with questions about why. No child likes to stand out—for reasons that make others shun her."

Stewart wanted to draw her close, stroke her long, thick hair and console her, but she wasn't asking for comfort.

Tairin scooched closer to Yara and wrapped an arm around her. "It's all right. I understand better than you think." Tairin's eyes held a pinched look. "My mother never told me the truth, either—until she had no choice—and by then it was too late for both of us."

"Romani women are all like that," Ilona said. "Stubborn and

strong-willed. It's what's kept us going, given us the ability to stand up to the men."

The truck rocked to an abrupt halt. Stewart pushed a cautious thread of magic outward. What was wrong? Were there roadblocks in this country too?

Raised voices reached him, demanding the driver's paperwork. When the driver asked for a reason, whoever stopped them said the truck had been seen illegally crossing the border.

Damn! Vampires must have located their dead companion and raised an alarm. Maybe they were aligned with law enforcement in this country too.

"I'm going out there to help the driver," Stewart murmured, kicking himself for not being more vigilant. He'd been so focused on Yara, he hadn't bothered to scan for threats outside the truck.

"I'm coming with you," Jamal announced softly

"Let's be smart about this." Stewart kept his voice low. "We'll be better off invisible."

"Already thought of that." The air around Jamal shimmered, and a corner of the canvas tarp lifted and fell back into place.

Stewart followed on Jamal's heels. Night had fallen, and there was no moon. Why hadn't Meara warned them? Vultures didn't need much light to see. He hoped she hadn't run into problems— or done something stupid like taking on several vampires by herself.

He crept around the side of the truck. A police van was parked across the road. Fortunately, there were no other cars. Two officers were engaged in a heated conversation with their driver. One brandished a set of handcuffs.

"We have to kill them," Jamal said.

Much as Stewart had hoped for a transit of the Netherlands that didn't draw attention to them, he didn't see any other way out. Rendering the men unconscious would buy them time, but the minute they recovered, they'd radio in a description of the truck.

"Stewart!" Jamal's tone was sharp even in telepathy.

"I'll take the one nearest me." Without stopping to think about it, he focused lethal magic to stop the man's heart.

Both police officers hit the ground at the same time. Stewart loosed the magic that had kept him invisible, grabbed the one he'd killed, and dragged him into nearby underbrush. Jamal did the same. The radio in the police car crackled to life.

"How's your Dutch?" Jamal asked.

"Not bad. Yours?"

Jamal stepped out of the tatters of his spell and gestured at the radio still spewing words. "Be my guest. If we're ever in Egypt, I speak that language."

Stewart picked up the mike and depressed the talk button. "Quiet," he hissed. "You will give us away."

He dropped the mike back into its slot and got into the car, moving it to the side of the roadway. For good measure, he raised the hood and pulled the distributor, tossing it into thick shrubbery. At least the next car traveling past wouldn't speed into the nearest town and sound an alarm because a police car was blocking the road.

By the time he was done, the driver was back behind the wheel and Jamal had disappeared into the truck. Stewart followed him inside, and the truck rolled forward.

He set his jaw in a tense line, crawled back to where he'd been sitting, and looked at the circle of grim faces. Leaving a trail of dead bodies and disabled vehicles would not work in their favor. He didn't need magic to know everyone was worried.

"We're going to have to leave the truck," he said. "It will make it much harder to remain together, but I don't see where we have much choice."

"It can't be much farther to Harlingen," Yara said. "This is a small country. We don't want to bring the truck into the city, anyway. It has really narrow streets. It's been a seaport since medieval times."

"What do you suppose happened to Meara?" Michael asked.

Aye, we'd all like to know that.

"I have no idea," Stewart replied.

"I hope she's all right," Ilona said.

"She's been taking care of herself for a long time." Jamal wrapped both arms around Ilona, and she leaned into him.

Stewart sent magic in a full circle. It was a risk, but running up against threats like the police car that had stopped them was a bigger one.

"Find anything?" Michael asked.

"Not yet. Hush. I need to concentrate."

*Y*ara hadn't been this worried since the early days after her caravan split up. Keeping this many people safe and out of trouble was an impossible task. She used her own earth-linked magic to determine how much farther it was to Harlingen. They'd been underway for something over two hours, so it couldn't be that much farther.

Stewart's dark gaze augered into her, and he gripped her wrist. "No magic. 'Tis bad enough I have my own deployed. Nothing like sending up a beacon announcing our location to anyone nearby who holds power."

Her first instinct was to pull her wrist away, but the heat and energy from his body were tantalizing, electric. "No one can see mine," she explained, resisting an impulse to lean closer to him.

"How is that possible, lass? I felt it," he countered.

"That's because you're right next to me. I can blend my power with the earth. No one outside this truck should be able to detect what I'm doing."

"Ye must needs say a wee bit more."

Yara nodded. "This was one of the reasons other Rom gave me

a wide berth. My magic was not only different from theirs, it defied any Romani ability they'd ever come across."

"Probably because the other half of your blood is something else," Jamal murmured.

Yara shrugged. "I have no idea. No one in our caravan was powerful enough to sort it out."

"Meara is," Jamal said.

"If we ever see her again," Michael cut in. He screwed his face into a grimace. "I shouldn't have said that out loud. It tempts fate, and not in good ways."

Jamal cast a speculative glance her way. "Priestesses from some of the sects in ancient Egypt held magic similar to yours."

"But my caravan never left Holland," she protested, and then closed her teeth over her lower lip. Just because she'd never left this country didn't mean someone from elsewhere couldn't have spent an evening with her mother. Perhaps one of the gadjo had offered extra coin… She closed off that line of thought fast. It was disrespectful, and her mother wasn't here to defend herself.

Stewart released her wrist. The place his fingers had closed around still felt warm from his touch. She had no idea exactly what he was, but his initial reassurance that he meant her no harm was true enough.

Hell, I'm not sure what I am. No reason to lose sleep because he's a mystery as well.

"What were you looking for?" Ilona directed her question at Yara.

"Huh? When?"

"Just now, with your magic."

"I wanted to tack down where we are. Harlingen is close. Something under forty miles. We could walk it in a pinch—in a couple of days."

"Now there's a piece of good news." Tairin smiled.

"Smart of us to invite her along, eh?" Elliott chimed in.

"Me. Inviting her was my idea," Aron said.

"So it was." Ilona sent an indulgent look at her younger brother.

Stewart straightened his back and tucked his legs beneath him. "I dinna find aught magical within the range of my ability to check, but it doesna mean we're safe. Those two police officers had zero power. They were clearly hunting for us, though."

"Vampires sicced them on us." Cadr spat the words.

"That was my take too," Jamal said. "If we can see into the future, no doubt they can as well. Perhaps Hitler sent them into this country and France and goddess only knows how many other places to pave the way for the Reich."

"Do they drive cars?" Yara asked.

"I have no idea," Stewart replied. "But ye do raise an interesting point. If they could drive, why wouldn't they come after us themselves? Why send local gendarmes to do their dirty work?"

"Doona look a gift horse in the mouth," Vreis muttered. "Ye dispatched those humans with far less fanfare than a pair of vampires would have caused."

"How is killing them even possible?" Yara clasped her hands together. She hated talking about it, but she might need the information.

"Silver," Stewart said. "Silver through the heart or beheading them, which is much harder."

"That's it?" Surprise flooded her. "Somehow I figured potent magic had to be part of their undoing."

"Doona underestimate how difficult 'tis to get close enough to a vampire to kill one. Silver stakes and beheading mean ye must get within range of their mesmerism—and their fangs. They're unnaturally fast and strong."

"But they're vain," Elliott said. "Flattery can sometimes engage them sufficiently to divert their attention just long enough to trap them."

"Divert their attention away from someone with a silver stake?" Yara furled a brow.

"Exactly." Gregor, a powerfully built shifter with black hair and hazel eyes, who hadn't spoken much since she got into the truck, nodded. "It's how Ilona and I managed a vampire that had Aron targeted in Sachsenhausen-Oranienburg prison camp. We engaged him in idle chitchat so Jamal could sneak around behind and stake him."

"Do we still have silver stakes with us?" Yara asked, determined to chase this line of inquiry to its conclusion. "If so, it would be good for me to know who carries them."

"Smart lass." Stewart nodded approvingly, and a pleased feeling started in her stomach, radiating outward. She wanted him to think well of her, and it surprised her. Back in her caravan days, she hadn't given a damn what anyone thought.

Yeah, but I was fifteen and a pariah. Easier to hold myself aloof than twist myself into knots trying to please anyone.

"I have silver," Michael said, the words breaking into her musings.

"As do both Vreis and I," Cadr said.

"Jamal, Aron, and Elliott," Tairin took over. "Stewart and Gregor too. The other thing we have, but not in such generous quantities, are these." She pulled a leather pouch out from beneath her jacket.

Yara nodded, recognizing the amulet at once. "I used to make them for the gadjo. What's in that one?"

"Holy water, consecrated earth, garlic paste, bits of a crucifix, and rosary beads."

Yara rolled her eyes. "Are the priests in Germany more kindly disposed to gypsies than they are here?"

"No," Elliott said, his tone somber, "but they recognize the need to fight evil and were willing to help us."

"Since ye brought out your amulet"—Stewart focused on Tairin—"we should take stock of how many we have and make certain they're allocated to Romani."

"Right you are." Tairin drew the leather cord out from around her neck and handed her amulet to Yara.

She took the leather, warm from Tairin's body, and held it taking its measure. Her palm prickled from its power. "What exactly will this do?" She looped it around her neck and tucked in inside her clothing.

"Give you some protection against vampiric ability to hypnotize you," Elliott answered.

Three more amulets appeared, but they were already with Romani, so no others changed hands.

"We could do with a few more, but it can't be helped." The shifter who'd identified himself as Nivkh said. "Half the Rom have amulets. If those of you who don't pair up with someone who does—" He dusted his hands together. "I'm certain you'll figure things out. Guard your eyes."

"Why?" Yara took in the broad-shouldered man with white blond hair and ice blue eyes dressed in hunting leathers.

"I'm worried about Meara, and I'm going to search for her. If nothing is amiss, we'll meet you on the docks in Harlingen."

"And if ye require our help?" Stewart asked.

A rumbling snort blew past Nivkh's lips. "If it's so bad she and I can't extricate ourselves, there won't be much any of you can do to intervene."

Light flared blue-white, absorbing Nivkh in its nimbus before it grew so bright Yara had to shut her eyes. When she opened them, the spot where he'd been was empty.

Questions tumbled through her mind. Who exactly was Nivkh, beyond being a bear shifter? Meara wore her power like a banner. If Nivkh held anywhere near her level of ability, he'd cloaked it well enough she'd barely given him a second glance.

Until a few moments ago.

No one said anything and minutes ticked past. Soon they'd be close enough to Harlingen to find a place to abandon the truck. She was getting ready to open her mouth and say as much, when the lumbering vehicle turned hard right and bumped along what had to be a primitive road.

She did a better job packaging up her belongings until everything was stuffed into four bulging cloth sacks.

Stewart leaned close. "Ye must pare it down to less than that. Take only what is essential and will fit in a single bag."

"I'll carry one of them," Tairin said, and Yara remembered her story about having nothing left to lose.

"And I'll take another," Ilona spoke up. "The Nazis threw me into Dachau with nothing. I know how that feels."

"I'll carry another," Jamal offered.

Yara blinked back tears. "You don't have to. I—"

"We want to," Tairin broke in. "In a way, it evens the score for the wrongs that were done to us."

Yara glanced at Stewart. "Do you mind if they help me?"

"Of course not. I was just concerned ye'd be so burdened, ye'd not be able to keep up." Emotion flickered in the depths of his eyes. Concern, but it was tempered with hope.

Yara handed sacks across the truck, touched beyond measure by how willing the others were to help her. She was a stranger in their midst, yet they'd accepted her without question. If the situation were reversed, would she have been as generous?

I hope so, but being alone has marked me, scarred me.

Not so much I can't reverse the damage.

She sat straighter determined to be worthy of everyone's kindness.

The truck lurched to a halt, and the driver killed the engine. "Those of you who aren't carrying Yara's things, grab a blanket." Stewart said. "They might come in handy." Wrapping one into a thick bundle, he tucked it beneath his arm and pulled back a corner of the canvas tarpaulin. Everyone jumped down from the truck.

A door slammed, and the driver walked back to where they milled about. "Where did Nivkh go?" he asked.

"After Meara," Stewart replied. "Do ye know exactly where we are?"

"More or less." The driver nodded. "I wanted a place no one would stumble across the truck unless they were looking for us. We're about five miles from the docks as the crow flies." He tilted his head and snuffled, scenting the air. "You can smell the sea."

Yara almost muttered that statement would be true about most of the Netherlands, but she kept her mouth shut. It was a know-it-all thing to say and not needed.

The driver pointed to their right. "A faint track heads in a mostly western direction. Once I picked it out with my headlights, I stopped."

"Plenty of night left," Michael observed. "We'll be on the docks well before dawn. What happens then? Do you suppose we'll find a ship's captain we can persuade to take us aboard?"

"Your guess on that is as good as mine," Stewart said. "We can deploy magic and make humans do most anything, but it won't be just the captain we'll need to bend to our will. He'll have crew."

"Do we have money for passage?" Yara asked, hoping that maybe they wouldn't have to do anything magical. Employing power in that way was forbidden, though she wasn't certain who'd decreed it so.

"Nay. No passage money. We have Reichsmarks, but I doona wish to take the time to trade them for Guilders," Stewart replied.

"No offense to our newest addition"—the driver glanced at Yara—"but the Dutch are a stuffy lot. We'd never find a bank willing to change our money since none of us have valid identification papers."

Yara shrugged. "How could I take offense to a true statement? The Dutch were narrow-minded enough to declare gypsies outcasts."

Stewart dropped a hand on her shoulder. "'Tisn't forbidden to convince a ship's captain we'd make good passengers. Or to magic our way through a bank transaction."

She ducked from beneath his hand and turned to face him. "You were in my head."

"Aye, lass. I'm in most people's minds much of the time."

"It is forbidden to use magic to take advantage of those without it."

Ilona muffled a grunt that might have been laughter. "And just what were we doing every single time we cast a Tarot spread or told a fortune? Or handed over a collection of aromatic herbs under the guise of it being an irresistible love charm?"

Yara squared her shoulders. "Giving good measure for coin offered." Heat suffused her face, and she inhaled briskly. "I see where you're going with that. Damn it. They programmed me to think a certain way in the caravan, and I never got over it."

"Because the programming came with a magical assist no doubt," Michael said and winked.

"Too bad about our clothes," Jamal cut in. "Travel would be easier in our animal forms, but then we'd be naked when we arrived on the docks."

"This forest doesn't extend more than maybe another half mile," Yara said. "The terrain when we get near town is open farmland. You'd risk getting shot as wolves."

"Good to know," Jamal replied.

"Listen well." Stewart clapped his hands together. "We're splitting into four groups. We'll be less noticeable that way. Yara, describe the dock area if ye can."

She nodded. "It's big. The entire western part of town fronts on water, and there are many, many docks. Lots of big sailboats too."

"Hmmm. That might work even better," Stewart said.

"What might?" Michael elbowed him.

"If we locate a sailboat no one's used for a long time, we'll take it, so long as it's seaworthy. Easier than forcing our way aboard a commercial boat. I know how to sail, as do Cadr and Vreis. Everyone from my part of the world does."

"Aye aye, captain." Jamal snapped off a salute. "Alexandria was a busy port, but I've never even been on a ship."

"Let's get moving. Yara, Elliott, Tairin, come with me," Stewart said. "We'll regroup when we're on the docks. Keep your eyes peeled for a likely looking sailboat. It doesna have to be huge to accommodate all of us."

"What about Meara and Nivkh?" Jamal asked, obviously concerned about his shifter kin.

"I'll try to reach them when we get closer," Stewart replied.

"I've been calling Meara for a while now," Jamal admitted. "Nothing."

"We shouldn't leave without them," Yara murmured. Worry filled her. It felt wrong to pull anchor—assuming they found a boat—when two of their group might be in grave danger.

"Meara would tell us to go." Jamal's tone was grim.

"So would Nivkh," the driver said. "Best gift we can give them is to not get ourselves sunk so deep into something we need their assistance."

No one said much after that, and the others were forming groups when hers left the truck behind. The track the driver pointed out was easy to follow at first, but it soon devolved into a tangle of roots and thick mud that tugged at her feet with every step. Her boot with the hole took on mud and became heavy. A steady drizzle started, the kind that meant she'd be wet to her skin soon.

The tree cover gave way to tilled fields crisscrossed by irrigation ditches. Yara hunted for the walkway she knew had to be there. Otherwise the farmer wouldn't be able to tend his crops without slogging through hip-deep water.

"Over here." She used telepathy.

"Nay, lass. No magic unless 'tis absolutely necessary," Stewart said softly.

"Sorry. Mind if I stop for a moment?"

"Is something wrong?" Elliott asked.

"My boot is full of mud. I'll be faster if I clear it out." She undid her laces and pulled off the boot, balancing on her other foot as she dug clods of squishy muck out of the worn leather.

"There." She slid her foot back into the boot and laced it. "I'm used to wet."

Stewart strode briskly along the path she'd found. She wanted to reach out with her magic and make certain the others had located easy passage through the interminable fields that surrounded every town, but Stewart had been most clear about not deploying power.

They reached the end of the field, skirting a darkened farmhouse. A dog barked twice, but then quieted. They followed a dirt road toward the sound of breakers crashing against a distant shore. Years back, the town's lights would have come into view, but everyone was conserving power these days. True to Yara's prediction, the persistent drizzle meant she was wet down to her underclothes. Not that she had much left in the way of such things. When she stole clothing, she'd focused on practical pieces like skirts and jackets. Panties fell into the *nice, but not important* category.

She gave herself a mental shake to rein in her wandering thoughts.

Dirt gave way to asphalt, and the salt tang of the sea stung her nostrils.

Stewart stopped until she drew abreast of him. "Which way, lass?"

She pointed to a street. "It's as good as any other."

Tairin and Elliott joined them. Tairin shook water off herself. "I'd feel better if we were invisible."

Stewart drew his brows together. "How much farther?"

"Maybe a quarter hour at a quick clip," Yara replied.

His gaze roved over the dark, silent streets with water running down them and into the gutter system. "Conserve your power for now. There's no one to see and remember us. If that changes, so will we."

The expression on Tairin's face said she didn't agree with his assessment, but Elliott slipped an arm through hers and tugged her forward. Yara followed them with Stewart next to her. They'd walked single file through the field and into town, but the paved road was plenty wide enough to accommodate them two abreast.

The central part of town was as silent as the outskirts had been. Not that Yara spent much time in towns, but usually taverns remained open well into the night.

Just because they used to doesn't mean they do now, she corrected herself.

Her brief forays into town always coincided with midday when crowds would help hide her presence. In truth, she had no idea what happened the rest of the time.

"Did the Dutch government declare a curfew?" Stewart breathed into her ear.

"I don't know."

He drew in a sharp breath, seeming to have come to a difficult decision. "Ye get your wish." He touched Tairin's shoulder. "If this town is under curfew, we risk more this way than we would being invisible."

"Thank the goddess," Tairin muttered just before she and Elliott vanished in a shimmery current of magic.

"Lass?" Stewart skewered her with his shrewd, dark eyes.

"I've never leveraged magic to do that, but I can try."

He shook his head. "Now isna the time for experiments. Stand near to me, and I will shield the both of us."

She was already so close her shoulder touched his. The scent of his magic, sea and winter greenery, rose around her, and she inhaled hungrily. Something about the man by her side sang to her soul. For just a moment, she lost herself in magic that was arcane, seductive, and weaving itself about her in a protective arc.

When he started walking, his power drew her along.

CHAPTER 5

Stewart wanted to add his arms to the magic he wrapped around Yara, drawing her against his chest, but that would be ill-advised. They had to find a ship and be well gone before daylight turned the docks into a bustling mass of humanity. He needed to sort out why he was so attracted to the gypsy woman, but that required time. A commodity he was short of just now.

Deployed magic made it easy to locate the rest of them, all of whom had opted to shroud themselves in invisibility spells. He worried about the surfeit of power surrounding them. More than a dozen magic wielders, all invisible, packed a hell of a punch, but so far no one had emerged from the shadows to confront them.

"Follow me. I think we located a boat," Ilona whispered.

"We got close enough to determine no one has used it in a long time. Maybe years," Jamal concurred.

"It's big and really, really nice," Aron added, keeping his voice low.

"Show me," Stewart said. "No conversation between here and there."

Everyone nodded, and Jamal turned and headed north along a

well-kept road. Two and three-story houses lined the side not fronting on the bay. From the looks of things, most had been built in the seventeen- and eighteen-hundreds. Mirroring the condition of the street, they'd been updated and were in good repair.

Letting go of the spell that kept him shielded from sight, Jamal tossed his leg over a barrier and led them down a wooden dock riddled with holes, some large enough to fall through. An enormous rat poked his snout through one of the hollows, whiskers quivering with curiosity and beady eyes trained on them. Once it discovered they were too big to eat, it vanished back through the hole.

The rat looked well-fed. Stewart smothered a smile. Rodents would survive any war. They always did. Corpses made for a rich diet.

Jamal stopped and pointed. "That one."

"Loose your spells, all of you," Stewart said as he took in an older cutter, maybe sixty feet long. Its naked mast rose, and he wondered what kind of shape the sails were in. He scanned it for signs of life with a quick blast of magic.

"What do you think?" Jamal had sidled next to him.

"'Tis floating, which is auspicious," Stewart muttered. Once they were aboard, they were committed. They wouldn't have the luxury of trying out several ships to find the perfect one.

Cadr scooted up a ladder and dropped onto the deck. Vreis followed his brother. Stewart didn't need to ask what they were about. They'd check for canvas that wasn't too rotted to make good use of wind. The vessel probably had an auxiliary engine, but the odds of there being sufficient fuel to move them across the North Sea wasn't good.

"Sails are decent," Cadr sent.

Stewart motioned everyone aboard, but Jamal hung back once he'd helped Ilona and Aron with the rope ladder. "What about the first shifters, Meara and Nivkh?" He focused his voice right next to Stewart's ear.

"They're not here, and we canna wait for them."

"Same conclusion I'd come to, but I don't like it."

"Nor do I. Now go. I'll untie the boat. Hope to hell it doesna sink."

"Is there a chance of that?" Jamal's normally calm veneer took on an anxious cast. "I did my best to assess the hull with magic. It's intact, and—"

"Go. We'll deal with the rest of this once we're out of here." Stewart glanced at the night sky. "'Twill be light in an hour, mayhap less. We have to transit the bay afore anyone notices us and alerts the authorities."

"Why would they? No one's sailed this thing in a long time."

"Aye, and it worries me a wee bit. Boats this large are expensive, and this one appears to be in good repair. Why abandon it if there's not something amiss we're not seeing?"

"The owner might have died. Or had his property confiscated by the authorities."

"Hang onto that optimism. I fear 'twill be needed afore we reach port on the far side of the North Sea." Stewart gave Jamal a small shove. "Get moving."

The shifter shut his mouth with an audible *clack* and tackled the rope ladder hanging down the side of the boat.

Stewart unwound ropes from the rusty bollards and let them trail into the water. They'd draw them into the vessel and coil them once they were underway. He double checked that he'd gotten everything and was ready to clamber aboard when the distinctive stench of vampire burned his nostrils.

Goddammit!

They were so close to freedom. To have a pitched battle with vampires out in the open would be certain to attract attention. The type of attention that would ensure they never left Holland. The presence of vampires so near the border crossing argued they weren't skulking about in the shadows. No doubt they'd cut some juicy deal with the Dutch government, much as they had with the Nazis in Germany.

Naught I can do about it other than move this craft away from shore as fast as I can.

He skipped the rope ladder and used magic to catapult himself over the railing. Cadr and Vreis were raising the canvas. "Hurry," he sputtered.

"Aye, we smell the bastards too," Cadr said and finished clipping the mainsail to the mast and the boom.

Stewart grabbed a halyard, pulling hard to get the sail in place. Vreis joined him. "I doona understand why this boat was abandoned. 'Tis in respectable shape."

"I mentioned that same discrepancy to Jamal," Stewart grunted, tugging harder to muscle the sail into place.

"What can we do?" Gregor asked. "I already gathered everyone who carries silver and amulets in one spot."

Jamal trotted close. "Vampires never did like water."

"Say more." Stewart gritted his teeth together.

"It mutes their power. I'm not certain of the mechanism, but it seems to push them closer to the death they skirted by becoming vampires. I've seen ones driven close to the Nile age dramatically."

"Let's hope they dinna locate an antidote," Cadr muttered and wrapped rope around cleats to secure the mainsail.

"Does this thing have an engine?" Michael cast a nervous look in the direction the vampires were closing from.

"Let's find out." Jamal took off for the stern with Michael right behind him.

"Engine room will be below decks," Stewart called after them.

"You can't leave," Gregor shouted. "You have silver."

"Back soon." Michael moved faster.

The boat rocked easily, freed from its moorings, but there wasn't much in the way of wind, and the canvas flapped where rain pelted it. After floating a few yards from the dock, the craft bobbed atop the incoming tide. Stewart dropped the illusion that had protected him for so long. Druids were weather workers. It was what made them such effective stewards of the elements. The next moments would reveal him for what he was, but that was bound to happen sooner or later.

"Sheathe your power," he cautioned the shifters and Rom standing in a tight group.

"Why?" Gregor asked. "Whatever you have in mind, we're stronger together—"

"I will be summoning the wind to our aid. If ye have skills in that regard, toss them into the mix. If not, doona make my task more difficult. Cadr. Vreis. To me."

The men flanked him and raised their hands skyward, gathering power. Part of the Druid brotherhood, they'd stood by his side before they left the Old Country. Perhaps proximity to him had kept them young, but neither showed any sign of their years.

"Whatever you're about, hurry," Ilona cried. "Goddammit! I see the vampires. Three of them. They're on the dock, but not moving all that fast."

"They wouldn't be," Tairin said. "Water saps them. That gangway had huge gaps in it, and they'll be doing everything possible to conserve their power."

"We're too far from the dock for them to jump," Elliott pointed out.

"You could jump it with a magical assist," Tairin countered. "Join your magic with mine. All the rest of us can do the same. Make a line and anchor it with magic. Let's not make this easy for them."

Stewart focused on Danu, Celtic mother goddess of the world and Arianrhod, whose moon was just dipping below the horizon. He asked for strength and aid against evil. A light breeze rose, pooching out the canvas a little, but not enough to move a boat this size.

He glanced over one shoulder to catch a glimpse of the vampires. There were indeed three, their unholy beauty illuminated in a glow that flowed from each of them. They chanted in a demonic tongue, and black-tipped flames brightened the glow around them. The smells of sulfur and ozone burned his nose and throat. The slight breeze he'd summoned pooled around him and died. Worse, the boat rocked harder. It was almost impossible to capsize a sailboat because of all the weight in their keels, but dark magic was afoot.

Dark magic that didn't want them to leave.

Water might weaken the vampires, but the effect didn't appear to be an immediate one.

Cadr grasped one hand, Vreis the other. "We can do this," Cadr said in Gaelic.

"We have to," Stewart countered and ripped his attention away from the vampires. If they could have bridged the gap and jumped aboard, they'd already be here.

He dug deep, down into the secrets hidden within the earth beneath them. Water shielded those mysteries, muted them, and he exhorted it to step aside and let earth's beauty and might shine through.

The moon brightened where it hung suspended above the place where water and horizon met, and a silver-strewn path formed along the water's surface. The wind that had been anemic, reluctant, moments before rose around them in a howling, punishing gale that drove the ever-present rain into his upturned face.

"Aye. Now that's more like it." Vreis shaped and formed power until it arced outward from his outstretched hands.

Cadr did the same, and Stewart herded their magic until it forced the wind to stop swirling mindlessly and do their bidding. The sail filled, and the boat lurched forward, narrowly missing a boat moored to the next dock over.

"I'll man the helm." Cadr shouted to make himself heard above the wind. "Just keep that magic flowing." He made a grab for the wheel, unlocking it from where it was tied to hold the rudder in place.

Stewart couldn't have shut off the flow of power if he wanted to. Long years had passed since he'd practiced magic as a Druid and not as a Romani. The experience was as different as fussing with finger paints compared to painting the Sistine Chapel's ceiling. One took very little skill. The other more ability than a man could master no matter how long he lived.

Breath whistled from his lungs as he and Vreis shaped the flow of wind, keeping it aimed right at their sail. As he'd hoped when he first noticed it, the silvery path of moonlight drew their vessel like a lodestone. They scudded along it as if Ariahrhod had formed it just for them. Who knew? Perhaps she had.

He wanted to know what was happening with the vampires, but couldn't move even an iota of his concentration from his spell. Druid spells were all-encompassing. They dragged every last whit of effort out of a man, and then demanded still more.

If the vampires had boarded, he'd know about it. They hadn't, and that would have to be good enough for now.

The hum of the boat's engine stuttering to life reminded him of Michael and Jamal. *"Shut it off."* He used telepathy because he could no more have left his post than he could have loosed the magic using him as a lightning rod. Once Druid power had him in thrall, it left when it was good and ready to leave. Not a moment sooner.

Vreis tightened his grip on Stewart's hand. "Damn, this feels good." He laughed into the face of the rollicking wind. "I'd forgotten."

"No ye hadna. Not really," Stewart countered.

The magic did feel good. More than that, it felt right, scouring him clean of everything non-essential. Under Cadr's skilled hands, the ship took full advantage of the wind and moved briskly toward the breakwater separating Harlingen's bay from the North Sea.

Jamal and Michael trotted into view wearing very different expressions. Jamal appeared fascinated, but Michael's face trod a line between distress and fury. He shook a fist at Stewart. "You lied to me. Bastard. How could you pass yourself off as Romani all the years I've known you?"

"Not now." Stewart lassoed a thread of power headed right for Michael. Druid magic was a jealous mistress, quick to mete out punishment for any who criticized it.

Jamal dropped a hand on Michael's shoulder. "Come on, man. Let's join the others. At least we got the engine going. Thanks to you. Never knew what an ace mechanic you were."

"That's because you don't know much about me at all." Fury and disappointment streamed from Michael, but he let Jamal lead him to where Stewart presumed everyone else was.

The moonlit path shone before their hull, veering left as it passed the breakwater. He'd been worried about transiting the barrier. Sometimes rocks were close to the surface, and he hadn't had a chance to hunt for a helmsman's cabin that might have nautical charts.

The tug of power lessened and then fell away, and the moon gave up its struggle to remain in view. None of that mattered. They were underway, the waters of the North Sea lapping beneath them. A brisk breeze that had nothing to do with magic powered them forward. He let go of Vreis and clapped him on the back.

"We did it! Thank you."

"Nay, thank you. Ye're the one with most of the power. I just went along for the ride."

"And quite a ride it was." Stewart offered heartfelt prayers to Danu and Arianrhod before considering what came next.

He grimaced. Time to face the music—with everyone. Once that task was behind him, they could plan for the future.

He turned to Vreis. "Take stock of what we have aboard. See

about extra canvas, provisions, anything ye can locate, and report back to me."

"Will do. I'm curious what we have to work with too. In truth, I'm still figuring out precisely why this ship was abandoned."

"Mayhap something ye unearth will answer that question."

"Perhaps." Vreis sprinted toward stairs leading to the lower decks.

"Where are we going?" Cadr tucked a hand around his mouth to make himself heard.

Stewart thought about it. They had two choices. Make landfall as soon as possible, or remain in the boat until they got to Scotland. He stopped next to where Cadr stood, gripping the large wheel. "Easier to travel north by sea."

"Edinburgh?" Cadr raised a dark brow.

"If we can get that far, 'twould simplify the rest of things."

Cadr grinned rakishly. "I'm so glad ye dinna force us south to Dover. I wasna looking forward to sneaking across the length of England. They booted us out once for the crime of practicing our magic."

"Aye, they did indeed." Stewart mock slugged Cadr. "Times have changed, though. Modern man doesna recognize magic—in anyone. We'd likely have been safe enough, but we can make far better time this way. Three days, give or take, and we'll sail into Edinburgh—so long as a storm doesna slow our progress."

"I agree with your time estimate, but ye're wrong about modern man failing to recognize magic. Hitler knows vampires are magical beings. He's unscrupulous enough to leverage any angle, if he thinks it will strengthen his thousand year Reich."

"Mayhap he simply sees them as a bizarre cult steeped in blood and death." Stewart shrugged. "I need to square things with the others. No use pretending to be Romani any longer."

He crossed the deck to where everyone huddled in a tight knot in the bow, watching the coastline recede in a damp, gray dawn. "What happened with the vampires?"

Tairin faced him and crossed her arms beneath her breasts. "It was the oddest thing. One moment, they were plying that black-tipped fire they throw around. The next, they were enveloped in a thick, gunmetal cloud."

"I could see them through it," Yara said, "but no one else could. It was like they'd been paralyzed. Frozen in place."

"What happened then?" Stewart pressed.

"Nothing," Yara replied. "The boat picked up speed, and water formed a vortex between us and them. When it cleared, the cloud was gone, but so were they."

Stewart raked a hand through his hair, much of which had come loose from its braids. "Did any of you feel them die?"

"I didn't." Aron's eyes shone with wonder. "That thing you did, it was astonishing. Were you born with power like that? Or did you have to work to develop it?"

Ilona drew her brother against her and mouthed, "Hush. Not now."

"I don't believe the vampires are dead," Gregor said and leaned close. "No smell of rot and no bones scattered on the quay. What the hell are you? Not a Romani. Not a shifter." He shook his head hard enough dark hair fell into his eyes, but he shoved it out of the way. "Not that I'm complaining or ungrateful, mind you. That trick you did where you called the wind to your bidding pulled our bacon out of the flames."

Stewart stood straight, his shoulders squared. "I'm a Druid. At one time, I was the highest-ranking priest in the British Isles. I'm old, but there are shifters far older than I, like Meara and Nivkh. Anubis too afore his fall from grace. Cadr and Vreis are Druids as well. When sentiment rose against magic wielders all across Britain, we left. 'Twas either that or risk being hanged."

"Why the hell choose Romani caravans as cover?" Michael spoke up. Bitterness underscored his question.

Stewart turned his hands palms upward. "Why not? 'Twas the

last place I'd be able to work magic of any fashion in the modern world. I owe you an apology for deceiving you and the other caravan leaders, but I never once took advantage of my position. I strengthened my caravans and cared for my people as a leader should."

"That's not the point," Michael broke in.

"What is?" Stewart countered. "Ye feel deceived. I broke trust by not revealing what I was, and I apologize for that. When ye're not as angry, ye'll see there were few paths open to me. I wished to keep Cadr and Vreis close, and I have utmost respect for the Romani people. I did everything I could to preserve and strengthen their magic, though 'twas an uphill battle."

Tairin pushed closer. "Seems many of us have experience hiding who and what we are."

"I certainly did enough of it." Yara trained her astute gaze on him.

"Good to know I dinna have a corner on that particular market." Stewart tamped back a grin that wanted out.

Vreis pelted toward them, a drawn look on his face and his blue eyes pinched at the corners. "I figured out why this boat sat unused." Breath whistled from between his clenched teeth.

Stewart faced him. Was this when they discovered they'd chosen badly? In the middle of the North Sea when retreat was impossible? No one had sensed the vampires die, nor seen their bodies wither into bony corpses, which probably meant they'd leveraged enough of their own power to escape. But maybe this wasn't about vampires.

"Well? Out with it."

"I found four bodies in the forward hold. They're wrapped in sacking, but they died of plague if I'm any judge."

"We're immune," Jamal said.

"We being shifters?" Stewart requested clarification, and Jamal nodded.

"I did what testing I could with magic," Vreis went on. "It

appears they've been dead for a few months. Doesn't that mean the infection would die along with them?"

Stewart thought back to when plague swept through England in 1665. "Did ye find any dead rats?" he asked Vreis.

"Och aye, many. How did ye know?"

"They fed off the corpses, got the disease, and died. My guess is we're safe enough."

"We can move the dead off the ship," Gregor said.

"And purify the hold with magic," Jamal added. Without waiting for Stewart to bless their plan, he and Gregor hastened away from the group.

"I want to come." Aron started after them, but Ilona sprinted toward him and grasped his upper arm.

"Nope. Not on your life. You're not a shifter, hence you're not immune."

"But Stewart said the disease can't hurt anyone."

She eyed him sternly. "I'd just as soon not test that theory. By the goddess, Aron, don't try my patience."

"Like you tried mine when you were missing for two days," he shot back.

Stewart made a chopping motion with one hand. "Enough. Everyone might want to get some rest. Once Vreis takes stock of what we have aboard, we'll assign—" The cry of a vulture on the hunt drowned out the last of his words.

He glanced skyward, relieved beyond measure to see Meara winging toward them. Where the hell was Nivkh?

The raptor circled, clearly intent on landing, and Stewart figured he'd find out soon enough.

CHAPTER 6

Yara glanced skyward, heartened to see the vulture shifter's wings cutting through a gray dawn. In the brief time since she'd been with the small group of shifters and Romani, they'd become like family. Perhaps she'd been far lonelier than she'd allowed herself to acknowledge. Watching Stewart shape and form magic to bend the wind to his bidding had kindled a bone-deep longing within her. The power flowing from him, Cadr, and Vreis resonated in a way Romani magic never had.

Why was that?

Was her magic more closely aligned with theirs?

She shook her head to clear her jumbled thoughts. Conversation ebbed and flowed around her as everyone waited for Meara to join them. She turned to Ilona, who stood closest to her. "Why does Meara have so much more power than the other shifters?"

Ilona's mouth twisted downward. "Keep in mind that being a shifter is quite new for me, so I don't know nearly as much as the other shifters might. Meara is one of the first shifters. Rather like a god to the rest of them. Except I guess it would be the *rest of us*."

"The other one, Nivkh. Is he a first shifter as well?"

Ilona nodded. "Yes. You really should ask Jamal or Gregor or Tairin. Each of the varieties of shifter has a first that represents them. Except maybe wolves. I was there when the first wolf was snared and killed because he'd sold out to a vampire."

"I bet that's quite a story," Yara murmured.

"It is. If you remind me, I'll tell you the parts I know. My wolf holds knowledge too, far more than I do when it comes to things that are related to being a shifter. Before I forget, your sacks are piled on the far side of the wheel. We put them there after we came aboard."

Yara patted her own sack that hung suspended on a strap slung over one shoulder. "Thanks. It seems silly for me to have brought anything, but since I did, maybe some of it will come in useful."

"Was it mostly clothes?" Ilona furled her brows. "My bag seemed too heavy for a few skirts and jackets."

"Most of my things are magical aids. Candles. Herbs. Wands. You must've gotten the bag with the grimoire in it. That old book weighs a ton."

"Grimoire? Are you a witch?" She grinned. "Come on. Fess up. This is a day for people to discard their disguises."

Yara closed her teeth over her lower lip. "I don't know exactly what I am. Rom magic never felt like a good fit even though I practiced plenty of it." She came close to sharing the odd attraction she'd felt when Stewart shaped the weather to his bidding, but it sounded so farfetched, she swallowed the words unspoken.

"Witches have grimoires," Ilona persisted. "Did you get the spell book from a witch?"

Heat rose from her chest until Yara figured she had to be bright red. "I— I found the book. I just called it that because it was a magical book, but not anything like Rom lore tomes. It was in the cave near where you first saw me. I waited for someone to return to claim it, but no one ever did." She shrugged, suddenly uncomfortable under Ilona's frank stare. "I asked the book if it were willing to go with me, and it flipped to a passage that urged me to take it."

Fascination lit the backs of Ilona's gray eyes with a warm glow. "A sentient book. I've heard of such things. I'd love to spend some time with it—if it would let me." She paused a beat. "I bet it's part of the reason you picked that cave in the first place. It was waiting for you."

Yara grew warmer still. She'd wondered the same thing Ilona had just given voice to, but a book with magic strong enough to craft its own destiny had seemed absurd. She had no idea how the leather-bound tome would react to anyone else dipping into its pages, but she didn't want to hurt Ilona's feelings so she smiled encouragingly.

The vulture slipped downward, shifting in an intense flash of brilliance. When the light cleared, Meara stood in front of them in her human body.

"Where's Nivkh?" Stewart asked.

"How should I know?" Meara's nostrils flared with annoyance. "He was with you when I left."

"He went to look for you," Aron said and then hurried on. "That thing you did to me. It made me immune to vampire mind control. Thank you so much." Before Ilona could make a grab for him, he launched himself at Meara and wound his arms around her.

"You're most welcome, young man. Now take your hands off me." Meara grasped his shoulders and held him at arm's length. "Touching another without asking first is disrespectful."

Ilona hurried forward and wrapped a hand around her brother's arm. "Sorry," she told Meara. "It won't happen again."

Aron twisted in her grasp. "You're supposed to ask before you touch me," he informed her loftily, unfazed by Meara's rebuke.

"That rule doesn't apply for people you're related to," she told him, looking like she was trying not to laugh.

Stewart glanced at the group still milling about. "There's a deck just below this one. It should have cabins and bunks. Take the blankets. Try to rest a bit while we sort things out."

"Grand idea." Ilona tugged on her brother. "Shall we?"

"No. I want to stay and listen to—"

"Didn't Valentin teach you to defer to your elders?" Michael's tone was harsh.

"Sure." Aron looked down. "But he's not here."

"I am," Michael said. "Go with your sister. In fact, we'll all join both of you."

Yara watched shifters and Romani leave in groups of twos and threes until only Stewart and Meara remained. She should leave too, but she didn't want to go. Keyed up from all the power still simmering in the salt air, she inhaled hungrily, sucking it down like nectar.

"Lass—" Stewart began.

"Let her remain if she wishes," Meara broke in.

A clatter of footsteps announced Jamal and Gregor with a body suspended between them. Yara pushed a thread of power outward hunting for the wrongness she associated with illness. It was there, but subtle. The men chucked the tarp-wrapped body over the side.

"We dropped the dead rats out a porthole on the lower deck," Jamal announced.

"Not sure we got them all." Gregor rolled his hazel eyes. "Figured once we moved the other three bodies out of there, I'd shift and make certain we didn't miss any."

"Any clues to who the people might have been?" Meara asked.

"Not on their corpses," Jamal replied. "Not so much as a wallet, watch, or ring, which suggests whoever dumped them here either didn't know enough about plague to be frightened by it—"

"Probably medical personnel," Meara interrupted. "Practical medical personnel with protective gear who understood money isn't worth much to a dead man."

"One was a woman," Gregor said.

"Odd they didn't burn the corpses and commandeer the boat," Stewart mused. "'Tis more to this tale. We have yet to reach to bottom of it."

Meara turned her hands palms up. "You needed a vessel, and this one presented itself. No need to dig too deep."

"Those bodies won't move themselves." Jamal prodded Gregor, and the two men disappeared through the door leading to a stairwell.

Meara cracked a wry smile. "Convenient you made it across the bay and into the North Sea. Breeze happened to show up precisely when you needed it?"

"What? Were ye airborne and watching the whole thing?"

"Now that you mention it, I was."

Stewart didn't know whether to laugh or punch her. "What happened to the vampires? Did ye intervene?" He moved a step nearer the vulture shifter.

"Yes. Saltwater weakens them. It attacks the blood castings that give them power over others. Eventually, they age, wither, and die the deaths they should have experienced long ago."

"Do you know why that is?" Yara clapped a hand over her mouth. "Sorry. I should listen, not ask questions."

Meara narrowed her eyes. "True enough, but I'll answer that one. Water is the oldest and most powerful of the elements. It's hard to control, and most magic wielders prefer to dabble with earth, air, and fire. The blood spells that make new vampires are aligned with fire. It explains why so much of what vampires do is accompanied by those disgusting black-tipped flames."

"I understand." Yara nodded, unable to quell her enthusiasm. "Water trumps fire every single time, but why would saltwater be more effective than, say, a lake?"

"Don't push your luck, child. That was one more question, but a well-considered one. If you think about the composition of blood, it's closer to saltwater than drinking water."

"Thank you." Yara clasped her hands in front of herself as a reminder to keep her mouth shut.

"What do ye think we should do about Nivkh?" Stewart asked and creased his forehead into a mass of concerned wrinkles.

"If that's a not-so-subtle way of sending me to hunt for him, it won't work. Nivkh is a first shifter. He has earth magic to burn, and he can take care of himself. Beyond that, he's close to immortal. He'll find us in Scotland."

"If he can. Damn it. I should have told him not to leave." Stewart exhaled noisily.

Meara quirked a silver brow. "Do you believe that would have done the least bit of good?"

Stewart's harsh expression softened. "Nay. He's been making his own decisions for longer than I've been alive." Another breath whooshed from him. "What comes next?"

"Aren't you going to ask where I went? What I did?"

"Has it come to where I must dig for information?" His brogue thickened. "If ye've something to tell me, by all means do so."

"Touché. Eh, maybe the news is disturbing enough, I'm looking for any excuse to keep it to myself."

Yara's stomach tightened into a knot. "I can leave." She took a step back, ready to locate her other three sacks and take them below decks.

Meara settled her odd gaze on Yara, stopping her in her tracks with magic that scoured her to her bones much as it had when she'd first met the vulture shifter.

"No reason to go. Everyone here will know what I have to say soon enough. Demons are afoot. Not the same one Elliott loosed inadvertently from Hell, but others just as powerful."

"They've teamed up with the vampires, right?" Stewart's tone held a dull, dead note.

"Of course." Meara rolled her eyes, and they looked even more feral than usual. "If I had to piece things together, my conjecture is Grigori was here just long enough to find a vampire or two. Hell, he might have located the nest we wiped out near Munich. Jamal and I sealed him back where he belongs, but his presence gave the vampires ideas."

Stewart fisted a hand and pounded it into his thigh. "Och aye. Bad ones. If a Romani had enough power to free a demon from the underworld, surely a determined vampire could loose an army." His nostrils flared. "How many did ye see?"

"Half a dozen. I didn't hang around to take roll."

"We dinna need this complication. Given the vampires' link with the Reich, the demons will sign on as well. Blood, misery, and death draw them like magnets. The prison camps will provide rich fodder, and Hitler is fool enough to court them. He doesna understand they could well be his undoing."

"By then, it won't matter." Meara drew her lips back from her teeth in a snarl. "The damage will be done, and Earth may not ever recover from the damage dealt to it."

Yara's mouth had dried so much forming words was a challenge. So was breathing. She finally squeaked out, "You mentioned Hell, but you can't mean the demon, Grigori. It's not possible."

"Oh yes, it is. Do you know any other by that name?" Meara narrowed her eyes to slits.

"I— I don't know him at all. I never believed he was real. Or any of the rest of them, either."

"Every single wicked name bandied about by your elders in an effort to scare the daylights out of you was like as not real." Stewart straightened his shoulders, but it looked as if the effort cost him. "I doona know why, but modern ways and magic have trouble coexisting. 'Tis almost as if the presence of one threatens the other."

"Vampires managed to work it out," Meara said dryly. "If they could, so can we."

"Apparently, the energy mismatch doesna slow demons, either." Bitterness lined Stewart's words.

Yara swallowed around the lump working on blocking her

airway. Without saliva, it was a losing battle. "These, uh, these demons," she choked out. "What happens if they don't go back to where they came from?"

"That place is called Hell, and 'tis real as well," Stewart muttered. "Demons on this side of the veil separating Earth from the underworld provoke an imbalance in dynamic energies. If they spend too much time here, chaos will ensue."

"Should fit right in with Hitler's grand scheme to rule the world." Meara made a sour face.

"We covered that ground. If the world he plans to rule devolves into anarchy," Stewart countered, "there willna be much left for him to sink his claws into. Ach, that one is mad, far too sunk in delusions of his own invincibility to play host to reason."

Yara's hands ached, and she realized she'd balled them into fists so tight her nails cut into her palms. Uncurling them, she spread her fingers. "The reason we're crossing the North Sea..." She ran out of words and started over. "The power you believe exists where we're going. Will it be enough to defeat both demons and vampires?"

"Not without help." Stewart dragged the words out.

"Who'd you have in mind?" Meara transferred her unsettling gaze from Yara to him.

"Who else? The Celtic gods are the only ones who might answer a plea from me."

Meara looked away. "Have you had any communications with them since you left Britain?"

He shook his head. "'Tisn't as if I havena reached out, but no one's answered until today when I asked Danu and Arianrhod for aid."

"I wondered where the moonlit path came from," Meara muttered.

"Aye. 'Twas Arianrhod's doing, and her intercession heartened me. In my worst moments, I've wondered if the Celts dinna pack up and leave for some other world. Magic withers and dies when no one is left who believes in it."

"That's what happened to Romani magic, isn't it?" Yara held up a hand. "Never mind. The erosion of Romani ability has no place here."

"Maybe it does," Meara said thoughtfully. "Shifters have kept to themselves. There's no place in any society for dual-natured people who can transform into animals. That's been true for hundreds of years. Because of that, we've been relatively immune to the dampening effects of a human population that no longer believes in magic."

"Whereas Romani have been dependent on interaction with humans to earn their way." Yara picked up Meara's line of reasoning and ran with it. "The ongoing proximity to people who think our power is nothing but smoke and mirrors has been a lynchpin to dull our ability."

"Precisely." Meara stared at her again. "But I'd not be so quick to dump yourself in with the rest of the gypsies."

The same discomfort whenever the topic of her origins surfaced pricked unpleasantly. "And why not? I may not know for certain who my father was, but—"

Stewart's dark, liquid eyes took on a thoughtful expression. "Ye may not know who your mother was either, lass. Ye know who raised you, but they're not necessarily one and the same."

"Of course, they are," spewed out before she could stop the words. Yara stumbled backward, staggered by the implication.

Meara exchanged a pointed glance with Stewart. "We're not going to solve the demon problem in the next hour," she said. "I'll alert the others. Perhaps once we're rested tand can devote a few more minds to the problem, better answers will emerge."

"Come with me, lass." Stewart beckoned.

Meara turned and trotted the length of the deck, disappearing into the same doorway Jamal and Gregor had been carting bodies out of.

Yara clasped the bag slung around her body closer, clutching it as if it were a lifeline. "Come with you where?" she stuttered.

"'Tis in everyone's interest for us to sort out your magic. I'm the logical one to do that." He hesitated. "I willna hurt you." He extended a hand but didn't touch her.

"What if we find something I don't like?" Fear left a metallic taste in the back of her throat, and she trembled from more than being wet through from the persistent rain.

"How could ye not like what ye are? Ye've been living with that woman for something akin to twenty-five years." His voice took on a low, persuasive tone, and she recognized the subtle prick of a compulsion spell.

Yara jerked away from the hand he'd snaked toward her. "Do not force me." She paused between each word for emphasis. "I may be stuck here on this boat, but we have to land sometime. When we do, I'll leave. Anywhere would be easier than living in the Netherlands. According to the man my sister left with, caravans still roam the British Isles. They haven't been outlawed yet."

"That was certainly true when I left, but 'twas well over a century ago. What frightens you most?"

She tossed her head, and wet hair slapped her in the face. "I'm not afraid of much of anything. Got over that once I found out I could manage on my own."

"Vampires scare you. So do demons." He held up a hand. "Before ye protest, they should terrify you. Fear is useful. It keeps us safe. Would ye like to know what I think?" He'd dropped his extended hand, but he moved closer until he was almost touching her.

Warmth radiated from him, and she had to stop herself from leaning closer still. The scent of his magic mingled with the salt smell of the sea, heady and intoxicating. A woman could drown in that smell and die happy.

Got to get hold of myself.

She squared her shoulders, but couldn't escape his heady magic.

"Not particularly, but I figure you'll tell me anyway." She turned her head away. She was being rude to a man who'd gone out of his way to provide for her, but she didn't want the protective shell around her shattered. Bad enough to not know who her father was. She needed to hang onto the memory of her mother. Letting go would cast her adrift. Would mean her entire life had been a sham.

Her eyes burned, but she commanded herself not to cry.

"What I believe," he went on despite her reticence, "is that deep down inside, ye already know. Ye have a great deal of power, some of which ye utilize to conceal what ye are. Ye've done it for so long, 'tis become second nature and ye no longer realize what ye're about. If ye focused the mirror of your third eye properly, ye'd know everything about your origins. All the missing pieces would fall into place, and ye'd be whole."

She blinked to relieve the pressure behind her eyes. He wasn't censuring her; he was being kind. She hadn't expected that. Not after she'd told him to leave her alone.

"The hardest path," he went on, "is continuing as ye've been. Now that your suspicions have been kindled, ye willna be able to let this rest until ye follow it to its end. Would ye like me to help? Or would ye rather I find you a berth below where ye can pursue this alone?"

One of the tears she'd struggled to hold back escaped and slid down her cheek. "You already know, don't you?" She forced herself to hold his gaze.

"Nay, lass, I doona. Nor does Meara, and she's looked you up, down, and sideways twice now. 'Tis as I said, ye learned—or were taught—to shield the core of what ye are. Your ability is potent enough, ye're not even aware of the energy ye're diverting to protect your magical identity."

She shifted from foot to foot, not certain what to say. She

wanted to accept his offer. If she closeted herself in a cabin, she wasn't at all certain she'd have the guts to do anything but patch up the denial that had held her together all these years.

"Come on then." He latched a hand beneath her elbow. "Join me and let's get this over with. We have many, far bigger problems, than the unknown nature of your magic."

Guilt rolled through her in a painful wave at the reminder. Her issues were petty balanced against vampires and demons. "I—uh, you—" Clearing her throat she tried again. "You should be with Meara and the others. I can do this. I—"

Stewart tightened his grip on her and tugged gently. "Let me be there, lass. I'm the one pressing you to expose your roots. If there are rougher spots than I anticipate, I want to be there."

"Rough spots? Like what?" Fear of the unknown rose, engulfing her in dread so profound she felt frozen in place.

"None of us know what your power will look like unleashed." He smiled softly. "The only thing I'm certain of is 'twill be far stronger than what ye're used to."

"I don't understand." She was stalling, but she couldn't help herself.

"Nor do I. Not completely, but 'tisn't a reason not to find out."

This time when he urged her forward, she followed him across the deck to steep metal steps leading down into darkness.

CHAPTER 7

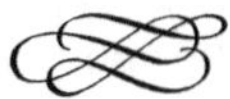

*Y*ara had descended partway down the first flight when she stopped and turned around.

"'Twill be all right, lass." Stewart wasn't quite certain what he'd do if she took a stand and flat out refused to sort through the power swirling around her. Either he could sense it more directly because he knew it was there, or it was delighted at the possibility of being set free. Regardless of the reason, it was far more palpable than it had been before.

"I didn't change my mind. It's my book."

"What book?" Stewart felt confused.

"The one I brought with me. I can't explain why, but it's kicking up a fuss about being left on the main deck."

"A magical book, eh? And a strong one at that." He quirked a brow just before he turned around. "Wait here. I'll fetch your bags."

Stewart loped across the deck and scooped up the pile of cloth sacks. He focused a calming spell, but kept it subtle, as he returned and handed Yara her things. She'd picked up on his earlier efforts to hurry things up, and he wanted to make damn sure he didn't spook her further. He chided himself for letting his impatience add fuel to her nervousness. Of course, she'd be terrified. Facing the unknown was bad enough, but if that *unknown* was a part of yourself, it made things far worse.

He sent out a tendril of magic, seeking to know more about the book he'd just delivered. His exploratory thread bounced back at him with a snap that would have hurt if he'd deployed more power to begin with.

Yara headed back down the stairs with him right behind her.

She'd accused him of already knowing what she was, except he didn't. Not for lack of trying, but his efforts to penetrate her layers of protections hadn't been any more successful than Meara's. Discomfort streamed from her. While they were still topside, he'd wondered if she were on the verge of making a run for the railing and tossing herself overboard.

Her magic wouldna allow that.

Once the words resonated in his mind, he recognized truth in them.

Yara stopped at the bottom of the first flight. A dark, narrow corridor extended toward the stern. "Which way?"

"I doona know, lass. I've not had a chance to look this vessel over. Let your magic lead."

The air around her brightened, taking on a shimmery aspect. One of the bags pulsed along with her enhanced power. Must be the one with the mysterious book. Stewart itched to hold it, examine it. He'd left most of his magical accoutrements behind when he fled the British Isles. He hadn't had much choice, but over the years of his exile, he'd longed for his library. Maybe the books would still be where he'd sequestered them in a decaying castle north of Glasgow.

Best not to get my hopes up.

Yara hesitated before one of` the string of closed doors on their left. "This one feels like the right place. Don't ask what I'm basing that on because I won't have an answer."

Reaching around her, Stewart unlatched the door and pushed

it open revealing a small cabin with bunk beds built into the bow side wall. A writing desk with its drawers hanging open was bolted to the floor on the stern side. Faded places on the wood-inlaid walls suggested someone had stripped something off them.

"Geez. It looks like someone was hunting for something." Yara dropped her sacks on the floor at the head of the bed and perched on the edge of the bare mattress.

"It does, indeed." Stewart pushed in the desk drawers, engaging the latches that held them in place during rough seas. He thought about the dead people in the hold and an expensive boat that had been abandoned for all intents and purposes. None of it was adding up.

Yara dug into one of the sacks and extracted a leather-bound book. From its cracked binding and the hand-drawn gilt runes on its cover, it had to be old. She cradled it against her chest, and the power spilling from it wove seamlessly with hers in a mix of blues, greens, and golds.

Stewart meant to hold silence, let Yara set the pace, but curiosity got the better of him. "That book, 'tis perfectly attuned to you. Have ye always had it?"

To his surprise, she laughed. "You're joking, right? You traveled with enough caravans to understand women have to learn to read on the sly, and no leader would ever entrust something ancient and magical to a mere woman."

He opened his mouth to protest he hadn't run his caravans that way, but changed course. Defensiveness wasn't called for. Many leaders, like Valentin for example, fit her description to a tee.

"How did ye come by it then?"

"It was in the cave where I worked my magic. I found it there." She closed her teeth over her lower lip. "After a year passed, I stopped expecting its owner to return. But I still asked its permission before I removed it from the cave once I made the decision to join your group."

The book's energy shaded to a darker gold and wove a thread of its magic around Yara's shoulders. She hugged it closer and latched onto his gaze with her own. "Can you feel its power too?"

"Aye, lass. A man would have to be dead not to."

She nodded, still chewing her lower lip. "I did what you said and followed my magic here. What happens next?"

"Close your earth eyes. Open your third eye." He adopted a hypnotic cadence and hoped she wouldn't fight him. "Imagine it just here." He tapped the center of his forehead between his eyebrows.

She kept her eyes, more violet than blue, trained on him. "I'm scared. What if I can't find my way back?"

If there'd been a chair to go with the desk, he'd have drawn it close and sat facing her, but there wasn't. He settled next to her on the mattress, leaving a respectable distance between them. He ached to cradle both her and the book in his arms, reassure her he wouldn't let anything harm her, but it was an empty promise.

Things were afoot in the world, evil things. Her best hedge was to locate the key holding her magic prisoner. He suspected whoever had left her with the caravan had swathed her in spells, so no one would suspect she wasn't Romani.

Nay, so no one would realize she held enough power to bring the caravan to its knees. Had they known, they'd have left her by the side of the road to starve or be set upon by marauding animals.

"What if I can't find my way back?" she repeated.

Stewart took a measured breath. How to answer her? He opted for honesty, rather than soft-pedaling the truth. "'Tisn't a gateway ye can kick open and hope to shut again. Once ye see who ye are, your life will change."

"So I'll never find my way back?" Her voice trembled.

"I canna lie to you. Nay, ye'll never be able to return to the state of being and knowledge ye hold right now, but when the blinders are off and ye view the world as it truly is, not as someone wished ye to see it..." He inhaled briskly. "Each of us has a destiny. Until ye stop hiding beneath the *geas* that was placed on you, ye'll never figure out what yours is."

Her eyes rounded. "Awk. You believe I've been cursed. Isn't that what a *geas* is?"

He shook his head. "Poor word choice. Aye, that is also a *geas*. In your case, someone decided 'twasn't in your best interest for the gypsies in your caravan to recognize ye werena one of them, so they leveraged your power, mixed in some of their own, and created an illusion. One ye've worn ever since. How far back can ye remember?"

She studied her hands, clasped around the book. "Maybe as young as when I was two."

"And ye were with the caravan then?"

"Yes. With Mother and Father, and my two sisters."

"That would argue someone specifically selected your parents to raise you."

Yara shook her head. "Not necessarily. I might have been a foundling. We came across abandoned babies from time to time; one wagon or another always took them in."

"I doona believe this was unplanned. Mayhap for a garden-variety infant no one wanted, but someone went to a lot of trouble to mask who ye are. I believe they chose your parents, and rather carefully."

She frowned, clearly taking in the implications. "But that would mean my parents knew…"

"Aye, lass, that it would."

She raised tortured eyes to him. "That might explain why Father drank. The truth ate at him. If the magic was that strong, he couldn't have told anyone about me, huh?"

"He might have been able to—if his magic was potent enough to overpower whomever cast the *geas* over you."

"It wasn't," she said flatly. "Father could barely summon enough power to steal a few coins and not have someone notice."

The book glowed brighter, and she started. "It's like it's urging me to stop procrastinating and get on with things."

Stewart let his instincts guide him and placed a hand on her thigh. He could do a better job infusing confidence that way—plus, he had to touch her. Holding back was damn near killing him. Something about her sang to his soul, and he was tired of arguing himself out of the attraction spilling through him.

"Impossible as it is to believe, since ye stumbled on it in a cave ye also stumbled upon, that is your book. Its magic blends perfectly with your own. 'Tisn't any way that can be accidental. Ye found it because it wanted to be found. Ye said ye were most of the way across the country when your caravan disbanded, yet ye ended up near the German border where the cave—and the book —just happened to be."

"That might be coincidence," she cut in, sounding rattled.

"Nay, lass. Not a chance. The book has your best interests at heart. It waited a long time for you. Trust it and close your eyes." He tightened his grip on her thigh. "This willna grow easier with waiting."

Her knuckles whitened as she clutched the book, but Yara closed her eyes, her breath ragged and uneven.

"Find your third eye," he urged. "Open a conduit to your power and imagine it tracking through you to the spot between your eyebrows that I showed you."

"Got it. Now what?"

"Breathe. Take a breath that goes to the bottom of your lungs. Blow it out, and take another." He didn't tell her she was strung so tightly, that the fact she could even find her magic was a miracle.

Nay, it speaks to just how powerful she is.

He resisted the temptation to push into her mind. She'd feel him, and it might make her skittish enough to ruin her tenuous commitment to delving into her origins.

"I— I'm seeing images. Visions."

"Let them come, lass. Tell me what ye see."

"Berlin. I'm in that huge, old Catholic church near the center of town. The one with all the stained glass. Rain is pounding outside. Lightning too. Between it and the votive candles, light is flaring all around me."

Anticipation filled him. Most priests didn't realize it, but churches were perfect for concentrating power. "Go on. I'm listening."

"There's a woman with long, red-gold hair dressed in wine-colored velvet. It's soft against my cheek—" Yara's voice faltered. "It feels like I'm there, watching, but the woman is carrying me, so I must be an infant. She's wearing lots of gold. Necklace, earrings, rings. Some of the gold is set with gemstones."

The scent of Yara's magic thickened around them. Wet pine trees with piquant vanilla undernotes. He wanted to weave his power in with hers, ached to blend with her on a magical plane, but he quashed his own desires. This wasn't about him—or them. She had to own what she was.

"She's crooning to me in Gaelic," Yara went on. "Telling me we won't have to wait long. I reach up and tug on one of her long curls. Her hair is beautiful. It reminds me of liquid fire. Oh!" Yara yelped as if she'd been bitten.

The book's magic thickened, forming a protective arc, and Stewart murmured, "Steady now. What did ye just see?"

"M—Mother and F—Father. They're walking toward us, looking uncertain. Mother holds out her arms, and the beautiful woman—she looks noble, like a queen—hands me to her. Father is talking, asking if the woman is certain she can't keep me. Her eyes get shiny, as if she's trying not to cry, and she says she'd like nothing better, but that I'm not safe with her.

"Father is stern, almost angry, but Mother reminds him she saw the noble lady in a dream or a vision. She's holding me close, but I reach for my first mother. I'm too little to have words, so I use my mind to ask if I'll ever see her again."

Stewart loosened his grip on Yara's thigh. He had to be hurting her, but she hadn't complained. They were close, so very close to the truth. "What did she tell you?"

Tears leaked from beneath Yara's closed lids. "It's so odd, I had no memory of this before, but right now, it's clear as day. She said, 'Aye, wee lassie, we shall meet again when the world teeters on the edge of destruction. By then, ye'll have claimed your birthright, and we shall fight side by side.'

"I asked her if we'd win, but she didn't answer. Her form took on an insubstantial aspect until I could see right through her. My mother was still holding onto me, and she cried out, 'Rhiannon, do we need to know anything special?'

"My first mother replied, 'Naught beyond what any parent would do. Love her. Keep her safe from harm. She has a role to play in history, and so do you for sheltering her when I cannot.'"

Stewart felt as if someone had slammed a nine-pound sledge into his chest. Rhiannon was Yara's mother? He lived with magic, was steeped in it, believed in it, yet he struggled to wrap his mind around evidence of the goddess presence in Yara. Now that he knew where to look, it was obvious.

So apparent, he felt stupid for missing it.

The *geas*. It had obscured her from everyone. Even him.

Yara was talking again. "I couldn't see my first mother, but her voice echoed around that empty chapel. She reassured my parents, thanked them, told them she'd make certain I was accepted as just one more Romani in their caravan. Her words faded, but I heard hoofbeats and the night cries of an owl on the hunt. The light that had pulsed through the chapel dwindled until the only thing left was the flicker of votive candles melting into pools of fat."

Her eyes flickered open, and she turned to look at him. "Is that all? Am I done with that part?"

He nodded. "Dig deep, lass. Tell me what ye feel and how ye're different."

She shut her eyes again, taking stock. When she opened them, she drew her brows together. "It's how I've always sensed myself, yet there's another layer I didn't have access to before. I'm still me —but not." She shivered "Maybe the differences will become obvious next time I try to cast a spell." Yara focused eyes that had shaded back to blue on him. "Who is Rhiannon?"

"Is your Celtic mythology so lacking?"

"Apparently so. I've heard of the Welsh goddess who rode a white horse and kept magical birds, but she's just a myth. Besides, she had to have died centuries ago."

Stewart swallowed hard, but he had to know for certain. No reason to get Yara riled up about being descended from a Celtic goddess if he weren't one hundred percent sure. "May I touch you and use magic to check something?"

She nodded and turned so she faced him. Doubt and confusion took turns on her expressive face, and her eyes developed an otherworldly aspect.

Stewart placed a hand gently on each side of her head. He wanted to lace his fingers into her thick, red hair, but if he did that, he'd be lost. At least he understood his attraction to her. Celtic magic called to its own, and she was stunning atop all that power.

He probed gently. He knew the feel of Rhiannon's power since he'd sat with her in council meetings. Her and Pwyll, her consort. Unlike when he'd tried to look into Yara before, this time, the obfuscating layers were gone, and he saw through to her clear, pure center. A center stuffed so full of power, it shone bright as a hundred suns. Even though he wasn't using his earth eyes, he still closed them reflexively against the pulsing light.

Definitely Rhiannon's blood.

But not Pwyll's. After her problems with Pwyll, Rhiannon had dallied with others, including an Irish sea god. One of them must have sired Yara.

At least it explained why the goddess had needed a home for her daughter. Men were far more unforgiving about infidelity in bygone years, and if Rhiannon envisioned a role for her daughter —one she needed to grow up to fulfill—she would have done everything possible to protect her.

Stewart moved his hands. He didn't want to stop touching Yara, but his reason for doing so was gone.

She focused on him. "Did you get the answers you sought?"

He nodded. "Aye, that I did. Ye're Rhiannon's daughter. Rhiannon the Welsh horse goddess with her flocks of magical birds, whose songs healed people. She was a good witch, a healer, and many other things. She suffered greatly, yet through her trials, she showed great courage."

"How is that even possible? How could she still have been alive twenty-five years ago?"

Stewart laced his fingers with hers. "The gods are immortal."

She gasped and drew back. "Does that mean I am too?"

"I doona know. Depends who your father was. That I couldna determine, which might well explain why Rhiannon thought ye'd be safer elsewhere."

She squeezed his hand before disentangling her fingers and getting to her feet. Yara laid the book on the desk where it glowed softly.

"What language is it written in?" Stewart nodded at the book.

Yara's lips curved into half a smile. "It changes. Sometimes I open it and get Dutch. Sometimes German, and on rare occasions, Gaelic. I taught myself to read, but only Dutch and German, which are similar." She turned her hands palms up. "No matter what language shows itself, I can find what I need and understand enough to make a spell that works."

"Of course, ye can." He smiled too. "Remember. 'Tis your book. Rhiannon left it where ye'd be certain to find it."

Yara rounded on him, but she wasn't smiling anymore. "Do you mean to suggest my real mother has been hovering on the sidelines watching me like some sneak thief all these years, but never showing herself? Never helping no matter how rough things got?"

The air around her crackled menacingly with power.

Stewart pushed to his feet. "Ye shouldna speak ill of the goddess. Even if she wasna your mother. And watch your magic. 'Twill be far easier to summon destruction now that ye have access to your full power. If ye're not careful, ye could burn down the ship."

"I'll speak any way I wish. What kind of mother was she, anyway? She dumped me when I was small. And in a Romani caravan no less. A place where women have no standing at all. She—"

Stewart clapped a hand over her mouth. "Stop. Right now. Else ye'll say something ye regret."

Electricity zinged up his arm, shocking him, and he pulled his hand away. Pain reverberated along his nerves, creating waves of discomfort.

Yara shook her head, eyes wide as her gaze flitted from side to side. "I hurt you. Jesus Christ! I'm sorry. I didn't mean to."

"Yara, I—"

But she spun on her heel, pulled the cabin door open, and raced through it.

Stewart stared after her, his arm still feeling like he'd stuffed it into a hill full of fire ants. He should go after her, but she was overloaded, overwrought. It might be best for her to have a wee bit of time to herself.

Rubbing his shoulder and the length of his arm, he left the cabin, intent on finding Vreis to see what his inventory had turned up. Yara might be outraged by Rhiannon's proximity, but the possibility of having a goddess near to hand gave him hope.

The battle was heating up, and they needed every ally they could lay their hands on.

CHAPTER 8

$\mathcal{Y}$ara ran the length of the corridor and located another steep staircase. She stared at it, but not for long. If she went down, it would take her to where other people were, and she wasn't fit company—for anybody. Grasping the metal railing, she clambered up the ladder-like stairs until cold salt spray blew in her face. The deck was slick with it, and she almost fell before magic intervened and kept her on her feet.

She hadn't summoned power to bail herself out. It was just there, and that added to a creeping discomfort that already threatened to suffocate her.

She hunkered next to a bulkhead and dropped her head into her hands. What was happening to her? Would she turn into something alien? She'd been a fool when she'd said she didn't feel different. It hadn't been obvious in the cramped cabin, or maybe Stewart's presence had a modulating effect, but magic pounded through her. Her head throbbed. Colors danced before her eyes, making the familiar world look like a Van Gogh painting gone bad. So much magic coursed through her, she clung to sanity by her fingernails, afraid if she wasn't vigilant, she'd shatter into a million motes of light. At least then she wouldn't have to live in a body that felt like it belonged to a stranger.

Yara winced. She'd longed for stronger magic many, many times.

Yeah, but people ask for all kinds of things. Wanting and having aren't the same.

She rubbed her temples. Maybe the touch of her fingers would jolt her back to normalcy. Why had she been so angry? She should be delighted she had a mother, and a supernatural one at that. It was the kind of news people dreamed about.

What was wrong with her?

A snort blew past her pursed lips. Not much wrong at all— other than having enough magic to flatten the entire Netherlands.

Stewart should have known better, a sly inner voice piped up.

This isn't Stewart's fault. I agreed. Besides this isn't about him. It's about me. Maybe my time to be more and do more is here. The book seemed to think so. It would have found a way to warn me if it thought I was making a mistake.

Yara dissected her thoughts. The book had stepped in a time or two, alerting her to danger outside her cave. She'd come to rely on it for many things. As a repository for just the spell she needed. As an early warning system. As a friend. To admit that last was hard since books were things, not people.

Yes, well, it's way more than a book, and I've always realized that whether I accepted the knowledge or not.

Out of all the things she'd brought with her, the book was the only one she'd never have left behind. When she'd asked it about leaving, it spontaneously flipped to a section that left no doubt about her path. She hadn't fleshed out that part when she was talking with Ilona, but the book predicted misfortune if she didn't go with the group of Rom and shifters. At the time, she'd rolled her eyes and thought it was being unduly dramatic. Not anymore.

The uncomfortable sensations cascading through her didn't

hold quite as bad a bite. Was acknowledging who she was the key here?

It is to everything else. Why not this?

Yara lifted her head and peered at a morning that was growing darker by the moment. Clouds roiled over the North Sea, and whitecaps formed on waves that looked bigger than they'd been an hour before. From her vantage point, she could see Cadr, his hands wrapped about the wheel. Magic streamed from him, and she suspected he needed it to keep the boat on course.

Vreis emerged from the same doorway she had and sprinted past her, arms extended to keep his balance on the rolling, heaving deck. He passed within a few feet of where she crouched, but didn't see her. Or maybe he was intent on reaching his brother.

The wind howled and shrieked, whipping around her, but she heard Vreis say, "Jamal and I found something else in that hold."

Cadr eyed the other man. "Besides the bodies?"

"Aye, true enough. Explains why the bodies were there. To discourage anyone from looking too closely."

Cadr readjusted his grip on the wheel that seemed to be straining to escape his control. "I'm all ears."

"'Tis a problem. Once someone discovers this boat's no longer in port, they'll come after us."

"Not in this weather, they willna. The storm surrounding us is widespread, and 'twill only grow worse. I tried to skirt it, but something keeps drawing us into the center."

"'Tis the current. It pushes hard across the North Sea. Always has."

"I scarcely require a lecture on seamanship. What else was in the hold?"

Vreis set his even features into grim lines. "There's gold in that hold. Lots of it. Mayhap a hundred pounds, and I doona mean British Sterling."

Cadr's eyebrows shot to attention. "Gold, eh? Bars? Coins? Sculptures? Mayhap a dragon lived aboard."

Vreis laughed. "Ye wish. Nay. No dragon. I'd have noticed the stench. They reek of sulfur and charcoal and fiery steam. 'Tis mostly coins with a few bars tossed into the mix."

"Coins from where? Can we spend them?"

Vreis punched his brother in the upper arm. "Always the practical one. I dinna take inventory, but the few I turned over are from 1500s Spain. I left Jamal sorting them into piles."

"Take the wheel for a bit," Cadr urged. "My arms are sore from fighting it."

The men changed places. "Jamal and I kicked it around," Vreis went on. "We'll need money after we land, and this is the kind of thing we can turn into cash. Any dealer in antiquities will buy them."

"So long as he doesna determine they're on a list of stolen goods," Cadr said sourly.

"True enough," Vreis replied, not sounding the least bit concerned.

A wave crashed over the rail. Water and foam slithered across the deck before they retreated. Cadr made a grab for a cable strung near the wheel. "First we need to get to land. 'Tis looking less and less likely. Mayhap we should forget Scotland and beat a path to our closest landfall."

"Tacking into the wind the whole way?" Vreis leaned into the wheel, muscling it into place and securing its position with lines. "We're only running the mainsail. We could pull it down and engage the engine, but…"

A hand dropped onto her shoulder and she started, twisting beneath it. Power bloomed within her. Defensive power she hadn't summoned.

"'Tis just me, lass. Sheathe your claws, now that we both know ye have them." Stewart dropped into a squat next to her. "How are ye doing?"

She turned to face him. "Better. I owe you a major apology."

He waved her to silence. "Not worth the time. How's all that magic feeling? Are ye stretching to accommodate it?"

The corners of her mouth curled with uncertainty, but honesty was essential to managing whomever she was turning into. "The key was to stop denying it was real."

"Aye, lassie. 'Tis the secret to almost everything."

"This storm…" she hesitated, but forged ahead. "Vreis said it's currents, but there's something unnatural about it."

"My take too. What are Cadr and Vreis talking about?" He glanced in their direction. "I was hunting for Vreis. Wanted to know what we have to work with aboard this boat."

"They haven't said much about the storm, but Vreis and Jamal found a fortune in gold in the hold with the dead people."

Breath whooshed from Stewart, and he balanced himself with a hand to remain hunkered next to her. "Gold, ye say? What kind and how much?"

"Ask Vreis. Or Jamal. He's still in the hold counting it."

Stewart scrunched his forehead into a thoughtful expression. "At least it solves the last of the mysteries surrounding this ship."

"You have to say more than that."

"Someone wanted to hide all that gold, so they put it in the hold and came up with bodies that died of plague. Nothing like a disease-ridden corpse to discourage anyone from looking too closely." He paused to take a measured breath. "The bad news is someone will come after us as soon as the weather clears."

"That's one explanation for why the gold was there." She licked salt off her lips from the ever-present spray.

"What might another be?"

"Rhiannon seems to be manipulating a whole lot behind the scenes. How do you know it's not her gold, and she meant for us to take this ship?"

He cupped the side of her face, his palm warm and enticing. "Your mother is rich as Croesus, lass. She has no need to sequester gold. When I knew her, she cared far more for her lightning fast steed and magical birds than any coin in the realm."

Yara swallowed hard. "How long ago was that?"

He glanced up, calculating. "Mayhap four hundred years, but I could be off by as much as a century."

Cadr pounded toward them, his stout boots slipping and sliding on the salt-slick deck. "There ye are. Vreis found gold."

"I already know."

"How?"

Stewart pointed at her.

Cadr blinked and then blinked again. "Yara? By all the gods, I dinna see you crouched there until Stewart pointed you out. I need to pour myself a wee dram."

"Is there liquor here?" Stewart asked.

"Aye, Vreis had a look about afore he found the gold. Freshwater holding tanks are two-thirds full, and there're casks of spirits. No food, but 'tisn't a surprise on that front."

He returned his attention to Yara. "Why in blazes couldna I see you? Have ye been here the whole time since Vreis came topside?"

She nodded. "It's all right. I had some thinking to do."

The rigging creaked and groaned and the boat canted at an unnatural angle, caught by increasing winds. "We've got to get that sail down now," Stewart said and pushed upright, bending so he faced into the wind.

"I'll help." Cadr sounded grim. "We need to preserve that canvas. Won't do us much good if it rips down the center."

"How will we make any progress?" Yara stood too, hanging onto a cable strung next to the bulkhead.

"The engine." Stewart glanced at Cadr. "Do we have any extra fuel?"

The other man nodded. "Aye, buckets to hear Vreis tell it. Ready, man?"

"Go."

They drew power around them until it formed a protective

bubble, but even that was distorted by the wind. Gusts buffeted her from one side, driving her against the stout wall of the ship. Standing was difficult since the deck canted at a severe angle, so she took up her crouch in the shadow of the bulkhead.

Yara wrapped herself in power, determined to control it rather than having it show up and dominate her will. She needed a purpose, so she sought verification for her hunch about the storm having magical underpinnings. Maybe someone had plans for them that didn't include landing in Scotland.

Rain pelted harder, and she clutched her cloak's hood tighter around her head. Long, wet hair trailed down the front of her jacket, but tucking the errant strands inside would only make her wetter. Water streamed from the sky, joining waves attacking the deck. The boat canted still more until one side almost touched the water's edge.

Power pulsed around her, warming her. For the first time since her journey into the subterranean depths of her psyche, she welcomed her enhanced ability, urging its assistance to think through her problems.

Which god controlled the North Sea?

Her mouth twitched into a knowing smile. The book. It knew everything. Surely, it could identify sea gods. The only one she could remember was Llyr, and he was ancient.

So's Rhiannon, and apparently she's still alive.

Canvas flapped as the sail slithered down the mast once the halyard was released. The men wrapped lengths of something around the canvas to secure it, and the ship—while still rocking and heaving—sat closer to upright.

Stewart and Vreis grappled with securing the expanse of canvas. Not much she could do here, so she trotted to the door leading to the stairs and made her way back to where she'd left her things and the book. Bending, she shook water out of her hair and face before entering her cabin. The salt smell of the sea was thick in her nostrils, and it reminded her of the scent of Stewart's magic.

Stewart.

A warm pulse beat through her at the thought of the tall, spare Scot. She'd treated him abysmally, but he wasn't angry. He'd dealt with her kindly as he hunkered next to her.

Kindly. I shouldn't assume anything. For all I know, he has a wife in the caravan he left behind.

She slid out of her cloak and hung it over a convenient hook placed near the door. It was wet clear through, and it might never dry in the cool, damp cabin. She fished a thick, black woolen sweater from one of her sacks and wrapped it around herself.

She'd been lucky to find that sweater. It had been slung over a deserted chair at an outdoor café in Enschede. She'd hung back, hiding in a shadowy alleyway for over an hour, but no one seemed inclined to claim the garment, so she'd walked casually by and picked it up, draping it around herself as if she had every right to do so.

Everything she owned had a story attached to it. Maybe that was why she valued each item. She'd just picked up the book and settled back on the bunk in the same spot where she'd sat earlier when someone tapped on her door.

A quick scan with the magic she hadn't yet sheathed confirmed it was Stewart, and she pushed a bit more magic to spring the latch. "Come in."

He swept through the door, kicking it shut behind him. Water streamed from him, puddling on the well-worn wooden floor. A glowing nimbus from his power followed the water, and it dried almost at once, creating clouds of steam as it evaporated.

"Sorry, lass. I dinna mean to make such an unholy mess in here." He crossed the small space in two strides and stood over her. "Casting spells, were ye?" He looked pointedly at the book in her lap.

"No. More like seeking information. The only sea god I could come up with was Llyr. There must be others."

He quirked a brow. "Aye, one or two. What did ye have in mind?"

She felt her cheeks heat. "It seemed to me that maybe someone didn't want us going to Scotland. If they have some other destination in mind, the storm could be a way of herding us in a different direction." She took a breath and hurried on before he could tell her she was being ridiculous. "Something bigger than us is pulling the strings. I feel it down to my bones. The boat we needed presented itself at just the right time. Then that magical moonbeam path was there. You might have helped the wind along with magic, but the moon showed us the way."

"Interesting." He still stood over her. "I'm not dripping much anymore. Mind if I sit?"

"Go ahead."

He settled at the far end of the bunk and twisted so he faced her. "Any idea what destination might earn us more commodious sailing conditions?"

She shook her head. "Of course not. That was why I wanted to find a sea god. Or a weather god. My mythology never was very solid." Embarrassment made her fidget where she sat. "Not that I expected a god to talk with me, but I was hoping if I found a likely name or two, you could communicate with them."

He cast a speculative glance her way. "Ye've more claim to godhood than I. Why not see if Rhiannon is close enough to do us some good?"

Yara let go of the book and twisted her hands atop its worn binding. She'd thought of that and discarded it out of hand.

He reached across the space between them and tilted her chin so she had to look at him. "What?"

"It's silly, ridiculous actually. She's a goddess, one who's been looking after me from the sidelines for years, but I can't summon her."

"Why not?"

"It's not my place. She'll come to me when she wants to, when she deems the time is right." Yara set her mouth in a tense line. "It's not like she hasn't had opportunity to show herself. I was alone in that cave and a nearby falling down shepherd's hut for a long time. She made certain I found the book…"

"Go on, lass." Stewart offered an encouraging smile.

"You're the one who planted that idea, the one about Rhiannon making certain the book found its way into my hands. It never occurred to me the book's presence was anything beyond happenstance." She shrugged. "I've found everything I have. No one ever gave me anything once I left the caravan."

"So the idea of another helping you makes you uncomfortable?"

She nodded. "Very. Means I'd be beholden to them, and I don't have much that's worth anything to pay back debts."

A shadow flitted behind his eyes. "Aye, I ken that logic all too well, but we must select a destination. If we do nothing, currents will drive the boat toward Denmark and Norway."

"What would you have me do?"

"Nay, I canna pick your path. Ye came in here to consult yon tome." He tilted his chin at the book still balanced in her lap. "'Twas ill-advised for me to suggest ye do aught differently."

"What if I only wanted out of the rain?"

He dropped his hand to his side, no longer touching her. She wanted to make a grab for him to reestablish contact, but didn't. Stewart got to his feet. "Find me once ye know something."

She chewed her lower lip. "What if nothing comes? There've been lots of times I've asked the book a question, and it's been stubbornly silent."

"Like as not because ye dinna need that particular answer. This time is different, and our need undeniable." He walked to the door and let himself out, pulling it shut behind him.

Yara stared after him. His scent hung in the room, and she

longed to race after him and twine her arms around his body. She shook her head hard. She was stalling, and whatever she came up with might be the difference between survival and death. Even absent magical storms, the North Sea in winter was deadly enough to founder ships far bigger than their sailboat.

She inhaled to center herself and anchor her magic, and then did it again. Power flared, close to the surface. At least summoning that part of herself didn't require any expenditure of effort. It was just there, waiting to see what she needed.

She let her hands hover over the book and asked three questions:

"Will the sea or weather gods help us?

"If so, how can we reach them?

"Where should we land to amplify our magic?"

The book's familiar energy throbbed, and the cracked binding took on a glow she knew all too well. The book had answers, and if she were patient, they'd come to her.

She peeled back her protections, making certain she'd be open to the book's particular way of communicating. It was harder now; lots more layers to dredge through until she revealed her essence. Trusting the book was a skill that had taken her months to master. The first time it gave her answers, she'd stumbled on them by accident. And it took still more time for her to connect the dots and recognize leaving herself open was essential to the way the book's magic operated.

The cover snapped open and pages riffled until the book quieted. When she looked at what it wanted her to read, a sketch identified as Manandan Mac Llyr stared back at her. She skimmed the description, written in Gaelic, and discovered Manandan was a lord of the mystical Otherworld as well as a mariner, aided in his journeys by supernatural powers. Some myths viewed him as master of the waves and believed he traveled beneath them, surfacing every dozen breaths or so.

She scribed her finger over the drawing, and the wild-haired man seemed to turn and stare right at her. "Mac Llyr," she mused. "Son of Llyr."

"Aye, woman. Llyr was my sire. And ye're a daughter of Rhiannon. What right have ye in my waters?" His accent was Irish, but lacked the softness she'd always associated with Irish brogues.

Yara's eyes widened; breath clotted in her throat. She moved the book off her lap and lurched to her feet so she could bow her head in deference to the god she'd inadvertently summoned.

"No right at all, but please help us find safe passage."

"Why? What benefit will I accrue for this boon?"

She swallowed around a thick place in her throat. She hadn't planned for this confrontation, never believing the book would do more than provide information. How could she explain Nazis to a sea god?

"I asked a question. I'm not accustomed to being kept waiting."

Yara straightened her shoulders. God or no god, she'd be damned if she'd let anyone push her around. "Vampires have grown stronger, my lord. They've joined with an equally great evil, and they feed off one another. If this wickedness is left unchecked, magic will die out of the world."

"How does that explain your presence in the North Sea?"

"Our magic wasn't sufficient to defeat either the vampires or the…other threat in Europe. One of our number is a Druid, and he believed we'd be stronger in Britain."

"I see. Who is this Druid? Do I know him?"

"Stewart. I don't know his last name, but his two companions are brothers named Cadr and Vreis."

Yara held her breath. Did she need to break the spell and run to find Stewart so she could unearth his surname? Power whispered around her, a susurrus of impossibility, yet she had no doubt the god was here with her. Maybe not his body—if he even had one—but his spirit.

"I know of them. All three are good and decent men."

Yara waited. Magic surging through the cabin started to dissipate. "Wait," she cried.

"Ye think to command me to your will?" Words thundered about her, and she sank to her knees, thoughts of holding her ground forgotten.

"No, my lord. Of course not. We must fight the wickedness that threatens us all. Where would you have us go?"

"I will see ye safe to Scotland. Once there, the lot of you are on your own. What will ye offer in return?"

She remembered the old tales well enough. Quid pro quo was how things worked. "I—I have no idea. There's gold aboard this ship."

"Och, I have no use for gold."

"What, then?" Asking seemed faster than playing twenty questions with Manandan, son of Llyr.

"Ye'll do, lass. Ye're no maid, but I shall overlook that. I shall round up Rhiannon and arrange things."

"What, exactly, would that entail?" she gritted out.

Power thrumming through the cabin cut off as abruptly as it had arrived.

Shock battled annoyance.

"I'll do, will I?" she muttered acerbically. "Even though I'm not chaste? We'll just see about that."

Old tales only went so far, and she'd be damned if she ended up a casualty to Manandan's whims. She shut her mouth with a *clack.* No reason to say one word about any of this to anyone until they were safe in port.

Surely her mother wouldn't see her sold into whatever scheme the sea god had in mind if she didn't agree.

Don't be so sure about that, an inner voice argued. *I have no bloody idea how gods view the world.*

CHAPTER 9

A little while before Stewart strode down the corridor outside Yara's cabin. He hadn't wanted to leave, but she needed to come to terms with her newly kindled magic. For that, she needed privacy, not him butting in at every turn. He reached the steep stairs and headed down, intent on doing his own reconnaissance of the boat so he wouldn't have to keep asking questions.

He started in the lower hold area. The faint stench of sickness still hung in the air. How in the goddess's name had someone managed to come up with plague victims to stash here? The disease had been all but eradicated. This wasn't the seventeenth century anymore where no one understood the bacteriologic underpinnings of illness.

When an answer rose, his gut contracted in disgust. The Nazis. They experimented on humans, injecting disease vectors into innocent men and women. At least that tacked down the most likely candidate for who'd sequestered gold aboard this ship. They must have had plans for it, otherwise the coins would have joined all the other loot the Nazis had stolen, much of it diverted to Swiss banks.

Germany doesn't control the Netherlands. Not yet at least.

Perhaps this stash was part of their plans to occupy the country. If that were the case, someone would surely miss this ship and set out after it. Stewart sent up a silent plea that whichever god controlled the storm harassing them would up the ante for any German vessel that had the temerity to track them.

No one in their right mind would set sail in the gale buffeting them from all sides, but it had to clear sometime. By then, they'd be well past the Netherlands coastline—or at the bottom of the North Sea.

He took stock of a tidy engine room. As Cadr had noted, fuel wouldn't be a problem. Other smaller rooms lined both sides of a central corridor. He found both water and liquor and a room that had once held food. Grain sacks had been decimated by rats. Too bad the little fuckers hadn't all died before they inhaled everything that wasn't nailed down.

Stewart lifted a hand and called his mage light. It glowed a soft blue, and he examined the bevy of shelves and cupboards. Heavy metal canisters had been pushed to the back. He dug them out and pried them open, delighted to find they contained rice and sugar. Both were crawling with weevils, but certainly edible. The weevils would rise to the top in a pot of boiling water and could be skimmed off.

He rolled his eyes. In the era he'd come from, all stored food was infested with something. It was only the twentieth century that had seen the rise of a squeamish population unwilling to share their rations with bugs.

"There ye are!" Cadr ducked into the storeroom. "Hey! Ye found food. Vreis should have taken more time."

"'Twasn't obvious. These containers were pushed to the rear of the lower cupboard. How are things topside?"

"Better, but the current is chasing us to the east. I came this way to fire the engine. We're still headed to Edinburgh, eh?" He raised a dark brow to punctuate his question.

"Not sure."

"What do ye mean by that? Has something changed?"

"Yara is seeing if she canna raise one of the sea or weather gods."

Cadr's blue eyes widened, and he stared at Stewart. "All right. Give. What is she? Surely not Romani since I truly dinna see her until she allowed me to. No Rom can do that. Druid magic outplays theirs every single time."

Stewart raked a hand through his hair, snagging wet strands that had come half unbraided with his splayed fingers. Soon enough, everyone would know about Yara, and he wasn't in the habit of keeping anything from Cadr or Vreis.

"Rhiannon's daughter. I have no idea who sired her."

A sharp intake of breath betrayed Cadr's surprise. "By all the bloody saints, 'twasn't the answer I'd anticipated. Not that 'tisn't welcome news, mind ye."

"What did ye think her to be?" Stewart cut the flow of power, and his light flickered and died, leaving them in relative gloom.

Cadr shrugged. "Mayhap a witch or even a Druid like us. She dinna have the feel of a Rom to me."

Stewart grinned crookedly. "Well, she's Celtic, right enough. So she's more closely aligned with us than the Rom are."

"Why was she masquerading as Romani? Was that story she cooked up about her caravan disbanding so much nonsense?"

"Nay. She dinna know who her mother was. I pushed her to figure things out, and she's still at the front end of that process." He took a measured breath. "Her initial reaction to the news wasna verra positive. She was furious—and scared half to death."

"Interesting. I wonder which of the other ancients will surface afore this is over. Back to the question of which way we're going, though. I'll engage the engine, but then I have to head back to the helm and tie in coordinates. If we do naught—"

"Aye, we'll end up in Denmark," Stewart cut in. "How about this? Let's assume our original course will work and do what we can to cross into the lee of the British Isles. Once we're there. We can sail up the coast."

"Leaves only the wee problem of getting across the North Sea." Cadr rubbed his hands together. "I love the simple challenges."

Jamal skidded into the small space. "There you are. Anyone want to take a quick look at the gold? I've sorted it." He frowned. "Someone's going to miss it. My estimate is it's worth better than half a million Reichsmarks."

Cadr whistled long and low. "Damn good news, if ye ask me. I'm off to work on the engine. Wait till Vreis hears that amount. He thought 'twould be far less." He pushed around Jamal and left, whistling an old Scottish folk tune.

Jamal crossed the small space and glanced into the open rice bin. "Excellent. I am hungry. I'll get a pot of this cooking in a little bit."

"Did ye find more gold?" Stewart asked. "Is that why the value went up?"

"Yes. I found more coins and several more bars stamped with Switzerland's seal." Jamal's nostrils flared. "The Swiss are a bunch of bastards. I'd rather not be caught with anything of theirs, even if we weren't the ones who stole it in the first place."

The deck beneath Stewart's feet hummed as the engine sputtered to life.

"Switzerland, eh? Nazis did stash resources in Swiss banks. Makes sense they'd have Swiss gold. It also lends credence to my theory about the coins being part of Germany's plan to occupy the Netherlands. They're readying resources for their push into that country, plus it's a handy spot to hide treasure they've laundered through Switzerland." Stewart dusted his hands together. "Two birds with one stone. Move money where ye expect to need it, and get purloined wealth out of a direct line of fire."

"Maybe so." Jamal blew out a tight breath. "The coins are mostly old, though. It's almost as if someone stumbled on an old galleon and plundered it."

"Old coins are worth more than new."

"Yes, I know that. I taught ancient and medieval history at the university in Innsbruck."

"How apt for a shifter who lived through that time." Stewart chuckled.

So did Jamal. "I'm not that old, but it's funny because Ilona said almost the exact same thing when I told her what I taught. Come on. Maybe we can figure out a way to hide the gold and magic things up so no one can find it."

The ship creaked and groaned as it fought the wind. Stewart followed Jamal out the door and back into the narrow, low-ceilinged corridor.

"How long will this journey take?" Jamal asked as he strode to another open door. "My wolf isn't happy. Ships aren't a natural environment for shifters. Except maybe Meara. Speaking of which, do you have any idea what happened to her?"

"Nay. I havena seen her since she announced she was going to alert everyone to take some downtime and get some rest herself. To answer your other question, I have no idea how long this crossing will take. With reasonable weather and good wind, mayhap three-and-a-half days. With the storm that's raging, it could take a week."

"A week? My wolf just barked insults and threatened to jump overboard and swim for the nearest shore. Good reason not to shift."

"Weren't ye planning to do that to scout out more dead rats?"

"Didn't need to. Between Vreis and me, we found them all. In here." Jamal pointed. "What Meara said was she was going to tell everyone to rest. She doesn't sleep. At least not much. She's up to something, which is why we haven't seen her."

Stewart looked at the gold. Jamal may have piled it in neat stacks, but the motion of the ship had spilled the coins in long arcs. The bars had fared somewhat better. He bent and sifted a few coins through his fingers, recognizing Spanish doubloons from their feel in his hand even before he saw the likenesses of Ferdinand and Isabella.

"Let me run this past you," Jamal said. "My suggestion is we parcel out the coins so each of us has a few. Not a huge number. The rest, we can dump inside a storage cask and spell it so no one can find it."

Stewart straightened. "And I have an even better idea. We each take a dozen or so coins, and then we fill a barrel or two with the rest of the gold and chuck it over the side."

A slow smile crawled across Jamal's austere features. "That way even if the Nazis catch up with us—and they're bound to locate this boat eventually—they won't find anything. I admit I wasn't certain vampires wouldn't see through any spell we put together."

"Exactly. No point in being greedy about the money. A few coins will buy us whatever we need in the way of shelter and supplies."

"I like it." Jamal shoved a few handfuls of coins into his various pockets. I'll begin parceling out the coins and tell everyone else to stop by here and help themselves. Meanwhile, I'll grab a wooden cask. I saw several lined up in a closet near the engine room."

"Get two. They won't be so awkward to move that way."

"How hard do you think it will be to find dealers in antique coins, so we can turn these"—Jamal waved a hand over the assorted piles at his feet—"into something a little more usable?"

"And ye're asking me why?"

Jamal shrugged. "You're from the British Isles."

"Och, laddie. I left there a verra long time ago. Not so long ago that coins such as these would have passed for legal tender, but long enough I have no idea how easy 'twill be to turn them into pound notes."

"Thanks. Guess we'll figure it out together." Jamal slipped past Stewart, his pockets jingling with coins.

So long as Stewart was in the hold where the corpses had been, he shut his eyes and deployed magic to see if he could figure out anything further about the disease-ridden bodies. They'd been dead when they were dumped here, and the illness may have looked like plague—he assumed open sores, blackened flesh, and lots of dried blood—but it didn't have quite the feel plague had.

He remembered it well from the times it had scoured villages and townships near him, decimating more than half the population. The more data he gathered, the more certain he was that the four hapless souls tossed into this hold had been the victim of Nazi medical experimentation. Even though plague was caused by bacteria, it was probably easier for the Reich's doctors to get hold of something simpler that would also kill in short order.

"Holding a wake for the recently departed, are you?" Meara inquired in a dry voice that snapped his eyes open.

Stewart bypassed her sarcasm. "Have ye explored this place with your power?"

The vulture shifter shook her head and extended her hands. Power crackled around her, turning the air blue-white. "Fascinating." She cut the flow of her magic. "Not plague. Was that your assessment as well?"

He nodded. "Any thoughts about the gold?"

She bent and turned a doubloon over in one long-fingered hand. "This one is real, so I assume the rest are as well. Explains why the bodies were here. Also adds urgency to us reaching land so we can jettison this ship."

"We're not going to reach anywhere requiring westerly travel unless we get a break in the weather."

Meara eyed him up and down. "You haven't been up on deck in a while, huh?"

"Nay. I've been taking stock of the ship's provisions and—"

Meara made a chopping motion with one hand. "The weather improved. Not all over. Just in a swath around us. We're making good enough time, Cadr and Vreis are ready to raise the sail again."

Stewart bolted for the door. "Means I need to cut the engine."

"I already did. It's why I'm on this level. I sensed deployed power, knew it was you, and got curious."

Stewart stopped in the doorway and turned toward Meara. "Did ye do something?"

"Like what?" She turned her hands palms upward.

"Alter the storm that wanted to kill us."

"I may be a first shifter, but weather working is beyond me. That's your purview, Druid. And it appeared it was beyond yours as well."

Hard-to-stomach truth slammed into him on the heels of Meara's observation. Yara had to be behind this. There weren't any other possible candidates.

He twisted on his heel, intent on finding her to see what kind of deal she'd struck with whichever god she raised.

Meara raced after him and closed her fingers around his upper arm. She was strong, and her hand may as well have been a vise. "Not so fast, Druid. You know what Yara is. Tell me."

He tried to jerk out of Meara's grasp, but she held fast.

"She's Rhiannon's daughter. Everyone will know soon enough."

"Indeed?" Surprise and grudging respect lined Meara's words. "Did you figure out—?"

"Nay. But I have a niggling suspicion we shall have the goddess in our midst sooner rather than later now that Yara knows who she is."

"Aside from the obvious that she might deign to assist us"—Meara stepped in front of him—"what good will having her here do? Surely, you're not planning to snoop into her long-buried secret. She went to a lot of trouble to hide her own daughter in a Romani caravan."

"She could not verra well have sequestered her in a shifter den," Stewart countered. "The elders would have exiled her once she hit womanhood and hadna shifted." Stewart augured his gaze into Meara. "Let go of me. I want to find Yara. Something happened after I left her with that spell book of hers. Sooner we know what it is, the sooner we can plan accordingly."

"What exactly was she doing with the spell book?"

"Locating a sea or weather god for me to talk with." He ground his teeth together. Given the abrupt shift in their fortunes, the god must have showed himself to Yara.

Christ! Was she all right? Worry left a sour taste on his tongue.

"Let go of me." He yanked away from Meara, breaking her hold on him. Either his desperation lent him added strength, or she was done with him.

It didn't matter. He swarmed up the first ladder to the center deck where he'd left Yara and pelted down the corridor. Her cabin door stood open. The book was there, but she wasn't.

He needed to be smart about this. The boat wasn't that big, and magic was the fastest way of locating her. He walked into the cabin, inhaling the scent of her power. Pine and vanilla and something unique to her. Air around the book pulsed warmly as if it approved of his presence. He had little doubt it had ways of making its displeasure known as well.

He sent his power spinning outward and found her on the main deck near the wheel. Made sense. He should have gone there first. If she'd cut some kind of deal with a god, they might want her outside to watch them work their miracle. The gods could be extremely narcissistic like that.

Stewart hastened back along the corridor. When he emerged on deck, he stopped dead. Meara certainly hadn't stretched the truth. Black clouds boiled behind them and off to both sides. Clouds so ominous, wind screeched and rain spat from them. Yet directly above, the sky was a lighter gray without a storm cloud to mar things. The mainsail was indeed deployed, and a brisk breeze drove them forward. Cadr and Gregor were hooking up more canvas to maximize their momentum.

They weren't even tacking. Vreis grasped the wheel with a

satisfied expression, meaning he wasn't struggling to hold the boat on course. Yara faced away from him, staring out to sea with her arms by her sides.

He hurried to her and said, "Whoever ye raised, 'twas a solid choice, lass."

She shot him an undecipherable look before resuming her thousand-yard stare out to sea. "Manandan mac Llyr said he'd see us safe to Scotland."

Stewart whistled long and low. "Aye, and I remember that one. He's verra powerful."

Yara did look at him then through eyes narrowed to slits. "He remembers you as well—and Cadr and Vreis. I believe that was why he deigned to help us. What is your last name?"

"Macleod. Why?"

She rolled her eyes and brushed hair damp from spray away from her face. "He asked me, and I didn't have any idea. Just your first name seemed to do it, though. I'm guessing you and Cadr and Vreis have been together for a long time."

"Aye, that we have." Stewart risked a brief scan with magic, but hers had formed an impenetrable shield again. Different from the one he'd come across initially, but the barrier was just as dense.

"If you want to know something, ask me."

What could he say? That he was worried the sea god had done something to her? "It's fine. I was just concerned ye were all right."

She folded her arms beneath her breasts. She was heartbreakingly lovely, and he longed to crush her against him, but he suspected she'd misinterpret his intentions. He didn't understand the intense attraction that made it hard to leave her side, but just because he felt it didn't mean she did.

"Ye needn't remain here—" he began. Perhaps they could talk a bit below decks. Clarify things. Cadr, Vreis, and Gregor had the ship well in hand.

She pointed at the sea, still rough, but not nearly as bad as the water behind them. "Need to keep an eye out for Manandan, if he shows up again."

"Lass. He's a god. He found you afore, and he can find you wherever ye might be aboard this vessel. He splits his time betwixt the Otherworld and the sea. I doona believe we will see him again once we dock in Edinburgh."

"What is the Otherworld?"

"'Tis the home of the Celtic gods as well as the dead. Fae and Dark Fae live there too."

She narrowed her eyes. "It's real? Have you been there?"

Stewart nodded. "I have. 'Twill exist so long as the gods remain here. Once they leave, the magical realm beneath the hills and barrows of the Old Country will vanish into nothingness. Or so legend promises."

Meara raced onto the deck with Jamal, Ilona, Tairin, and Elliott right behind her. The screech that emerged from her mouth would have done her vulture proud. "Everyone who doesn't have to be here to keep the ship from foundering, come with me," she shouted.

Stewart ran to her. "What is it?"

Breath steamed from her open mouth. "Vampires might hate water, but it doesn't faze demons. Two just materialized in the hold."

"This is my fault." Elliott drew his lips back from his teeth in a snarl. "If I hadn't loosed Grigori, the fuckers would have stayed put in Hell."

"You have no way of knowing that," Meara said. "Come on. Let's not just send them packing but make them so miserable reinforcements don't show up."

"We can do this," Tairin said. "I defeated one in Munich."

Stewart pushed around everyone and surged down the ladder. Yara's power was new. So new, it might make her a prime target for demons who could sense such things. Defending her was at the very top of his list.

Nay, I must do my best to protect everyone. 'Twas my idea to cross the North Sea. I will do whatever I have to so those who trusted my judgment doona come to folly on account of that faith.

Yara's energy closed from behind him. "You can't face them alone," she protested.

Hope raced through him. Maybe she cared more than he thought. Before he could craft a reply, Meara flew past in her vulture form cawing fiercely.

Stewart ran faster. How hard could it be to drive two demons back to Hell?

Doona underestimate them, an inner voice cautioned. *Demons loose in the world doesna bode well for any of us.*

Sulfur and the stench of dead things left to rot in a sun far hotter than it ever shone in this part of the world twisted his guts into a knot.

"Stay behind me," he told Yara.

"Like hell I will." She tried to push past him, but he grabbed her arm.

"Lass—"

"Don't lass me," she grunted.

They came to the same hold where Jamal had stacked coins. Brilliant black-tinged light flared, so bright it hurt his eyes.

"Damn. I thought she said two." At least Yara wasn't barreling around him.

Stewart loped into the hold. Meara shrieked viciously. Jamal and Tairin crowded into the small space, followed by Michael, Elliott, Ilona, and Gregor. Magic kindled, light against dark.

Three red-scaled demons leered at them. From their horned heads to their forked tails, they bled confidence.

Stewart squared his shoulders. "Why are ye here?"

"Turn the ship back the way it came, *Druid.* The gold doesn't belong to you." The demon's inflection made Druid sound like a curse.

Stewart snorted. "It doesna belong to your Nazi masters, either."

"Not their opinion," another demon countered. "Do not make the mistake of calling them our masters. We have only one master, Lucifer, as you know all too well."

Stewart stared them down, unwilling to dignify the dig about his run-in with the Dark Angel. It hadn't gone well—for him—and apparently everyone in Hell knew about it.

"The way I see it, ye have a problem," he went on smoothly. "The only reason this boat isna at the bottom of the North Sea is we solicited help from a quarter that would just as soon see ye back in Hell. If ye kill us, the boat will sink. If ye—"

"Shut up, Druid." Fire roared from the center demon, and a small, wooden cask burst into flames.

The demon to the left of the fire-crazed one grabbed his arm with a taloned hand. "Stop that. If the boat catches fire, it will founder." Magic atop magic doused the fire before it could spread to anything else.

Stewart pulled power like a madman. No better opportunity than when the bastards were squabbling to launch a forward attack. *"Weave power in with mine,"* he commanded. *"Doona hold back."*

"Finally!" Meara squawked into his mind and launched herself in a flurry of feathers right at one of the demon's eyes.

CHAPTER 10

*Y*ara blinked hard, but the demons didn't go away. She'd heard Meara announce demons had boarded the ship, but it hadn't sunk in. Not exactly. A million times worse than vampires, the three abominations stood easily, balancing on the balls of their feet as if they had every right in the world to be there.

Stewart racing past, clearly intent on taking down the threat singlehandedly, had gotten her moving, but nothing in her life had prepared her for the reality—or the brimstone stench—of denizens who belonged in the underworld.

Not walking about in the light of day.

Their presence sullied the goddess's light and was an affront to every single living creature. Buck naked with genitalia hanging free, the three demons sported thick hind legs. Smallish forearms were tipped with long, red talons just like their feet. Horns protruded from their foreheads and their eyes were a swirling mass of red and amber. No one could ever mistake them for human. Not so much as a scrap of humanity clung to them. None had hair, but maybe hair couldn't grow on their scaly hides.

Stewart told her to hang back. She made a good show of

protesting, but what she wanted to do was turn tail, run back to her cabin, and lock the door. Since that might not be enough, she'd seal it with magic.

Stop it! I've never let anyone fight my battles for me, and I'm not about to start now.

Meara was in vulture form, and she shrieked a battle cry just after Stewart ordered them to blend their magic. More Rom crowded into the small space. Aron, lithe and with his dark hair bundled out of the way, darted toward the demons with magic sloughing from him. He wore his power proudly, like a banner, with hubris only the innocent could muster.

"Aron!" Ilona shrieked. "No!" The gypsy-turned-shifter threw herself after her younger brother and grabbed his arm before he reached the demons.

"Sissy. Let go of me! I can do this. Vampires can't touch me. Maybe these fuckers can't, either."

"We're not going to find out. I—"

The hold dissolved into chaos, obliterating the rest of Ilona's words. The air teemed with flames and smoke until Yara struggled to see anything. Grunts and cries filled the room, and the coppery stench of spilled blood didn't bode well. Unsure how she knew, Yara felt certain the demons' blood wouldn't smell anything like hers.

To her shame, she realized she'd wound wards around herself, much as she'd used in her cave or the shepherd's hut when she wanted to escape notice. Embarrassment scoured her like a hot, bitter tide. She'd thrown in her lot with the shifters and Romani fighting for their lives. Now wasn't the time to hide behind an invisibility she'd cultivated for years.

Yara took the power she'd shrouded herself with and used it to form a clear area in front of herself so she could see. Her heart constricted. While she'd been buried in self-preservation, the demons had been wreaking havoc. Only two remained, but

Michael lay on the floor with another Romani next to him, chanting over his inert form.

She drew the amulet on its leather cord out from beneath her clothing and tossed it to the Rom next to Michael. "Use this," she cried. "It might give you some protection."

The Rom draped it around his neck, but never stopped chanting. Michael didn't stir.

Power flared from Stewart's outstretched hands, power that flayed scales from one of the demons. It bellowed in pain and outrage while Stewart surged forward, refusing to give any quarter. Meara attacked from the air, digging her beak into the thing's eyes. One orb burst under her assault, and the rotten egg stench intensified until Yara's gorge rose, burning the back of her throat with bile.

Elliott and Tairin had the other demon cornered, and it hissed at them, following the hissing with guttural words. Though she didn't know the language, demonspeak was easy enough to interpret. The demon mocked the shifters. Told them they were insignificant bugs to be crushed beneath his clawed feet. Brilliant light flashed around Tairin, and a black and gray wolf formed where she'd stood. Wonder at the transformation filled Yara.

Simple and elegant and terrifying, Tairin skinned her muzzle back from her fangs and rushed the demon, aiming for his Achilles tendons.

Breath congealed in Yara's throat. Were the bastards configured like humans? If not, Tairin's risk would be for naught, and might well spell her doom. Yara stopped thinking. She could philosophize all she wanted later—if she survived. Magic jumped to her summons and crackled from her outstretched fingers. Careful to keep the flow of her power well above Tairin, Yara thrust it forward with instructions to fry the thing's brains.

She had no idea how much power she commanded, but she ran full open. No reason to titrate the current boiling through her.

To hell with sending the demon packing. Killing it would work better because then it couldn't come back to harass them again.

She crossed the few feet separating her from Elliott and gripped his shoulder. "Do this with me."

He didn't question her, just unlocked his magical well, so she could join with him. Together, they upped destructive energy until the demon's scales began to smoke and shrivel. It shrieked and redirected the flow of its fell magic, intent on flight now that it was beaten.

"Oh no, you don't," Yara cried.

"We need to let it leave," Elliott protested.

"Why? We can destroy it. That wouldn't be true if it were still in Hell, but they're weaker here. Maybe then ten others won't show up on his heels."

After a moment's hesitation when Elliott started to close his magic off from her, he reestablished their link.

Yara wanted to thank him for believing in her, but she couldn't transfer her attention from their adversary. She also wanted to know how Stewart and Meara were doing with the other demon, but she didn't have anything extra to finesse so much as a sideways glance. One hundred percent of her focus rained destruction on the demon dead ahead.

Tairin snarled, growled, and snapped. Black ichor shot from the demon, coating her fur in a thick, stinking gore that mocked normalcy.

Nothing about this is normal. We're fighting for way more than our lives.

She inhaled raggedly. They were fighting to keep magic alive in the world. Once it withered, every living thing that was good would fade right along with it. The demons knew that too. Maybe they were sick of being confined to the nether regions. Anxious for a shot at freedom from endless darkness.

The thought had no sooner formed than she understood what the Nazis must have promised. Hitler was a genius at figuring out what motivated people. Offering unlimited blood and sex had snared the vampires, coopting them to play on his team. Freedom was the key that had lured demons.

"Good to know what we're up against," she snarled.

"What?" Elliott asked, keeping most of his attention trained on Tairin.

"Later. Let's do whatever it takes to annihilate this bastard."

Surprisingly nimble given the thrashing he'd taken, the demon leapt away from Tairin's strong jaws and threw itself over Michael's prone form. Either Tairin had missed its ankle tendons, or it didn't have any. It dug its talons into Michael's shoulders, leaving bloody tracks.

He groaned. Magic flared from him, but a pitiful amount. The demon might have been weakened, but Michael's power couldn't be more than an annoyance to it. The amulet didn't appear to be any deterrent at all.

The demon snapped his head back, and its unearthly gaze bored into her. Still in demonspeak, it said, "Release me, and I will go peacefully. If I must force my way out of here, I shall take him"—the demon stabbed a talon through Michael's upper arm —"with me."

Michael screamed, writhing to get away from the demon.

The creature laughed uproariously, pointed a talon at the Rom who'd been chanting over Michael, and barked a single word. The man clutched his chest and gurgled as a ripping, tearing sound burst from him.

"We have to let the demon go," Elliott said into her mind. *"Michael is like a father to me. We can't let the demon kill him too."*

Tairin sprang over debris. Hunkering next to Michael and the demon, she growled furiously.

"Goes double for the wolf," the demon went on, sounding more confident his plan would work. "Call the abomination off and I'll be on my way."

"Who the hell are you calling an abomination?" Tairin screeched.

Even telepathically, her outrage rang through. Fury sheeted from the wolf. It circled behind the demon so fast it was a blur. A staunch leap positioned Tairin on the demon's back where she closed powerful jaws around the thing's neck.

"Now!" Yara urged Elliott. "Give it all you've got."

She opened channels she'd never even known existed until magic gushed, blotting out everything but their adversary. Careful to avoid Tairin clinging to the wolf like a limpet, she instructed power to boil the thing alive. Noxious smelling smoke filled the hold, but the demon's scales began to blister and peel away from the hide beneath.

Still more black blood poured from its many open wounds, and it crumpled atop Michael.

"Tairin! Let go!" Elliott cried.

She hurtled backward off her perch just before the demon's body exploded.

Elliott scrambled forward and got hold of Michael, pulling him out from beneath what was left of the demon. Michael retched weakly, and Elliott turned him on his side so he wouldn't choke on vomit.

Yara made a dive for the other Romani who'd been kneeling next to Michael. His face was gray, and when she felt for a pulse, she couldn't find one.

"Goddammit!"

Losing anyone to the demons was unacceptable. Worse than deaths at the hands of the Nazis or the Dutch government or vampires. It was irrational. She felt that way because demons outplayed everything else evil rolled into one.

She shook herself hard and sent magic auguring into the Romani in her arms. If the damage wasn't too severe, maybe she could repair it. An inner voice argued she'd lost it. Dead was dead. No matter how powerful she'd become, no one could defeat death.

The gods can.

She shushed the voice in her head and continued her assessment of the gypsy man's injuries. Heat and light bombarded her, accompanied by shrieks and growls. Who else had shifted? Why wasn't the other demon dead?

Doesn't matter. I can't look now.

The man's heart had shattered inside his chest. Yara gazed at the damage with her third eye. Horror spilled through her. All the demon had done was point at the man and speak a single word. What hope was left for any of them against an enemy this strong?

I can't think like that. If I do, I'm doomed.

She placed the man down gently and turned her hot, gritty gaze outward in time to see the third demon dissolve into a smoking ruin. Stewart and Meara's magic still pummeled it—bright white and blue white—but Meara was in her human form again. Two wolves prowled through the hold. Tairin and a larger wolf that looked like her.

Probably Jamal.

Meara cut the flow of her power; so did Stewart. He scanned the hold and shook his head. "Three dead. We canna afford another visit from the underworld."

"While I'd prefer not to entertain demons a second time, likely we'd fare better than we did today." Breath whistled through Meara's teeth. "It took a while for us to hit our stride. If demons do show up again, we'll be more efficient."

Emotion pummeled Yara. Fury. Hopelessness. Sorrow. She looked at Elliott, with Michael cradled against him. "Will he be all right?"

Elliott nodded. "Yes. But he won't be in any kind of shape to do much of anything until he recovers his strength. The demon was desperate there at the end, and he siphoned a piss pot of Michael's essence to defend himself."

The air shimmered, and Tairin transformed back to human. She hurried to Elliott and knelt, threading her arms around him and Michael. "I'm glad you're still here," she told Michael.

"That makes two of us." He flailed against Elliott. "Let go so I can get my feet under me. And stop worrying for chrissakes. I'm not as fragile as all that."

Elliott and Tairin straightened, and Elliott extended both hands for Michael to grasp, hauling him upright.

Tairin pursed her lips into a tight line. "Not sure what I'm going to do for clothes. Mine ripped nine ways from Sunday when I shifted."

"I have things you can borrow," Yara said. "Knew there was some reason I brought all that stuff."

"I'd appreciate it." Tairin's expression softened. "It would only be until I can locate a needle and thread and repair my things."

"You're in luck. I have those too." Yara shut the dead man's eyes and got to her feet, murmuring the Romani prayer for the dead. Stewart had mentioned two others. She scanned the hold. One of the shifters and another Romani lay sprawled in spreading pools of blood.

Stewart intercepted the angle of her gaze and nodded curtly. "Och aye, they got a wee bit too close to the line of fire. Meara's right about one thing."

"Oh I am, am I?" She furled her gray brows.

Stewart tipped his chin her way. "I'd forgotten how much collateral damage demons spew in their wake. Now that we know, we can instruct everyone who's left to take greater care to give them a wide berth—if they return."

Elliott gave Tairin a quick hug. "You might want to take Yara up on that offer for something to cover yourself."

"Come on." Yara hooked an arm beneath Tairin's. "Let's get something on you before you freeze to death."

"Not much chance of that." Tairin spread her arms wide to encompass the smoke-filled hold. It still stank of sulfur and brimstone and was just now returning to a tolerable temperature. When the demons were in full destruction mode, the space had grown far too hot for comfort.

Ilona, a naked Jamal, and Aron trudged past, their faces smeared with sooty stripes. Yara figured she didn't look any better. Ilona and Jamal carried handfuls of clothing scraps, probably the remains of what he'd been wearing.

"If you'd like, you can borrow some of my clothes too," she called after Ilona. "I have an oversized shirt or two that might fit Jamal."

"Thanks!" the other woman stopped in the doorway and turned to face her. "It may come to that, but I think I can patch these with a combination of magic and my sewing kit."

"If there's a way to bend magic to repair cloth, I want to learn," Tairin spoke up.

Ilona rolled her eyes. "Let's see how well this works. I haven't actually tried it yet."

"Meet you back in our cabin," Elliott told Tairin and left the room with Michael leaning on him.

Stewart hoisted one of the bodies over his shoulder and staggered upright, grunting from effort. "Got to get him up on deck," he explained. "Cadr or Vreis will help me with the invocation to drive any remaining taint of evil from this man so his death will be clean and his spirit free to find the Otherworld. We'll repeat the same blessing for the other two as well."

"Can I help?" Yara asked.

"Nay, but the offer is appreciated." Stewart trudged past, twisting sideways to fit through the narrow door with his burden. Magic bloomed, forming a coruscation around him and the dead man.

"He'll need that power and then some to hoist that body up two flights of stairs." Tairin recovered the tatters that had been her clothes off the gore-stained floor.

"I offered to help." Yara stared after Stewart, still prepared to follow him.

"Men like him rarely require assistance." Tairin's mouth twisted wryly. "I recognize the mindset from my years in caravans." She headed the opposite way Stewart had gone since both ends of the corridor running from bow to stern had stairwells.

"How long did you bury your shifter side, pretending you were Romani?" Yara asked.

"I didn't *bury my shifter side*." Tairin's words vibrated with rebuke. "My wolf wouldn't have stood for that. We'd slip away from time to time so it could run free. And I wasn't pretending on the Romani side of things. My mother was Rom."

Yara winced. "Sorry. It was a really poor choice of words on my part. I'm not at my best right now."

"It's all right. No offense taken. I'm a little shorter-fused than normal. That go-round with the demons rattled me." Tairin took a measured breath. "I had to move from caravan to caravan to hide my longevity. Michael's was the fourth one I joined over the last hundred years."

"Before that?" Yara reached around Tairin and pushed the door of her cabin open.

"I spent my first hundred years in wolf form. Egypt wasn't a safe place for a young woman by herself. My wolf saved me from being raped, imprisoned, and like as not killed."

"Smart of you to pick that path." Yara kicked the door shut and crossed the small space to root in her sacks.

"Not all that smart. I was a wolf so long, I almost couldn't find the human part of me. After all that time, it took me a week to shift, but it all worked out." Tairin took a skirt and sweater from Yara, sliding them on. "Thank you. That book makes its own magic, doesn't it?" She tilted her head at the book laying open on the desk.

"Yes, it does. In truth, I'm still figuring it out. In terms of the clothes, you're welcome. Keep them as long as you need to. Hang on a sec." She drew an embossed leather case holding her needles and thread from another sack.

Tairin's eyes widened. "That's lovely. Wherever did you come by it?"

"It's one of the few things I kept from the caravan. My oldest sister laid claim to damn near everything, but she never knew about a few items, and this sewing kit was one of them." Yara shrugged, suddenly uncomfortable. "Over the years I've added thread and buttons and hooks to it. You know how it is."

"Indeed I do." Tairin grinned and scooped Yara into a hug. "Never walk by something you might be able to use."

Yara hugged her back. "It's the gypsy way."

"No. It's the smart way. I'm proud of my Romani heritage. And sad we've gotten such a bad name."

"I feel exactly the same way." Yara let go of her and pressed the sewing kit into her hands.

"Looking forward to getting to know you better, and I'll return this as soon as I'm done with it."

"No rush." Yara followed the other woman out of her cabin, intent on joining Stewart on deck.

With a smile and a wave, Tairin vanished through a door a little farther down the corridor.

Yara had just started up the stairs when she felt Stewart's distinctive energy moving toward her. Retreating to deck level since there wasn't room for two in the narrow stairwell, she waited for him to reach her side.

"Done already?" she asked.

He shook his head. "I need you topside, lass. Manandan mac Llyr is less than pleased about accepting bodies killed by demons into his waters. He may well be rethinking his aid."

She chewed her lower lip. "Is the storm back?"

"It never really left. The only clear waters are near our boat."

"It's days yet until we reach Scotland, isn't it?"

"Aye. At least two."

"What exactly did Manandan say?"

Stewart drew his brows together. "'Twas more what he dinna say. He was most clear about having had no idea our presence would draw demons."

"So if he'd known, he'd never have promised us passage to Scotland?" Yara wanted to make certain she understood clearly.

"He dinna come out and say that, but 'twas the meaning I gleaned from him. Ye're the one who summoned him, and ye're who he wishes to converse with."

She balled her hands into fists.

Stewart narrowed his eyes. "What havena ye told me?"

Yara switched to telepathy, not at all sure it would stymie a god—if Manandan were even listening. *I was the bargaining chip. He agreed to help us in exchange for me joining him. He was going to rustle up Rhiannon to cut some kind of deal.*

Stewart pounded a fist into the wall. Fury erupted from him, and he grabbed her shoulders and shook her. "Just when were ye going to get around to sharing that with me? Nay. Never mind. The last place ye're going is up on deck." He shook her again. "Back to your cabin."

Yara jerked away from his grip, using a healthy jot of magic to break free. "You cannot tell me what to do. I'm my own person. I struck that bargain, and I'm going to where Manandan is to talk with him." She gripped the handrails on either side of the stairs intent on a confrontation with the sea god.

Stewart ripped her hands from the railing, twisted her until she faced him, and slashed his mouth over hers, pinning her between his body and the wall. At first, she struggled, but the heat of his body and his firm mouth fused to hers woke something primal in her. Something that wanted to crawl up his body and bury the hardness jutting into her stomach deep inside.

His enticing scent rose, capturing her, and she twined her arms around him, kissing him back as if they were the last two people left in the world.

CHAPTER 11

Stewart had been troubled—but not surprised—about the sea god's annoyance at having demons aboard the ship. Manandan's displeasure had spurred his sudden change of heart, which wouldn't become worrisome unless the god acted on it. If that happened, the roiling, heaving sea would close around them once more. Not necessarily a death sentence, but it would make their lives far more unpleasant.

He'd spent enough years kowtowing to the Celts to have experienced their fickleness in all its iterations. When you were immortal, the rules everyone else lived by flew out the window. Manandan hated demons, but that wasn't a reason to penalize the rest of them. It wasn't as if they'd conjured the bastards.

He knew Manandan, remembered him from endless Celtic council meetings. When he'd attempted to reason with him, the god grew increasingly restive and strident, demanding Yara's presence.

Stewart figured the god wanted Yara because her magic was what had drawn him in the first place. What a miscalculation.

Yara's disclosure cast Manandan's summons in an entirely different light, and Stewart reacted violently. Yara was his. *His*, by every god and goddess in the pantheon. He'd be damned if he'd acknowledge the sea god's claim to her.

Never mind no words of love had passed between them. Never mind she'd have no reason to consider herself his. He'd been giving her space to adapt to her parentage—and her magic. That space had just shrunk to nothing, though. He'd face down Manandan before he'd allow the god to make off with the only woman to penetrate his barriers in hundreds of years.

What the bloody fucking hell had she been thinking to agree to such a proposal? Had she figured Rhiannon would swoop in and save her?

Hah!

Being a god outplayed being a mortal, and Rhiannon would bow to the sea god. Hell, she might well see him as a good match. Far better than her well-hidden daughter deserved.

Two pieces of truth slapped him hard. He'd lose in a direct confrontation with Manandan. And he had no idea who Yara's father was. She might be a full-blooded god after all, and Rhiannon may have concealed her for a host of reasons he couldn't verify.

It doesna matter what she is. I'm falling in love with her.

Fury and dismay about her bargain with the god made it hard to get words out, but he pounded a fist into the wall and sputtered, "Just when were ye going to get around to sharing that with me? Nay. Never mind. The last place ye're going is up on deck." He shook her. Not hard, but he needed her full attention. "Back to your cabin."

Yara jerked away from his grip, using a healthy jot of magic to break free. "You cannot tell me what to do. I'm my own person. I struck that deal, and I'm going where Manandan is to talk with him." She gripped the handrails on either side of the stairs intent on a confrontation with the sea god.

Anger spilled from her as she ripped away from his grasp and mounted the stairs. His normal, methodical way of approaching the world frittered to nothing, and he spun her in his arms and crushed his mouth over hers. If she'd been entranced by Manandan, he'd drive the opportunistic god from her mind.

And everything else as well until the only one in Yara's heart, mind, and soul was him.

The sea god was a player with women stashed in every port city, the Otherworld, and goddess only knew where else. Yara had caught his eye, and he thought to add her to his stable.

Not on my watch, he willna, Stewart swore to himself.

Yara thrashed in his arms, but she wasn't trying very hard to get away. If she'd tossed her considerable magic into the mix, he'd never have been able to hold her. Her nipples pebbled where they pressed against his chest, and she opened her mouth to his questing tongue. With his desire unleased from the iron control he usually imposed on it, his cock strained against the front of his kilt and pressed into her belly.

When she wrapped her arms around him, holding on tight, and the vanilla-pine scent of her power enveloped them, his desperation lessened a notch. She did care. You couldn't fake the emotion sluicing from her as she clung to him.

He sucked and nibbled her lips, trading off kisses with raking his tongue inside her mouth. She sparred with it, and then explored the inside of his mouth in return. Her hands, which had been splayed across his shoulders, moved lower, leaving trails of liquid heat in their wake.

When she gripped his ass and pulled him hard against her, he groaned. Now that the floodgates were down, he wanted her with a singlemindedness that ran through him like quicksilver. His breath sped up, mingling with hers as they ground their bodies together.

The ship, heaving and rolling with renewed vigor, jarred sense into him and he tore his mouth from hers. Moving his hands from the curves of her hips, he settled them onto her shoulders. "Lass, we must do what we can to appease Manandan, but"—he leveled his gaze at her—"I willna go so far as to agree to his proposal that ye become his mistress."

He hesitated, faltering. "Unless, 'tis your wish, but even if ye doona want me, linking your life to Manandan's is a verra bad idea for many reasons."

She eyed him with an unreadable expression. "Forget him. What do you want?"

Stewart sucked in a breath, his nostrils flaring. "I want you, but I also want you to be happy. Were ye overcome by Manandan's charms? Was that why ye dinna tell him—?"

"Tell him what?" Yara broke in. "How the hell do you say no to a god? Besides, I didn't exactly tell him yes. I asked a question, and he disappeared. Granted, I didn't try to call him back. It would have been absurdly selfish of me to put myself before all the other people on this ship."

"So ye werena smitten, lass?"

She smiled. "Sometimes you sound unbelievably archaic. Nay," she aped his brogue, "I wasna smitten. Merely practical. Besides, I figured my mother wouldn't force me into something I didn't want. Once we were safe in Scotland, I would have addressed this."

"'Twas a gamble. The gods may squabble like rats over a rotting corpse, but they stand together against any outsider, which is exactly what they'd consider ye to be."

The deck pitched violently beneath them, and he scrambled for balance. "Come on. Manandan's temper appears to be deteriorating."

"It wasn't his strong suit when he was in my cabin. Let me go first."

"Nay." Stewart gripped the handrails and hauled himself one deck up with Yara right behind him. They needed a plan, and he didn't have one. Manandan had always been quick to anger, and he didn't like to lose.

The deck canted hard to port; Cadr and Gregor were scrambling to get the canvas down. Vreis stood at the helm. Lines of strain carved deep into his face as he fought the wheel.

Manandan was turned away from them, facing out to sea with his hands raised. Power arced from his fingers, burning blue-white against the darkness where sea and sky merged into each other. It should still be daytime, but you couldn't prove it by the inky darkness surrounding the ship. Water raced over the rails, retreating as it rejoined the sea.

Yara started forward, but Stewart gripped her upper arm, and then slid his hand down until their fingers laced together. The god knew they were there. No need to say anything.

Stewart rocked from foot to foot to stay upright. Perhaps the god would give him something to work with if he waited. Patience had never been one of Manandan's virtues. In this instance, that might work in their favor.

Manandan spun. Anger shot from his black eyes. Dark hair swirled around him, falling to the middle of his back. He'd always preferred robes to trousers, and today's was the color of old claret, sashed in deep blue.

He pointed a long-nailed index finger at Yara. "Faithless whore. I offered you a great honor, and ye throw it in my face by rutting with yon Druid. What? Ye couldna wait until I had the time to take you to my bed?"

The god marched toward them, his arm still extended. "We had a deal. A bargain. Granted, 'twas not sealed with your blood, but ye're Rhiannon's daughter. I assumed ye'd be an honorable wench. Not a faithless slut."

Stewart stepped between them. "That is enough. Ye insult the woman who shall be my wife."

A muted squawk emerged from Yara, but she didn't follow it up by telling him he'd just presumed a whole lot without asking her.

"Wife, eh? Appears she's a wee bit surprised by your proposal."

"If I'm surprised, it's because I can see you," Yara spoke up, her voice surprisingly steady. "In my cabin, you were nothing but a disembodied voice."

"So?" Manandan stared at her. "Surely ye've seen Rhiannon in all her forms."

"In truth, I've never seen her at all. Not that I remember, anyway. She fostered me in a gypsy caravan when I was just a babe."

"Details." He waved a dismissive hand and more seawater sluiced over the deck, swirling about his feet. "We had an agreement. Will ye maintain your end, or would ye prefer to leave this flimsy piece of wood masquerading as a boat to the whims of the sea?"

"I see many more options than that," Stewart cut in smoothly. "Ye surprised the lass when ye materialized below decks. She was flustered and dinna wish to put her own needs above those of the rest of us traveling with her."

Manandan nodded knowingly. "Indeed. All good and salient reasons for her to leave with me now. I'll instruct the sea to see you safely across to Scotland as I promised."

"Did you talk with my mother? With Rhiannon?" Yara asked.

"When would I have had a chance to do that?" he countered. "I've been here, holding the storm at bay." He tossed his head. "Keeping my end of the bargain."

Stewart clacked his jaws together and jumped in with both feet. "Ye just contradicted yourself."

Manandan transferred his unnerving black eyes to Stewart. "I should kill you for that impertinence."

"Hear me out, then decide." Stewart squared his shoulders. "First, ye said ye could instruct the sea to guide us safely across, implying ye dinna have to be here overseeing things. Next, ye announced ye'd been holding the storm at bay. Ye canna have it both ways. Either your presence is essential. Or 'tis not."

"Your point, Druid?" Manandan skinned his lips back from his teeth, looking annoyed.

At least he hasna called down lightning to smote me. Yet.

"My point was this." Stewart plunged ahead. If he stopped to organize what came out of his mouth, his courage might fail. "Ye dinna believe aught stood betwixt ye and yon lass, so ye werena in any rush to leave. Your behind-the-scenes motive was to make certain the ship made port with her aboard. Now that ye recognize I have a claim where she's concerned, ye're anxious to spirit her away regardless of whether the ship founders."

"I would hear from her whether she sees herself as yours." The sea god shoved past Stewart and stood nose to nose with Yara. "I take what I want, lass, but ye agreed to—"

"I asked a question," she broke in. "I never said yes to anything. You left too soon."

Stewart winced. She'd interrupted a god, and that wouldn't end well.

"We had an understanding," Manandan shouted. "Ye asked what I wanted when I turned down your offer of gold. Since my request was well within your ability to acquiesce, of course I left."

"I asked a question," Yara persisted. "You never used the words *mistress* or *marry* or *have sex with*. From where I'm sitting, your meaning was vague. For all I knew, you were planning to shanghai me to be your housekeeper."

Stewart bit back an inane desire to laugh. Clearly not cowed by the god, Yara was brave and resourceful, countering his opinions with reason. Stewart wanted to hug her, but there wasn't much point in making Manandan even angrier.

"Housekeeper?" His voice rose. "Housekeeper? I'm a god, woman. Magic accomplishes such tasks."

Yara shrugged. "Since I wasn't raised by Rhiannon, all I understand is life in Romani caravans—or by myself after the Dutch government made it a crime to be a gypsy." She crossed her arms beneath her breasts and stood as straight as she could manage on the pitching deck.

A crafty look crossed Manandan's craggy features. "Ye've had little enough of ease in your life, lassie. I could make up for the hard times. Ye'd never want for aught."

"It takes more than that to make someone happy. I may be Rhiannon's child, but until less than a day ago, I viewed myself as human."

"I know what women like. Come with me. I have a lovely corner room in mind just for you. It looks down on gardens such as ye've never laid eyes on afore. Flowers grow that bloom only in the Otherworld. Ye'd have servants to tend to your every need."

Stewart both saw and felt compulsion weave itself with the sea god's offer. He fisted his hands, wanting to drive them through Manandan's handsome face.

A closed-off look etched into Yara's features, and she tilted her chin at a defiant angle. "Sorry. God or no, I'm not for sale."

"I tried to do this nicely," Manandan snarled. "Let's see if a year or two in the dungeons doesna improve your attitude. I can afford to wait ye out." The sea crashed over a railing and formed a glittering nimbus circling him and Yara. Brightness grew around the two, edging upward.

Stewart pulled power like a madman. He had to intervene before the god's spell reached its zenith. When that happened, he'd disappear and take Yara with him.

"Let us help." Jamal and Elliott closed on either side of him, weaving their shifter magic with his. It was a more potent blend than Stewart would have guessed. Power flared around them in a mixture of blues, greens, and browns, and the scents of their combined power gave him hope all wasn't lost.

"Yara! Break free while ye still can," Stewart exhorted.

Rather than answer, she extended her arms. Lightning bolts crackled from her fingertips. The wind turned her flame-colored hair into a twisting mass that took one bird form after the next.

Was it conscious? Either she was channeling her mother, or Rhiannon was on her way. Stewart upped his link with the two shifters and focused more power to break through the pulsing maelstrom of seawater surrounding Manandan and Yara. Even if Rhiannon were racing to her daughter's side, she might arrive too late.

As if drawn by the avian tableau playing itself out in Yara's long hair, Meara flew between the god and Yara, cawing fiercely. Stewart felt like cheering, but his spell required all his attention. Surely, the god couldn't stand against all of them.

He doesna have to. All he needs to do is create enough of a power vacuum to spirit himself and Yara out of here.

Aye, and once he's gone, we shall feel the full brunt of his resentment.

No help for that last. Once Yara was safely beyond the god's reach, Stewart wanted him well and truly gone. He'd faced rough seas before, and he could do it again. The boat was solidly built. It would see them safe to port—with an assist from everyone's combined magic.

He hoped.

I have yet to lose a ship. This willna be the first.

Manandan shot a blast of blue-tinged power at the vulture shifter, but she evaded him easily with a tilt of her extended wings. Yara took advantage of the momentary break in the god's attention to fashion an opening in the pulsing water. Once she slithered through, she dropped back until a few feet separated her from Manandan.

He roared his displeasure. A vortex crafted from seawater swished outward from where he stood, enveloping Yara. She fought against it, power spewing from her as she tried to break the god's grip.

Meara went on full attack mode, flying right at the god with her beak angled to take out one of his eyes. Just when she got close, she smacked up against something Stewart couldn't see.

Must be the god's warding. Shit! How would they drill through that? He was holding his spell around Yara and defending himself without expending much visible effort at all.

Stewart focused his magic, combined with Jamal's and Elliott's, at various points in the cyclone around Yara, but couldn't penetrate it. "I need more," he cried. "Give me more."

"There isn't any more," Elliott said, his tone grim as death. "We need to be smart about this. Water is the most potent of the elements, and it's his strong point. The rest of us use earth and air."

"Fire comes to my call," Jamal panted, "but it's less than useless against water."

"We have to do something." Stewart shouted to make himself heard above the howling wind and pounding sea.

Oblivious to the rest of them, Meara flew around Manandan's head, getting in blows from her beak from time to time. How she determined where rents were in the god's warding was beyond Stewart since the shielding around the god all looked the same to him.

At least Meara's diversion kept the god's net around Yara from reaching full velocity. Stewart stripped warding from himself and plunged toward Yara. Where the sea touched him, it burned so hot he imagined skin sloughing from his bones, but he kept going until he stood within the circle of water by Yara's side.

"That was stupid," she screeched, her face contorted into a rictus. "Now you're trapped right along with me."

Her lack of faith in him stung, but he pushed it aside. "I hold Jamal's and Elliott's magic in addition to my own. Join yours to the mix. Together, we can blast through the enchantment. Ye must believe we can do this, lass."

Hope flared in her eyes, turning them deep violet, and the unique feel of her magic augered into him. He didn't hesitate, just braided it with what lived within him, working as fast as he could.

The sea pushed against them now with the same hungry icy-heat that had burned him when he blasted through its barrier. "Earth trumps water," he shouted. "Channel as much as ye can."

"It's my strongest element." A feral expression made her look like something out of legends, otherworldly and fierce enough to bend fate to her will.

"On my count of three." Stewart didn't bother with telepathy. Meara was still keeping Manandan busy, and if this worked, things would happen fast.

"One. Two. Three."

Magic scoured its way through him; he welcomed its cleansing path. Extreme power always did this, made him feel like he came within a hairsbreadth of dying and being reborn as something pure and innocent, yet ancient and wise at the same time.

The circle of seawater burst around them, turning into nothing more than foam racing across the tilting deck.

Stewart didn't hesitate. He wrapped his arms around Yara and dragged her backward until they were behind Jamal and Elliott.

Manandan focused a gimlet gaze their way. "Ye think to stymie me with cheap parlor tricks? My sea will make certain this ship founders. I'm done with good deeds. And with faithless sluts who doona appreciate me." He raised both arms over his head and began to chant in Gaelic.

Meara pecked his outstretched hands until blood flowed, but the god ignored her.

Magic with a different feel spilled around them, enveloping them in a multihued ball of light. Wind still howled and waves still roared, but the ship righted itself, no longer fighting the restless sea.

"What the hell is happening now?" Yara sputtered.

Stewart tightened his grip on her. "I might be mistaken, lass, but I believe your mother is about to make an appearance."

Yara tried to evade his grasp. The air around her developed a reddish tinge as anger exploded from her. "I hate this," she yelled. "I'm more than a goddamned pawn on a game board. You hear that, Mother?" She shook her fist skyward. "Take your fucking help and choke on it. I may have needed you once, but I don't anymore."

Shock ricocheted through Stewart. He opened his mouth to chide Yara for her disrespect, but silvery laughter cut through the howl of wind and the slap of waves.

A gateway pulsing with violet light formed next to Manandan, and Rhiannon stepped through. Long red hair, twin to her daughter's, flowed to her feet. She was wrapped in lengths of silver and gold brocade, and an owl sat on each shoulder. A copper torc circled her throat, and rings with violet gemstones adorned the index fingers of both hands.

She turned her golden eyes on Yara. "Well met, daughter. 'Twould be a sad day, indeed, if ye suffered for want of a mother ye never knew."

CHAPTER 12

*Y*ara stared at the goddess, who could have been her twin—except for the owls and the eyes—and smothered an inane desire to fall to her knees in a curtsy. She made a grab for her anger, but finding it wasn't as straightforward as she might have liked.

"Rhiannon. Timely of you to drop by, dear heart." Manandan's words dripped honey.

She returned her otherworldly eyes to the sea god. "I dinna drop by for you, ye pompous boor."

Yara's ears perked up. Clearly her mother wasn't thrilled by Manandan, or likely to be taken in by his charms. She'd bet a story lay behind their antipathy, perhaps one Rhiannon might share with her.

The false smile on Manandan's handsome face slipped a notch or two, but he plowed ahead. "Your daughter"—he jerked his chin in Yara's direction—"entered into a bargain with me. Tell her she's bound to fulfill her end whether she likes it or no."

Rhiannon laughed, tossing her head back on her graceful stalk of a neck. "She has no cause to listen to me. I've not laid eyes on her since she was two years old." Her expression sobered, and she narrowed her eyes to slits. "Describe the terms of this *bargain*."

"'Twas simple enough. I'd ensure this boat made it safely to Scotland. In return, she'd come with me."

"Come with you, eh?"

Rhiannon's expression hardened, adding a ferocious element to her beauty. The owls ruffled black-edged gray feathers in unison and hooted menacingly. "For what purpose and how long?" Rhiannon continued. "Were the precise terms of your proposal laid out, or did ye keep things vague? As I recall, that was one of your favorite schemes."

"I doona have *favorite schemes*," he sputtered. An owl flew at his head and he batted it away.

"Och, but ye do. Ye make it sound as if your requirements are elementary when, in truth, they bind others in servitude. Come on." Rhiannon crooked two fingers. "Out with it. What exactly did ye tell my daughter?"

Yara stood straighter. "You scarcely need him for that. Once he agreed to see us to Scotland, he asked what I was offering in return. I suggested gold since there's a lot of it aboard this boat. He told me he had no use for gold, and out of the blue, he said, '"Ye'll do, lass. Ye're no maid, but I shall overlook that. I will round up Rhiannon and arrange things.'

"I didn't care much for the way he put things at the time," Yara went on. "I started to ask a question, but by then, he'd left."

The goddess twisted her mouth into a moue. "Aye, and I hear the truth in your words." She extended an arm, index finger pointing at Manandan's chest. "No wonder ye thought it fortuitous I showed up, but I can fill in the blank spots well enough. My daughter, with her newly-discovered, enriched magic, asked the spell book for assistance—"

"So long as ye mentioned the book," Manandan cut in, "that tome is an affront. The etching of me is a verra poor likeness. And the description." He rolled his eyes. "Woefully inaccurate. I demand all of it be removed."

"After your misuse of its power, that can be arranged. Best watch it, or I shall see you expunged from far more than that book. I ensured it fell into my daughter's hands to keep her safe from harm—but I dinna count on your interference."

The owl that had been flapping about Manandan's head returned to Rhiannon's shoulder, hooting and ruffling its feathers.

"Humph." Manandan inhaled noisily, and tendrils of sea raced across the deck to swirl about him. "Not much reason for me to remain—or that daughter of yours. She needs a staunch lesson in respect. Stand aside, and she and I will be gone from here."

"Not so fast." Power sparked from Rhiannon, and the water retreated. "I am not done. Ye felt the tug of summons from the book and saw Yara, her head bent over its pages. She's a comely lass, and ye believed her easy pickings to add to your overflowing stable of women."

Rhiannon dusted her hands together. "Neat trick, if ye could pull it off, which ye verra nearly did. Agree to aid the ship, which costs you nothing, and secure an indentured wench." Fury blazed from the goddess's golden eyes. "Ye took advantage of my daughter's altruism and naiveté. She was willing to place the well-being of her shipmates above her own needs."

"I did no such thing." Manandan adopted an injured tone and expression. "What about my altruism in offering to save the ship?"

"'Twould be far more believable if ye hadna sent the storm in the first place. It has your stench all over it. Ye enjoy playing with vessels, particularly ones forced to attempt a crossing during the dark months. 'Tis naught but sport to you."

Manandan extended a hand. "Rhiannon. Ye're angry. We dinna part under the best of circumstances, but 'twas hundreds of years in the past. Surely ye can find it in yourself to forgive me."

She made a chopping motion with one hand. "I'll never forgive your deplorable behavior, but doona flatter yourself. I forgot about you long ago."

There is a story there, Yara told herself. *And a juicy one at that. I bet they were lovers and he cheated or lied or did some other despicable thing.*

"Release her!" Rhiannon commanded.

"Whatever do ye mean?" Manandan countered.

Rhiannon moved until she faced the sea god squarely and enunciated her words, biting them off one at a time like bullets. "Release. My. Daughter. From. Her. Bargain. Do. It. Now."

Both owls screeched, clearly driven by their mistress's ire.

"Fine. Is that all it will take for me to be done here?"

Rhiannon cocked her head to one side, but didn't answer, just continued to stare at the other god.

"Very well." Manandan flicked a finger Yara's way.

It was a small gesture, almost insignificant, so what happened next stunned her. Sensation began in her feet and shot to the crown of her head, making her skin first prickle, and then burn unpleasantly. Her eyes widened. She hadn't realized the god had wrapped her in a spell until it shattered around her in a hail of crackling so unnerving she hunted for glass shards. Even Stewart hadn't known since he'd been shocked—and furious—when she told him about Manandan's terms.

"W-what would have happened if…if—?" Yara wasn't certain how to word what she was asking.

"Had his spell remained," Rhiannon said, "ye'd have been bound to his will—forever. 'Tis how he ensnares the unsuspecting. Ye had to agree at the beginning, which ye did because ye dinna have the full story. Once ye said yes, though, ye became his."

Yara took an unsteady breath, followed by another. She strode a few paces closer to her mother and bowed her head slightly. "I didn't exactly say yes, but nor did I say no. Thank you. I'll need to be more careful. Hiding out from the Dutch government was easy by comparison."

A soft smile formed on Rhiannon's ageless face. "Aye, daughter. Never underestimate the gods. They're old and canny, and almost never have aught but their own advantage close to heart." She skewered Manandan with a pointed glance and added, "Particularly the men."

"I resent that," Manandan muttered.

Rhiannon shrugged. "Resent all ye wish. What ye shall do is this—"

"I doona take orders from you," he huffed.

"In this instance, ye may wish to. If ye doona comply, I shall recount what ye've done to our Council, and they can determine an appropriate punishment. Ye dinna exactly lie to Yara, but nor did ye give her enough of the truth to base her decision on. Additionally, she dinna acquiesce to your plan, yet ye bound her anyway. 'Twas a violation of our compact with humankind."

"Anyone with your blood is scarcely human," he countered.

Not bothering to dignify his comment with a reply, she continued. "Withdraw all your spells from the North Sea, the protective and destructive ones. This ship will survive or founder on its own merits and that of those sailing it."

Manandan shook himself from head to foot. "That's all?"

"Aye."

"If I agree, ye'll release me without me having to fight my way through your magic and your owls?"

"Aye," she repeated, "but I demand your word, sealed by a blood oath." A silvery blade materialized in her hand.

"My word is my bond. Blood is scarcely—"

"I say it is." She bore down on him, blade extended. "If ye doona pick a body part for my blade, I shall."

Yara had no idea where her courage came from, but she leapt toward Rhiannon. "Let me cut him. It's my right since I'm who he trapped in a false bargain."

Rhiannon directed an appraising glance her way that chopped

all the way to her soul before extending the blade with its carved bone handle.

Meara, who'd been perched on a piece of rigging, flew at Manandan, talons extended. If there was blood to be had, she clearly wanted a piece of the action. The owls joined the fray, circling the vulture as all three birds took turns chivvying the sea god.

Manandan yanked an arm upward to protect his head from the birds' sharp beaks. It gave Yara a perfect opportunity to slice her blade through the ball of his thumb. Blood spurted. Along with it came the sound of Rhiannon chanting in Gaelic.

Magic swirled, adding shades of blue to the salt-tinged air. Squawking angrily, Meara and the owl duo got in several good pecks to Manandan's head before he vanished in a flash of booming light. The gray curtain that had separated the boat from the rest of the landscape dissipated, leaving a stiff breeze and a sea with four-foot waves. They looked like child's play compared with what they'd fought before.

Yara blinked spray from her eyes, hunting for her mother. The glittering gateway was forming once again, and the goddess turned toward it.

"Wait! You can't leave," Yara protested.

Rhiannon turned. "Of course, I can. 'Twas accurate when ye said ye dinna need me."

Anger surged. "What? You're going to drop in and out of my life as you choose?"

"Be grateful I showed up this time…daughter. Had I not, ye'd be tied to Manandan forever."

"If you're expecting me to—"

"I expect nothing. Until we meet again. And we shall." Rhiannon twisted and launched herself through the gateway, which closed behind her and the owls clinging to her shoulders.

Yara stared at the spot where her mother had disappeared. A

riot of emotion rocked her, from fury to disappointment to astonishment at the reality of Rhiannon's power.

So much for that comfy mother-daughter chat where she disclosed all the lurid details about her and Manandan.

Yara blew out an annoyed breath. She'd been worse than a fool to believe she'd finally have the kind of mother who cozied up with tea and cakes for intimate little talks.

Stewart walked to her side, and conversations broke out all around them. Meara shifted back to human in a blaze of light so bright, Yara squinched her eyes shut.

"We can begin to shape your power"—Stewart's brogue washed against her —"so it warns you about those such as Manandan."

Everything Stewart had said about her being his rushed to the fore, and she ducked from beneath the arm he'd slung around her shoulder. "You presumed far too much below decks. I'm relieved to not be shackled to Manandan, but I'm not yours, either." Yara winced at how snippy she sounded, but there wasn't any way to soften her message and still get it across.

"But, lass—" Dismay displaced the relief that had been stenciled into his features.

"But lass, nothing," she retorted. "Don't you have a ship to deal with?"

Yara didn't wait for an answer. Turning, she pelted down the ladder. If she hadn't caught the handrails on both sides, she'd have fallen to the deck below because she missed the first two steps.

Footsteps sounded behind her, and she whirled ready to give Stewart another dose of reality.

"It's just me," Tairin said. "I heard all that and thought maybe you might want a sympathetic ear. I was alone—just me and my wolf—for a long time. It's hard to give up that level of freedom, no matter how drawn you are to someone."

Kindness in the other woman's words made it hard to swallow around the thick place that had formed in her throat. Yara fought the press of tears behind her lids. She nodded because it was easier than talking and led the way to her cabin.

Tairin followed her inside and shut the door behind them.

Crossing the small space, Yara walked to the book and flipped it shut. Part of her was curious if Manandan was still inside, but a bigger part didn't care. A shudder coursed down her spine, and she turned to face Tairin, who'd perched on the end of the lower bunk.

"How could I have been so stupid?" she demanded and crossed her arms under her breasts.

Tairin smiled slightly. "You have to say more than that. Stupid about what?"

"Jesus! Everything. I should've known better than to fall for Manandan's cheesy deal. Once he said *I'd do* in that patronizing tone, I should've said, 'Oh hell, no,' and been done with him."

"From what I pieced together listening on deck"—Tairin waved a hand upward—"you found the sea god in that book of yours. You must trust the book, or you'd never have carted such a heavy, unwieldy thing with you. Because the sea god was in your book, you trusted him the same way you have confidence in the book. It's a logical extension."

Yara made a wry face. "You're right, but what this means is I can't trust the book anymore. Not totally, anyway."

"Not the worst thing in the world. Nothing is a sure bet all the time." Tairin shrugged. "Where does Stewart play into all this?"

Yara rocked back on her heels. "You're pretty direct."

The other woman shrugged again. "I've been alive for a long time. I've found it's best to get the difficult parts out on the table, shed a little daylight on them."

Yara bristled. "Stewart's not a *difficult part*. He caught me at a weak moment is all. I'm better off without him."

Tairin got to her feet and angled her head to one side. "You know this how?"

"I've always been by myself—" she began.

"Precisely." Tairin cut in. "And because something has always been a certain way, does that mean it can't change? We offered you a chance to come with us. You didn't stew over it very long before you accepted."

Yara opened her mouth, but Tairin waved her to silence. "Coming with us was a good decision. Best one you could have made under the circumstances. You thought the Dutch were bastards. They're pikers compared with the Nazis, and they'll overrun the Netherlands before the summer solstice. Elliott and Meara and Ilona are seers, and they've seen it in their vision states."

"Okay. I get it that change isn't necessarily a bad thing." Yara closed her teeth over her lower lip. "But leaving a place I've been hiding out for years isn't in the same league with letting a man into my life."

"You like Stewart. I sense it."

Heat began in Yara's chest and slithered over her head. "I'm attracted to him. I have no idea if there's anything there beyond wanting to invite him into my bed."

"How can you find out?"

"Why do I want to?" Yara countered.

Tairin pursed her lips into a thin line. "This is personal, but did you have any men in your life after you left the caravan?"

The heat turned into a fire, and Yara figured she'd turned bright red. "A few," she mumbled. "Mostly after my sister and her lover left the Netherlands. I tried to steer clear of everyone, but sometimes I just got so lonely I ached for the feel of someone next to me."

"Did you care about any of them?" Tairin pressed, adding, "Don't worry if the answer is no. I'm not here to judge you. I considered taking a few men into my bed for exactly the same reason. In the end, I chose not to, but if I had, my heart would have been closed to them."

"What made the difference in choosing not to?" Yara angled her head, wanting to know.

"I always had my wolf. It meant I was never truly lonely."

Yara nodded, grateful beyond reckoning that Tairin understood. She'd lived the gypsy life, a life where casual sex wasn't frowned upon so long as it remained in the shadows.

"It was sort of the same with me," Yara murmured. "Except I didn't have a bond animal to keep me warm at night. The men—and there weren't all that many—weren't anything special. They didn't expect anything beyond my body, and I didn't want anything else from them, either."

Tairin nodded. "Yup. That's easy, right? No worries about getting hurt or abandoned or cheated on."

Yara sucked in a ragged breath and took a chance. "You and Elliott seem happy."

A smile bloomed, illuminating Tairin's exotic beauty. "We are, but I almost kicked him to the gutter before we had a chance. Shifters and Romani aren't exactly slated soul mates. Both races forbid contact with the other, and for the most ridiculous reason."

"What is it? I always wondered about that." Yara made her way to the far side of the bunk and balanced on its edge. "Sit," she urged. "The boat's rocking enough standing requires work."

Tairin grasped a wall hook, but remained on her feet. "The short answer is that long ago a mixed blood shifter mated with a mixed blood Rom. They produced a devil child who murdered hundreds before he was apprehended. Of course, no one understood genetics in those days. They assumed it was a problem that would always plague Rom-shifter matings. No one paid one whit of attention to the witch and other magical blood that were also part of producing the damaged seed."

"Interesting." Yara tucked her legs beneath her and leaned against the wall. "I remember all the hush-hush warnings from the older women. They cautioned us about bunches of things. So many, it made the world feel very unsafe, but they harped on shifters more than everything else combined."

"I had the same experience, except since I was half shifter, those discussions always made me feel naked and exposed. Like my secret was about to be my undoing."

"Was it?"

A muscle twitched in Tairin's set jaw. "Not exactly. In the end, I revealed what I was willingly, but that's another story.

"Back to Stewart. I've worked side by side with him for several months. He's a decent man, and you've seen how powerful his magic is. Yeah, he lied about what he was to the caravans, but so did I."

Yara twisted her mouth into a grimace. "So did I by default. I didn't know, but I didn't dig too deep, either."

"I asked before, and you hedged. What do you feel for Stewart?"

"I honestly don't know." The memory of being crushed against him raced back, and heat suffused her face again. To avoid saying more, she asked a question. "Did you have any reservations about Elliott, beyond him being Romani?"

"Oh my goodness, yes." It was Tairin's turn to blush. "I came very close to closing the door to him permanently."

"What changed your mind?" Yara bent toward Tairin, not wanting to miss any part of her answer. Words or nuances.

"My wolf. And me too, I suppose. Elliott had been attacked by a gravely wounded vampire intent on finding another vessel so he wouldn't die. I couldn't let him join the damned, and my wolf said there was a way to save him. Father tried to hold me back, said it was too dangerous, but by then I'd shifted and taken off after Elliott."

Tairin stopped to draw a breath. "Elliott knew he wasn't strong enough to defeat the vampire, so while he was still more man than vampire he ran toward a precipice, intent on destroying himself by jumping off the edge."

Yara's throat tightened. "By the goddess! What did you do?"

"It was more my wolf than me. It located a wolf willing to bond with Elliott, and we jumped on him and bit him before he made the edge of the cliff. Even then, it was nip and tuck and took all Meara's magic to strengthen Elliott's wolf enough for him to shift."

"What would have happened if he couldn't?"

"I'd have been dragged into darkness with him. My wolf and I both. His wolf too." Sadness streamed from Tairin. "That would have been the worst part. The bond animals are good and pure and beautiful. To become the cause of their suffering for all eternity would have been too much to bear."

"It was your wolf's idea," Yara began, wishing she had a bond animal to help her with the hard decisions.

"That doesn't mean it stopped being my job to keep us both safe." Tairin edged toward the door, but stopped on the near side of it. "I can't make your choices for you, but I hope you give Stewart a chance. It's a lonely life." She slipped out the door, latching it softly behind her, before Yara could reply.

Lurching to her feet, she paced from one side of the cabin to the other cataloguing pros and cons. It didn't take long before she understood how profoundly frightened she was of anything that looked like an emotional commitment.

"Okay." She spoke out loud to steady herself. "Now that I know what a coward I am, the question is whether I'm willing to do anything to change it."

She swallowed hard. Even if she was, she'd been bitchy enough maybe he'd already written her off.

CHAPTER 13

*N*ight came and went, followed by much of the following day. Stewart made a point of finding things to busy himself with on deck. He hadn't wanted to run into Yara, and apparently she felt the same because she hadn't poked her head out since telling him he had a ship to tend to.

He pressed his lips into a tight line, tasting salt from the ever-present spray. So far, they'd had decent winds. Absent anything unexpected—and he hadn't sensed a thing to suggest adverse weather—they'd make port sometime tomorrow. They'd been fortunate demons hadn't staged a return visit to exact revenge. By now, whoever sent them surely knew they hadn't been successful retrieving the gold, and they must be frantic and furious.

A lethal combination, if ever there was one, but he didn't dwell on that.

He checked the rigging, adding more canvas at a nod from Vreis who stood at the helm. He, Cadr, and Vreis had taken turns as helmsman, with Jamal, Gregor, and Elliott hanging about anxious to learn the fine points of sailing. Back in bird form, Meara squawked encouragement from the rigging. Or maybe it was criticism. If she'd wanted to be understood, she'd have switched to telepathy, and she hadn't been so inclined.

Days were short this time of year. A gray-toned sunset splashed across the western horizon. Not particularly colorful, but at least it wasn't raining, and the wind was manageable.

Yara's absence bothered him. A lot. It had taken all his considerable self-discipline not to hunt her down for a heart-to-heart. The only reason he hadn't was because he couldn't stand to have her repeat her message that he'd presumed too much.

Aye, if I give her a wee bit of time to mull things over, things may improve.

Or not.

Her absence argued for the *or not* side of things. She was outspoken enough she'd have let him know if she changed her mind. He ground his teeth together. There it was. When he next laid eyes on her, the wisest path would be to give her plenty of space. No reason to make the lass even more uncomfortable than she already was, regardless of the pain carving its way through him.

Alone had become a way of life, and it wasn't about to change.

As he thought about it, Rhiannon hadn't acknowledged him, either. He didn't consider what that might mean until long after she'd left. It was always possible she hadn't seen him. She'd been focused on Manandan and Yara, but the gods weren't limited in the same way humans—even humans with magic—were.

Omnipotent and invincible, the gods might not choose to act on knowledge, but it was there for the taking if they focused their attention on it.

I'm overthinking this. She knew I was there, but 'twasn't a situation for exchanging pleasantries. Besides, if she realized what happened betwixt Yara and me below decks and dinna approve, I'd be dead.

The backhanded reassurance didn't wipe away his concerns. Rhiannon's parting words to Yara had been that they'd meet again, which meant something was simmering and about to unfold…

He stared at the vulture. She was a seer. Perhaps she knew more than she'd shared. "Meara. I have a question."

She cocked her head to one side looking like a garden variety vulture.

"Have ye scryed our future lately?"

The bird squawked and bobbed its head.

Stewart had finished with the sail, so he trotted closer to the vulture. "Well? What did ye uncover?"

With a toss of her head and excessive feather rustling, Meara transitioned to her human form in a blaze of brilliance. Stewart was ready for the starburst of light and looked away before her transformation seared his corneas.

Meara's long hair trailed behind her, and she wore a solemn expression with pinched places in the corners of her amber eyes. "I need to locate Ilona and Elliott. If our combined power yields the same future as my individual scrying, then I will be more inclined to discuss this."

"I'm here." Elliott strode to where they stood. "I heard that. Want me to hunt down Ilona?"

"I can," Jamal called from over by the wheel. "Be right back. She and Yara and Tairin have been working on a sewing project." He loped across the deck toward a stairwell.

Aron edged out of a shadowed alcove. "Excellent! I'll stand in for Jamal while he's gone."

Vreis ruffled the lad's dark hair. "Step right up and place your hands on the wheel where mine are."

"Really?" Excitement thrummed through Aron's voice, and he wrapped his slender hands around the polished wood.

The boy's delight heartened Stewart. Pain and terror and disillusionment dragged at the soul until all a person saw was bleakness. The lad had lived through hell, but it hadn't dimmed his spirit. Perhaps it was a sign hope hadn't died out of the world, no matter how grim things appeared.

He focused his gaze on Meara. Probing her with magic was pointless. If she had something she wanted to hide, he'd never unearth it.

As if she'd determined his line of thought, she drew her brows together and met his direct stare. "If you're about to inquire why I was wasting time in bird form when I could have been fine-tuning my take on our future, don't bother."

Stewart screwed his face into a grimace. "That did occur to me." He took a measured breath. "What I came up with was this. Sometimes, when a thing is so terrible I canna bear to look at it, I take a wee break. Not that I expect what's bothering me will change, but a bit of distance adds perspective. Sometimes I see more clearly after a few hours or days have passed, and the event I feared doesna look quite so devastating—"

Meara waved him to silence. "You'd best hope the gods come to our aid once we reach Great Britain. And all the other magical creatures as well. A darkness bears down on us that's so encompassing I can't see its beginning or its end."

Elliott leaned closer, his features creased into a worried expression. "Why didn't you summon Ilona and me before this?"

The vulture shifter rolled eyes that still held a decidedly avian cast. "You weren't listening. I was hoping time might lend perspective. Stewart understands well enough."

"But there must be things we could do to be better prepared," Elliott broke in, but then clammed up fast. He must have remembered she was a first shifter and he a newly made one. Color rose, splotching his features. "Sorry. I was out of line. It's hard to go from the top of the magical realm, where I used to be, to the bottom."

Ilona hurried to where they stood. Long, dark curls tumbled around her, and her gray eyes glistened with concern. She latched her gaze onto Meara. "Jamal told me we're going to activate our seer gifts. Where do you want to do this?"

"That's part of the problem." Meara thinned her lips to a straight line. "We'll expend a lot of magic. So much, we could jeopardize the boat."

"Let me take care of that part," Stewart said. "I can deflect your combined power afore it threatens our craft."

Yara's unmistakable energy drew near. Shock vied with pleasure. Stewart didn't mean to look her way, but he couldn't help himself. Her hair hung in two plaits down the front of a green, woolen cloak. Dark circles etched beneath her eyes, and it didn't appear she'd slept the previous night. His heart went out to her. She looked young and vulnerable and pushed beyond her depth.

Had the magical book delivered a message similar to what Meara had seen in her vision? It made sense and might be what had kept Yara from her rest.

He wanted to go to her, draw her close, and reassure her he'd take care of her, but it would be the wrong thing to do. He made a grab for his resolve to leave her be. If it had taken her better than twenty-four hours to gird herself to face him, he needed to be unfailingly proper. He'd treat her with the dignity and respect he'd afford any of them.

Nothing more. Nothing less.

She came to a halt next to Meara, avoiding making eye contact with him. "If you're going to scry the future to determine what we face, you must include me," she told the first shifter.

Meara narrowed her eyes. "And why might that be? Your power is strong but untaught and untried."

Yara smiled wryly. "Is that a diplomatic way of telling me I'd be more of a liability than an asset?"

"Something like that, but you didn't answer my question."

Yara tossed her head back and squared her thin shoulders. The gesture tore at Stewart's heart. She was frightened, but determined to not let it stop her from doing the right thing.

"Ever since Rhiannon showed up here, the book has changed. It doesn't wait for me to ask things anymore. It just starts glowing, and the pages rustle until they fall open to what it wants me to know." Her nostrils flared. "I'm exhausted. I was up all night with it. Kept telling it to save the next revelation for today, but it was like it was excited to finally be free of goddess-only-knows what."

She shook her head. "Sorry, I'm rambling. The short answer is it told me you three"—she pointed at Elliott, Ilona, and Meara—"were going to look into the future. It made it abundantly clear I was to be part of that. Me and the book," she clarified.

"Mmph." Meara sucked in a noisy breath. "Hard to say no to that. If I did, it might jinx our efforts. All right." She nodded once. "The hold where the dead bodies were should do. The four of you will meet me there in half an hour. It will give me time to arrange the energy in that space."

"Arrange the energy?" Ilona furled a brow.

Meara flapped both hands, clearly annoyed. "Goddess preserve me from new shifters. I'll be clearing out anything that might interfere with our efforts." Before anyone could question her further about anything, light flashed and she vanished.

The corners of Elliott's mouth twitched. "Guess she's not used to having to answer to anyone about anything."

"Ye'd be correct," Stewart replied. "See all of you verra soon. Take this span of time to empty your minds of aught that might get in the way."

"You said that for a reason." Ilona angled her head. "What is it?"

"Demons attacked us once. They're sneaky. I havena felt their presence, but it doesna mean they're not watching us. Do whatever ye can to purify yourselves. 'Tis what Meara is doing to the hold."

To reduce the temptation to talk with Yara, he made his way to Vreis and Aron. The young man's eyes were wide. "I want to be there with the rest of you," he announced. "Ilona needs me."

Stewart dropped a hand on his shoulder. "She needs to know

ye're safe with Vreis and Jamal. If everyone is in the hold, who will take care of the ship?"

Aron still clutched the wheel. "I don't really know anything about sailing, but I do know about magic, and—"

"The hallmark of a good sailor is taking orders without question." Stewart spoke over Aron. "Ye're worried about your sister, but naught will happen to her."

"Promise?" Worry spilled from Aron's eyes. Leftovers from the misery he'd endured in a concentration camp where vampires fed from him.

"Aye, lad. I canna guarantee anyone's safety over the long haul, but today's endeavor willna harm any of us."

I hope.

He turned his attention to Vreis. "Everything under control?"

The other Druid nodded. "I know this stretch of sea well. I'm not expecting anything untoward betwixt here and Edinburgh. Cadr will be along soon enough to take his turn at the helm."

"About Edinburgh." Stewart moved his hand from Aron's shoulder. "Aim for the next decent place we could put in north of there. I doona want to have to deal with the port authorities in case someone reported this vessel stolen."

"Got it." Vreis rolled his eyes. "Ashamed I dinna think of that myself."

"Ye will remain here." Stewart focused his words at Aron and anchored his command with a small spell.

"Yes, I will." Aron snapped off a sloppy approximation of a salute that made Stewart smile.

He turned and made his way to the stairs leading below decks. Jamal passed him near the top of them. "Thanks for your kindness to Aron," he murmured low.

"No thanks needed," Stewart replied. "The boy is a treasure."

"He scarcely sees himself as a boy, which is part of the problem." Jamal shrugged. "But he's bright and coming into his own magically. I'm more inclined to push him a bit than remind him of his youth and inexperience."

"Wise choice." Stewart made his way down the steep stairs to the lowest level. He deployed power, pushing, sensing, probing for anything wicked that might have taken up residence while they weren't looking.

Not finding anything amiss, he strode to the small room where everyone else had gathered.

Meara gestured him to a spot in the circle opposite her, and he squatted balancing on his haunches. A large basin of seawater sat between them, its surface rocking with the motion of the ship. Ilona and Elliott sat across from each other.

"Where do you want me?" Yara stood near Meara, the book clasped between her hands. She still hadn't so much as spared a glance Stewart's way. Her indifference burned, but they had bigger things to worry about than his bruised feelings.

"I've been trying to figure that out," Meara replied. "This circle is balanced. If I add you, it won't be."

"Odd numbers hold power." Stewart kept his voice soft, so Meara wouldn't think he was contradicting her. "Ye'd planned to proceed without me originally, which would have left ye three."

Meara glared at him before shutting her eyes for a moment. When she opened them, they were her vulture's eyes, feral and untamed. "You and that book of yours will be next to Stewart, directly across from me," she told Yara.

A look Stewart couldn't decipher washed across Yara's face, but she didn't argue, just walked around the circle and crouched next to him, laying the book in front of her.

A glowing nimbus surrounded it, and it opened, pages turning on their own until it settled to a particular spot.

"What does it say?" Meara asked, the words strained as if it pained her to accept magic that wasn't of her own making.

"That you chose well and we should begin," Yara replied.

"Nice to have its permission," Meara muttered acidly and began to chant.

Elliott and Ilona joined in, and the surface of the basin turned clear as glass, no longer at the mercy of the rocking boat.

Stewart wasn't certain if he should look at the basin. He'd never been a seer, and he didn't want his particular brand of power to muck up their efforts. Instead, he focused on building a container around the five of them. Once he had the basic structure, he strengthened it doing his best to ensure nothing from Meara's incantation could leak through and threaten the ship's integrity.

He was painfully aware of Yara's presence next to him. Her vanilla-pine scent kindled desire and an ache that pierced him through and through. Why had the goddess seen fit to place her in his path only to have her spurn him?

Questions like that had no answers.

The seers' chanting gained intensity, and the water in the basin developed an ominous black tinge. His spell started to unravel about the edges, and he shored it up. Golden darts flew from Yara's outstretched hands securing places resistant to his efforts.

He glanced sidelong at her only to catch her looking away. That she'd made any kind of eye contact pleased him, but he chided himself for being pathetic and a fool. She probably needed a visual to guide her efforts and gauge the type of magic he was using.

"This will take all of us. Something bad is coming. I feel it hovering, and they're helpless right now." Yara jerked her chin toward Elliott, Ilona, and Meara. Their eyes were shut, hands extended over an increasingly restive basin. Water slopped over the edges, and it had turned almost entirely black.

Stewart felt wickedness bearing down on them too. The air grew thick and stale until drawing breath took effort.

Meara jumped to her feet. Power sheeted from her, and her eyes snapped open as she exhorted the water to yield its secrets.

Instead, it rose in a black vortex spinning from basin to ceiling. An ominous booming sound, followed by high-pitched squealing, pounded against Stewart's ears and twisted his gut into a knot of tension.

Elliott and Ilona were standing now too. The seers still did their damnedest to shape the water to their will, but it had leapt its bounds and escaped any semblance of control.

Stewart rocketed upright, followed by Yara.

Meara switched tactics, chanting an incantation to vanquish evil. Apparently, she'd given up on wringing information from the swirling maelstrom. The tower of black water whirled so fast it showered him with noxious smelling drops that burned where they landed.

Stewart reached for Yara's hands. She grasped his outstretched fingers without question, and he felt a jolt as the contact increased his power tenfold. Touching Yara added enough magic to strip away illusion, and everything driving the darkness slammed into him. He didn't need to be a seer to see dancing, laughing demons cavorting with vampires. Men in SS uniforms darted in and out of the evil creatures' revelry, laughing as if they'd been handed the world on a sulfur-stained platter.

He blinked hard, but the vision remained stenciled into his brain. No matter what happened, that scene would stay with him for the rest of his days.

Stewart battled incredulity and horror. It was bad enough when it had just been vampires and Nazis. Although he'd suspected demons had joined the alliance, the certainty of them adding their power to the mix was appalling. He concentrated on maintaining the barrier he'd erected. The book glowed crimson at his feet, adding its own brand of enchantment to their efforts.

Yara tightened her grip on him and when he looked at her, tears leaked from her eyes.

"We canna give up, lass."

"I know. It's horrible, though. So much worse than…" She shook her head.

Meara's voice rose to a screech, and the tower of water crashed to the deck, sloshing harmlessly around their feet.

"Fuck!" Elliott managed through panting breaths.

"Double that from me," Ilona gasped in a thin, strained voice. She inhaled in a series of jagged breaths and focused her next words on Meara. "Was *that* what you saw?"

Meara nodded. She looked as rattled as Stewart had ever seen her. "Demons aren't just flirting with being part of this anymore. They've signed on as full partners." She snorted derisively. "In their minds, they likely see themselves as leading the charge."

"Someone needs to let Hitler in on that secret." Elliott screwed his face into a grimace.

Stewart looked right at Meara. "There's more."

She swallowed visibly. "Yes, there is. This time around was far worse than in my previous trance state. We came very close to losing control of the gateway."

"What exactly does that mean?" Yara asked. She let go of him, bent, and picked up the book, holding it tight against her chest.

"Whenever ye summon vision states," Stewart answered to spare Meara the trouble, "ye open a portal to the thing ye're gathering information about. If ye canna control the gateway, whatever is on the other side can force its way through."

Color drained from Yara's face, leaving her skin the shade of old ivory.

Meara clapped her hands together three times. "Focus. We can't afford to lose our way in the face of the unthinkable."

"It is better for us to know what we face," Ilona said, but she didn't sound convinced.

"I have to let Tairin know," Elliott muttered. "Won't be much of a surprise to her since she fought Grigori once before."

"Hold on for a moment." Meara's voice rang with command. "Everyone needs to know we will face an army of darkness, and not too long after we set foot on Scottish soil. I was able to glean that much before the water got away from me."

"We can't take them on by ourselves," Elliott protested.

"We may not have a choice," Ilona countered. "There's nowhere for us to run to."

"This journey is my doing." Stewart stood straighter. "I will gather what allies I can to our side after we make land."

"Best be quick about it," Meara said. She moved until she stood in front of him. "This isn't happening because you pushed us to cross the North Sea. It would have happened no matter where we were."

"Ye canna know that," he protested.

"Oh yes, I can," she retorted. "Every single vision I've summoned has contained nothing but blackness. There's no escaping it. Not here. Not in Germany. Not across the ocean in the States. When the Reich came into being, human energy fueled nascent evil. Hell's denizens grew reckless feeding on chaos and anarchy. It's why Grigori was able to penetrate Hell's veil and why vampires are suddenly in our midst after centuries of keeping themselves well-hidden from human notice."

She bent and swiped her index finger in a long stripe across the wet deck. "We must build a line and hold it. If we fail—" She shook her head, either unwilling or unable to flesh out her line of thought with more words. "We will meet at first light and decide how our initial hours ashore will unfold."

Meara stalked out of the hold followed by Elliott and Ilona, who looked shaken to their cores.

Yara started after them, but Stewart said, "Thank you for trusting me when I held out my hands."

She stopped walking and turned her gaze on him. Her eyes held a haunted, otherworldly aspect. "The book told me—"

"Nay, lass. Ye joined your magic with mine unstintingly. No book could have managed that. Ye held nothing back."

Her harsh expression crumpled, and she fled out the door but not before he saw the same longing he wrestled with stamped into her features.

Cursing himself for not leaving well enough alone, Stewart bolted after her. He yearned for her and wouldn't rest until he'd either smoothed over their earlier argument—or she told him to go to hell.

The world might be teetering on the edge of annihilation, but he'd take whatever time he could carve out with Yara. She was his mate. The woman he'd waited lifetimes for.

She might not agree, but he had to find out for certain.

CHAPTER 14

$\mathcal{Y}$ara ran out of the hold because if she didn't, she'd throw herself into Stewart's arms. She'd spent the last day not only wrestling with the book, but going back and forth about her feelings for the tall, spare Scot with his red hair and penetrating eyes. Tairin had dropped by to talk twice more, but Yara changed the subject when she mentioned Stewart. The shifter meant well, but this was one decision Yara had to make by herself. Other's opinions would only cloud things.

She bit down hard on her lower lip.

Apparently, she wasn't as ambivalent as she thought. When Stewart had extended his hands intent on joining their magic, she dove in headfirst, delighted to have a viable excuse to touch him. Their power harmonized so well it stunned her. If she inhaled, she could still smell the clean scent of his magic: ocean tang mingled with gorse and heather. Exactly how she imagined the Highlands would smell, even though she'd never been there.

Footsteps pounded behind her. She didn't have to turn around to know it was him. They'd run out of words in the hold, and only one reason remained for him to come after her. He'd made his feelings clear enough. Either she gave them a chance—or she kicked the door closed once and for all.

I already did that, and he didn't give up.

That he cared enough to keep trying kindled a warm glow in her midsection. She was drawn to him in a way that both thrilled and mystified her. But the possibility of sharing her life with anyone scared the stuffing out of her.

"Yara." The single word was laced with entreaty. "Please."

She'd reached the end of the corridor and faced two choices. Either she scrambled up the ladder and ignored the man closing on her. Or she stopped long enough to find out what he wanted.

Jesus. Who am I kidding? I know what he wants because I want the same thing.

She gripped the sides of the ladder bent on flight, and an ineffable sadness filled her wiping out everything bright and good in her world. Had he cast a spell to make her feel that way? It wasn't like her to do anything beyond living in the moment. The last eight years hadn't lent themselves to anything akin to long range planning.

Stewart reached her and stood facing her back, so close the warmth from his body seared her. "Lass. Turn around." Something thick and desperate lay beneath his words, and she didn't have it in herself to spurn him. Not when he sounded like that.

Letting go of the handrails, she turned and looked at him. The corridor had very little illumination, so she kindled a mage light. Raw pain twisted his features into a mask of sorrow and hopelessness. Anguish knifed through her, and she extended a hand, cradling the side of his face.

"I'm sorry. I never meant to hurt you. It's just…"

Just what? What can I say besides I'm a terrible coward?

He leaned into her touch. "No need for apologies. I understand, and better than ye might think. When ye've had only yourself to answer to, even contemplating changing that is frightening."

She opened her mouth, but he shook his head. "Let me finish. Regardless of how this conversation goes, ye and I will remain allies. Our two magics complement each other. 'Tis far too potent a combination to not leverage when darkness attacks—and it will. 'Tis out there gathering forces, even if I canna sense it directly."

Warmth from his stubbled cheek warmed her hand. "Maybe anything between us should wait until we see what happens with the demons and vampires."

"Aye, and I've thought the same, but we may not be alive at the end of what's coming." He smiled crookedly. "Ye may be on account of Rhiannon. I suspect if she leaves Earth for one of the other worlds, she'll take you with her. But I've never forgotten I'm mortal. The Celts may have needed me once, but that time is long past."

She should stop touching him, but she couldn't make herself move her hand. "I'm not sure you're right about Rhiannon spiriting me off somewhere. Hell, I might refuse to go even if she wanted me to, but that part doesn't matter."

His direct gaze bored into her. "Ye know less than naught about me beyond me hiding what I was in order to travel with the Romani. Mayhap if ye understood a wee bit more, 'twould set some of your fears to rest. Would ye be willing to listen for a small span of time?"

Touched beyond words by how hard he was trying, she nodded, swallowing around a thick place in her throat.

"Druid priests werena bound by celibacy like their Christian counterparts." He rolled his eyes. "Not that they practiced celibacy, mind ye. Mayhap because 'twas forbidden, they rutted with anything they came across—and all in the name of their god, but 'tisn't important.

"Even though sex wasna forbidden me, I rarely indulged. Mostly only during the festivals—if then. I always thought I'd find a woman I could love, but it never happened. Centuries passed, and things grew difficult for anyone practicing a non-Christian faith. Came a time when even if I'd found a woman I wanted to take to wife, I'd have walked away because I'd not have willingly placed her at risk. Her or our bairns.

"Once I left Britain and inveigled my way into the Romani culture, I also steered clear of entanglements. I saw plenty of caravan leaders who misused their power that way, and I vowed to not be one of them."

He took a measured breath. "That brings me to the present. I felt attracted to you the first moment we found you in that forest near the German border."

"How do you know I didn't find you?" she countered. "I know that territory well and could have hidden myself if I'd wanted."

"Why didn't you?"

She was rubbing the side of his face now, exploring the stark lines of bone and muscle. "I'm not certain it was as formal as my weighing plusses and minuses and coming to a conclusion. If I'd done that, the lot of you would have been long gone."

"Would ye like to know what I think?" A soft smile played about his chiseled lips.

"I have a feeling you're going to tell me, regardless."

"Aye, that I am. This may be self-serving on my part, but I lean more toward it being the truth. Ye came out of hiding because of me. Oh, ye dinna know I was there, but ye were drawn to my energy. Mayhap that book of yours made certain ye were in that precise place at the proper time to intercept our group.

"We were only there for a short time. Long enough to dispatch the vampire, and then we'd have been gone." He angled his head to one side and continued to spear her with his direct gaze.

Yara thought back to the day she'd sensed the others and come out to investigate. She'd been curious—and afraid—but not so fearful she was immobilized. She closed her teeth over her lower lip.

"I sensed the vampire. When I figured out how near it was, I kept a close eye on it. Those things can trap you. I also knew shifters and Romani were moving toward me. An odd energy, one I couldn't catalog, was there too." She glanced up shyly. "Turned out that was you."

"What drew you out of hiding?" He stood so close, heat from him enveloped her, along with his alluring scent.

"I'm not entirely sure. I felt the vampire die and was elated. I had no idea you could kill them. It gave me courage to leave my cave. I planned to remain hidden and just watch from behind some trees, but Aron knew I was there."

Stewart nodded. "Aye, the lad is surprisingly powerful for one so young. I knew you were there as well, though. 'Twas I who told him."

Yara's other hand snaked around Stewart's shoulder. The need to touch him was overpowering, and she didn't have the willpower to resist. "I wondered about why I agreed to leave so readily. It's not like me. Usually, I'm very cautious about anything that changes my life."

She took a deep breath. "Things have been hard since my sister left. There's only me, and my survival has depended on being vigilant—and guarded. Ready to take flight the second I sensed something wasn't right. I had a system in place, but it wouldn't have taken much for it to blow up in my face. That vampire, for example, would have put a real crimp in things. Normal invisibility spells don't work predictably with them."

He smoothed stray hairs away from her face. His fingertips sent small shivers running through her. "You're so lovely. And we have so little time. I doona wish to speak of vampires."

"I'd be happy if the lot of them disappeared off the face of the earth."

"They remained on the sidelines for years. Modern life isna compatible with their magic. It mutes it, much as it does for the rest of us. Hitler and his Reich breathed new life into their abilities, and may they be damned to Hell for all eternity for their meddling."

He continued to stroke her face. "I said I dinna wish to speak of vampires, and launched into an explanation of their newly risen strength. Apologies. Vampires will bother us soon enough, but I'll not invite them back into this conversation."

He cradled her face in his hands, and his magic rose, surrounding them in a warmth that made her long for things she could barely remember. For home and hearth and family. For passion and tenderness. For a world not teetering on the brink of annihilation.

"I would kiss you, lassie, but this time I'm asking, not taking." His voice rasped with unquenched need. Promise smoldered in the backs of his eyes, twin flames that could kindle and burn them both to cinders.

"I want you too." The words surprised her. Not so much that she'd said them, but that she wanted his lips on hers more than she'd ever wanted anything.

Stewart angled his head and brushed his lips over hers. Sweet, tentative. Nothing like their last kiss where their bodies had crashed together. She pressed her mouth against his, savoring the contact and increasing the pressure as she bit and nibbled her way from his mouth across one cheek to an earlobe and back again.

This time when she reached his mouth, he slid his hands backward, threading them into her hair and holding her head steady while he urged her to open her mouth for his questing tongue. He tasted of honey wine she remembered from her days with the caravan, and she sucked on his tongue, desperate to inhale all of him.

Her breath quickened, and her nipples peaked where they pressed against his chest. It had been months since she'd lain with a man. Maybe years. Her lifestyle hadn't been conducive to letting anyone know she existed. Hunger burned through her. Desire for the simple contact of flesh against flesh. For the dance where bodies ruled and minds took a backseat. Heat slicked her women's parts, and the empty place between her legs screamed to be filled.

He ran his tongue down her neck to the hollow between her collarbones, leaving a trail of hot breath and kisses. She wrapped her arms around him, wanting to never let go. A small voice in the back of her mind urged caution, but she shushed it. Maybe this wasn't a good idea, but Stewart's lust was so sharp, so palpable, it carried her along like an inexorable tide.

It's not just him. I want this or I'd find the strength to break away.

He lifted his head and snared her gaze with his own. "We do this together or not at all. Do ye want me, Yara? Not just for the momentary joy our bodies can bring, but for what I am?"

The timing of his words couldn't have been coincidental. "You were inside my head."

"Aye, but only because ye're the most important thing in the world to me." He smoothed his thumbs over her cheekbones. "Ye're so lovely and so elemental. I've waited many lifetimes for you, but this must be right for both of us."

Yara leaned into his touch, reveling in the press of his body against the length of hers. She turned her mouth upward, hoping for more kisses, but he shook his head.

"Nay. If I start kissing you again, next thing, I'll have your skirts rucked up, and I doona wish to take you like a common serving wench." His eyes glittered with promise and danger. "Come with me."

Desire flashed through her like molten quicksilver. She opened her mouth to say she'd ruck up her skirts in a heartbeat if it would quell the hunger beating a path from her belly to her core, but her throat was too thick to form words, so she just nodded.

The untamed look in his eyes deepened. "I ken well enough, for my cock is so full 'tis a wonder I havena spent holding you. Up the ladder, darling. My cabin is at the verra top of this flight."

Yara wrenched away from him and started upward. The place he'd been pressed against her felt empty, hollow, but his unique energy pulsed behind her. She wondered which door was his, but one clicked open, unlatched by magic, and she walked through.

The small space was twin to her own except devoid of any belongings. It made sense since she was the only one who'd brought more than the clothes on her back. The door snicked shut and she turned slowly, suddenly shy now they were alone. Because they'd only be in the way, she bent to unlace her boots and kicked them aside.

Heat shimmered around him creating a golden nimbus as he crossed the short distance to her and began pulling pins from her hair. It had half fallen down before, but now it tumbled past her shoulders.

He fingered a curl or two. "Ye have hair that would make any dragon worth his salt weep with envy. 'Tis like a curtain of living flame. And your eyes shade from blue to violet. Right now, they look like amethysts, deep and full of mystery."

He unwound her cloak from her shoulders and tossed it across the desk. The outline of her nipples had to be clearly visible beneath her thin shirt because he made a decidedly male noise deep in his throat and filled his hands with her breasts, rubbing his thumbs over her erect nipples. Leaning forward, he fastened his mouth over hers once again.

A hungry moan ripped from her, so fraught with desire she hardly believed it was her. She'd always been a silent lover, mostly to ensure she wasn't caught. He twirled her nipples harder and sank his tongue inside her mouth. Sensation spilled through her setting her on fire.

The outline of his cock tented the front of his kilt. Yara reached for him, closing a hand around his ridged flesh. He groaned, and his cock swelled still more, pulsing against her touch. With her other hand, she searched for how to undo the tartan wrapped about him, but if it had buttons or some other fastening, she couldn't find them.

Their breathing quickened until it filled the room with evidence of their need. Stewart wrenched his mouth from hers and let go of her breasts long enough to snatch her top over her head. He whistled long and low at the sight of her naked breasts and undid the buttons holding her skirt on her hips. It slithered to the floor, and she stepped out of it pushing her soaked panties down her legs in its wake.

Beyond aroused, she reached for his tartan again, intent on removing it, but he pushed her hands away. "Let me. 'Tisn't difficult, but there's a trick to it."

She tried to pay attention, but her mind was mush from wanting him. A twist here, a turn there, and the finely woven, woolen plaid fell to the floor. Next, he drew his shirt off over his head. Breath hitched in her throat as her gaze played over his nakedness. It might have been a trick of his magic, but his skin glowed a rich golden copper. Muscles slabbed his shoulders, arms, and legs, shapely and powerful. His nipples, also copper colored with a fine dusting of red hair around them, were puckered just like hers. Hard and proud, his cock jutted from a mat of tawny curls.

"You're amazing," she managed and grinned. "I even like the boots. They're a nice touch."

The magic surrounding him intensified, and the laces unwound themselves until he could step out of his stout leather footgear. He held out his arms. "I could look at you forever and die a happy man, but—"

She dove into his arms, cutting off his words. The shock of his body against hers, skin to skin, made her forget everything she'd ever known. None of her lovers had kindled desire so rampant it filled her entire universe with longing. She splayed her hands across his back, tracing lines of bone and muscle until she kneaded his high, firm ass in both hands.

He kissed her with a ferocity that left her even more breathless, and then slammed his consciousness into hers, joining their minds with magic. She saw his yearning for her, felt it with a poignancy that swept all her barriers away.

His cock jumped against her belly, and she couldn't wait any longer. He crooned to her in Gaelic and swept her into his arms as if she weighed nothing. Two strides brought them to the edge of the low, narrow bunk, and he laid her tenderly atop it. She scooted over to make room for him, and he lay beside her, cradling her against him.

She stroked all of him she could reach. Her fingertips came alive where they connected with his skin, and she couldn't get enough of him. He was still murmuring Gaelic endearments as he turned her onto her back and slithered to where he could take a nipple into his mouth. He teased and bit until her belly clenched with need, and desire threatened to swamp her. She wanted to kiss him, touch him, lick him, absorb him into herself. Worship him with touch and tongue and her body until she lost track of where he ended and she began.

Squirming into a better position, she reached between them and curled her hand around his cock. It felt even better without layers of wool between it and her fingers, and she teased it from base to tip and back again.

He made the same sound he'd made before, like a big cat on the prowl, and let go of her breast. "I canna wait, lassie. There isna much room in this bunk. Turn so your back is toward me."

She fitted her ass into the hollow of his flat stomach and felt the press of his cockhead against the entrance to her body. He pushed inside her slowly, letting her stretch to accommodate his girth. She wriggled to seat him within her. Each tiny movement felt better than the last, and joy cascaded through her.

Reaching around, he rubbed the center of her sensation. Her nub was engorged and slick with her fluids, and she covered his hand with her own, showing him the rhythm she needed. At first, he just twitched his cock where it rested within her, but then he withdrew and plumbed her again and again, moving harder and faster as he rubbed her nub.

Sensation exploded as orgasm caught her up and spun her around. She'd thought he'd come when she did, but he kept on rubbing her, all the while fucking her from behind.

"Ye can do this, Yara. Let yourself go. Come again with me."

Maybe it was the words, maybe their joined magic, but a second climax seeded itself from the embers of the first one. Time slowed until the world consisted only of their bodies and pleasure blazing through her. His cock shuddered. Jets of scorching semen pushed her over the crest a second time.

He held her tight, hand cupped around her vulva and cock buried inside her body as their panting breaths quieted. His magic ebbed and flowed around them, cradling her in warmth and caring. Yara relaxed into Stewart's embrace, wanting the enchantment flowing between them to last forever. It might be illusory, but she felt safe in a way she hadn't since her caravan split up.

A stout knock pounded against the door. Stewart cursed in Gaelic, but then called out, "Cadr. I'll be topside presently."

"Sooner rather than later. The coastline's in sight, but another storm blew up out of nowhere, and it has the stink of magic about it."

"Times will be hard once we make land, but it's as if the world's against us even getting that far," Yara murmured.

"Nay, lassie. The Fates gave us exactly what we needed. Time to love one another. All the rest will come together exactly as it should."

"I hope so." She stopped shy of voicing her concerns about facing vampires, demons, and the angry owners of the gold that had been hidden aboard this ship.

He pulled himself from her embrace and stood, dressing quickly. The complex wrap of the tartan looked easy when he transformed it from a length of wool to a garment with a snap of his wrists. "Remain here as long as ye like."

Unspoken endearments shone from his eyes before he turned and slipped from the cabin.

Unlike her cabin, this bunk had a blanket, one of the ones they'd brought from the truck. Yara pulled it to her chin and wrapped her arms around herself. She felt different, changed in a way she didn't fully understand. Part of her was frantic because maybe she'd ceded a small piece of her freedom, but the other parts didn't care.

Stewart was amazing. Incredible. Her future. Her everything.

She smothered a snort and told herself to get a grip. It was all the magic. She was still in its thrall.

Yes. That had to be it. Just because she'd shared her body didn't mean she'd lost her ability to function as an independent person.

The ship's motion intensified, and she tossed the blanket aside and reached for her clothes. If they were under some variety of supernatural attack, she should be there helping, not luxuriating in the warm afterglow from lovemaking.

Annoyed with herself for her self-indulgence, she set herself to rights and headed for the helm. Stewart was one thing, but she'd damn well better keep her eye on the bigger picture. The others needed her magic, and she had no intention of ending up at the bottom of the North Sea.

CHAPTER 15

Stewart hurried up the single flight separating his cabin from the main deck. Loving Yara held a rightness that made him even more certain she was his fated one. The woman the universe had been holding in abeyance all these years, but she was well worth the wait. Her beauty stole his breath. Not only her physical attributes, but her pure, shining spirit. He'd joined his soul to hers when they made love, given her a piece of himself and taken a wee bit of her in return.

They were joined now. As surely as if the gods had blessed their union. Did she know?

He smiled wryly. How could she? She wasn't steeped in Celtic lore, which meant he'd have to find a way to tell her. Not that she couldn't still walk away, but if she did he'd long for her for the rest of his days.

Spray slapped his face, and the deck sloshed with sea water. Darkness reigned, and he extended power to figure out what they faced. Land was close, so near he could smell the tang of growing things. To be so close to their goal and have it ripped out of their hands was unthinkable.

Vreis and Cadr bent over the wheel, holding a course. Barely.

The boat canted alarmingly, its sails so full of wind it was a wonder they didn't split. Stewart reached the other Druids. "We need to bring the canvas down," he shouted over the howl of the storm.

Vreis nodded, his expression carved into forbidding lines. "Aye we thought the same, but this rogue wind just cut hours off our journey. We hoped if we could make the lee of the eastern side of the Isles, 'twould become more manageable. That hasna happened yet, though, and I agree running under full sail isna wise."

As if they knew they were a topic of conversation, the sails creaked and groaned. They hadn't been designed for hurricane force winds. "Sails. Now. Afore the mainsail shreds," Stewart repeated, still testing the raging waters with his magic. Try as he might, he couldn't sense fell power afoot. Only bad weather. The North Sea was notorious for storms that blew up out of nowhere.

He turned his attention to Cadr. "Why did ye believe this storm is unnatural?"

Cadr strained to hold the wheel steady. "Why else? I felt the thrum of something. Demons or Manandan or something that shouldna have been present. If I hadna been paying attention, though, I'd have missed it. 'Twas here and gone that fast. I sent Aron below to stay with his sister. The boy dinna want to leave, but there was no choice."

"Did ye feel it?" Stewart asked Vreis.

"Och aye, that I did. Damn it! 'Tis back again. Barbed needles driving into me from odd angles. It comes and goes, never remaining long enough for me to identify it."

Barbed needles certainly had the feel of demons' dark enchantment, and Stewart girded himself to do battle with the bastards again. He'd do damn near anything to ensure Yara made shore safely.

The ship leaned another notch or two, so low the edge of the sail trailed in the water. Dark magic pinged against Stewart's extended senses, harsh and prickly, but like Vreis had described, it left as suddenly as it had arrived.

What the fuck was it? He needed more than a few seconds' snippet to determine how to annihilate it. If he summoned a spell to vanquish demons, and that wasn't what they faced, it could backfire badly.

Jamal and Gregor fought their way across the heaving deck, sloshing through water cascading over it. Meara caught up with them, her long, soaked hair plastered against her body.

"What do you need us to do?" Jamal asked.

Meara ignored him. "What the hell happened?" she demanded, staring at Stewart. "Your job was making certain our magic didn't escape the confines of the hold."

Understanding hit him like a fist to his gut. The magic Cadr and Vreis sensed had to be the dark power that had formed the maelstrom below decks. He called magic like a madman, chanting for all he was worth. If Meara was right, and she likely was, he could fix this.

Vreis jumped in, helping anchor Stewart's incantation.

Meara rolled her avian eyes and hissed, not unlike her vulture would have.

Stewart shaped air to quell the wind. When his first effort didn't make any difference, he tried again, altering the composition of his casting.

Vreis sang a few notes to mix earth into their working. Not just any earth. Vreis called for grave dirt. It would lure their opponent close enough to make a difference.

Tension settled between Stewart's shoulders feeling like Sisyphus's rock must have. He understood why Vreis altered things. It was a brilliant move—if it worked. If it didn't, the gateway he'd just blown open to better disable dark energy could suck them into its maw.

"Steady," he exhorted and redirected the flow of his magic to help Vreis.

Brightness hurried toward him. He didn't see it so much as feel it in the depths of his being.

Yara.

He wanted to yell at her to go back to his cabin and shroud herself in spells, but he couldn't redirect an angstrom of attention away from his casting. They'd reached a critical juncture.

Meara's unique energy threaded itself between his and Vreis's, strengthening their efforts. She and Jamal and Gregor were talking, but he had no idea what they'd said. His third ear was tuned to his magic, shutting out everything else.

Yara didn't say a word. She didn't ask questions, which was just as well since he couldn't have answered them anyway. Instead, she wrapped a hand around his upper arm. Power surged into him, augmenting his own by a factor of a hundred or better.

Earth magic was where she lived. It turned Vreis's gambit into a sure thing. Colors sheeted around them. Blues, greens, and golds. Lured by grave dirt, demons rushed forward, surrounded by black-tipped flames. Laughing, snarling, taunting, they had no idea what they'd just lumbered into.

"Hold," Stewart yelled. "Let them come closer. Closer still." He waited, power balanced between his hands until half a dozen demons were so close their burned sulfur stench choked him.

Adrenaline hummed along his nerves and left a metallic taste coating his tongue. Vreis, Jamal, Meara, and the others formed a tight line with him and Yara at its center. He gathered everyone's power, aiming for a lethal mass, but marshaling it into a cohesive whole was worse than directing lightning to do his bidding. The magic held a mesmerizing quality and had a will all its own.

"Give me more!" he shrieked. "Doona hold back." Working by instinct, Stewart focused earth magic, let it use him for a vessel as it expanded into a deadly mass.

Yara tightened her hold on his upper arm. *"Let go."* She screamed the words into his mind. *"Before it turns on us."*

He screeched die in Gaelic three times. *Faigh bás, Faigh bás.*

Faigh bás. And loosed their assembled magic. The air caught fire. The demons weren't laughing anymore. They clawed for purchase as a mountain of rocks and dirt bore down on them, driving them back into the Hell-spawned hole Stewart had ripped open.

He staggered, almost fell to his knees, but didn't abandon his casting until the chasm was sealed, vanishing into gray-black mist.

"Nice work. I'll take it from here, not that there's much more to be done." Meara stepped in front of him, power flaring from her outstretched hands.

The wind died down to a dull roar, and the ship returned to its normal sailing position. Thank all the gods the canvas was unharmed. They didn't have an extra mainsail. No one had expected this vessel to ever leave port; they'd been far more focused on plague-ridden bodies and purloined gold.

Stewart was breathing as if he'd just run a race. "Thank you," he told Yara. "Goddess only knows what might have happened if ye'd not given me that push to loose our power."

She shrugged. "Our combined power had reached maximum velocity, but it felt unruly, like it might turn on us if we didn't give it free rein. What happened? Is everything all right now?"

"For the moment, lass." He gulped more air. "When that much power is drawn together—particularly from disparate sources—it does what it wants. I needed the boost ye provided since it damn near mesmerized me."

A dismayed look crossed her face. "Not exactly the answer I'd hoped for."

He screwed his mouth into a grimace. "Aye, but 'tis the truth. Magic is a harsh mistress. Ye must keep hold of the upper hand— no matter what the cost."

"What if I hadn't said anything?"

He chuckled wryly. "Meara would have pecked my eyes out."

She let go of him, and it took strength of mind not to grab her hand and put it back. He craved her touch, far more than was good for either of them. They'd won the latest skirmish by the narrowest of margins.

Meara stalked over to them. "The darkness we thought we contained in the hold leaked out. Not all of it, or the ship would have foundered, but enough fell energy got loose to put out a cry for reinforcements."

The first shifter made a disgusted snorting noise. "Good you got a jump on this," she told Stewart. "It was spiraling out of control fast."

He inhaled sharply. "If ye hadna recognized it for what it was, I'm not sure Vreis and I would have settled on the proper spell to defeat it."

"Ye picked the spell," Vreis said. "I just added magic and a wee twist to things." He shifted his gaze to Yara. "Have ye always had this level of magical ability?"

She looked away. "More or less, except I didn't do anything beyond lending my magic to your spell."

Cadr relaxed his death grip on the wheel and whistled. "I wasna even part of the spell, and I felt shockwaves from where I stood. Goddess help us if anything ever stands in your way, woman. Ye'll flatten the world if ye're not careful."

A small smile played about Yara's mouth, and she shook her head. "You're giving me far too much credit, I fear."

Stewart glanced at a sky where stars were starting to show through the clouds. "How long afore we're abreast of Kirkcaldy? 'Tis as good a location as any other."

"Soon," Cadr replied. "That bitch of a storm made this bucket of bolts sit up and fly."

"Soon as in before it's light?" Meara spoke up.

"Aye," Vreis concurred. "Mayhap another hour. Do ye still plan to drop anchor and use the life rafts to row ashore?"

Stewart opened his mouth to say nothing had changed, but Meara beat him to it. "We'll pull up to a dock," she said, "and scatter magic like yesterday's blossoms to wipe people's memories that they've ever seen us. By the time the spells wear off, we'll be long gone."

"By that token, we could've landed in Edinburgh," Jamal muttered.

"Nay," Stewart said. "'Tis heavily guarded. Far more so than Kirkcaldy." He angled his gaze at Meara. "Ye wanted to meet with everyone at first light. Correct?"

"That meeting must occur right now." She made shooing motions at Jamal and Gregor. "Go get everyone. Wake them if need be. Once everyone is here, we'll figure out the next part."

The two shifters scooted away, moving fast.

"Do ye have a plan?" Stewart asked Meara without preamble. The tone of his question was blunt, but he needed to know.

"Not exactly. You know Scotland far better than I, but the quicker we get to where magic burns brightest, the better our chances will be."

"So long as we're sprinkling magic about—in clear violation of the compact betwixt our kind and humans," Stewart said. "My suggestion is we borrow enough vehicles to beat a path to Fort William."

"How long will it take to drive there?" Yara asked.

"Depends on the kinds of vehicles, but not more than three or four hours. We could abandon them outside the town and cover the last bit on foot.

"Last bit to where?" Vreis asked.

"Och, and that might help," Stewart muttered. "My thought was to scoot up the track to the top of Ben Nevis, gathering the little folk as we go. The mountain concentrates power, and 'tis a beacon of hope for our kind. I'll do everything in my power to entice a god or two to our side as well."

Cadr drew his brows into a thick line. "I like it. 'Tis a defensible position—most of the time."

"What changes?" Yara asked.

"Visibility," Stewart replied. "Betimes thick fogs obscure everything, but 'tis a mixed curse. If we canna see our enemies, neither can they pinpoint our location. An intricate cave system leads deep into the mountain. If we're sore pressed, it will provide shelter and an escape route."

He stopped there. No telling who might be drifting in the ether listening in on them. Just because the demons had been forced to stop chivvying the ship didn't mean they'd left.

Shifters and Romani streamed toward them. An almost full moon joined the stars, illuminating everyone in a pale, golden glow. Perhaps Arianrhod looked down from Caer Sidi and was offering her blessings. Stewart mouthed a silent prayer to the virgin goddess who controlled both moon and tides.

Elliott and Tairin came last with Michael leaning heavily on both of them. It would take more than a hand span of hours for him to recover. As if he gleaned the direction of Stewart's thoughts, he looked right at him.

"Don't waste a moment worrying about me. I'll keep up. Somehow."

Meara circled the group, probably making certain everyone was accounted for. Seemingly satisfied, she strode to Stewart's side and addressed everyone in a clear, ringing voice. "This next part will go quickly. Be ready to leave the ship as soon as we tie up at the dock. That means making certain you have at least half a dozen gold pieces. More if you're comfortable carrying them. If there's aught else aboard you believe would be useful, by all means, bring it along so long as it's easily portable." She glanced at Stewart.

He smothered a snort. She was going to let him do the dirty work. He took a deep breath and blew it out. "Doona stint on magic when ye leave this vessel. We must ensure no one either notices or remembers ever having seen us."

"But that's forbidden," Ilona protested. "We can't use magic to delude humans."

He leveled his gaze at her. "And ye never used so much as a wee, tiny bit to coax a gadjo to part with one more coin?"

Color stained her face, obvious in the moonlight, and she tossed her head. "Never mind."

"Does anyone else have any reservations?" Stewart let his gaze settle on each person in turn. "If so, speak up now."

No one said a word, so he went on. "We will put as much distance as we can betwixt us and the docks as fast as we can. Those of you who can drive, hunt for vehicles that will be easy to steal and will blend in. Neutral colors, common brands. Keep scattering magic.

"No one will see or remember us if we join our magic and make certain to keep it flowing. Once we're all in cars, we will head west toward Stirling, and thence northwest to Fort William."

"What if we need fuel?" Jamal asked.

"Plan ahead," Meara cut in. "Switch cars if yours is close to running out. We can't risk stopping for petrol and trying to pay for it with gold coins that dropped out of use centuries ago. Or Reichsmarks that scream we're from Germany."

"An old inn marks the base of the trail up Ben Nevis," Stewart said. "We will meet near there. Telepathy should suffice to keep track of where all of us are while we're en route." He swallowed hard. "If ye're set upon, spare nothing. If ye canna immobilize whomever stands in your way with magic, kill them."

Solemn nods met his gaze, along with murmurs of assent.

Meara clapped her hands smartly together. "Ready yourselves. I want this ship empty within minutes of our arrival."

"Once everyone has what coins they want," Jamal said, "Gregor and I will pile the remainder into casks and drop them into the sea." He glanced at Stewart for affirmation.

"Aye, 'tis still the soundest course. That way it willna be there for whomever turns this ship inside out once they discover its whereabouts."

The deck cleared fast until only Cadr, Vreis, Yara, and Meara stood ringed around him. "Ye do realize all that expended magic will draw other magical creatures like a lodestone," Vreis muttered.

"Of course, I do," Meara snapped. "I don't see any other options. If you've a better idea, out with it."

Vreis made a forked sign against evil. "Let us hope vampires doona read it as a prime invitation to add us to their ranks. We can deal with two or three, but more than that will slow us down and drain our power."

"Better not to borrow trouble," Cadr said. "How about if ye get some gold for us both and mayhap a wee bit of those food stocks Stewart found, but we never had time to prepare."

Vreis nodded and vaulted across the deck.

"I'm not certain I understand why vampires would be a problem in daylight," Yara said.

"They're worse at night"—Meara's nostrils flared—"but they're plenty strong during the day as well. Those tales about them going to ground because sunlight burns them aren't true."

"Aye, like as not vampires themselves perpetrated those myths to enhance their odds of luring the unsuspecting." Stewart turned toward Yara. He longed to sweep her up and carry her back to his bed. Tell her how much their time together had meant to him, but such things would have to wait. Maybe for a long time.

He attempted to infuse some of what he was feeling into the way he looked at her as he asked, "Do ye need help? Ye're the only one of us with aught to put together."

She shook her head. "I'll go take care of everything right now. I've parceled out enough of the clothing I brought, it won't take me long to arrange things." She sent a shy smile skittering his way and ran lightly toward the stairs.

Meara glanced from Yara's retreating form to Stewart and back again. She waited until Yara had disappeared from sight and angled her head to one side. The scents of rosemary and clay baked hard under an Egyptian sun rose, and Stewart understood she'd wound a ward around them.

"We dinna need privacy," he protested. "Cadr knows everything I do."

"My decision, not yours," Meara retorted. "This isn't the best of times to launch an affair of the heart. Or was it only sex?"

Stewart winced, pursing his mouth into a hard line. "'Tisn't any of your business from where I sit."

She marched directly in front of him and thumped his chest with an extended index finger. "Of course, it's my affair. I need every single one of us a thousand percent behind getting off this ship and into the Highlands. You may have forgotten"—she thumped again for good measure—"but you're a key element in securing aid from the magical elements here. I can call shifters to our side, but we need the Fae and the Celts. If you're mooning over a new love interest, you might not—"

Stewart's temper flared as anger rushed through him in a steamy tide. He slapped Meara's hand aside. "I doona need someone prescribing what I should and shouldna do. That approach may work for your shifters, but I doona report to you. If we are to work together effectively, ye'd do well to remember that."

She narrowed her eyes. "That serious, eh?"

"I am not discussing Yara with you."

"Fine," Meara countered. "Don't, but have you thought how the Celts will react to your pleas for assistance if you're no longer Stewart, the Druid priest who eschewed everything to serve them?"

"That wasna how 'twas at all," he protested.

"Really?" she quirked a gray brow. "Did you never think it odd no woman ever materialized who appealed to you?"

He bit back a harsh rush of words. Maybe the first shifter was onto something. The Celts had kept him exactly where they wanted him, able to spring to their beck and call at a moment's notice. A wife would have interfered. His choice to keep to himself once he left Scotland had been of his own making. He was no longer so certain about the hundreds of years before that.

He shook his head and exhaled briskly. "No reason for them to know."

Breath hissed from between Meara's teeth. "They're gods. They know everything, plus Rhiannon is bound to show up. She said as much, and Yara carries her blood. For all we know, she might have her daughter's future planned out."

"I doubt it. She hung about the sidelines for years. If she had any stake in Yara's choices, she'd have made her presence known long afore now."

"Not necessarily." Meara frowned. "I haven't had much truck with the Celts, but from what little I know, they're an odd lot. Quick to cast blame and squabble among themselves, but equally quick to defend one of their own if an outsider has the temerity to criticize them—or seeks to bond with them."

"'Tis a fair encapsulation." He shrugged. "Naught I can do about how they react. I learned that long ago."

Meara focused her gimlet gaze on him. "You could lay this new love interest of yours aside until after the next spate of events unfolds."

"Nay. I willna do that." He leaned close. "Yara is mine. *Mine*. Do ye ken that?"

"All too well. The question is if she understands it the same way you do, and whether your lack of attention to our mission will doom us all. Each of us has only so much energy and magic. You may not agree with my assessment, but the amount you squander on Yara won't be available for the task at hand." Turning on her heel, Meara stalked away and her spell splintered around him.

Stewart stared after her. Fury vied with an almost profane need to possess Yara. He'd already branded her, but he wanted to deepen his marks, make certain the world knew she was his woman.

His and his alone.

He sucked in a breath and blew it out. Then he did it again. Damn if Meara's observations weren't too accurate for comfort. His focus—his total focus—had to be shepherding them across Scotland and persuading every magical creature he could locate to join their effort.

Anything less than his best effort might, indeed, doom them all. Cadr and Vreis could help, but it would take all three of them to convince magical creatures, who'd steered clear of anything that smacked of interference in human affairs, to do anything other than burrow deeper into the hills and barrows of the Highlands.

If they became really annoyed, it wasn't beyond them to retreat to the *Dreaming* and remain there to wait out mankind's latest disaster.

Vreis loped back to the helm and dropped a handful of coins into Cadr's pocket. He patted his own. "We're set. Do ye wish a break from the wheel?"

"Sure." Cadr strode to Stewart. "What the bloody hell was all that about? I saw Meara's spell."

Stewart shook his head. "Nothing. Naught to be concerned with." Before Cadr could question him further, he hurried away. Not being totally truthful with his companion went against the grain, but he couldn't very well admit he'd been about to make a huge mistake by placing his infatuation with Yara above his responsibilities to them all.

That had almost come back to bite them when the magical maelstrom jumped its bounds, and the only thing that saved them from ruin was Yara screaming at him to release the rebellious clump of enchantment.

He clacked his jaws together. They'd vanquish the demons and vampires and send them packing. Their absence would weaken the Nazis and pave the way for the Allied Forces to conquer them. Perhaps there'd even be a way to encourage the States to jump into the fray and lend their considerable military power.

Feeling a little better, he hustled to the ship's bottom deck intent on making certain they didn't leave anything behind that might come in useful.

He wasn't giving up on sharing his life with Yara, merely putting it off until after the heavy lifting was done. Surely, she'd understand.

Aye, but will she agree to keep our attraction under wraps until afterward?

The certainty that all would be well deserted him. He could stumble through an explanation about being the Celts' lackey and them preferring him unattached to better serve their needs, but it made him look like little better than a trained lapdog. Scarcely the image he wanted to project for the woman he was falling in love with.

Since no easy answers rose, he turned his thoughts to the task at hand and pulled open cabinets and drawers. Soon a respectable pile of moth-eaten cloaks and foodstuffs lay at his feet. Stacking the items, he summoned magic to transport them to the main deck.

He'd figure out a way to square things with Yara. He had to. Nothing could get between them...

A sinking feeling left a bitter taste in his mouth. Something had already driven a wedge in the closeness he yearned for. He hoped to hell it wasn't the leading edge of such a long laundry list Yara gave up in disgust.

$\mathcal{Y}$ara whistled a cheery folk tune as she sorted and stuffed items into sacks. True to her prediction, two sacks held everything this time. The book's magic pulsed, which meant it wanted her attention, but she dropped it into a bag with promises she'd attend to it later.

The worn, leather binding heated beneath her fingertips before she let go of it. Clearly, the tome didn't agree with her decision. It was used to commanding her attention, and it demanded it now.

She glanced around the cabin, making certain she hadn't missed anything. She needed to run down to the hold and gather a few coins. Once that was done, she could let the book's latest gambit unfold. Telling it as much, she fled out the door with magic prickling from her feet to the crown of her head.

She smothered a snort. Ever since the book had come into her possession, she'd figured it was a tool, something for her to leverage to maximize her power.

Yeah, I had no idea it actually ran the show and was just waiting for an opportunity to turn into a taskmaster. For all I know, it's how Mother keeps an eye on me.

That last thought was disquieting enough she squelched it. Rhiannon's presence was plenty daunting, without envisioning her skulking somewhere behind the book to follow Yara's every move.

The distinctive feel of Stewart's magic enveloped her long before she reached the bottom of the ladder. She hastened her footsteps, thrilled by the prospect of another hug and perhaps a kiss or two.

"Hi! What a lovely surprise," she called when he came into view. After she reached him, she extended a hand. "What are you doing?"

A look she couldn't decipher washed over his face, and the power that had shimmered about him faded. "Taking inventory and moving a few things to the main deck. We can split up who carries them. Not much point in leaving anything aboard that might help us."

His words held a formality that surprised her. He'd never sounded this distant, not even the day they'd first met. She dropped her hand—a hand he hadn't grasped—and asked, "Is something wrong?"

"Nay, lass. What could be wrong? Odds are excellent we'll reach port. From there, 'tis anyone's guess, but our luck should hold." The stilted aspect to his words deepened, almost as if he'd understood her question well enough, but was choosing not to answer it.

Her happiness at seeing him faded, replaced by a sodden certainty he saw her as a slut. Men were like that. They pushed for sex, but once you gave in, you joined the ranks of fallen women. She puffed out a ragged breath. She would not make a fool of herself.

I will not cry.

I will not flatten him with magic—even if I could.

I will leave this hold with my dignity intact.

A tall order, but she'd pull it off. Part of her wanted to dissolve into inane laughter. Talk about the quintessential shipboard romance gone bad.

"Yara. Are ye all right?"

Yeah, sure, fine. You slimy bastard. You led me to believe you cared about me.

She smiled brightly, wondering if her face would break. "Why wouldn't I be? I'm just down here for a few coins. See you when it's time to disembark." Spinning, she ran to the room that held the gold.

Unbelievably, he followed her. Jesus! Wasn't it enough he'd just given her the brushoff? She bent and stuffed two handfuls of coins into her pockets. When she turned to leave, he blocked the doorway.

"Ye doona understand, lass."

"Oh I understand plenty," she sputtered. "I wasn't born yesterday. Nor was I a maid, so I know how these things work." She bit off a string of words about thinking he was different, pushed past him, and pelted down the corridor. The sooner she got back to her cabin and found out what the book wanted, the better.

Tears pricked behind her eyelids, but she blinked them away.

He ran after her, reaching her before she could escape up the steep stairs. "Ye doona understand," he repeated.

Yara spun and faced him, hands extended in front of her. "Oh I don't, do I? Let me be abundantly clear. I won't bother you. No tears. No recriminations. Let's just forget we ever had sex, okay? It wasn't that great anyway."

She winced internally at the lie, but hoped he'd be too wrapped up in guilt—or whatever he was feeling—not to notice.

The pained expression on his face hardened. Apparently, her jibe about his lack of bedroom skills had sunk in. Men all fancied themselves Lotharios. To suggest otherwise was the worst disparagement imaginable.

"Ye doona really mean that, lass—" he began.

She leveled her gaze at him and broke in. "Oh yes, I do." Without waiting for what tripe he'd come up with next, she pulled herself hand over hand up the ladder-like stairs.

This time, he didn't follow her.

She didn't know whether to be relieved or devastated. Tears were far too close to the surface, but she made it into her cabin and sealed the door with magic before they leaked from both eyes. Yara scrubbed at her cheeks. Why the hell should she be so upset? She'd had one-shot lovers before. In truth, it was all she'd had.

She sank onto the end of the lower bunk and wrapped her arms around herself. The answer to her question was obvious. She was upset because he'd promised more.

"And I believed him. Fool that I was," she muttered.

Yara inhaled deeply, blew it out, and did it again. At least it kept the tears from turning into a full-blown crying jag. She wasn't the first woman to be taken in by a smooth-talking man intent on taking his cock out for some exercise. And she wouldn't be the last. When Ian had first begun courting her sister, she'd been certain he was only in it for Ilse's body.

"I was wrong about him. And wrong about Stewart too, it appears." She went on talking out loud to steady herself. "Perfect track record. Guess I should give up trying to predict what anything with a dick between its legs will do."

A muted squeal from the sack containing the book reminded her she'd made it a promise. It had never made any noise before, so this must be truly important. Relieved to have something to do beyond stewing about a love affair that had never existed except in her imagination, she plucked the book from its sack and let it flop open across her lap.

As she expected, the pages rustled, driven by magic she didn't control. When they stopped, she studied the indicated section. It was devoted to the Celtic pantheon and outlined the various gods and goddesses in excruciating detail.

Yara thumped the open page with her fingertips. "What? You expect me to memorize who all these deities are right now? It's not going to happen."

Light pulsed and glowed, and the book moved to another section. Yara's eyes widened. This part was about Stewart. It had a likeness and his name. She flipped through over a dozen closely-written pages before anger got the better of her and she slammed the book shut.

"I am not going to waste my time reading about him." She slapped the flat of her hand against the book's binding for emphasis. "What I don't comprehend is why you'd even want me to. Don't you understand? He lied to me."

Yara bolted to her feet and dropped the book back into its sack. "Leave me alone for a while. I'm done with you and Stewart."

The golden light that had shimmered around the tome faded until it looked like it had most of the time it had been in her possession: a very old grimoire that contained spells.

Yara stared at it, waiting for it to do something, but it lay inert at the top of the sack. Maybe it was done with her.

If it was fueled by Rhiannon's magic, did that mean her mother was done with her as well? Yara cinched up the sack. It didn't matter. How could she lose anything that had never been hers in the first place?

"Excellent question," she muttered and snatched up both sacks intent on carting them to the main deck so she'd be ready when the boat pulled up to a dock. She made her way up the stairs in two trips since she needed one hand to hang onto the railing.

Almost everyone was milling about the deck. Stewart was there handing out goods. Avoiding him, she walked to where Tairin, Elliott, and Michael sat with their backs against a bulkhead.

"How are you feeling?" she asked Michael.

He shrugged. "Better, but still weak. I'm doing my best to

consolidate my magic so I won't be dependent on the rest of you to hide me."

Elliott patted the older man's arm. "I already told you, I'll take care of you."

"Maybe I don't want you to have to," Michael grumbled.

Tairin got to her feet and moved next to Yara. *"How's it going?"* she asked in telepathy and slanted her gaze Stewart's way.

Yara rounded on her, but clamped her jaws shut before something harsh escaped. Tairin cared. It was why she'd asked. Yara just shook her head. Anything she said would come out wrong, so silence was her best bet. She was still raw from Stewart's abrupt dismissal cloaked in some higher purpose she "wouldn't understand."

Mercifully, Tairin didn't say anything else. She only nodded sympathetically.

"How long before we reach port?" Yara asked. "It's too dark to see much, but I smell land."

"Soon," Elliott replied. "I just asked Vreis much the same. He and Cadr have some kind of shrouding about the ship. It means others can't see us, but it keeps us from seeing much as well."

Yara frowned, not familiar with a ward that was opaque. She remained with her small group in silence, waiting. The scrape of wood against wood was followed by a jolt, and she shot forward along with Tairin, straining to see through the murk. Elliott helped Michael upright. Soon was one thing, but she hadn't been ready for landfall quite that quickly.

She slung her sacks over one shoulder. Tairin and Elliott tucked clothing beneath their arms, but not so much they didn't keep one hand free to help Michael. He grunted, but didn't pull away from where they linked their hands around his upper arms to steady him.

Yara walked behind, just in case they needed more help. She was touched by the way they cared for Michael. It reminded her of everything she'd lost when her caravan split up, scattering them to the four corners of nowhere.

No one to help.

No one to care.

No one to share things with.

The loneliness she'd lived with ever since her sister left hit her like a physical blow, and it was all she could do not to double over. That was one of the reasons she'd been so quick to hang on Stewart's every word, never doubting he cared about her.

She closed her teeth over her lower lip and bit hard. Goddammit if she hadn't been the easiest of easy marks. Maybe he'd scanned her with his considerable power and figured that out. Particularly after her fiasco with Manandan when she was feeling guilty and vulnerable for not having been assertive enough.

Stop it. Just stop. She made her inner voice stern. What was done was done. No way she could go back and undo it. The important thing was not compounding her errors with yet one more.

They reached the rope ladder, and she joined the queue as everyone abandoned the ship as fast as they could. About half of them were already on the dock in a murky quarter light that created an eerie glow. At least no one was hurrying over to see who they were.

Their magical barrier must be working.

She waited until Elliott and Tairin saw Michael safely down the ladder. Elliott went first and steadied the ladder while Tairin hung onto Michael from above. Getting herself down would be awkward since she only had one hand, so she tossed the sacks onto the dock, and scurried after them.

The second her feet hit the planking of the dock, Stewart urged, "Hurry, lassie. Ye're the last of us."

"Don't *lassie* me." Yara stared at gloom stretching in all directions and made an attempt at civility so she didn't get left behind. "Which way?"

"Follow me." He sprinted lightly into the roiling darkness. It developed a silvery cast where it touched him, which lent him an appealing, otherworldly aspect.

She bit down on her lower lip to flush positive thoughts of him from her mind. They'd just make things harder. Try as she might, though, she couldn't shutter her longing—not entirely.

Yara moved fast, scattering magic and *don't look here* spells as she ran. She'd been remiss about warding herself getting off the ship, but enough ambient magic simmered around the vessel, it probably didn't matter. The dock gave way to cobblestones, and she kept running. Stewart's spell surrounded her. She knew it was his because it carried the scent of his workings.

When she reached out with her magic, she sensed the others fanned ahead of her. The plan had been to steal vehicles. What if they couldn't find any? She shook her head hard. They had to find something. They hadn't come this far only to end up in a Scottish jail.

Yara reminded herself this wasn't the Netherlands. Even if some official suspected she was Romani, it wasn't a crime here. The reason they were running was to distance themselves from the ship in case someone had reported it stolen. Given the demons that had come after them, it was a sure bet whoever owned the gold wouldn't be far behind.

She'd learned years ago to not give in when bleakness surrounded her, and she borrowed heavily from that training ground. Yara narrowed her focus to the ground beneath her feet and the handful of shifters and Rom around her. She traded breath for keeping spells circulating around herself and running. They left the cobblestones for a smoother surface, which gave way to packed dirt. Kirkcaldy must not be very large, or she'd done a better job than she thought holding the world at bay.

Beyond the spells swirling about her, daylight peeked through. Not bright, but they'd left night behind them, along with the ship and the docks. The simmering sphere of their combined magics ratcheted to a halt. Yara wanted to know why, but held silence. She could have used telepathy, but she'd find out soon enough.

Metal creaked, car doors slammed, and the tang of gasoline stung her nostrils. Magic crumbled, traded for a gray, drizzly morning. A battered sedan sped away from where the rest of them stood. A quick nose count told her Jamal, Ilona, Aron, Elliott, Tairin, and Michael had left in the car.

Widely spaced houses that had seen better days lay scattered nearby, so they'd apparently left the city behind.

Cadr scuttled next to Stewart. "We need to get moving."

"Aye, agreed.'Tisn't likely we'll come upon another car. Mostly countryside lays beyond this point."

Vreis pried one of her sacks out of her hands. "I'll take this one. Ye'll move faster with less of a burden."

She noted he'd left her the one containing the book. Not surprising since it probably wouldn't leave her side without pitching a fit. "Should we resurrect our spells?"

Stewart shook his head. "Nay. We're far enough from the ship, no one can tie us to it." He creased his face into a thoughtful expression. "Mayhap 'tis the goddess's hand in this after all. Part of my task was to summon aid, and I canna do that nearly as well from a moving car."

He started off in a westerly direction with Cadr, Vreis, Gregor, and the others following. A squawk from overhead reminded her of Meara. The shifter was tracking them in her vulture form. Yara made a wry face. About now, having wings would be a great boon —so long as the book could figure out a way to remain by her side. The way things had shaped up, she had faith in its ability to overcome damn near any adversity.

Unless it was done with her as she'd suspected earlier.

Thinking about the book and wondering if she'd alienated it, Yara sent her mind voice spiraling outward as she trotted after the ragtag group.

"Mother. Are you out there?"

Silence met her query, and she felt like a fool. Even if Rhiannon had been closer than Yara ever guessed all these years, she hadn't been inclined to make her presence known. Why should that have changed?

Unfamiliar magic swirled and thickened. The scents of heather in bloom and gorse berries tickled her nostrils. When Yara focused her third eye, she saw tiny people, not more than two or three feet tall, surrounding Stewart. Wonder filled her at the sight of what had to be Fae, the faery people, with hair in a bevy of rainbow colors and eyes like hammered silver. Bits of cloth wound about their stocky bodies, and their feet were bare.

One must have a nose for gold because he snaked a hand into Stewart's pocket and withdrew a single doubloon.

"If 'tis the price for your help, 'tis small enough," Stewart murmured.

The little people crawled all over him then, riding on his shoulders and grabbing onto his clothing until he pulled two of them into his arms. They chattered in Gaelic so ancient, Yara only picked up one word in three, but the sight of Stewart cradling the magical beings smote her, and she understood it would take a lifetime to get over him.

Maybe more than one.

Nothing so simple as walking away and closing her mind and heart to him.

Whatever did he do to me?

"Nay, daughter." Rhiannon's musical voice was so unexpected, Yara almost tripped over her own feet. *"Twas what ye did to each other. It canna be undone, nor should it."*

"You have to say more than that." Yara hesitated a beat before adding, *"Mother."*

"I will, but now isna the time. Have faith. He will not fail you. Nor will I. Ye were born for what is almost upon us. 'Tis sorry I am I dinna do more to prepare you, but ye're courageous and resourceful. Believe in those things. In yourself. And in Stewart."

Yara started to reply, but there was no point. Rhiannon was gone. She knew it as surely as she'd ever known anything. Light flickered and pulsed around Stewart, Cadr, and Vreis. They'd attracted a veritable army of Fae, interspersed by other shining creatures who were taller and dark-haired. Unlike their smaller cousins, they were garbed in leather trousers and jerkins, shading from buff to almost black.

What were they? Dark Fae, or some other manner of being?

Yara didn't want to ask for fear they might think her rude. Or turn their magic against her. She'd never believed the tales about the fair folk. None of the Rom did.

Almost against her will, she focused on Stewart only to find his gaze fixed on her. He looked so hopeful—and so desolate—her heart cracked wide open. He'd wanted to talk with her earlier, and she'd shut him down.

Worse than that, she'd said some cruel things. Not as many as she could have, but enough.

Meara squawked knowingly, as if she'd been inside Yara's head, and dive-bombed her. After a last-minute somersault in midair, she fastened sharp talons into Yara's shoulder.

"Ouch. That hurts." Yara glared sidelong at the vulture using her shoulder for a tree branch.

"Get over yourself and listen up, child." Meara clacked her beak for emphasis. *"And keep moving. It's a hundred miles to Fort William. That's quite a distance for someone without wings."*

"I'm scarcely your child." Yara bristled.

"Get over yourself and listen anyway." The talons dug deeper.

Blood trickled down from her shoulder, and Yara thinned her lips into a determined line. "I'm listening. Sooner you've said your peace, the sooner you can get off my shoulder."

She cringed. She was being insufferably rude to a strong, ancient magic wielder. If she didn't shape up, the first shifter could flatten her with magic.

"*Better.*" Another beak clack. *"I'm the reason Stewart backed off courting you. I had solid motives, and they still stand..."*

The Fae's rapid response to Stewart's call both surprised and heartened him. According to them, they'd been waiting for his arrival, which had been foretold by their seers. That last got his attention. If knowledge of the conflagration to come was so widespread the entire magical community knew about it, that meant the other side knew as well.

No possibility of springing a surprise attack and gaining the upper hand via stealth.

The dark Fae were here too. They'd swallowed their built-in antipathy for the other half of their race without so much as a sarcastic rejoinder. None that had happened in his vicinity, anyway. At the point when he'd left Scotland, the dark Fae would rather eat nails than breathe the same air as the waifs clinging to him and filching gold from his pockets.

He'd forgotten the Fae's attraction to the shiny metal, and it made him smile. The world might be ending, but a bunch of delighted Fae would drag gold coin into the *Dreaming* with them if their hills and barrows became uninhabitable.

The *Dreaming*.

The faery folk retreated there when they tired of human

foibles. Stewart had never fully understood if it was linked to Earth energy, or existed in a separate plane. He hoped the latter since if demons won this round, magic and the faery folk had to survive. He'd been raised on tales of Armageddon, threats that Earth needed magic to survive, even though humans didn't know that.

Wars had come and gone over his long lifetime, but there'd never been a war when evil aligned with one side or the other. Magic, either. The unseen world had always kept to itself. Why was this time different? It had to be vampires. Up until the end of the nineteenth century, they'd added to their ranks without much difficulty. Modern life, where cars replaced walking or traveling by horseback, had cut down their opportunities for snatching the unsuspecting and turning them.

Stewart was as guilty as any of them. He'd all but forgotten about vampires until Tairin and Elliott unearthed a nest outside Munich.

Out of sight.

Out of mind.

Aye, and badly underestimated.

He made a wry face. The blood and sex rituals with the SS infused new life into what had probably been a slowly-dying race. The rise of dark power weakened the gates holding Hell's denizens captive. Arawn, god of the dead, used to ride herd on his charges. What the hell happened to him? For all Stewart knew, the Celts had abandoned Earth for more promising worlds. Those not being torn apart by power-mad humans.

Rhiannon is still here. So's Manandan.

She showed up to keep an eye on her daughter, but his presence argues the Celts havena left—at least not yet.

He hadn't let himself reflect on Yara, but thinking about Rhiannon gave him a stiff push in that direction. He'd botched things badly. He hadn't been sure quite what to say. It had seemed clunky and awkward to launch into a whole explanation about the

Celts maybe being more inclined to help if he were unattached—since they'd always preferred him that way. Because words hadn't risen to do his bidding easily, he'd said nothing at all.

She'd been hurt—and then angry. The open longing stamped into her features when she first saw him in the hold dug into him. He'd wanted her too, wanted to draw her close and cover her lips with his. Instead, he'd turned into a bumbling schoolboy tripping over his own feet.

Duty and responsibility came first, but because he'd put them first, he'd hurt Yara. The reality was like a physical blow, but he couldn't rewind time and override Meara's advice with a different choice. Yara was a proud woman, not one who'd ever stand still for being taken advantage of. He'd seen the truth of her thoughts etched into her expressive face without needing to peek into her mind. She felt used, like he'd taken the path many men did when they ached for release, saying whatever would coax a woman to open her legs.

He wasn't like that, though. Making love to her had been one of the most intense experiences of his life. Not something to walk away from. Why hadn't he been able get the words out? Words to reassure her he was falling in love with her and would protect her with his dying breath. He'd come close, but her jibe about his lovemaking not being up to par rankled.

Aye, I became angry, defensive, and then she was gone.

He risked a glance her way. Meara rode on her shoulder, and he'd bet his last gold coin—if he had any left—they were conversing telepathically. He could have checked with magic, but it felt disrespectful to bother them.

He took stock of where they were. He'd been walking mindlessly. Planes roared overhead, but the unpleasant, fear-saturated energy of an occupied country hadn't yet reached Scotland. Stewart uttered a silent prayer it never would. It occurred to him that the shifters still with them might be better off traveling in their animal forms. They'd make better time that way.

A collection of vehicles in front of what appeared to be an abandoned farm caught the corner of his vision. He directed a thread of magic in that direction to double check his impressions about the untidy spread being unoccupied. Nothing living pinged against his magic.

"Hold up," he told the others.

A chatter of questions in Gaelic from the Fae rattled against him. He explained that while they had a magical network from one end of the U.K. to the other allowing quick passage, it wouldn't accommodate the rest of them.

Gregor and the bear shifter who'd driven them out of Germany intuited Stewart's intent. They loped to the motley group of farm trucks and older sedans, moving easily from one to another. Stewart hurried after them. They could squeeze into two cars—if they found two that still ran.

An engine stuttered to life, and Gregor motioned to Stewart. "Solves half our problem," he said.

"Aye. How's the fuel?"

Gregor shrugged. "Who knows? The gauge is broken. I'll siphon what I can from the ones that will never run again. It should be enough. While I'm doing that, sort who goes with me. Be sure someone knows the way to where we're going."

Stewart nodded sharply and set down the faeries who'd been nestled against him. One of the dark Fae marched dead in front of him and said, "Your destination is Ben Nevis. We shall meet you there." His words were stilted, formal. He wasn't asking. He was telling.

Stewart adopted the same formality and bowed slightly. "Thank you. Open fires and safe travels."

A chorus of, "Open fires," rose around him, and the faery folk shimmered to nothingness in an iridescent haze of droplets. Their scent remained, and the heather and gorse kindled a bone-deep longing for home and hearth. For Yara by his side... Meara still rode on her shoulder, and Stewart headed toward them.

"Ye'll go with Gregor," he told Yara, then added, "I presume ye'll fly," to Meara.

The vulture squawked and launched herself off Yara's shoulder. Wincing, Yara rubbed it gingerly. "Bird weighs more than she looks like." Yara leveled her gaze at Stewart. "I'm not going with Gregor. Pick someone else. I'm fine."

"But lass," he protested. "Ye'll be safer that way."

"Pick someone else," she repeated and made a grab for the sack she'd dropped to rub her shoulder. The bear shifter was working on another car, and Yara strode toward him. A brilliant flash of light presaged Meara's shift just before she joined Yara. The two women converged on where the bear shifter bent over the vehicle's open hood.

Gregor was ready to leave, so Stewart herded half of them his way, including both Cadr and Vreis. Even though the farmhouse appeared deserted, he breathed a sigh of relief when the car rolled up the rutted drive, and no one materialized out of the ether shaking a fist and screaming imprecations.

Only four of them remained. Stewart picked his way through the rusting junkyard to the accompaniment of cursing from the bear shifter. "Do ye know what's wrong with it?" Stewart asked.

"More or less," the bear grumbled. "Spark plugs are shot."

"Can you cannibalize something from these other cars?" Yara asked.

It was a good question. She'd been living off her wits for years, and it showed, but Stewart kept his thoughts to himself. She might think he was patronizing her, trying to make up for his earlier blunder. At least she hadn't jumped at the chance to put as much distance as possible between them when he'd offered her a spot in Gregor's car.

It might not mean anything, but Stewart clung to it anyway as a good omen.

Like most of his Romani companions, he'd never bothered to learn much about cars. He could drive one in a pinch, but he far preferred not to. Feeling out of his league, he peered at the engine. Rust streaked it and circled the spark plug holes. Maybe a spot of directed magic might help.

"Stand back," he said.

"What do you have in mind?" the bear shifter asked. "I was about to see if any of the rest of these junkers"—he spread his arms wide—"used the same type of plug, except I don't have any tools. Anybody's guess whether whoever used to live here left any."

"What I had in mind was cleaning the rust off," Stewart replied.

"Might be all that's holding it together." The shifter smothered a snort, and then added, "Don't mind me. It's definitely worth a try. If we can fix the sparking problem, this thing should roll."

"Does your magic work on manmade, inert materials?" Meara quirked a skeptical brow. "Mine doesn't."

He didn't know the answer, but didn't want to give up before they'd even begun, so he extended his hands and pushed exploratory bursts of power outward, saying, "Let's find out."

Yara stepped to his side. He felt a jolt at the base of his spine when her magic joined his. No matter what misunderstandings had passed between them, their power was made to be joined. The vanilla-pine smell unique to her rose around them, and he inhaled hungrily. Yara's ability stunned him and was like a balm to his soul at the same time.

"Do you think we could reach through the metal casing and see how corroded the sparkplug tips are?" she asked.

"I doona see why not, but let's clean what we can see first."

Rust turned to a fine powder as they worked, and the bear shifter blew it aside, clearing residue away with his thick, stubby fingers.

"Deeper," Yara urged. "My magic's strong linked to yours."

Stewart nodded. "Aye, lassie. Worst that will happen is the metal will defeat our efforts."

Magic swelled, pulsing around them in waves that emanated from him and Yara. His skin prickled from the surfeit of energy, and he closed his earth eyes, focusing his third eye on the chunk of metal in front of them. At first, all he saw was the rectangular outline of the newly clean engine.

Yara closed a hand around his lower arm. The contact boosted their combined spell, and the gray metal developed a translucent aspect. If he could see through it, maybe working magic wasn't as farfetched as he'd believed.

Stewart chided himself. Trusting your ability was half the battle. Visualize. Believe. Expect results. He knew the drill, but he hadn't actually expected to be able to reach inside the engine block. Before he could run with this new development, Yara snapped up their magic and focused it on the line of spark plugs. Each one flared beneath her ministrations.

"Damn!" the bear shifter muttered. "They're sparking. This might work after all."

"Is that all of them?" Yara's voice sounded strained, and she didn't turn her head to look at the bear shifter.

"Yes," he replied.

Yara let go of Stewart's arm and cut the flow of their combined magic. He loved the feel of her inside his magical center, but trying to hold her close when she clearly wanted to leave was wrong. He reeled in his power and stepped back.

The bear shifter slid behind the wheel and changed a few settings. The engine coughed and sputtered before stumbling to life.

Meara clapped her hands together. "I should have had more faith. I didn't believe it was possible to alter one of those things with magic."

"Why not?" Yara send a sidelong glance at the vulture shifter.

"Our magic was forged in a time before machinery existed. I've never doubted my ability when it came to modifying anything in the natural world, but I've never tested it on something like that."

She pointed at the car. Its engine still sputtered, but it was moving toward smoother operation.

The bear shifter stuck his head out the door. "We're in luck. Gas tank's mostly full. Get in. We're leaving."

"Eh, I'm still flying," Meara said. "Never did develop a fondness for cars." Light flashed. Before it cleared, the vulture was airborne, her wings beating hard.

Yara slid into the front seat. Stewart started to get into the back, but someone had removed the seat cushions. The only thing in the space was mouse nests, the mice having long since departed.

Yara glanced over one shoulder. "Come on up here," she said. "You don't want to sit on the frame."

He slammed the back door, and got in next to Yara, sandwiching her between himself and the bear shifter. The car started rolling before he secured the door. "How'd ye come to know so much about cars?" he asked her. "Most Romani don't."

She turned a wry smile his way. "True enough. Cars came in handy after I left the caravan. I've slept in deserted ones and figured out how to make them run when they were more convenient than walking."

He felt impressed by her ingenuity and flexibility, but awkward saying so. They weren't alone, and he didn't want to make her uncomfortable if the conversation turned too personal.

The bear shifter saved him from further rumination by asking, "What happens after we reach Ben Nevis?"

"Och, I wish I had an answer for that. The faery folk will meet us there. Mayhap a Celt or two. We'll follow the track to Ben Nevis's summit. From that point, we wait."

"Why?" the bear shifter persisted.

"What's your name?" Yara broke in.

The man grinned, and it lit up his austere features. "Rylan."

"Thanks." Yara grinned back. "It beats calling you *the bear shifter* in my mind."

Rylan turned his attention back to Stewart. "Why should we wait?" he demanded. "The strongest defense has always been a staunch offense."

"True enough." Stewart drew in a breath, blew it out, and did it once more. "For one thing, I'm not certain where to find our enemies. Vampires are widespread. Demons mostly live in Hell, which isna a place we can get to easily."

"I was part of the group that took on the vampire nest outside Munich," the bear shifter said. His words were calm, but his knuckles whitened where he clutched the steering wheel. "It required planning and split-second timing. We formed groups of five, and each targeted one vampire. More than that, we practiced working together the day before. In retrospect, it might not have taken all five of us per vampire. Three or four would have done it, but the timing was critical. So was each group having a silver spike. The Rom used amulets to offer some protection from vampire mind control. We had them too in hopes holy water and consecrated earth would slow the vampires down."

He stopped to take a measured breath, and Stewart stepped into the silence. "What ye're saying is we're not prepared to face off against more than a handful of vampires, never mind demons."

Rylan nodded once. "That's exactly what I'm saying, but waiting may not be in our best interest. Once we have a solid plan, we need to launch an attack. Meara put out a call to shifters in this country. I'm hoping many will join us. It's hard to refuse Meara. She has a long memory, and she knows all the other first shifters."

Stewart brightened. The shifter call to arms was an unexpected piece of good news, one he hadn't anticipated. "Many thanks for letting me know. The more of us, the better our chances are."

"Do you really believe so?" Yara asked.

"Aye, lass, that I do. Why would ye think otherwise?"

She drew her brows into a thoughtful expression. "Well, my

caravan disbanded because too many of us in one spot posed a problem. In one way, it's not quite the same, yet in another it is. We lost the strength we had in sheer numbers, but…"

Yara shook her head. "I'm babbling. It's what I do when I'm worried."

He placed a hand over her thigh but removed it quickly. He'd meant to comfort her, but the heat from her body seared him. To mask his discomfort, he started talking. "Your assessment is accurate so far as it goes. Small groups have an easier time escaping detection, but that willna be our goal."

"Say more," Rylan urged.

Stewart debated a watered-down version of the truth, but that wasn't how it worked with allies. You were straight with them.

"What I suspect," he began selecting his words with care, "is that the enemy sees us as weak. 'Tis why they only sent three demons to intercept the ship."

"They doubled the number next time when we were almost to port," Yara muttered.

"Because they doona like to lose," Stewart retorted. "Let's think this through. Vampires canna function near water. They're the demons' primary ally. After the demons' last fiasco, they must have decided to wait and take us on once we landed. That way, they'd be able to leverage their vampire associates."

"Do you know that for certain?" Rylan demanded.

"Nay. Of course not. 'Tis conjecture, but I've spent enough years battling darkness, I understand how they reason. They'll not make the same mistake of being undermanned a third time." Stewart tapped the windshield. "Angle left at this intersection."

He took in the almost empty countryside as they rolled along. Once this part of Scotland had been a bustling agricultural center. What had happened to it? The empty farm they'd taken the cars from appeared to be representative of a declining population.

"Where'd everyone go?" Yara's question mirrored his thoughts.

"I have no idea."

"We're coming to a village," Rylan noted. "With people. Maybe they thought it would be safer to live close together in case the Nazis launched an offensive."

"Maybe so," Stewart muttered. He tried to raise the Celtic gods again, but no one answered. The car probably muted his magic, but they hadn't been inclined to reply when he'd been on foot, either.

A thought occurred to him, and he asked Yara, "Have ye heard aught from Rhiannon since we left the ship behind?"

She turned her eyes on him, full violet in this light, and nodded once but didn't add words to the gesture.

"Did she say she'd help us?" he prodded.

"I have no idea. The topic didn't come up." Yara chewed on her lower lip. "She may be my mother, but I don't have any kind of a relationship with her. She shows up when she chooses, and departs just as fast."

"Aye, but—"

Yara made a chopping motion with one hand. "If she shows up again, I'll make a point of asking. We'd do better using this time to plan our offensive. At least then we'll have a strategy we can share with everyone else when we're all together."

"First, we need to figure out who has silver and amulets," Rylan said.

"None in this car," Yara murmured and cast a pointed look Stewart's way.

Her criticism hit home. He could have planned their flight across Scotland better, a fact she'd been quick to remind him of. Apparently, he'd been wrong about her having forgiven him.

"We should be fine until we get to the bottom of the Ben Nevis track," he countered, doing his best not to sound defensive. "Shouldn't take more than another hour or so."

"Do you think the vampires and demons will be waiting there, so they can pick us off one by one?" Yara asked. Color drained from her face, leaving a resolute expression that tugged at his heart.

"'Twould be a good tactical decision on their part," Stewart replied, "but I doona believe they're that organized—or that smart. Like as not, they're still trying to locate us. I'm hoping we'll have time to traverse the distance to the top."

"If we were driving into an ambush, Meara would have told me," Rylan said, and then added, "How far it is to the top of Ben Nevis?"

"Four miles. Stone huts sit atop the mountain, as do the entrances to several cave systems."

The car jolted forward as Rylan laid on the gas. "We'll be the last car to arrive," he explained. "I just contacted Meara, and she'll make certain everyone starts up the track and doesn't wait for us."

"Since ye're talking with her," Stewart cut in, "have someone leave at least one amulet and one silver stake. They can mark the location with a magical beacon."

"Done."

The highway widened and grew busier, which made sense. The Highlands had always been a popular destination. Stewart muted their presence with cloaking spells. The fewer people who remembered their dented-up car, the better.

"Want some help?" Yara asked. Her body pressed against his from thigh to knee in their cramped quarters. He'd been doing his damnedest not to pay attention—or react to—her proximity, but it was a losing battle.

"Sure."

Her magic slid seamlessly in with his. Clearly, they were becoming more proficient working as a team. Soon, they'd be in the thick of things. Stewart vowed to open his heart to her while he could, no matter what kind of a blundering fool he made of himself. As soon as they were walking uphill, he'd do everything he could to make certain she understood how important she was to him.

The rational portion of his mind—the sector that had always had the upper hand—tried to talk him out of it, but he didn't listen. Listening to advice got him into this mess. From now on, he'd follow his instincts.

And his heart.

CHAPTER 18

*Y*ara marveled at how powerful she and Stewart were when their magic was conjoined. She'd mostly worked alone in the caravan, and her sister had been weak as a kitten when it came to magic. It felt right sitting next to Stewart with their power woven together. Her ability enhanced his, and the reverse was true as well. Rhiannon had been clear he was the man for her, and Meara's explanation went a long way toward clearing her hurt feelings from Stewart's behavior in the ship's hold.

They needed to talk, but for that they needed privacy.

Stewart had been feeding Rylan directions as they passed through the outskirts of Fort William. They'd turned off onto a side road, and she saw the other two cars a few hundred yards away.

Rylan pulled up behind them. "Excellent," he said, pocketed the keys, and pushed his door open. It creaked on rusty hinges, but the vehicle had done well for them.

Stewart withdrew the spell he'd kept around them. The place her magic dwelt felt empty, incomplete, without it.

"Let's get moving," he said and piled out the passenger door with her right behind him.

Meara's winged form came into view, flying slowly. Screeching, she flew in gradually widening circles as she gained altitude.

Rylan must have talked with her because he loped a short way up the trail and bent to retrieve something from beneath a bush.

Must be the silver stake and amulet.

Yara hurried to where he stood waiting for them as he tucked the items into pockets in his jacket. "Meara says the weather's really going to hell above the lake." He eyed Stewart. "I'm guessing you know where that is."

"Aye, that I do."

The ground around them heaved and rolled, reminding her of the ship. Magic surged, and she dropped the sack she'd carted ever since she left the ship to extend her hands. Balance was a challenge, and she rocked from foot to foot to remain upright.

"'Tis just the faery folk. Sheathe your power." Stewart snatched up the bag and slung it over one shoulder. "Come on."

A golden glow shaped itself into a gateway, the air shimmered with an abundance of power, and Fae poured through. Far more than there'd been earlier. Something about the little folk made Yara's heart lighter. Dark Fae followed, and the mass of their magic surged uphill, carrying everyone with it. A whooshing sound drew her attention in time to see the portal whisk shut as if it had never existed.

"Where'd they come from?" she asked, adding, "Or maybe a better question would be how they traveled here."

"They bide in the hills and barrows beneath Scotland—Ireland and northern England too," Stewart replied.

"Have you ever been there?" The concept of a subterranean network that linked entire countries via an enchanted tunnel system fascinated her.

He smiled softly. "Nay, lassie. I'm a wee bit too big to fit, even if I were invited, which I havena been."

She thought about her sister. Maybe once they were done here, she could track Ilse down. Stewart trotted on one side of her with Rylan on the other. No chance for the privacy she'd hoped for with Stewart. Not yet, anyway.

My total focus should be on the battle, she chided herself.

She'd been quick to project her thoughts beyond the battle to locating her sister, but the reality was she might not live out the day. Yara scrunched her hands into fists. They had to win. If they didn't, it would be the beginning of a long, downhill slide for Earth and all its inhabitants—magical and otherwise.

They moved quickly up the rocky path. It was wide enough to accommodate carts, and she guessed it had been used by farmers and ranchers for hundreds of years. No one said much. The Fae's magic surrounded them. It held a healing, hypnotic quality, and she had to pay attention or she'd have tossed vigilance aside in favor of the childlike innocence surrounding the faeries.

"They're nothing like what they appear." Stewart spoke low, placing his mouth close to her ear.

Her head whipped around. "You were in my mind."

A sheepish expression twisted his stark features. "Aye, guilty as charged."

She wanted to reach for his hand, but Rylan was right next to her. Instead she said, "It's all right. I wasn't complaining. What did you mean about—?"

He shook his head and switched to telepathy. *"They may look like children. Like innocents, but they purposely deploy magic to lull people into underestimating them. They've lived off humans for hundreds of years. One of the ways they've accomplished that is by appearing meek and nonthreatening."*

"Could have fooled me," she murmured. "How are they really?"

"Skilled warriors. Better at mind control than vampires, when ye cut to the bones of it."

"Good that they're on our side."

Stewart nodded. "I'm about to see if I canna raise the Celts—again. Ye might check if Rhiannon is about."

Yara peered through mist that had thickened as they gained altitude. They'd just entered a hanging valley, and a lake sat off to her left. Wind whipped around them, and she tugged her cloak closer about her, drawing its hood over her head. It might not be raining right yet, but she could both smell and taste it in the unsettled air.

Stewart handed the bag back to her. "Do ye mind, lassie?"

"Not at all." She repositioned it so it hung over one shoulder. "Was the book getting restless?"

He snorted. "Aye, ye might say as much. It dinna like it overmuch when I snatched up the bag down below, and it grew increasingly edgy as we moved uphill."

The book's power throbbed against her back. She might have read recrimination in its emanations, but maybe that was going too far. Gratified it hadn't written her off, she crooned to it, told it she was happy to have it back.

"Is that the lake Meara meant?" Rylan jerked his chin at a substantial body of water with whitecaps rolling across its surface.

"Aye. 'Tis Lochan Meall."

"How much farther to the top?"

"Perhaps an hour and a half," Stewart replied. "Why?"

Rylan shook his shaggy head, displacing a shock of dark hair that had fallen across his eyes. "I believe I'll shift. I'm a far stronger fighter in my animal form, and I can make better time as well." He glanced at Yara. "I know it's an imposition, but might I trouble you to keep my clothes in that sack of yours until we reach wherever we're stopping? You could offload them then."

"Of course."

Stewart eyed them. "We canna bide here. We're too exposed. Wait until the next bend in the trail. If I recall rightly, an overhang there will afford us some protection from the wind. And provide a defensible position if we're set upon."

As if it had heard him, a gust rattled through that was almost strong enough blow them off the track. "You're a weather worker. Can you do anything? Stave off this storm?" Yara asked.

"Aye, but it would drain my magic quickly. I must conserve my power for what lies ahead."

Stewart hurried forward. Rain began, large, fat drops that pelted down from a gunmetal sky and made Yara grateful for her woolen head covering. Rylan pushed past her. "If you could wait even for a minute, it would spare you the sight of my nakedness."

Yara nodded. Maybe she waited longer than that, or maybe he was faster than he'd expected. By the time she rounded the bend in the trail, a large, shaggy, dark brown bear was loping away from them. She stared after him, amazed at the transformation.

Stewart handed her a folded stack of clothing, and she stuffed it into her bag. The cloth was doing less than nothing to keep the sack's contents dry, but the book's ancient binding seemed immune to anything as mundane as weather.

She tossed the bag over a shoulder. "I assume you have the silver and amulet."

"Aye, at the ready." Stewart knotted Rylan's bootlaces together and draped them across his shoulders so one boot dangled on either side of his chest.

Half a dozen Fae swarmed over Stewart. "We can carry the boots," echoed in a discordant mixture of old and new Gaelic.

"Aye, and I'd be a right fool to fall for that," Stewart scoffed.

A plump Fae with hair the deep violet of sunset on a winter day hauled himself up Stewart by gripping handfuls of his clothes, ending up with his arms slung around Stewart's neck. "We may play such tricks on mortals, but there's nowhere betwixt here and the top of *Beinn Nibheis* to turn a battered pair of boots such as those into coin. Besides"—he angled his head at a mischievous angle—"ye gave us more than sufficient gold. 'Twould be wrong to lighten your load further."

Yara stared at the engaging little man. It was all she could do not to reach out a hand to touch his violet curls.

As if he could read her thoughts, he turned his hammered silver eyes her way. "Ye're a comely lassie, but any get of Rhiannon's would be."

Yara swallowed a snort. "How is it everyone knows I'm her daughter but me? I know now, but for a really long time, I had no idea."

The Fae shrugged and winked broadly. "Och, ye need to hang around a better class of magic wielder."

His deadpan expression made her want to laugh. "Quite the charmer, aren't you?"

He mock bowed from where he'd draped his round body over Rylan's boots. "I'm sure I havena any idea what ye're nattering on about." The Fae turned his gaze on Stewart and rattled off a string of Gaelic. Stewart answered in kind. All the while, they climbed higher on a track that zigzagged back and forth across Ben Nevis's broad western flank.

A stiff wind howled, and remaining on the track took most of her attention. Rain worsened, turning first to sleet and then to snow. Water squished through holes in her boot soles, and her feet turned to cubes of ice. She funneled a thread of magic to keep blood flowing. The track wasn't difficult, but it was both long and steep, and she was growing tired. She still wanted a few private moments with Stewart, but at least so far, the Fae had kept up a steady stream of chatter. Following their rapid-fire Gaelic while she fought the burgeoning storm was impossible.

Who knew? Maybe he and Stewart had been buddies before Stewart was forced to flee the British Isles.

They had to reach where they were going soon. They'd been on the move for better than three hours since leaving the car. Maybe longer. Water dripped off her nose, and her braids were covered with ice and snow. The track steepened, and a rock obelisk rose to her left. Visibility had eroded to only a few feet.

"Nay on the boots? 'Tis your final word?" the Fae asked in his lilting, musical voice.

Stewart's reply rumbled, most of it torn away by the wind. Yara plodded beside him. She didn't want to make a pest out of herself by asking how much farther. A shiver slithered down her spine, followed by another. If she had anything warmer to put on, she'd have stopped and done so. Most of her remaining clothes were in the sack Vreis had taken. Beyond that, anything traveling in this weather had to be as soaked through as she was.

"Watch the edge to your left." Stewart's warning was timely when a momentary break in the endless gray surrounding them displayed a jumble of rocks leading to a steep drop off.

Squawking presaged Meara's arrival. The vulture shifter plummeted to the ground right in front of them, water sheeting off her black feathers. She clacked her beak twice and shifted in a muted haze of light. Her long, gray hair was soaked, and it clung to her body in a sodden, tangled mass.

Yara fell back a pace. Was the shifter so depleted, she couldn't manage her usual blaze of brightness?

"What's wrong?" Stewart gripped both her shoulders, but Meara pulled away from him.

"Any luck with the Celtic gods?" She bit off the words.

Stewart narrowed his eyes to slits. "Nay. And I've been trying to raise them most of the way up here."

Meara focused her untamed, avian gaze on Yara. "How about your mother?"

Yara looked away. She hadn't tried to summon Rhiannon. "I— I'll see if I can't find her now."

"What's wrong?" Stewart repeated.

"Great wickedness is heading right for us. I left the others near the round stone building at the summit because it seemed more defensible."

"Will we arrive in time to help them?" Stewart asked.

That he didn't question Meara's assessment might mean he'd sensed approaching darkness as well. Yara ground her teeth together. She'd been remiss not to have deployed her own power to scan for threats, so she sent it zinging outward.

And reeled it in just as fast. The wall of evil bearing down on them scared the daylights out of her. It was endless. Bottomless. Her throat thickened with fear, and sweat slicked her sides despite the cold. Hopelessness threatened to swamp her.

"We'll be there to meet our enemies," rose from the Fae and Dark Fae in a chorus. The magical nimbus surrounding the fair folk split the darkness ahead of them as the Faeries hastened toward the mountain's top.

Meara crossed her arms over her soaked hair and made a sour face. "Let's hope they're stronger than they look. About fifty shifters have joined us, but I fear it won't be near enough. Plus, there's not much space to maneuver up there."

Stewart set his mouth in a determined line and held out his hands. "Mountains are the bones of the earth, and the source of my power. Take hold of me, and I'll transport us into a chamber that opens behind the stone building."

"What about raising the Celts?" Meara pressed.

"One thing at a time," Stewart countered. "We must rejoin the rest of us afore we're attacked."

Yara halted her unsuccessful attempts to communicate with Rhiannon and grasped one of Stewart's outstretched hands. After a brief pause, Meara took the other. The Druid's magic wrapped them in its clutches, and the ocean scent of his power mingled with Meara's sunbaked clay and rosemary smell. The latter was so out of place in the middle of a blizzard, Yara could have laughed.

She might have if their situation wasn't so grim.

The rocky path beneath their feet fell away. Yara blinked against darkness until a cave studded with small, iridescent lights formed around them. Rocks placed strategically every few feet glowed as if lit with an inner fire. Were they always like that, or had Stewart triggered some mechanism to coax them to life?

He disentangled his hands from theirs. "If ye walk dead ahead, ye'll find a boulder blocking the entrance to this cavern. It will yield to magic. The stone building is just beyond. I shall make one last effort to entice the gods to come out of hiding and help us afore I go outside."

He dropped Rylan's boots in a corner, raised his arms, and chanted in Gaelic, the words poignant, thick with desperation.

Yara shook water off her head and brushed snow out of her hair. She untangled the sack's handles and placed Rylan's clothing atop his boots. The book glowed brightly, so she drew it out, intent on seeing if it had a way to locate Rhiannon.

Meara stalked away from them, clearly intent on joining the gaggle of shifters and Rom outside. The scrape of stone against dirt confirmed Yara's hunch. Crouching, she let the book fall open on her lap and visualized her goddess mother.

She didn't have to wait long. Rather than rustling pages, Rhiannon shimmered into being off to her right. Her flame-red hair was braided in an intricate Celtic knot pattern, and her golden eyes glowed. She held out her hands in clear invitation. Yara set the book aside and walked close enough to clasp them.

Power flowed into her. Ancient, potent, almost painful as it filled her with a burning sensation that made her want to shuck her skin and begin anew. She met her mother's eerie gaze—not an easy task—and asked, "What are you doing?"

A soft, sad smile played about the goddess's mouth. "Daughter. This is your battle, not mine. My era, the Celtic gods' era, died long ago. That we remain here is one of the mysteries. We canna help—not much, anyway—but nowhere is it written I canna shift a piece of what is left of my power to you."

Fear shot through Yara, along with a certainty she'd never be strong enough to pick up the banner her mother had carried. She tried to pull away, but Rhiannon held fast.

"Aye, but ye're wrong, daughter. The only element missing is believing in yourself and your power."

"I— I don't understand." Yara chewed her lower lip, biting so hard she tasted blood. "Manandan was one of you, and he seemed plenty powerful enough."

Rhiannon laughed softly. "He's a mere shadow of who he used to be, but ye canna tell him that. He insists his magic survived intact." She shrugged, and the golden chains beneath her torc clattered against each other. "Men. Poor, deluded fools, the lot of them."

Yara slanted her gaze at Stewart, and Rhiannon laughed once more. "Och, he canna hear us. I made certain of that." She leaned close. "The Celts fashioned his power so it potentiates ours. Ye need him in this battle, and he needs you. Together, ye can lead the others to victory."

Her form began to shimmer, taking on a translucent aspect. "No. Don't go," Yara pleaded. She sounded like a child, but this was her mother, and she wanted her with a fierceness that rivaled the power pounding through her, turning her blood molten.

Rhiannon disentangled her hands from Yara's grasp. "I must. This isna my battle, but we shall meet again, daughter. If ye are victorious, 'twill be at your wedding."

"What if we're not?" Yara pressed.

"Then I will see you in the Summerlands where we shall pass our days on sun swept moors drinking mead."

As quickly as she'd arrived, Rhiannon faded until nothing but a faint glow marked the place she'd been.

Stewart hastened to Yara's side. "Will the Celts help us? No one answered me." Worry eddied from the edges of his eyes in a series of fine lines.

Yara held out her hands in a precise replica of what her mother had just done. He grabbed hold, his gaze never leaving hers. "No Celts," she replied, trying for a voice and words that didn't tremble. "Their time on Earth has passed. Rhiannon said we—you and I—can do this. That our combined power will be enough, but that we must believe in ourselves."

A slow smile split his face, and he bent his head, slashing his mouth over hers in a quick, hard kiss. When he lifted his mouth, he let go of one of her hands and tugged her forward with the other. "Rhiannon gifted us her blessing—and her confidence. 'Tis good enough for me."

Yara wanted to protest that they had things to say to each other. Bad water under the bridge to clear away, but he shook his head. "I love you, lassie. All else can wait."

"I love you too. There, I said it. In case I don't get another chance." Her eyes sheened with sudden tears, and she blinked them back. A riot of conflicting emotion filled her until she feared she'd crack wide open.

Tenderness and promise spilled from his gaze. "Och, Yara. My Yara. We'll write the script as we need to for ourselves. We can do this. We can do anything, so long as we're together."

Yara ran by his side, their hands still joined. Magic flashed, and the boulder moved aside. Evil was almost here—dank, stifling, oppressive—but confidence filled her. Vampires were too depraved to live, and demons needed to return to Hell.

"We can do this." She echoed his words and believed them to her bones.

"Aye, lass, that we can."

Stewart pelted into a blinding snowstorm barking orders. The faerie folk jumped to his commands. Yara felt like a different woman. Who knew? Maybe she was channeling her mother, but she called out to both shifters and Rom, and they gathered around her, ready to do her bidding without question.

Yara sent a quick prayer skyward that she'd be worthy of the trust etched into the sea of faces turned her way. Stewart was gathering a group to face down vampires, so she raised her voice, shouting into the storm raging around them.

"Who among us has fought demons?"

Tairin stepped forward, a resolute expression on her face. Meara came too, and a handful of others including Elliott.

Yara skinned her lips back from her teeth. "Excellent. Killing them is a lot of trouble, but we can make their miserable lives so horrific they make an end run for Hell to escape us."

"I like it." A Dark Fae drove a pikestaff into the earth in front of him.

"Aye, we hate those bastards," the other Fae screeched.

They didn't look innocent anymore, and Yara remembered Stewart's words. *They may look like children, but they purposely deploy magic to lull people into underestimating them.*

Bright magic rose in a cloud of gold, silver, and a rainbow of colors. It prickled where it touched her, so full of power it wasn't possible to contain it.

Darkness swooshed out of the east, and Yara turned to meet it head on. Something fey and untamed kindled within her, and she recognized Rhiannon's unique brand of energy.

Love and gratitude for the goddess surged, running high. Yara extended her arms and clear, white light flashed from her fingertips. "Come forward," she cried, aiming her words at the darkness. "Approach and meet your doom."

War cries rose around her. Many voices. Many languages. Yara wrapped them all in a protective spell. They'd fight together and, by the goddess and everything good, she'd see to it that they won.

CHAPTER 19

Stewart had been beyond elated by Rhiannon's unexpected appearance. His first hope had been that she'd bring her fellow Celts to fight by their side, but the way things played out was even better. Somewhere, someone recognized his claim to Yara when he'd snatched a piece of her soul, swapping it with a bit of his. The intensity—the rightness—of having his body buried deep within hers had driven him, but given a choice, he wouldn't change a thing.

He wanted to shout his joy to the heavens, but chaos bore down on them. The kiss he and Yara shared in the cave would have to be enough until the battle ended. She'd told him she loved him, and no matter what happened today, the sweetness of her words would always live inside him.

A wave of fresh panic raced from his toes and swooshed over the top of his head. She had to survive, and he fought an urge to bind her with magic and stuff her back into the cave.

As if that would work.

She'd break through his spell as easily as a child dragged a grubby finger through a spider's web. Besides, Rhiannon's message was that they were invincible together.

Together. Stewart savored the sound of it.

Yara had always been strong, but whatever Rhiannon did made her formidable. They hadn't discussed strategy. There hadn't been time, but she was gathering a cadre to fight demons. He was proud of her, awed by her strength and courage, and he vowed to be a worthy mate.

Stewart blinked against wind and ice pellets pummeling him from above. Believing in the power of their combined magic was paramount, and he surged forward, summoning fighters to coordinate their offense against the vampires headed their way. The rotten, decayed blood smell of them was thick now, and Stewart sorted silver stake wielders from those with amulets.

"I'm immune to them," Aron reminded him, shouting over the din of the wind. Fear sheeted from the young Rom, but he held himself proud, ready to do his part.

Stewart divided the shifters and Rom into groups of three. Thanks to Meara, they had a preponderance of shifters of all persuasions. Wolves, bears, mountain lions, coyotes, and birds.

He cupped his hands around his mouth. "At least one person in each group has to be human to wield the silver stake."

Amid snarls and grumbles, several naked men and women emerged from their animal forms, snatching up stakes from the pile in front of Stewart.

Blackness bore down on them in a choking miasma that stole his breath. Vampires stank. They toned it down when they were luring their next meal, but now their full power was focused on destroying the puny group of shifters and Rom standing in their way. Who knew if they were even aware of the faerie folk?

Stewart shook a fist at the black cloud settling over them, choking out everything pure and honorable. "Ye willna win," he screamed and joined one of the groups armed for vampires.

A swarm of them converged from all sides, each one beautiful in an unholy way. He'd never understood how something so profane could catch the eye and tease the soul with unmet promises. He felt the same way about demons, but most of them lacked the vampires' striking features.

None of that mattered. Vampires were a scourge. They should have been wiped out by the priests in Egypt. That any had escaped, existing in some subterranean well only to resurface in Hitler's Reich, infuriated him.

His eyes burned and his throat stung. He held a silver stake high and drove it into one vampire chest after another. The third one, a woman with stunning copper curls, emerald eyes, and a lush figure, wrapped a long-nailed hand around his arm.

"Druid." Light was fading from her eyes, but the older vampires took a while to die.

He glared at her. "Aye. 'Tis what I am."

She smiled. Slow, lazy, seductive in stark contrast to the black ichor pouring around the silver stake protruding from her chest. "Remove the silver. I can gift you with immortality." A fat, black beetle slithered around the stake and onto Stewart's hand where he held the silver in place. Three more bugs raced after the first.

Stewart vaporized them with magic. "Save your beasties," he snarled. "I know what they do." He didn't waste his breath telling the abomination twisting in death throes that the same beetles had almost been the death of Elliott when another of the master vampires tried to hijack his body so it could keep on living.

"Immortality." The vampire tried again. Black blood burbled from her mouth, staining her chin and marring her otherworldly splendor.

Stewart didn't bother to reply. More beetles crawled out of the vampire, mouths opening and closing hungrily. She must be one of the truly old ones. After a quick glance around himself to make certain none of the bugs had glommed onto anyone else, he killed the ones he could see and summoned fire to immolate the vampire before she could harm anyone.

She was still alive, and her screams joined the howl of the storm as magic-driven flames consumed her. He pulled out his stake before it turned into a useless pool of molten metal. The vampire reared up. Not dead enough. Not yet. Stewart worked fast, winding cords of magic about the undead abomination. He wouldn't have to immobilize it for long. Good thing, because it was strong.

The vampire shrieked curses while she struggled and fought her bonds. Black ichor flew everywhere. Her head whipped from side to side, but at least the cavalcade of beetles had stopped.

"Die!" Stewart exhorted and fed more magic to the flames. *"Faigh bás."*

The fire completed what the stake began, burning with a vengeance until nothing was left but a pile of charred bones. It had taken a continuous infusion of magic to keep it going in the midst of constant, punishing sleet that left a coat of ice over everything it touched.

Stewart straightened, assessing where he could do the most good. Vampires still poured out of the murk surrounding them on Ben Nevis's summit. Fae and Dark Fae had joined each of the groups of three fighting them. A pair of vampires converged on two shifters, a Rom, and three faeries to Stewart's left. He started their way to add his silver stake to the mix when the Fae and Dark Fae extended their hands. Power jetted from them in a river of green and gold. The vampires saw it, but discounted its significance.

So did Stewart until the green-gold river formed a long chord that knotted itself around one of the vampire's necks. The Dark Fae barked one word in Gaelic, and the rope turned into a guillotine severing the vampire's head from its body. The second vampire's eyes widened, and he spun, intent on escape, but the rope followed him and repeated its lethal act.

Blood spurted, thick, black, noxious, from the two severed heads. Stewart grinned—vicious, grim, feral. For the first time, he truly believed they'd rid Earth of the vile creatures for once and for all.

"What the bloody hell?" Cadr pushed next to Stewart.

"'Tis the power of the two estranged halves of Faerie. The Fae split ranks so long ago, I'd forgotten what they could do when they combined their ability."

"I'm not sure I ever knew," Cadr muttered and joined a nearby group battling a lissome, blonde vampire pleading for her life in a voice that would have done a Siren proud. Fortunately, no one was taken in by her silken tones.

Stewart hunted for Yara, but she and the others who'd been battling demons weren't anywhere in sight. Between the punishing storm still pounding them and the dark cloud obscuring anything more than a few feet away, his eyes were almost useless.

He deployed magic, hunting her and her cadre. Nothing pinged back in reply to his seeking spell. Panic coated his tongue with a sour, metallic tang, and he ran, threading his way between the groups fighting vampires that were scattered across the mountaintop.

Magic hadn't found her, but maybe one of the demons—or more than one—had deployed wards, obfuscations. Aye. That had to be it. His circuit of the battleground didn't take long. By the time he returned to his starting spot, he couldn't escape the fact that Yara wasn't here. She'd vanished along with about twenty Rom and shifters who'd been fighting alongside her.

Stewart balled his hands into fists so hard his nails cut into his palms and shrieked, "Nay! I'll not let you have her."

Rhiannon snapped into view right in front of him. No shimmers this time. She was just there, her eyes glittering dangerously. "What?" she demanded, her voice shrill and edged with something that sounded suspiciously like alarm. "Ye let those bastards make off with my daughter."

Stewart choked back an entire string of words. Excuses had no place. Not in front of a Celtic god. "Where is she?" he demanded.

"Where else?" Rhiannon's beauty contorted into a sneer. "In Hell."

Ice spilled through Stewart's blood until he felt as if he'd turned into the storm still ranging about them. He'd never been to the netherworld. Its portals were closed to mortals. "Quick! How can I get there?"

Rhiannon shook her head. "Ye canna."

"But I must." An idea formed. "Ye altered something within Yara. Do the same for me."

"Ye're not my blood," she protested. "'Tisn't possible."

"Ye doona know that. Not for sure." Stewart closed the short distance between himself and the goddess. "I have a piece of Yara within me. It might be enough for you to work with."

Hope flared in Rhiannon's golden eyes, sharp and painful. She laid her hands on either side of his head and began to chant. Pain shot through his skull, and the worst headache imaginable burst behind his eyes. Aching, throbbing, burning. Nausea twisted his guts into fiery knots, but he stood still. Pain was a small price if it gained him entrance to Hell.

Scorching, raging agony tracked from his head through his chest. Bile rose, splashing the back of his throat, but he swallowed it back. Threads of prickling anguish attacked both his legs, and the soles of his feet burned with exquisite torture.

He stared at Rhiannon. "Nothing left to torch, goddess." When he swallowed, he tasted blood and figured he'd bitten through something. The battle raged around them filled with screams and the stench of blood, entrails, and vampire. Smoke from multiple pyres joined the rest in a stinking mélange, but his entire attention was focused on Rhiannon. Had what she'd done been enough?

She dropped her hands to her sides and angled her head, casting a speculative glance his way. "I do believe that will work, Druid."

He rolled his eyes, surprised his body responded to any

command after the punishment it had just taken. "Fine. Where's the portal to Arawn's world?"

"I'll do you one better. I'll show you." Power flashed around her.

Stewart latched onto the tail end of it, not wanting to lose her. The faerie folk, shifters, and Rom were drilling huge holes in the vampire population. They didn't need him here, but Yara did.

He should never have left her side. Maybe if he hadn't…

Nay, I'd be trapped in Hell with her. I needed whatever Rhiannon just fed into me.

In a distant corner of his mind, he was curious just what that was, but experimentation with his newly augmented power would be tested soon enough. Contrails of light marked the goddess's passage, and he jumped through a black void. The air seared his lungs, and the reek of sulfur and ozone scraped his nostrils raw.

Hell had to be on the other side.

He rolled out onto hard-baked, cracked red earth that stretched as far as he could see. Fumaroles bubbled all around him, making him wonder just how stable the clay beneath his feet was. Heat buffeted him from all sides. Dry, relentless, it would suck the life out of anyone human damned fast. The air scorched his lungs, and the sky was a sickly yellow-green. Incessant brightness was almost worse than the heat. It seared his corneas, already raw from Rhiannon's intrusion.

A loud, cracking noise battered him, and Cadr popped out of the ether next to him, followed by Vreis. Both men hit hard and rolled to their feet. Stewart blinked hard, thinking maybe he was hallucinating, but his fellow Druids didn't disappear. "How—?" he began.

"Not easily," Cadr replied.

"Aye," Vreis walked over, dusting himself off. "We saw you with Rhiannon, and suspected something was up. The Fae and their dark cousins had the vampire problem well in hand, so we borrowed on an old magic."

"The one where we hide in each other's essence," Cadr clarified. "Neither Vreis nor I were sure it would work, mostly because we had no idea where ye were bound, but we dinna want you to face danger alone. So we snuck along. If ye'd been paying closer attention, ye'd surely have noticed."

"'Tis Yara, right?" Vreis narrowed his eyes. "She and the ones fighting demons are missing, so my guess was ye'd forge a path into Hell." A smug smile crossed his face. "For once, I was right."

Stewart punched each of them in the upper arm. "Ye brave, crazy sods. Damn my eyes, but I'm glad we're on the same side."

"Be glad enough to help us out of here the same way we got in," Cadr countered. He shielded his eyes with a hand and turned in a circle gazing out at the dead landscape. "Any idea which way we're headed?"

Stewart sent magic zinging outward. Yara's unmistakable energy pinged against his seeking spell, loud and clear. "That way." He pointed, and then set off at a lope, avoiding areas close to the smoking fumaroles that spit red-hot rock.

"What happened to Rhiannon?" Vreis asked. He flanked Stewart on one side with Cadr on the other.

"I have no idea. She did something to make me strong enough to follow her, and then vanished in a haze of light. If I hadna been quick, I'd never have been able to track her."

"Aye, well, she was certain ye'd be motivated." Vreis chuckled. "So this is Hell. I've always wondered what it looks like."

"Not me," Cadr muttered. "Figured I'd find out soon enough. Ye know, at the tail end of things."

Stewart elbowed him and ran faster. He had no idea what they'd find, but he'd deal with it, and then craft some way to extricate them from Hell. This wasn't like annihilating vampires. Creatures born of night, they resulted from a blood pact between the devil and Sekhmet, Egyptian goddess of death and slaughter. As Stewart remembered the story, the goddess parlayed with Satan in exchange for something that would immobilize her enemies and offer her endless power.

Aye, not so different from Hitler after all. No wonder the vampires dinna overthink his offer much. 'Twas familiar territory for them.

His thoughts tracked back to demons as he ran. They'd always existed. An army of evil, counterpoint to angels, who jumped to a brighter call. He rolled his mental eyes. The Christian god might have overshadowed his earlier prototypes, but the Celts were real, as were the Greco-Roman pantheon. The Norse gods as well. Today's humans had definitely missed the mark in their choice of a deity, but Stewart learned a lesson when he'd been tossed out of the British Isles. No one wanted to hear his opinions about which gods had the most power.

Or any power at all.

He angled more to his left. Yara's energy drew him like a lodestone. She might be under siege, but goddamn it if she wasn't still very much alive.

"I count fifteen with her," Vreis said. "Two dead, thirteen still alive, although one of those is weakening."

"Aye," Cadr concurred. "Mostly shifters, but a few Rom."

Stewart pushed himself to run faster. He'd been so focused on tracking Yara, he hadn't done a nose count of her companions. They'd be there soon. "We need a plan. Odds of killing those bastards in the middle of their own realm are nil."

"We'll have to give them a good enough scare they scatter like the cowards they are," Vreis retorted.

"Aye, and one look at your smarmy visage should do the trick," Cadr jibed.

"Och, if mine doesna manage it, yours certainly will," Vreis shot back.

Jagged, red cliffs came into view in the distance. Yara and her crew were backed up against them. Stewart offered her kudos. Out of a dearth of possibilities, she'd chosen a defensible position.

He made hand motions to cut the flow of their magic and circle around behind the gaggle of demons that had Yara and her people pinned against the cliffs. At least so far, no one had noticed them. He wanted to maximize their element of surprise. The reek of sulfur had expanded into a choking miasma as they drew closer, and the sky had developed streaks of red in defiance of every natural law.

He wanted to rush into the midst of the demon horde that was scattering lethal magic—except it would be a waste because it wouldn't kill them.

Yara was outlined clearly now. A circle of pure, white light surrounded her, and she'd clearly worked to extend it to shield as many others as she could. Lines of strain carved into her face, but magic blazed from her, and it was keeping the demons at bay.

For now.

Jagged bolts of red and black lightning flew from the demons' outstretched hands. An even dozen of them surrounded Yara and the others who'd been sucked into Hell along with her. Stewart ground his teeth together. His guess was they'd only wanted Yara because of her Celtic blood. Everyone else had been standing too close.

Aye. Collateral damage. Poor sods.

He was close enough to marry his magic with Yara's. Her head snapped up at the contact, and her mouth stretched into a grim smile. The coruscation surrounding her brightened still more.

Stewart hurried forward, no longer worried about concealment. Cadr ran on one side, Vreis the other. They wove their power into a barrier that should deflect an elephant. It was second nature since this was how they faced off against evil. That they'd followed him without question warmed him. They were his family. Them and Yara.

He raced into the thick of things with a bloodcurdling Scottish battle cry intent on standing by Yara's side with his companions. Strike fast. Strike hard. Once the demons were falling over each other's pikestaffs and cudgels, they'd marshal their magic and forge a path back to Earth.

He hoped.

Remaining in Hell wasn't on his agenda. Everything about the place was an affront to his senses. No wonder demons were such bastards.

Aye, no wonder they're in a right hurry to escape this place. Earth must look fair decent to them after a span of time biding here.

CHAPTER 20

arlier on Ben Nevis's Summit

Yara felt quietly pleased. At least so far, demons hadn't gotten close enough to kill anyone, and her ward was prevailing with magic to spare. Not that she'd had much breathing space, but the few times she'd glanced Stewart's way, his group was more than holding its own against the vampires. She was nonplussed when more kept coming, but what worked for the first batch would surely continue to mow through new arrivals.

A burst of green light caught her eye, and she looked up in time to see a magical noose that had Fae stamped all over it choke a vampire to death. No silver needed. She felt like whooping for joy. Plenty of Fae stood with them today. Enough to eradicate vampires for good.

Yeah. Right. Once those fuckers lose enough men, they'll go to ground just like they did when priests threatened their survival in Egypt.

Yara analyzed her thought. She had very little knowledge about vampires, so that pithy little tidbit must have arrived in her head courtesy of Rhiannon's infusion of power. She shrugged and shored up her warding where a constant barrage of black-tinged flames had weakened it. Even if they only crippled vampires

249

enough to drive them into the shadows for a few centuries, she'd consider it a victory.

She made a face, twisting her mouth into a moue. Would that demons were quite so cooperative. This batch—twelve of them—were better organized than the three who'd boarded their ship and the six who'd hounded them near Kirkcaldy. So far, this batch had taken their time and hadn't made any foolish mistakes. She'd kept a close eye out for chinks in their coordinated offense, but had yet to find any.

So far, neither side had made significant gains. Or any gains at all. It was almost as if the demons were engaged in some kind of holding pattern waiting for the stars—or in their case pitchforks—to align properly. A shudder rippled down her spine, followed by another.

Had she stumbled onto something?

Were the demons playing them? Holding down the fort until something cataclysmic occurred?

"Not much I can do about it if they are." Yara didn't realize she'd spoken aloud until she heard herself.

"What?" Tairin shouted from right next to her. The storm with its hooting, howling wind made communication a challenge.

Yara met Tairin's gaze and shook her head. It was too soon to share her worry the demons had a non-obvious agenda that would somehow come around and catch them unaware.

Elliott sidled close enough to position his mouth near her ear. "I don't like this."

Breath whistled through her teeth as she sucked air. She wasn't the only one who'd noticed something odd afoot, which didn't bode well. "Neither do I. Which part bothers you?"

Elliott frowned. "They're not trying very hard. Your ward is good, but not bombproof, especially at the ends."

"I was coming around to the same conclusion," she admitted, "but I don't know what to do about it. We can't very well just vanish back into the cave and turn these bastards loose on the Scots."

She felt a rumble—low and menacing—in the pit of her stomach before it escalated into gnashing, discordant notes. No time to cull through Rhiannon's treasure trove of memories and spells. Nor was there time to retrieve the grimoire.

"Crap! The jaws of the trap just snapped shut." Elliott raced to Tairin's side and wrapped a protective arm around her shoulders while whispering frantically into her ear.

Yara battled helplessness. What should she do? She had no idea what the demons were up to. How could you counteract something that remained a mystery?

She poured power into the ward surrounding her people.

It didn't make any difference.

The dissonant notes escalated until she slammed her hands over her ears; it didn't blunt the noise. A wave of magic hit her from the side, knocking her to her knees. In the split moment when she wasn't riding herd on her ward, the whole lot of them were swept into a black, airless void.

Her lungs burned, but fury blazed brighter. Why had she believed demons would play fair? They were the original con men, shysters, tricksters. Demons made Loki look like a choirboy. How could she have forgotten? Or had they done something? Woven a web to dull her suspicions?

Doesn't matter. I bet we're headed straight for Hell. Those fuckers wanted to even the odds.

She shook her head hard enough her teeth rattled against each other. This was not a time to ask rhetorical questions. Once they stopped falling through blackness, she'd do a better job of taking care of the shifters and Romani caught up in this trap with her.

Guilt bit deep, but it felt like a selfish indulgence. She'd had only herself to consider for years, but that had changed and she had to do a better job. If she fucked up and her stupidity hurt her, it was one thing. If her lack of insight or judgment or paying attention to her instincts snared others in the same net, it was a whole other universe of culpability.

Her mother had passed some kind of torch. At least so far, Yara hadn't done very well as its mistress.

The Celts never watched out for humans.

Maybe so, but I'm not them.

She made the mistake of trying to breathe, and her lungs seized painfully. She clawed at her throat, desperate for air. Her vision hazed, and she fell faster. With the last of her consciousness, she cushioned magic around herself. When she tried to extend it to the others plummeting through blackness right along with her, the lack of air stymied her efforts.

Had whoever snared her grabbed Stewart too?

She gasped like a landed fish, but this time, her reflexive efforts to breathe were rewarded. Hot air that stank like a charnel pit, but air nonetheless. If she could breathe, she could work magic, so she sent out feelers to determine who'd been caught in a trap she felt certain was meant for her. The ground raced up to meet her. If she hadn't had the foresight to soften her landing, she'd have hit hard.

Shifters and Rom fell, landing on all sides of her, some more elegantly than others, but no one appeared injured.

"What the fuck?" A shifter she didn't recognize scanned the place they'd ended up.

"What the fuck, indeed." Elliott skinned his lips back from his teeth. "This has to be Hell."

Everyone scrambled upright, amid curses, groans, and growls.

Yara bounded to her feet and stared out at cracked red earth, fumaroles, and a sky streaked putrid yellow-green. It was bright, and she squinched her eyes to slits. Where could she take a stand and protect her people? She spun in a circle and spied wickedly sharp red cliffs not far behind them. They could put the cliffs to their back. It would mean they'd only have three sides to watch, not four.

A quick nose count confirmed fifteen had been spirited to Hell along with her. More shifters than Rom, which boded well from a magical perspective.

"Quick." Yara didn't bother with telepathy. "Ward yourselves and head for those cliffs."

Once she had everyone headed that direction, Yara draped her own ward around their retreating backs and followed them. So far, a greeting party hadn't materialized, but that luck wouldn't last. Someone wanted them right where they were. If she could find out why, it might be the key to escape—and survival.

She sucked in a deep breath, and the overheated air of Hell scorched her lungs. They couldn't remain here—not long, anyway. They'd weaken in the oppressive heat, and die from lack of water. This barren world might host a subterranean spring or two, but she'd bet her ass they were both guarded and well-hidden.

One step at a time.

Establish a defensive perimeter by the cliff and erect the best wards we can.

She ran hard and joined her small group.

"Good choice," Jamal said.

Yara rolled her eyes. "Thanks. Not like we had a million options. Where's Aron?" She held her breath. Had the young Rom gotten trapped in the airless void between worlds?

"I sent him to get something for me right before we were taken," Ilona replied. "I had a feeling something hideous was almost upon us, so I told him to find me a dry cloak in the cave. He'll be furious—and worried about Jamal and me—but at least he's safe for the moment."

"Strong work." Yara wondered what else the gypsy-seer-turned-shifter knew, but didn't quiz her. "Have any of you been here before?"

A wave of head shakes met her question. "I don't figure getting out of this place, which I presume is Hell, will be as easy as getting in, but that's a way down the road. First, we have to survive."

"The demons want something," Elliott said.

"It's not us dead," Tairin countered. "They could have just left us in that void and we'd all have suffocated."

"We need to figure out why we're here," Jamal said. "Once we know that, we might be able to strike a deal."

"Might be as simple as offering up some of that gold they were after on the ship," Tairin said. "We all have some."

The purulent stench of demon rose in a harsh haze. Her gorge constricted in protest at the cross between rotting vegetation, meat so putrid it was sloughing off the bones, and long unwashed bodies.

"Forget cutting deals for now," Yara shouted. "Form a line two deep with the stronger magic wielders in the back. I'll ward us all, but you each need to reinforce my spell by weaving yours in with it."

She paid out a casting worthy of Arachne as she wound layers of protection about the fifteen people who were here because of her. She wasn't certain why she kept coming back to that, but she never doubted her culpability. This had something to do with Rhiannon, and she'd become her mother's stand in.

Goddammit, Mother! Did you know this would happen? What in Danu's name did you do to piss off demonkind?

Maybe it's not her. Maybe it's all of us and the godforsaken gold on that ship.

She emptied her head and prepared to fight. If the demons were in a chatty mood, she'd ask why she and her companions had been shanghaied.

The ground pitched and heaved, reminiscent of the boat and their North Sea crossing. Holes formed, jagged portals in the scorched earth, and the reek of sulfur from the fumaroles joined all the other noxious odors. One of the excavations grew larger and stone-colored liquid jetted from it, spraying the ground with clods of burning mud.

Demons, some with red scales, some with black, swarmed out

of the openings. She counted twelve. Was it the same dozen who'd faced off against them on Ben Nevis? She stared, but couldn't tell. They all looked similar with their horned heads, clawed feet and hands, and sharp, pointy teeth. Forked tails swished behind some but not all of them.

The heat ratcheted up a few notches, and she shucked her woolen cloak, letting it fall to the ground at her feet. She split her power. Some kept the ward whole, but the rest blasted outward. May as well come into this strong. Maybe if they didn't just roll over and give up, the demons might decide they were too big a problem, and—

"And what?" she muttered. "Offer us an escort back to Earth? All they have to do is walk away. The heat and lack of water will do us in soon enough."

Yara squared her shoulders. That was not going to happen. She'd find a way back to Earth for them, no matter what it cost her.

Black lightning forked from upraised demon claws. It battered her ward and upped the temperature still further. Stinging sweat ran into her eyes and dampened her hair. Sparks flew where their magic collided with the demons' attack. Colors, each more unpleasant than the last, rolled across the sky, and the ground continued to heave in worrisome waves.

She glanced at it. Had the demons upset some seismic balance when they'd blasted through the fragile crust separating them from a river of red-hot lava? More importantly, she'd always drawn her power from her connection to the earth beneath her feet. What would happen if she asked this particular stretch of packed, parched dirt to come to her aid?

An idea bloomed, and she sent an exploratory tendril of power into the dirt. Maybe she could communicate with it, heal some of its fissures. In return, perhaps it would decide she was a better bet than its demon masters. Almost anyone would be. She focused her third eye. What she saw was far from encouraging. While the layers that butted up against the cliff where they'd taken a stand had substance to them, the rest of the cracked mesa's crust was shockingly thin. It was amazing they'd made it across without someone breaking through and falling to their death in a river of molten lava.

They'd have to be damned careful if they ever fashioned an opportunity to leave.

She tried various greetings. Anything to open a line of communication, but the earth remained stubbornly silent. Nothing like the dirt back on Earth. It jumped on chances to talk with her. She'd always suspected it was lonely, hungry for any kind of contact.

Yara had no idea if the insubstantial crust was even sentient. Long exposure to demons might have killed off its essence, but she tried anyway.

"My heart hurts for what's happened to you. I'm here because I offer succor, support. If you can hear me, I will have need of you soon. When I ask for your help, crumple to dust beneath where the demons stand. It's simple enough." She paused before adding. *"They haven't been good to you. You owe them nothing."*

The demons had escalated their attack, adding a hypnotic tone sequence in between the lightning strikes. It was seductive, and when she tuned in to it, honeyed words about dropping the barrier and joining forces with demonkind ebbed and flowed. Surely everyone would see through the demons' chicanery.

She went back to orchestrating the dance that pitted their magic against the demons' onslaught when movement toward one end of her line caught her eye. Before she could deploy magic to stop them, two shifters and a Romani dropped their warding and ran toward the demons, hands outstretched as if they were racing toward loved ones.

Lightning found them before they'd covered half the distance, and they fell where they stood, clutching their chests and screaming in agony. Black flames engulfed them.

Yara choked back horror. "Do not listen to them! Not now. Not ever." She raised her voice, projecting it with magic. Next, she straightened her spine and yelled at the demons, "What do you want with us? Why are we here? If it's only me you want, let my companions leave."

The demon who'd positioned himself near the center of their formation stomped closer, avoiding two bubbling fumaroles. They splashed hot mud on his scaled feet, but he didn't react.

"You are here because Satan wishes it."

"All of us, or just me?" she persisted.

Jamal edged to her side. "Don't even think about cutting a deal where you offer yourself up like a sacrificial goat to free the rest of us. We're in this together."

"Mostly you." The demon grinned, displaying broken, rotting teeth. "The others are an unexpected bonus. Gets boring down here. Boring as hell." He tossed back his head and laughed uproariously at his own joke.

Yara rolled her eyes. Great. A comedian. "Why me?" she persisted. His answer pretty much ruled out the gold as being their rationale, but she figured she'd get as much information as she could. The other demons continued to bombard their ward with power that cracked and boomed every time it hit. The heat and the stench escalated. She had to breathe, but every time she did, nausea spilled through her.

"You're a Celt."

Yara stared at him. "That's all? What'd they ever do to you?"

He shook his scaled head, spittle flying from his gaping jaws. "They've been trying to seal us in here permanently forever." He stalked closer. The earth beneath one of his taloned feet caved in, and he jumped sideways.

Yara inhaled raggedly. Had the earth heard her? Was it about to swallow this arrogant bastard whole? She willed it to happen, but the surface stabilized.

The demon moved closer still until the rotten meat smell of

him made her lightheaded. "War feeds us. There's another brewing on the heels of the one a few years back. Hitler is far better for us than Kaiser Wilhelm. More brutal. Fewer scruples."

Yara considered shooting back that Hitler had no scruples and that demons should have tapped the Dutch government if they were hunting for coldhearted associates, but she kept her mouth shut.

"That explains why I'm here," Yara retorted. "Let the rest of my friends go."

"Save your breath," Jamal said. "We're not leaving you behind to save ourselves. It's not how battles are fought."

Smoke from the three who'd been immolated in demon fire mocked his words. "I appreciate the—"

"Save your breath," Ilona cut in sounding fierce. "I've seen variations of today in my glass, and I believe we'll find a way out."

Yara considered digging for more information, but seers titrated what they told you. If Ilona wanted her to know more, she'd have offered it up.

The demon had been eyeing her. "Are you requesting a deal or not?" He leered at her. "It's been a while since Satan's welcomed a new bride."

Yara choked on her own saliva. Out of all the possibilities she'd envisioned, this one wasn't anywhere on the list.

"No deals." Jamal spat the words, sounding outraged.

The demon shrugged. "Have it your way. More sport for us, although the heat will do you in soon enough." He dropped back into line with the other demons. Several laughed and pointed at her. Yara wanted to punch their arrogant lights out, but killing demons on their home turf wasn't possible.

Forked lightning crackled against their shielding. She fought back, herding power in its wake. Maybe Ilona was wrong and there wasn't a way out of here, but she'd go down fighting.

Power slammed into her. Familiar magic that magnified hers tenfold.

Stewart!

Stewart was here. How had he managed to breach Hell's boundaries? She tamped down elation racing from her head to her feet. No reason to let the demons know their odds had just taken a nosedive. A big one.

She and Stewart were made to fight side by side. They were so strong, she couldn't imagine them losing anything they took on, but it wouldn't do to get cocky. He could die here right along with the rest of them. So could she. Her excitement faded. If he got himself killed because of her, she'd never forgive herself. Why the hell hadn't he stayed put?

Yara shook herself. The odd energy in this wasted land was getting to her, twisting her thoughts into pretzels. Taking care to be subtle, she scanned the horizon. Dust swirled in vortices that obscured her view. Stewart was out there, and he was moving closer.

She latched onto that thought and redoubled her strikes, aiming right for the demon who'd made the crack about her being Satan's bride.

Fucker.

Bastard.

Anger was a welcome respite from the worry that had carved deep channels into her. She reached for it with both hands. She and Stewart were linked in ways she didn't understand. Eagerness to be reunited with him—and his proximity—fueled her efforts.

The demon who'd mocked her yelped when a bolt of power caught him square between the legs. He closed a clawed hand over his dangling genitals just before the earth beneath his feet caved in.

"Yes!" Yara screeched and directed her next words at the earth, an earth that had clearly taken her promises to heart. "Thank you. I won't forget you. Ever."

The other eleven demons surged forward. Any semblance of a staged attack fled. Fury poured from them in waves, and they battered Yara's ward with renewed energy, screeching their rage. If they had even the slightest concern about the fragile, cracked surface swallowing them too, it didn't show.

Yara gathered power from everyone and heaved it into the center of the batch of demons. One yelped. Another's scales took on a disgusting liquid aspect as its hide began to smoke.

Light flared brilliant white, and Cadr, Vreis, and Stewart joined them. She wanted to wrap her arms around Stewart and never let go, but that would have to wait.

"Good to see you, lassie." Stewart grinned rakishly at her.

She couldn't help herself. No matter how dire their straits were, Stewart—her heart, her life—was here. She grinned back. "Focus on the earth," she told everyone. "It's our friend."

The three Druids wove their magic in with Yara's perimeter. It strengthened until it became visible. Bands of power arced around them, and the demons' fire and black-edged spells bounced off.

"Our ward will hold the demons for now, but not for long," Stewart yelled. "Ye must needs say a wee bit more about the earth."

CHAPTER 21

Stewart sliced through Yara's warding, sealing it fast behind himself, Cadr, and Vreis. Their shared magic made it possible. A shining nimbus—something he'd always associated with the Celts—surrounded Yara. She looked beautiful and formidable with her hands extended and power sheeting from her. He searched for words to tell her how relieved he was to find her unharmed, but nothing sounded right.

Of course, she'd be unharmed. She was a goddess. To suggest he'd been concerned might come across as demeaning, as if he had no faith in her. He settled for, "Good to see you, lassie."

She gifted him with a quick smile and blew out a tight breath. "Focus on the earth. It's our friend."

Stewart wasn't certain precisely what she meant, but their comrade's death had incensed the remaining demons. He marshaled magic from Cadr and Vreis and threaded Druid power into Yara's warding until the demons' renewed attack bounced off it, falling to the cracked earth. Wherever it hit, the mottled surface heaved and bubbled.

"Nicely done, everyone. We saw that demon vanish," Vreis said.

"Aye, and we were damned careful where we stepped crossing the mesa after that," Cadr added.

"Our ward will hold the demons for now, but not for long," Stewart yelled. "Ye must needs say a wee bit more about the earth."

Yara closed her teeth over her lower lip and switched to telepathy. *"That demon was no accident. I promised the earth we'd help repair its faults."* Her nostrils flared. *"It's a chance, and it might not work, but if all of us drill beneath where we stand, healing as we go, I believe the other demons will meet the same fate as the one who fell through into goddess knows where. He didn't return, so my guess is either he's stuck, or he decided we were too much trouble to bother himself with."*

"Aye, they're a selfish lot. If there isna clear gain for them, they willna cooperate." Stewart couldn't stop staring at Yara. She'd changed from the woman who'd crept from shadows to intercept their truck on the Netherlands' border. He hoped she'd still want him, but she was goddess through and through, and might well have moved beyond whatever he could offer her.

"Some of us should continue fighting," Tairin said. *"So the demons don't get suspicious until it's too late."*

"Good point." Stewart squeezed Tairin's shoulder.

"The four of us will take care of keeping the demons occupied," Elliott said, joining hands with Tairin, Ilona, and Jamal to strengthen their magic via physical contact.

Stewart eyed the demons. Three had rushed the ward, and were pummeling it with their fists. One swung a cudgel. Where it connected, the ward shuddered, but held. Had they listened in just now? Their minds were closed to him, but their actions suggested they didn't see any reason to placate the fractured dirt they stood on.

Jamal moved in front of Stewart, along with Tairin, Elliott, Cadr, Vreis, and Ilona. Power poured from them, slicing through the ward as if it weren't there. Made sense. Bright magic recognized its own. The remaining shifters and Rom joined the front line, adding their magic to the mix.

Jamal shot a glance at Stewart. "Hurry, man. We can't keep this up forever." Sweat streaked his face, and his dark hair was matted to his head.

Yara stood next to Stewart, her spine arrow-straight. "Ready?"

Instead of answering, Stewart augured power into the earth beneath his feet. Cautious at first, he spread more magic when the earth didn't rebuff him. Perhaps it recognized his earth-linked power, understood that earth provided the substrate for his magic. The damage he found made his heart hurt, and he extended arcs of healing energy to bind the damaged places that cried out to him.

He hoped to hell the others were holding the demons at bay since there wasn't much he could do to help. A quick scan through his link with Cadr and Vreis reassured him. At least they hadn't lost any more men, but neither had the demons slowed their onslaught one whit.

"We need to hurry," he told Yara.

"I know."

She worked alongside him, crooning to the ravaged earth. Where their power touched, the magma-infested crust cooled immediately. He sent the molten rock back toward the center of this borderworld where it belonged. Without its constant presence, layers could form. Layers that would support the dirt and rocks and make them whole again.

"The land needs water. How can we do that?" Yara asked.

He clasped her hand, the hand she'd slipped into his. *"We'll look. If we find a subterranean channel, I'll open a way through for it."*

Yara had good instincts. Water would complete the healing process—so long as Satan left things alone. Not a safe bet, but at least the earth would get a respite from evil. Perhaps their help would encourage it to fight back next time. He sent his consciousness outward, weaving through tunnels of rock and underground rivers where lava flowed, all the while alert for the cooling scent that meant water.

"Nothing's here." Yara sounded desolate. *"The demons are gaining. I feel it. We have to help the others."*

"Deeper," he urged. *"We can do this."*

"I don't want any more deaths on my conscience," she argued.

He tightened his hold on her hand. *"'Tis a gamble, but if we appease the earth with water, it may well suck the remaining demons into its maw. Doona underestimate its power."*

"All right." Her words held a terse quality. She didn't agree, but she trusted his assessment.

"Ye willna be sorry." He wanted to thank her for believing in him, but that would have to wait.

Stewart thrust their combined power downward. All worlds had held life at one time or another. Life meant water. Even demons couldn't exist without it, which argued for at least one source that reached the surface. Likely one heavily guarded by demons to ensure none of the cooling liquid could leach into the surrounding earth to restore it.

"Look! Look at this! I might have found something." Her mind voice vibrated with elation, and she directed their shared magic to a slender channel with a sluggish flow of brackish water.

Stewart didn't hesitate. He blew through the channel until it widened. Water, pure, sweet water, chugged through the path he'd just cleared. Working fast, he created multiple channels branching from the main one to spread the water across a broad area.

The earth sang to him, its song merging with the roar of the newly freed water. He sang back, and Yara joined her high, sweet voice with theirs. They urged the water to seek its old pattern and drive the magma lower, where it belonged. The clean, fresh scent of orchards and growing things exploded until it muted the stench that pervaded Hell.

"Take the demons," Stewart suggested to the earth. *"Draw them deep into the heat of your center and barricade them in with water. 'Twill be fewer to ruin you next time."*

"*Yes!*" Yara added compulsion to his suggestion. "*Punish them for what they did to you.*"

Because his consciousness was linked to the earth beneath him, he felt it gape open, shuddering as it sucked the demons under, tumbling them into an earthbound prison.

"*Thank you. Oh, thank you so much,*" Yara cried.

"*Ye made us whole, goddess.*" The earth's reply rumbled through water rushing to fill its ancient byways.

Stewart added his thanks to Yara's. This was far from a permanent fix, but he didn't want to ruin the moment by saying so. He didn't harbor illusions about Satan packing up his demons and leaving for a place where he could establish dominion over elements that weren't quite so unruly. Regardless of the ultimate outcome, they'd done good work here today.

"*'Tis time, lass,*" he said and withdrew his focus from the earth.

Shifters and Rom cheered, slapping each other on the back in a celebration that had obviously begun while he was joined with the earth's spirits.

Vreis grabbed Stewart's arm. "They're gone!" he crowed. "The demons are gone. 'Tis a bloody miracle. The ground opened and swallowed them whole."

"Aye, and when the chasm sealed itself, the temperature dropped a good ten degrees," Cadr added, wiping a sheen of sweat from his brow.

"Eh." Stewart snorted. "'Tis still Hell. Just a wee bit more comfortable."

Yara was still joined with the earth, her gaze unfocused, her hands extended downward, including the one still sheathed in his. Her essence seeped back into her, rich with the smell of loam and harvests. She smiled broadly and inclined her head.

"I did a touch more damage control so long as I was there." She drew her brows together. "The earth spirits wanted me to stay, but they understood why I couldn't."

Tairin grabbed her arm. "I don't know how you did it, but the demons are gone."

Yara nodded, still smiling. "I know. I felt the earth tumble them downward. They're not dead. If the earth fails to hold them captive, they'll bounce out elsewhere in this accursed place, but it's a sure bet they won't bother us again."

"Satan will have a dickens of a time luring any of his other minions to take us on once they hear what happened to their kinsmen," Elliott said in a satisfied tone, his blue eyes crinkling at their corners.

Stewart glanced around. They needed to get back to Earth. Tarrying here was a bad idea. Satan would be so furious, the old bastard just might show up himself.

Yara tilted her head to one side as if she were listening.

"What is it, lass?" he asked, but she held up a hand.

A wall of magic rolled toward them as intimidating as the black cloud that had descended atop Ben Nevis, but this was Celtic power. Stewart recognized it and batted back a desire to run the other way. When the Celts banded together with their power joined like that, he'd generally taken cover. They always wanted something, and it was rarely to congratulate him on a job well done.

Best case, it always meant weeks to months of backbreaking effort—for him.

Yara swung her gaze around the group. "Rhiannon's coming. She'll see us home."

Stewart considered pointing out that far more than a single Celt was headed their way, but Yara sounded so relieved, he kept his knowledge to himself. The worst was over. For now. Soon he could gather her close and kiss her until they were both breathless with need.

She quirked a brow his way. "Great imagery. Keep it coming," she murmured, having clearly been inside his mind.

He winked broadly. "I will."

The still, dead air of Hell didn't feel quite so dead when a shower of white light coalesced into a shimmery portal. Rhiannon stepped through, clothed in a pure white robe sashed in crimson. The owls were back on both shoulders. Others came behind her. Arawn, Gwydion, Bran, Arianrhod, Manandan, Llyr, Fionn, and a few others as well.

Stewart's heart swelled in his chest. Despite everything, damn if he hadn't missed the Celts. They might have been harsh masters, but they'd usually treated fairly with him. He bowed low. When he straightened he said, "Well met, my lords—and ladies."

"We're not your lords, not anymore," Rhiannon said. "We have forged a path for you to escape from this world. We shall seal it behind us to ensure nothing sneaks through that doesna belong."

The portal glowed warmly. The Celts stood aside, motioning everyone through. Apparently, they planned to go last to ensure their exit point was well and truly impenetrable to Hell's minions.

Stewart detoured and slung one of the piles of bones that had been a shifter over one shoulder. Vreis and Cadr did the same for the other two corpses. Leaving them in Hell wasn't right. Once they returned, Meara could take charge of the shifters' remains. He'd see to proper rites for the Romani.

The Celt's corridor felt soothing after the spine-jarring reality of Hell. He'd been under attack the entire time, and it had taken a toll. Unlike his transit from Ben Nevis, this route had air. Not much, but anything was an improvement over nothing. The Celts' solid presence closed behind him.

Yara walked by his side and slipped her hand into the one not stabilizing the corpse thrown across his shoulder. "No matter what happens next, I'm grateful to be out of that place. I feel horrible about the three who died, though. Demons lured them out from behind the ward. If I'd been more vigilant..."

"Och, lassie. Casualties are part of war. There's never been a commander who dinna lose a man."

She grimaced. "I'm sure those leaders come around to living with their failures, but I still feel like I could have done better."

"Ye came up with the idea to ask the earth for help. 'Twas little shy of brilliant, and in the end 'twas what saved us."

She smiled shyly. "Thanks. Do you suppose today will at least slow the Reich down?"

He considered it, not wanting to utter false words on the altar of making her feel better. "I believe so. We made a hell of a dent in the vampire population. Not that there aren't others, but Hitler likely seemed a sure thing to them afore now. If aligning themselves with him means they have to fight for their lives, they may well come to a different conclusion about helping him."

She smiled wryly. "Too bad none of this will touch Dutch officials and their bigoted decision-making."

"I never had to deal with them." Stewart took a measured breath. "But ye may recall, Druids were run out of the British Isles for many of the same reasons. Everyone has to have someone to look down on, someone to persecute. Like it or no, 'tis the way of the world."

The dimly lit passageway brightened before falling away. Ben Nevis's summit came into view. It was still snowing, but the storm felt clean somehow, not driven by malevolent energy. The shifters and Romani they'd left to battle vampires raced to them amid a flurry of hugs, kisses, and good wishes, jubilant despite the rotten weather.

Aron pelted toward Ilona and Jamal. "You sent me away on purpose," he screamed at his sister.

She opened her arms, and her brother hurtled into them, face contorting with emotion. "I did," she agreed. "And I'd do it again to keep you safe."

Jamal slung an arm around them both. "Your sister loves you. It's not a bad thing."

Stewart peered through driving snow. "No more vampires?"

Michael clumped to Stewart's side. "No more vampires. Not here, anyway. Open fires, old friend."

"Aye, open fires indeed. Nice work."

Michael shrugged. "After a while, vampires stopped coming. I have no idea if we killed all of them, or if an entire batch decided fighting us wasn't worth it."

"Eh, likely the latter," Stewart replied, "but the outcome is the same. What happened to the Fae?"

"They left once it was clear no more vampires were in the offing. Said to give you their best and that they'd see you again. Sooner rather than later was how they put it."

The Celts emerged from the passageway between worlds. It slammed shut with a boom, and the glittering portal scattered into motes of multihued light that were gobbled up by the storm.

Rhiannon clapped her hands smartly, and her owls flew this way and that, hooting and herding everyone toward the cave behind the stone building.

Meara caught up to him. "Thank you for bringing my shifters back from Hell, although I'd have understood if you had no choice but to leave them. Come along into the cave. I'll take over the remains from there."

"Do ye want me to tell Vreis? He has the other body."

She shook her head. "I already did." Meara shot forward and slithered around the boulder still partially blocking the entrance. Once she turned, Stewart handed the charred remains to her, and she laid what was left of the body gently next to the other corpse Vreis had carried inside.

Stewart brushed charcoal bits off his clothing. He stank of death, but so did everyone else.

"Inside, everyone. Now." Rhiannon's tone left no room for dissent.

Stewart moved away from the doorway and pushed the boulder back into place with magic once the last of them was within. He summoned a different type of magic to kindle lights within clear, quartz rocks placed by Druids hundreds of years before. Air sprites lived within those rocks, and they glowed obligingly when called upon.

Rhiannon circled around until she faced everyone. The other Celts formed a wall behind her. After a final series of hoots, the owls landed on her shoulders, beaks clacking shut in unison.

"I would share a story with you," she began. "'Tis a tale I hope will grow into myth that outlasts us all. One of my magical birds came to me years back. 'Twas a raven, and it foretold today's battle. It also foretold the Celts egress from Earth, so I was loath to pay it much heed.

"Shortly after the bird's visit, a beautiful man came to me in a vision. His hair was like spun gold, and his eyes the shade of uncut amethysts. I invited him to lay with me, and we remained in my bower for weeks loving each other. To this day, I have no idea who he was—or if he was even real. He told me we'd made a daughter and that she had to survive. He left how her survival happened up to me."

Rhiannon turned and ran her sharp gaze over her fellow gods. "I dinna trust your goodwill toward any get of mine where ye dinna know her bloodlines, and I couldna afford to have ye set her out for the crows or sell her into servitude."

She turned back to face everyone else. "I knew my child's magic would be strong, which precluded placing her into a human home. Romani caravans were the only place left where a creature with magic might bide unnoticed, so I found a likely Romani couple and paid them extravagantly to raise my child.

"To ensure my plan would unfold undisturbed, I threw myself on Arianrhod's mercy. She invited me to bide in Caer Sidi, the place she oversees both moon and tides. I gave birth there, and kept my daughter close as long as I dared. She was able to communicate telepathically almost from birth. By the time she was two, it was past time to let her go. Had she grown much older, I feared she'd reveal the secrets of her parentage.

"I located the gypsy couple and had them meet me in a Berlin church where I handed over my daughter. It tore out a piece of my heart, and I wept for months."

Yara took a step toward her mother. Tears sheened her cheeks, but Rhiannon waved her back. "Let me finish. There's not so very much more. I watched over you while ye were in the caravan. When it broke up, I watched you still and made certain the book found its way to you."

Rhiannon spread her hands in front of her. "Out of everything I've accomplished over my millennia of existence, this was by far and away the most difficult. I have my birds and my horse, but I wanted my daughter with an ache that was all-encompassing.

"And now my job is truly done. Yara rose to the task she was born for. 'Tis proud I am of who she's grown into, even though I canna take credit for a whit of it. While I am certain she was born to conquer far bigger undertakings than today, 'twas the only challenge that's made itself known to me."

She held out her arms. Yara barreled into them, and the two women clung to one another.

Gwydion moved next to them and laid a hand on Rhiannon's shoulder. Golden hair spilled down his wine-colored robe. "'Tis sorry I am, sister, that ye felt forced to trod the path ye did. Yet I understand your reasoning full well. Mayhap 'tis an omen that 'tis time for all of us"—he leveled a pointed glance at Manandan—"to fade out of time and memory."

"Mayhap so." Manandan looked away.

Rhiannon met Gwydion's direct, blue-green gaze. "Ye may leave. I would bide a bit. Long enough to see my daughter married."

Whoops and cheers rang through the cave.

Rhiannon let go of Yara and beckoned to Stewart. He walked forward, brimming over with emotion. Love for Yara. Gratitude to the Celts. Maybe in some distant corner of their minds, they'd known he had to remain single. To save himself for his one true love, who had yet to be born.

None of that mattered and he covered the distance to Rhiannon's outstretched hand, clasping it. "Ye have my blessing to wed my daughter," she said, her voice loud and clear. "Three weeks from today, we shall gather in Invelochy Castle outside Inverness at sunset."

Before he could craft a response, the Celts vanished in a blaze of light and a mélange of scents from cinders to aged whiskey to new-mown hay.

No one said a word for long moments, and then myriad conversations broke out at once. Yara wrapped her arms around him, and he hugged her back. "Where would ye like to go, lassie?"

She hugged him tighter. "Somewhere I can peek under that kilt of yours. And take a bath. Not necessarily in that order."

He thought about it, playing possibilities through his mind. He'd left several trunks scattered throughout the Highlands. One of the deserted manor houses had a natural hot spring nearby, but so did Ben Nevis.

He raised his voice so everyone could hear him. "Quiet for just a moment." It took a while, but all the side conversations died away.

"I hope all of you will come to our wedding. Ye heard Rhiannon. Three weeks from today at sunset at Inverlochy Castle. It looks like a falling down ruin, but use your magic to enter. Once ye're inside, go up to the third floor. The Celts' council chamber is at the end of the hall."

"Wouldn't miss it for the world. Can we follow this corridor within Ben Nevis down far enough to get out of the storm?" Jamal asked.

"Aye. Give me a wee moment to see this Romani laid to his rest, and then I'll lead you to a spot close to that lake we passed halfway up."

People scuffled about picking things up. Stewart carried the dead Romani past the boulder to Ben Nevis's summit. He placed him tenderly inside the uppermost of the stone buildings, chanted the Druid prayer for his soul to find eternal rest, and set mage fire burning to purify his remains. When the fire was done, there'd be naught left but ashes, and the wind would blow those away.

When he returned to the cave, Meara was bent over her fallen shifters near its entrance. She stopped chanting long enough to say, "I'll find my own way down. See you at your wedding."

He gave her a quick, hard hug, and the old shifter hugged him back.

Everyone else was ready to leave, and he took his place at the head of the line with Yara next to him. "Want me to take one of your sacks?"

"No. They're not heavy anymore. My book is gone. I searched everywhere while I was waiting for you."

"Ye doona need it any longer, lass." He clasped her hand in his and started down the winding passageway, calling on air sprites to light their way.

"I didn't think about it quite that way." Yara sounded thoughtful. "Maybe I don't. Mostly, that book was Mother watching over me, and she doesn't need to anymore."

Cadr and Vreis were right behind him. "Where are ye headed tonight?" Vreis asked.

"The hot springs behind the inn at the bottom of Ben Nevis, first. After that, I have no idea," Stewart replied.

"I know of a spot not far from here," Cadr said. "They're kin of mine, and they'll let us bide a night or two."

"That's terribly kind of you," Yara said. "Maybe just until we figure out how to turn a gold coin or two into pounds."

Cadr snorted. "Aye, they may kick us out after a day or two, lass."

Stewart tightened his grip on Yara's hand. No matter what came next, they'd be together with magic strong enough to tackle damn near anything. Even absent their combined power, knowing Yara would be his bride ignited a bone deep longing. They'd need lifetimes together to quench that yearning, and even that might not do it.

"Lassie," he murmured. "Love of my life."

"Och, such a sweet tongued boyo." She aped his brogue. "Speaking of which, we have to find Ilse. I want my sister at my wedding."

"Where is she?" Vreis asked.

"Ireland."

"'Tis a big place," Cadr said. "Can ye narrow it down at wee bit?"

"Sure. I mentioned it that first night I joined my fortunes to yours. She and Ian are in Galway."

"Vreis and I will find her," Cadr said. "'Twill be our wedding gift."

Stewart's throat thickened with emotion. Cadr and Vreis were the best of companions. "Thank you."

"Hear that?" Vreis demanded.

"Och aye, and I certainly did," Cadr countered. "He finally thanked us for something. He doesna deserve us, but we'll stick to his hide like burrs no matter what."

"Through thick and thin," Vreis managed before he broke out laughing. It was so infectious, everyone close by joined in.

CHAPTER 22

*Y*ara strolled outside the decaying ruins that marked where Inverlochy Castle once sat. Her wedding day had dawned clear and cold, and rain had yet to mar it. She snugged a plain, black cloak tighter over a long dress of cream-colored linen. Rhiannon had come up with it from somewhere, and it was delicate and lovely, sewn with seed pearls and tiny diamonds and emeralds. Its original owner had been shorter than Yara, and the gown hit her mid-calf, but that made it easy to keep it out of the muddy streets.

Sunset would be in less than an hour, and she'd escaped the flurry of preparations within in favor of peace and quiet. She would have liked to share the pearl gray sky and brisk air with Stewart, but he'd been banned from her side these last two days to honor some Celtic tradition about the groom not laying eyes on his bride before the wedding.

Ilse and Ian had shown up a few days ago. Seeing her sister again warmed her, and they'd picked up the threads of their closeness as if no time at all had passed. Perhaps thinking about Ilse drew her because footsteps marked a staccato rhythm as they hurried nearer.

Yara turned and waited for her sister to catch up. "I thought you were working on dinner," she said.

Ilse rolled her dark eyes and blew strands of coal black hair out of her face. "There are Celtic goddesses in that kitchen. Goddesses, I tell you. Half a dozen of them, and each wanted to order me about," she sputtered. "Wouldn't have been so bad, except their instructions contradicted each other. Some were using magic to prepare food. Others wanted a more natural approach."

"I'm surprised they let you leave." Yara smiled.

"They didn't. I slipped out a side door while they were arguing about your cake."

"Really? It's not baked yet?"

"I guess when you command as much magic as they do, these things happen instantly." Ilse shook her head, and huge, gold hoop earrings danced about her face. She was short, buxom, and had the dark, exotic beauty typical of Romani women. "I'm used to how the Rom plied magic. Ha! We were rank amateurs by comparison."

"Speaking of the Rom, it's encouraging the caravans in Ireland are still alive and well. After the Netherlands and Germany, I was beginning to wonder if our heritage would die out entirely."

Ilse smiled softly. "It was a relief to me as well. Even though I left with Ian, I wasn't totally certain he was telling me the truth."

Yara quirked a brow. "More like inducements so you'd run away with him?"

"Something like that." Her smile widened. "I really, really like Stewart. He's a good man, and he'll make you a fantastic husband."

"How can you tell?" Gypsy women were inveterate matchmakers, and Yara wanted to figure out if something beyond wishful thinking lay behind her sister's words.

"It's how he looks at you. His heart all but spills out his eyes." She bit her lower lip in a thoughtful expression. "He looks at you as if you're a princess, and the most precious gift of all."

Yara's face grew warm. She wanted Stewart to love her because she adored him. Even though they hadn't known one another long, it was as if they'd been soul mates in another life. She'd floated the idea one night when they were wrapped in each other's arms, and he'd explained that their souls were indeed joined.

Rhiannon's twin owls flew right at them, hooting indignantly, and Yara burst out laughing. "It appears they're ready for us."

"No." Ilse corrected her. "They're ready for *you*. No one cares if I show up except me, but it looks as if they're ready to begin."

Yara turned back toward the front of the ruins with Ilse next to her.

"Good thing you're with me," Ilse noted. "When I first got here, it took every scrap of power Ian and I could gin up to get into this place. I was afraid I'd have to wait for someone with real magic."

Yara didn't say anything for fear she'd hurt her sister's feelings. The castle had yielded easily to her, and she focused a jot of magic at splinters that had once been part of a massive front door. Light glowed warm gold, and a wavery gateway formed. She herded Ilse through before following her.

Inside, the place looked much as it probably had during its heyday centuries before. Paintings and statues and thick rugs graced its halls. Light flared from sconces inset into thick walls, kindling on their own when she walked by. They mounted two winding flights of stairs. Once they gained the long hallway spanning the castle's top floor, Rhiannon poked her head out of a side door and beckoned.

"There ye are. I had to locate you with magic. Once I did, I sent my owls to round you up." Reproach scored her words.

The owls in question whizzed past Yara and Ilse, still hooting, and settled on the goddess's shoulders, their black and gray plumage bristling with outrage.

"Yes, indeed. Here I am." Yara smiled, hoping to defuse her mother's ire.

"See you soon." Ilse bent close and kissed her cheek.

Rhiannon dragged Yara into a side chamber big enough to host a small army and pulled her cloak aside, brushing her dress into place. "Good. Ye dinna wrinkle it."

"I don't think that's possible. It's a magical gown. Surely, it's moved beyond anything so prosaic as an iron."

The corners of Rhiannon's mouth twitched, and she settled a veil into place over Yara's head, arranging its folds. Standing back, she cocked her head to one side, made a few adjustments, and nodded.

"Will I do?"

"Aye, daughter. Quite well. Come along. 'Tis time."

Yara walked next to her mother. "Lots of Celts are here. Did they decide not to leave Earth after all?"

"Nay, not at all, but they're waiting until after the ceremony. They may not know you, but Stewart was near and dear to them all. Beyond that, they respect me."

Rhiannon pulled a door open, the owls hooting softly. "In ye go."

Yara's eyes widened as she entered a chamber lit with hundreds of candles arranged in elaborate golden candelabra. People filled the hall, and the very air vibrated with their various magics. Where had all of them come from? And then she recognized banks of Fae and Dark Fae. Tairin, Elliott, Jamal, Ilona, Michael, and Aron nodded at her, smiling warmly. Ilse rose from her spot next to Ian and ran to her side long enough to give her a quick hug.

Bagpipe music, haunting and lyrical, rose. When she hunted for its source, she saw Cadr and Vreis garbed in tartans, piping. They stood off to one side at the front of the room. Their plaids were different, and she assumed it had to do with their clan affiliation.

The music gathered speed, and Stewart emerged from behind a crimson curtain near the bagpipes. Her knees weakened; breath whooshed from her. He was so striking, he was impossible not to stare at. His red hair was braided with jewels and beads in a Celtic warrior pattern. His tartan—red with black and green markings—wrapped around his tall, broad shouldered frame with a silver sporran spanning his waist. A cream-colored linen shirt with full sleeves sat beneath the tartan. Knee length boots fashioned from buff leather laced to his knees.

He swept the room with his gaze until he found her, and then he held out both hands. She walked to his side to the accompaniment of the pipes. Fae and Dark Fae rose like a sweeping wave as she passed, bowing and cheering in Gaelic. When she got to Stewart, he clasped one of her hands and they walked the rest of the length of the room to where Rhiannon, Gwydion, and a dark-haired Celt she'd not met before waited.

Yara had asked about the ceremony itself, but everyone told her all she had to do was be there, that everything would unfold as it should. She'd protested that all of them had been to a Celtic wedding, but she had no idea what to expect. Rhiannon had just smiled, told her to be patient, and then clammed up.

"Ye're so lovely, lassie," Stewart whispered into her ear.

She tightened her grip on his hand and whispered back, "You're gorgeous. So extravagantly handsome, I could eat you up."

"I'll hold you to that just as soon as we've gotten through the festivities."

They halted in front of the triumvirate. Stewart bowed formally, so Yara did the same.

Rhiannon squared her shoulders. "I am Rhiannon, white witch and Welsh Horse Goddess. I give my permission for my daughter, Yara, to wed Stewart, a Druid High Priest."

Gwydion stepped forward. Today, his robe was heavy, embossed white silk, sashed in teal. "And I am Gwydion, master enchanter and warrior magician. I agree to this joining and shall sanctify it with my blood."

The dark-haired Celt stepped forward. "I am Arawn, god of

the dead. I, too, agree to this joining and shall sanctify it with my blood."

Rhiannon inclined her head toward Gwydion and Arawn. "Thanks be to you for your assistance today." She plucked a silver chalice from an elaborately carved table and drank from it. When she was done, she handed it to Gwydion who did the same. From there it went to Arawn, and then to her and Stewart, who handed the chalice back to Rhiannon.

"Of what have ye drunk?" she demanded, sounding stern.

"Of Celtic blood and glory," Stewart replied, punctuated by a roar from the crowd.

The chalice made the rounds once more, and Rhiannon repeated her question.

"Of Celtic splendor," Stewart replied to more roars from the crowd. Apparently, they were familiar with this ritual and adored it.

Meanwhile, the bagpipes continued playing, filling the hall with achingly sweet music that plucked at Yara's heartstrings. It had to be imbued with magic to evoke such a potent response.

Once they'd cycled through "of Celtic magnificence" and "of Celtic glory enduring forever with no beginning nor end," the owls left Rhiannon's shoulder and circled them. One landed on Yara's shoulder, talons digging deep, and the other landed on Stewart.

Rhiannon extended a finger and dragged it through blood welling through Yara's gown from the owl's claws. She swabbed it over Stewart's wound and then repeated the motion twice more.

"We have shared blood," Rhiannon intoned.

"Aye," Arawn said. "We have shared blood."

"We have shared blood. Now, 'tis your turn." Gwydion fastened his sky-blue eyes on Stewart, who nodded.

"Repeat after me." Stewart turned to face her, and the owls returned to Rhiannon, their part apparently complete. He gripped both her hands in his, and his dark gaze seared her to her bones.

"Ye are blood of my blood and bone of my bone." His voice was so deep and rich, chills ran through Yara as she repeated his words.

He gripped her hands harder. "I give you my body that we may be one. I give you my spirit till our life shall be done. Ye are blood of my blood and bone of my bone."

Tears prickled as she repeated the ancient binding. It ran deeper than the mere words, and her sprit took flight. Stewart let go of her hands and tossed her veil back over her head. Bending, he closed his mouth over hers amid a bevy of cheers.

Yara wrapped her arms around him, never wanting to let go. Never wanting the kiss to end. The ceremony had been driven by magic, and it held her in thrall.

Something sharp pecked her, then something else. She dragged her mouth from Stewart's to find not just the owls, but Meara in vulture form. She cawed merrily. *"You'll have your life-times for the bedroom. Come dance the night away, drink your fill, and throw cake for the birds to share."*

"What?" Yara didn't bother with telepathy. "Cake throwing, eh? Another ancient custom?"

The vulture didn't answer, just flew down the hall and out the door.

Happiness sluiced through Yara until she felt she'd burst from a surfeit of emotion. "What happens next?" she asked Stewart.

"We move to the grand hall across the corridor, so everyone can wish us well and toast us and share our wedding feast."

Yara walked tall by his side as they crossed the large room. She'd assumed this was the grand hall, but perhaps one even larger was waiting for them next door. The owls were gone, but so were the Celts. "Where'd Rhiannon and the other two go?"

Stewart shrugged. "My guess is they're putting the finishing touches on the food and drink." He leaned close enough to whisper into her ear. "In all the long years I've known them, they've never, never gone out of their way to do aught for anyone not one of them. Today is verra special, lassie. This may well be the last deed any of them do here, and they did it for us."

Fae and Dark Fae surrounded them, chattering merrily in Gaelic. The group pushed through the arched doorway into the hall, and a flash of powerful shifter magic hurtled toward them. Yara glanced up expecting Meara, but Nivkh barreled their way. Garbed in leather, his burly form was welcome indeed. Yara had asked Meara if she knew what happened to him. She'd said no, but that had been a few days ago.

Apparently, things had changed.

The faerie folk parted to let him through amid cries of bear and first shifter. Many bowed to him. Power poured through the hall, redolent of the sharp tang of icy tundra, and he wrapped his powerful arms around Yara and Stewart. "I may have missed the wedding, but I shall drink to your good health, a long life, and many cubs."

Meara flew to them, shifting midair.

Nivkh nodded at her. "Thank you for finding me in time. I'd finally crossed the North Sea, but I had no idea which part of the British Isles to search first."

Rhiannon and Gwydion crowded into the broad hall, along with her owls. "Come within," she urged. "Food awaits. Drink too."

The Fae and Dark Fae surged around everyone, hustling through an open door that glistened with silver motes of power.

Rhiannon gazed fondly after them. "We should hurry or they'll eat the tables down to the wood."

Nivkh let go of Yara and Stewart and bowed low before Rhiannon. "Nice to see you again, my lady."

"And you." She inclined her head. "How did ye come to be here for my daughter's wedding?"

"I invited him," Meara said. "He became separated from us before we crossed the North Sea." She shifted her eerie gaze so it rested on him. "You have excellent news. Be sure to share it before we get immersed in toasting the newlyweds."

Yara's ears perked up, and she cast an appraising glance at the bear shifter. "Stewart wanted Meara to go after you, but she said you could take care of yourself."

Nivkh snorted, sounding suspiciously like the bear he was, and elbowed Meara. "Vote of confidence, eh?"

"Something like that." She hooked an arm through his. "Come on. I don't know about you, but I'm hungry."

"Bears are always hungry." Nivkh chortled and strode after the Fae.

Rhiannon trotted after the shifters. Her owls flew behind Yara and Stewart, wings brushing their faces. "Aye, we're on the move," Stewart informed the birds. It seemed to satisfy them because they flew after their mistress.

Luscious smells wafted through the door. Yara still held tight to Stewart's hand. "Husband."

"Aye, that would be me." He led them into a room even grander than the one where they'd been wed. Tales of Celtic glory were depicted in wall hangings and thick rugs running the length of the hall.

Someone thrust glasses of mead into their hands. She took a sip and said, "Husband, I like the sound of it."

"And I love the way it sounds rolling off your tongue." He clinked glasses with her. "To us, my love, my heart, my darling."

They hooked their arms together and drank from each other's glasses in a Rom-style toast.

Nivkh and Meara mounted a raised dais at one end of the room, and Meara clapped her hands smartly together. The sound wasn't loud, but everyone turned to face her, and conversations quieted.

"I'll be quick about this," Nivkh said. "After all, we have a wedding to celebrate, yet there's still more cause to rejoice. I couldn't find a simple way out of the Netherlands and ended up sneaking back into Germany in bear form. I stopped by the caravans Stewart and Michael left outside Munich and am pleased to report all is well with them."

"Even better, though, the vampires have cleared out. They apparently decided helping Hitler held far too high a price tag. They were angry at how he manipulated them, and they transferred that ire to the Reich. Before they left, they mowed through every camp in Germany killing SS and anyone associated with Hitler. The demons have decamped as well. I have no idea if they've retreated to Hell where they belong, but demon taint faded and died away until I couldn't find it anywhere."

Cheers broke out, building to an enthusiastic cacophony of applause, hoots, and hollers. Music burst from the bagpipes. A rousing victory song that swept fears away. Cadr and Vreis were elated by the news, and it shone through their piping.

"There's more than one tale to be told here. It appears you fought and fought well. I suspect you're the reason vampires and demons decided retreat was in their best interest." Nivkh cupped his hands around his mouth to make himself heard. "Someday, I'd like to hear what happened."

Meara bent close to him, probably assuring him she'd tell him everything.

Stewart wrapped an arm around Yara. "Och aye, lassie, and that's a fair bit of excellent news. Means we can return to the caravan that calls me leader—if such would please you."

A smile started in her heart before spreading to her mouth. To be part of a caravan again would be the best thing ever. "I'd love it. Doesn't matter if I don't have a shred of gypsy blood. Caravans are my home, and I've missed them."

"Och and we'll make a fine pair. Me with my Druid magic, and ye with your Celt heritage. Seems fitting, somehow. My people will welcome us, regardless."

"Can Ilse and Ian join us?"

"Of course. If they want to." He took a measured breath. "We'll have to remain in hiding until after the war ends, but I'm confident 'twill end someday. Not having vampires to fuel his hideous agenda will cripple Hitler and ensure that good triumphs in the end."

"When will we leave Scotland?" Yara knew they'd have to, but something about the magic-saturated land captivated her.

Stewart shrugged. "No one says we canna bide a wee bit afore we depart. I'd like to pass through Glasgow on our way south. I left my own collection of magical books in a moldering castle. If aught is left of them, we can bring them along."

"I bet they're still there. If they're anything like the book Mother gave me, they're indestructible."

He bent close and kissed her cheek. "I hope ye're right."

A plump little fae with hair the green of a summer bower waddled over and handed her an overstuffed plate. Another with pink curls did the same for Stewart. "Hold up," the first Fae said. "Chairs are on their way."

A pair of Dark Fae dragged overstuffed chairs close by, and Yara dropped into one taking care to keep her full plate balanced.

"Can I get my lady anything else?" the green-haired Fae asked.

He was so earnest and so utterly magical, she grinned. "No thank you. This is perfect."

"We'll bring cake just as soon as you're done." The pink-curled girl giggled, curtsied, and fled.

Yara leaned against the seat's padded back and popped sweetmeats and other morsels into her mouth. Stewart sat by her side, his gaze never leaving her.

She set her fork down. "Why aren't you eating?"

He shrugged. "I'm enjoying watching you. I still canna quite believe ye agreed to marry me. 'Tis like a dream, but one I never wish to waken from."

Yara laid her plate on the floor and did the same with his. Once his lap was empty, she sat in it and closed her arms around him. "Have I told you lately how much I love you?"

He hugged her back and brushed his lips over hers. "Aye, darling lassie, but I'll never tire of hearing it." His tone turned formal. "Thank you for the honor of joining your life to mine."

She snuggled her head into the hollow of his shoulder. "Thank you for wanting me. It's an honor on my side as well."

Rhiannon walked to where they sat. "'Tis good to see you happy. Makes up for all those years ye were miserable and there was naught I could do but hope ye'd find answers in the book."

Yara disentangled herself from Stewart and stood to face her mother. "What happened to the book? I looked and looked for it in the cave."

"Ye doona need it any longer. 'Twas a magical construct, but ye already guessed that." She held out her arms. "We shall take our leave. I'm grateful to have gotten to spend even this wee bit of time with you."

Yara hugged her mother. "I'm grateful for it as well. Will I ever see you again?"

"Nay, daughter. The lot of us are leaving Earth forever. Our time here is done. In truth, 'tis been done for the last hundred years, but I had one last task—and now that it's been dispatched, I have no more justification to remain."

Stewart stood too. "Will Arianrhod bide in Caer Sidi?"

Rhiannon nodded. "She will, for who would ride herd on the moon and tides if not for her?" She let go of Yara and squared her shoulders. "When the bairns come, show my grandchildren to the moon. Arianrhod will let me know."

Yara's throat constricted with emotion. "I wish we'd had more time."

"Be grateful we had any." Rhiannon whistled once sharply. The owls whisked onto her shoulders, and a shining white steed formed in the air. Rhiannon vaulted astride it, and it turned, galloping until it vanished.

Yara remembered those hoofbeats. She'd heard them that

night in the church. Tears formed, leaking from her eyes, and she brushed them away. "I shouldn't be sad. Not today of all days."

Stewart pulled her close. "Ye love fiercely, lassie. Doona wish it away."

She melted into his embrace. She'd gone from having nothing but herself to knowing who she was and having a stalwart man by her side. Yara let go of Stewart and said, "Let's greet our guests and thank them for sharing today with us."

"Did ye have enough to eat?"

"We can eat anytime. Come on."

Together, hand in hand, they walked toward the group of Fae closest to them.

You've reached the end of the *Soul Dance* books. If you enjoyed them, you might also like my Dragon Lore quartet. A sample from *Highland Secrets*, the first book of that series, follows.

The four books in Dragon Lore are:

Highland Secrets

To Love a Highland Dragon

Dragon Maid

Dragon's Dare

ABOUT THE AUTHOR

Ann Gimpel is a USA Today bestselling author. A lifelong aficionado of the unusual, she began writing speculative fiction a few years ago. Since then her short fiction has appeared in a number of webzines, magazines, and anthologies. Her longer books run the gamut from urban fantasy to paranormal romance to science fiction. Once upon a time, she nurtured clients. Now she nurtures dark, gritty fantasy stories that push hard against reality. When she's not writing, she's in the backcountry getting down and dirty with her camera. She's published over 60 books to date, with several more planned for 2018 and beyond. A husband, grown children, grandchildren, and wolf hybrids round out her family.

Keep up with her at www.anngimpel.com or http://anngimpel.blogspot.com

If you enjoyed what you read, get in line for special offers and pre-release special reads. Sign up for Ann's newsletter on her website or her blog.

Furious and weary, Angus Shea wants out, but no matter how he feels, he can't stop the magic powering his visions. The Celts kidnapped him when he wasn't much more than a boy and forced him to do their bidding. He's sick of them and their endless assignments, but they wiped his memories, and he has no idea where he came from.

Dragon shifters are disappearing from the Scottish Highlands, and the Celtic Council sends Angus to investigate. He meets up with Arianrhod, legendary virgin huntress from Celtic myth, in Fire Mountain, the dragons' home world.

Arianrhod prefers to work alone, mostly because she harbors a dirty little secret and guards her privacy for the best of reasons. She's not exactly a virgin, and she'd be laughed out of the Pantheon if the truth surfaced. Despite the complications of leading a double life, she's never found a lover who tempted her to walk away from her fellow Celtic gods.

Attraction ignites, hot and so urgent Arianrhod's carefully balanced life teeters on the brink of discovery. Angus is everything she's ever wanted, but he's far too close to her Celtic kin to keep her secret safe. Angus wants her too, but she's a Celt. He's hated them forever, and she's part of everything he's lain awake nights plotting to escape from.

Can they risk everything?

Will they?

If they do, can they live with the consequences?

HIGHLAND SECRETS, CHAPTER ONE

DRAGON LORE, BOOK ONE

*A*ngus Shea stroked beneath icy waters off the northern tip of Ireland, blending his energy with a pod of Selkies. The sea creatures cut through choppy waves in front, behind, and above him. He'd rather dive and play in the deeps with them—and if it were any other day, he would have—but he needed to keep an eye on the skies, so he edged toward the surface, pushing his head free.

Celene, a coal black Selkie he'd done more than swim with, drew close enough her lush pelt stroked his skin. He draped an arm around her, and she nuzzled his neck with her snout.

"Where have you been?" She spoke deep into his mind. Accommodating vocal chords were part of her human form, not her seal, and he'd never learned the Selkies' lyrical language.

"I spent a little time at my home in Scotland, but mostly I've ranged far from the Irish Sea."

"That doesn't tell me anything." She nipped playfully at his shoulder with her squared-off teeth.

"Prying ears are everywhere." He leaned into her warmth, enjoying a respite from the cold water.

"We could go where no one would hear."

He was tempted, so tempted he toyed with saying yes and taking a break from watching for the dragon he expected. Dragons interpreted time in their own way, and the damned thing might not show up today or tomorrow or even this week. If it showed at all.

How much could he tell the Selkie?

An answer crowded on the heels of his question.

Nothing.

Angus shuttered his mind, so the creature swimming by his side couldn't read it. Much as he yearned to talk with someone, anyone, about the impossibilities the gods tasked him with, prudence won out. Not that this assignment was worse than any of the others, but he'd finally figured out they'd never end.

I could say no. Tell them I'm done.

He cut off the bitter laugh that wanted out. Whoever had the balls to refuse the Celts risked swift and certain punishment. He could hear Gwydion, master enchanter, or Ceridwen, goddess of the world, laughing their heads off—before they cut out his tongue or killed him on the spot.

"You don't have to say a word." Celene went on, almost as if she'd peeked into his thoughts before he took care to protect them. Selkie laughter buffeted him, spraying him with a warm, rich melody mixed with salty water. *"I'm curious, but I miss your body."*

He missed hers too. She'd been his only break from solitude for more years than he wanted to admit. He cast another glance skyward. Though he tried to be subtle, he heard a smug murmur near his ear and knew he hadn't fooled the Selkie.

"You wait for an Ancient One." The tenor of her mind speech shifted as she shielded it from anyone who might be close. Without stopping for him to corroborate, she forged ahead. *"We can take up the banner and watch for you. My kin will let us know."*

Angus picked his way carefully, as if he walked through a field of unexploded ordnance. "I appreciate the thought, but no one can know of my comings or goings, lass."

"We know more than you think." Celene batted him with a flipper. *"In truth, very little escapes us, but here isn't the place to share what I heard about your latest mission."*

Concern rippled through him. If the Selkies knew, who else might? Hell, he didn't know much beyond his assigned meeting place with the dragon, and they'd be heading into danger.

What else was new? Danger was so second nature, his adrenaline pumps barely flinched at anything these days.

"Come with me." Either Celene was oblivious to the turmoil rumbling through him, or she ignored it. She swam from beneath his arm and herded him toward shore. *"There's a secluded glade deep in marsh grass. No one will find us, and my kin will keep watch for the dragon. I already asked."*

The Selkies would do their best—and maybe today it would be enough—but they were no match for evil that had sunk its roots deep into the fabric of the Old Country and the rest of this world. It was why the gods stooped to using him—half-mortal, half-divine, or whatever the hell he was—to do their dirty work. Arawn, god of the dead, revenge, and terror, caught him skulking in the time-travel tunnels when he wasn't much more than a boy and trapped him, cutting off any possibility of return. To make certain Angus remained, the god altered his memories, so he had no idea where he came from.

Now almost twenty-five years later, Arawn and the others still came up with enough for him to do that a life to call his own was out of the question. The carrot they dangled was the truth about his birth, but they never came close to divulging it. The stick was his fear of what they'd do, if he told them he was done.

Over time, he'd stopped asking about his origins. He cared, but it wasn't worth the energy to run up against their stony faces and cunningly crafted half-truths that revealed exactly nothing. Despite his reservations about a quick dalliance with Celene—and maybe missing his rendezvous with the dragon—he was sick of his self-imposed isolation.

She chivied him into shallow water. Once she was certain he'd follow, she drew ahead easily. As if the other Selkies understood, the pod dispersed. When he peered through gray-green water for their multi-colored pelts, they weren't there.

By the time he clambered onto the rocky shore, Celene had shucked her skin. In human form, she opened her arms to welcome him. Long black hair shrouded her almost to her feet. Violet eyes gleamed in welcome. Her generous breasts peeked through the curtain of hair, their copper-colored nipples already pebbled with wanting him.

Angus had tucked his clothes beneath a rock before joining the Selkie pod. Because he swam nude, nothing was in the way as he plunged into Celene's offered embrace. God, how he'd missed the touch of another against him, skin to skin. Celene's body felt warm against his chilled one. She closed her arms around him and ran her hands down his back, lingering over the curve of his butt.

He hugged her in return. The scent of her, salt and mint, flooded his mind with images of their lovemaking, and his cock hardened between their bodies. He trailed his fingertips down her smooth skin, marveling at how different she felt from a human woman. Velvety and charged with electricity. Some Selkies walked among humans, even took permanent partners. Angus didn't understand how they eluded discovery.

Celene closed her mouth over the junction between his neck and shoulder, licking, sucking, biting. He moved a hand from her back to cup the side of her face and lowered his lips over hers. Desire engulfed him. Hot, urgent, desperate, he sank his tongue into her waiting mouth.

She grappled with his ass, pulling his body hard against hers as her hips writhed and breath hitched in her throat. Tearing her mouth from his, she gasped. "Too long. It's been too long."

Liquid heat trailed the path of her mouth as she licked her way down his chest, stopping to tease his nipples. He kissed the top of her head and wove his fingers into her long hair. Every nerve came alive with wanting her, but it ran deeper than that. Touch was such a basic need, and he'd denied that essential part of his humanity—along with every other comfort.

For what?

No matter how much he gave the Celts, they took every shred —and him—for granted. He wanted to get a job, blend in with humans. Something mundane like driving a cab, or flipping burgers in a grill, but his requests were denied. The Celts provided for him. So long as they housed and fed him, why would he need to clutter his time with anything as humdrum as earning a living? What if they needed him, and he was in the middle of washing dishes in some nameless restaurant? He could almost hear Gwydion's voice. See the master enchanter with a long-suffering look on his face—

He wiped his Celtic masters from his mind. This time was for him and Celene. No one else belonged in his head. Just because he'd chosen a semimonastic existence was no reason he couldn't give her everything she needed. Months had passed since they'd last been together, maybe as much as a year. He moved back enough to fill his hands with her breasts, rubbing her erect nipples before he bent to suck on them, remembering the little biting motions she loved.

A low, guttural moan escaped her, and she threaded her fingers through his hair. Holding him against her breasts, she began to sing as he loved her. A series of low, sweet notes rose in cadence and intensity as she lost herself in his touch. He'd asked her about the music once, and she told him it was how sea people vocalized their joy. The music filled him with unbearable hunger —poignant, mind-bending need for another person's touch.

Although he'd never done it before, he raised his voice and joined her song. The change was instantaneous. In that moment, he sensed her loneliness and isolation, twin to his own and recognized that both of them needed more kisses, more touches—even more than they needed sex.

"Lay on your belly." His voice rasped with wanting her. He tore tufts of marsh grass and arranged them to make her a bed on a sandy stretch between rocks.

She lay down, continuing to sing. Angus sang too, as he straddled her and ran his hands down her back rubbing tension from her muscles. He followed his hands with his mouth and strung kisses across her shoulder blades and down the line of vertebrae from her neck to the curves of her ass. Between their song, the feel of her skin beneath his fingertips, and his cock getting stiffer by the moment, waiting became almost painful, yet he held back, not quite sure why.

The rhythm and cadence of her song shifted as he alternated his mouth and hands across the sculpted planes of her back. The intense pressure in his balls receded almost as if he'd reached a peak, though he hadn't come. Maybe she sensed his need for warmth, contact, much as he'd sensed hers.

"Move off me so I can look at you." Celene flipped over to face him, kneeling above her. Rose and gold splotched her pale skin, and a broad smile split her exotic, high-cheek-boned face. "Today was different. You sang with me. You've never done that before."

He shrugged, suddenly self-conscious. "It felt right. Even though I wasn't inside you, what happened between us felt right."

She cocked her head to one side and trained her gaze on him. "Are you sure you don't have sea blood?"

A flicker of annoyance at the Celts' staunch refusal to disclose anything about his birth narrowed his eyes. "I have no idea what I am." He ticked what he did know off on his fingers. "I'm not immortal, but I'll live well beyond human lifespans. My magic is closer to seer and witch than anything else, yet I'm neither of those. The covens acknowledge me as one of theirs, but only because the local witches are too kind to tell me to go away. The time-travel portals accept me." He shrugged again. "I don't suppose knowing more would make a hell of a lot of difference."

"You're not from Scotland, even though you live there." She stated it baldly, as fact.

He frowned. "Why would you say that?"

"Your speech. There's something about the lilt of Scotland that's impossible to rid yourself of. You don't sound Irish or British, either, at least not from the time we live in." Her nostrils flared. "Maybe that's it."

"Maybe what's it?"

"You could be from the past, and not just a few years back, perhaps hundreds—or even more. I'm not old enough to recall what human speech sounded like then, but some Selkies are."

"Fine." Frustration tightened his chest, like it always did when the mystery of his origins became a point of discussion. "My first memories are when the god of the dead dragged me out of a time-travel portal when I was fifteen."

"I'm sorry." She draped a hand over his hip, cradling it. "I've upset you."

He started to protest, but she silenced him with a look. "Don't insult me with a lie, Angus, but you don't have to talk about it, either. Such a pretty man." She stroked hair back from his face. "With your deep brown hair and amber eyes. Did you know they shade to dark gold when you're angry?"

She was trying to divert him with flattery, but he wasn't buying it. "You have no idea what it's like not knowing—" He shook his head, and the rest of his words died unspoken. It didn't matter what she knew or didn't know about him. She'd never be more than an occasional lover, and both of them knew it.

"It could be more," she said softly, obviously having been in his mind.

Angus took her hands in his and gazed at her. "You get more of me than anyone, and you see how pathetically little that is. There's nothing more to give."

"There could be," she persisted. "You could refuse next time they send you on—"

He bent toward her and laid a hand over her mouth. "I'm not free. Not now. Not ever."

"I don't understand." She pushed his hand away and closed very white teeth over her full lower lip.

He smiled crookedly. "Not sure I do, either. Every man has a life's work. No matter how I feel about it, this appears to be mine."

Even though it wasn't wise, he started to ask what she knew about his current assignment, but a flash of unusual energy drew his gaze skyward. He leapt to his feet. A copper-colored dragon circled to land not far from him. Maybe the Ancient One had seen him with Celene and decided to be considerate.

Not very fucking likely. Dragons were a force unto themselves.

"I have to go," he said. "Let me walk you to your skin, so I know you're safely on your way home."

A sad expression crossed her face, creasing the skin around her eyes into a network of fine lines. "It's right here." She scrambled to her feet and gripped both his upper arms, forcing him to look at her. "Thank you."

"For what?"

"Being you." She brushed her lips over his and moved to a marsh grass thicket. In moments, she'd dragged her pelt over her human body. Transformed into a seal, she waded into the surf.

Before it engulfed her, she turned to gaze at him. *Be careful, and think on what I said.*

He didn't answer, just watched her head bob in the waves before turning toward his clothing. It wasn't far from the place Celene had led them. His body felt vibrant, alive, and he still tingled from her touch. He longed for a woman of his own, children, a home, before he stuffed the impossible so deep under wraps he couldn't mourn the loss.

Angus moved the large rock he'd placed over his clothes to protect them from the wind. He pulled a ragged dark blue fisherman's knit sweater over his head and stepped into thick, black woolen trousers. Settling on a log, he pulled on socks and laced up stout leather boots. Though the breeze was raw, he'd worn neither hat nor gloves.

Ready as he figured he'd ever be, he covered the fifty yards to where the dragon had settled up the beach. He didn't recognize this one, but he'd only met a bare handful of the hundreds living in Fire Mountain and on other worlds as well. When he drew near, he stopped and bowed his head respectfully, waiting for the dragon to speak first.

"I don't like this any better than you do," the dragon muttered. "Come close enough I don't have to broadcast our business to the world."

Angus walked closer. He could've suggested the dragon use telepathy since all the Ancient Ones were conversant in the technique, but he kept his mouth shut. The dragon was smaller than many he'd seen. Copper scales shaded to burnished gold on its chest, and dark eyes with golden centers whirled so fast they held a hypnotic quality. Lethal, six-inch-long red claws tipped its stubby forelegs. The dragon stood upright on hind legs tipped with the same sharp claws and kept its gaze averted, not saying anything.

What the hell? Every other dragon he'd met was proud, imperious, and quick to remind Angus of his inferiority. This one seemed young, but was it? After another long few minutes, Angus tossed respect—and caution—to the winds.

"What's your name? And what are we supposed to be doing? All Ceridwen told me was to meet you here."

The dragon opened its mouth, and a gout of flame landed scant inches from Angus's boots.

He frowned and drew his brows together. "If we're going to work together, I need to know what to call you." He sent a speculative gaze across the air between them. "If you annihilate me, they'll just assign you a new partner, and I'm a hell of a lot easier to get along with than any of the Celts."

"Tell me something I don't know," the dragon rumbled and

belched smoke.

Frustration in its voice struck a note in Angus's soul, and he gestured with both hands. "You may as well tell me who you are and what we're supposed to do together." He infused his words with subtle persuasion. If the dragon didn't care for the Celts, either, they'd likely get along well enough.

"Why? What I should do is leave." The dragon sounded sulky—and scared.

"If you could, you'd already be gone." Angus was as certain of that as he was of anything. The dragon needed him for something, and whatever it was, the Ancient One wasn't particularly proud of it. "What happened? Am I some sort of punishment for you?" Tension settled like a steel bar across his shoulders, and he curled his hands into fists before he realized what he'd done.

"Oh I'd be gone, would I?"

The dragon ignored Angus's questions, and it mimicked his tone with eerie precision. It furled its wings and flapped them a time or two. Dirt swirled; small pebbles slapped Angus in the face. The creature belched steam and looked so distraught, he felt sorry for it.

"My life's not exactly a picnic, either," he ventured, on a hunt for common ground. "I'm a permanent mercenary, with no time off and no possibility of parole."

That got the dragon's attention, and it focused its whirling gaze on him. The golden centers of its eyes deepened with fiery motes that looked like little shooting stars. "Why would you want a respite from being a warrior?"

Good question.

"Because I'm tired. I'd like what most men have."

"What's that?" The dragon raised its brows, and its scales clanked against each other in a dissonant tinkling.

He shook his head. "It doesn't matter. The sooner you spit out whatever you need to say, the easier it'll be. The worst part about holding something you're ashamed of inside is it eats at you until you're nothing but a hollow shell."

Wings flapped, and those intense, whirling eyes shifted to the rocky beach. "I'm not *ashamed* of anything. I've been banished. Ceridwen said if I worked with you—and we were successful—I might be able to return."

Angus kept surprise out of his voice. "Banished from Fire Mountain?"

Steam puffed from the dragon's open mouth. "No. Idiot. I could live with that. They've banished me from the Highlands. My home."

"What happened?"

"It doesn't matter." The dragon threw his words back at him. "We have to go to Fire Mountain, where I'm to find one of the First Born. Once we have him—or her—"

"One of the six First Born dragons?" Angus broke in, scarcely believing the dragon's words. "They'll never show themselves— unless it's in their best interest."

Another wing flap and a defiant head toss. "There are actually ten. One of them was my father."

"When's the last time you saw him?" The words slipped out before he could stop them. Dragon males frequently didn't hang about once mating was over with, but the trembling mass of scales in front of him likely didn't need to be reminded.

"Never. Mother said he was too immersed in battles on another world to return for our hatching."

Angus unclenched his fists and hunted for something soothing to say that wasn't an outright lie. Dragon energy poked past his wards and into his mind. He tried to block it, but couldn't.

"You believe locating a First Born is hopeless." The dragon sounded resigned. "I may as well throw myself into a crater at Fire Mountain. I'll never see the Highlands again—or my mate." More wing rustling and the dragon rose a few feet off the ground, clearly intent on leaving.

"Hold on." Angus loped forward until he was right beneath the dragon. "I didn't say that—or think it, either. I don't know enough to make any sort of judgment. How about if you start at the beginning? If we're going to work together, I deserve that much."

The dragon circled a few times, indecision stamped in its erratic flight pattern.

"I know what it is to be alone." He kept his voice gentle. "And to not have anyone who cares if I live or die."

Maybe it wasn't totally true. Celene might shed a tear or two, but she'd be the only one. He kept his gaze trained on the sky, relieved the dragon wasn't putting distance between them. Something about the creature's pain tugged at his heart and made it feel like a kindred spirit.

The copper dragon folded its wings and settled heavily to earth a few feet from where Angus stood. It straightened its shoulders and tipped its chin defiantly.

"My name is Eletea," the dragon announced, revealing its gender.

"Angus Shea, though you likely know that."

"Yes, I do. I killed a mage, who fancied herself a dragon shifter." Eletea's eyes whirled faster, as if she dared Angus to say something.

He crinkled his forehead as he dredged up what he knew about dragon shifters. "Don't mages take their chances when they show up seeking a dragon to pair with?"

She nodded once, sharply. "The mage seduced one of us into believing her. I saved him by killing her, but he turned on me. Reported me to the Dragons' Council, and they roped the Celts into deciding my fate, since the one I killed had Celtic blood." Eletea's scales rippled in the dragon equivalent of a shrug. "I don't understand why they're bothering. It's not like I went after one of the gods. They're immortal. The one all the fuss is over barely qualified as a Celt."

Angus kept his expression neutral. "Celtic blood aside, I thought mages only bonded with same sex dragons."

"That was another problem," Eletea said, sounding vindicated. "No one saw it but me, though."

Sensing the worst was out on the table, Angus settled on a nearby rock and invited, "Start at the beginning. We have time."

"No, we don't," Eletea protested. "We should've been at Fire Mountain yesterday." She hung her head. "I didn't know what I wanted to do, so I flew and flew and flew. I almost didn't land this afternoon."

Angus did his best to project optimism. "Let's open a time-travel portal and be on our way to Fire Mountain." At the dragon's reluctant nod, he went on. "I understand you have your own ways of returning home, but if you travel with me, you can fill me in as we go."

What he didn't say was it probably wouldn't matter when they arrived at the dragons' home world. First Borns wouldn't give them the time of day, whether they showed up early, late, or right on time. He held many concerns, such as what would a First Born do, assuming they could locate one? But he held those cares inside for now.

He could've dreamed the future. Instead, he summoned a spell to take them to a time-traveling portal. Once the undulating gray-pink tube admitted them, he gradually paid out questions.

Reticent and quiet at first, Eletea finally began to talk.